OCEAN STIRRINGS

ALSO BY MERLE COLLINS

Fiction
Angel
Rain Darling
The Colour of Forgetting
The Ladies are Upstairs

Poetry
Because the Dawn Breaks
Rotten Pomerack
Lady in a Boat

Non-Fiction
The Governor's Story: The authorised biography of Dame Hilda Bynoe

MERLE COLLINS

OCEAN STIRRINGS

A WORK OF FICTION AND POETRY
IN TRIBUTE TO LOUISE LANGDON NORTON LITTLE
WORKING MOTHER AND ACTIVIST
MOTHER OF MALCOLM X AND HIS SEVEN SIBLINGS

PEEPAL TREE

First published in Great Britain in 2023
Peepal Tree Press Ltd
17 King's Avenue
Leeds LS6 1QS
England

ISBN13: 9781845235529

Supported using public funding by
ARTS COUNCIL
ENGLAND

"A novel is, after all, not a historical document, but a way to travel through the human heart."
— Julia Alvarez, *In the Time of the Butterflies*.

"… Poetry is concerned with the massiveness, the *multidimensional quality*, of experience."
— Cleanth Brooks, *Understanding Poetry* (Boston, MA: Holt, Rineheart & Winston, 1976), 6.

"The story of her life was an epic one. The epic began in Grenada, continued in Canada, and ended here in the States. In all three countries there are parts of her life waiting to be resurrected."
— Wilfred Little, brother of Malcolm X, about his mother Louise Little in Jan Carew, *Ghosts in Our Blood* (Lawrence Hill Books, 1994), 112.

CONTENTS

Part 3. The United States of America. 1919-1931

Part 4: Premonitions and Endings 1931-1939

Part 5: Leavings and Returnings. 1939-early 1960s. Poems

1917: ON THE WAY TO CANADA

I turn to the ocean
That swallowed my ancestors
I stand on deck
Dare the waves to be calm
I'm here again, Atlantic
I want to visit the place that Hudson claimed
I want to walk where the Iroquois walked
I want to see more of the Lamèwik that made and divided Europe

I want to listen to what the ocean says
Whisper to me, ocean
I want to find a way to tell my story
Mwen vlé twouvé yon manyè pou wakonté listwa mwen

PART 1
Grenada Beginnings

CHAPTER ONE

1896. A La Digue Morning

From the hills of La Digue they can look down at the ocean, talking secret to the sands, shoo-shooing, playful, intimate, running up and easing back, down there near La Baye, the town that is theirs. People say it is the second town of their island, Grenada, but for those who live there, La Baye, which some also call Grenville, is the first. Sometimes town people act as if *town*, which is what they call St George's, the capital, is the centre, but to people around La Baye, *their* town is really the main place for everything – for good king fish from the sea, for crayfish from the river mouth, for a nice new market these days, for cocoa, now that cocoa is in swing, for nutmeg, for everything. It is where they meet and greet each other by Mr Lamotte liquor store, by Mr Rennie on Victoria Street, by the Revenue Office, by the Colonial Bank agency, by the market. They pretend not to see Miss Doodoose, as underneath as ever, standing up at the corner by the pillarbox, watching everything and waiting to run she mouth. Or Mr Joseph, waiting by that same pillar box in his khaki shirt and khaki pants, waiting to see the government workers clear the mail out of the pillarbox at half past two, waiting as if somebody paying him to do that job. Fast he fast so, they thinking. But there is nothing of that in their shouts to one another.

Makoumè, kouman ou yé? How tings?
And
What you know good? Sa ou ka di la?
Épi
Ti fi, ou gadé bèl, wi! Girl, you lookin nice, yes!

And

You don't have to tell me something in the mortar besides the pestle. Uh Uh Uh!

Ou pa ni pou di mwen i ni kéchoy nan pilon-an pasé manch-la
Épi

Woy-o-yoy! *Denmou an plas la!* Trouble in the place!

Sometimes they have to help up two languages – *dé lanng* – to tell the story going on around them; sometimes one is enough. And always they laugh out loud, sounding gleeful, as if they have secured the secret to survival. Not that life is easy. Life has never been easy. Sometimes on the hill in La Digue and the surrounding areas, when the rain don't fall to water the hillside land, and when the estate acting as if labourer is river dog, things hard like *boli*, which is the name their ancestors left them for the calabash, but anyway God good – *Papa Bondyé bon* – and they making it.

And this thing self they call the estate! All round the place the situation different and some people getting rid of the land because they say it not doing too well, but whether is Vincent in La Digue or those that inherit from Garraway in Union or is Patterson in Marli Cottage or Patterson and Whiteman in Mirabeau and St Cyr, it don't matter who it is, you have to listen out for when land become available and try to make sure you get a piece because land becoming available more and more and a little piece o land is the answer these days for poor people who don't have it. Because even when it there for *you* to work on and put money in *their* pocket, that is another story. They say they getting rid of the big estate and helping out poor people, but what they doing is trying to help deyself first. *Épi, si ou katjilé asou'i, ou sa konpwann.* And if you think about it, it stands to reason. *Tout moun ka gadé pou kò-yé.* Everybody looking out for theyself.

They tell you they going give you an acre of land so you could work it and they ask you to plant cocoa for them in between your crops on your acre while you plant yam and dasheen and other things for yourself. But don't be fooled. *Mé pa kité yé kouyonné'w.* Oh no! As soon as you finish planting the cocoa for them, they taking away that piece and saying how willing they are to give you another piece. They laughing with you *kya kya kya* while all of this happening and you just have to watch them and do as if you stupid. You know that is their land, but that as soon as you manage to buy a piece for yourself where you could grow your own food, you done with this nonsense. *Ou fini èvèk bétiz sala*. And is not only here it happening. My cousin in Sauteurs tell me is the same thing up there.

Maryam is thinking all of this as she stands with arms akimbo, on the dirt road below the hill where their house sits, looking down through the trees at the sea in the distance. She gives a quick swish to the light blue cotton skirt, stamps her feet, puts her hand up to touch the plait circling her head, and stamps her feet again. A cricket or a *mybone* or something. Some insect trying to bother her. She moves a hand across her shoulders, brushing, looking around; she sees nothing, focuses again on the grey-blue sea, foaming down below.

She can't hear it, but she can imagine that swhooshing sound of the sea as it moving in and out, looking so calm over there near La Baye. These days, is like she always hearing talk about how blue and peaceful are the seas around the island. Hmm. Is the children she hearing the talk from. Is high-up people that does talk that talk, and it come to her mainly through the children, who get it wherever they get it, but the sea looking good down there in truth, *wi*, even from far – the white foam on the blue, speckling it up like – well, it lookin good – well good.

Maryam thinks of her big son Eero. At seventeen, eh – seventeen *dèggè dèggè* years! – and with what his father calling a *independent streak*. At seventeen, what kind of independent streak is that he having? *Ki kalité andépandans i ni a dissèt lané?*

Anyway, *mouth open, word jump out, yes*. At seventeen, me self already had more than enough on my plate. *Hay-a-yay!* And in spite of herself, Maryam laughing out loud at this thought so that Dolly – walking down the track just at that moment, coming from her garden further up the hill along this road that they calling Waterfall, with a bundle of wood poised over a straw hat on her head, a brown skin *mami sipot* in one hand and a short-blade cutlass in the other – Dolly stop and talk.

"Ay ay, Maryam! *Blag sala byen dou*. That joke well sweet. I want piece of it. *Mwen vlé yon mòso.*"

Maryam turns to face Dolly, smiles, stands with her feet apart on the track, and moves the outside part of her right thumb across her chin. "*Kouman ou yé*, Dolly? How you do?"

You have to be careful, she thinking. The same ones laughing with you *kya kya kya* just waiting to pick up story and run with it.

Dolly looks at Maryam curiously. "*Mwen la*. I dey. But you self, Maryam, you more than dey! *Mé ou menm,* Maryam, *ou plis ki la.* You and who else enjoying thing so? *Ou épi ki moun ki ka pasé bon tan kon sa? Bagay bon?* Thing good?"

Maryam is still smiling, calm, watchful. "Me and me alone, girl. *Sé mwen épi mwen tousèl.* Is my mind giving me good joke like that. *Sé lèspwi mwen ki ka ba mwen bon blag kon sa. Épi sé lanng épi dan ki ka édé mwen kon sa.* And is tongue and teeth that helping me out so." Maryam laughs out loud again, and Dolly smiles, still looking curious.

"*Lanng épi dan, sé dé sala, yé danjéwé, eh.* Those two, tongue and teeth, they dangerous, you know." And Dolly moves her head slightly to one side to give emphasis to the point. Maryam smiles too, her face crinkling as she lifts a hand to rub it across eyes gone suddenly cloudy, as if rain does fall when you least expect it. She thinks, *Yes, I know. Wi. Mwen konnèt.* She turns to her right, jumps over the cocoa leaves, across the small drain, indicating that she is going to walk back up to her house on the hillside.

"Well, see you again, Ma," says Dolly. "Let me put foot to road and go make sure pot on fire. *Kité mwen mété pyé asou chimen èk alé mété chòdyè mwen asou difé-a.* Take care of yourself, okay? And say howdy for me."

"*Wi, doudou. Mèsi.* Yes, my dear. Thank you. *Di bonjou pou mwen osi.* Say howdy for me, too."

Dolly, her dark face glistening with sweat, her long brown skirt down over black waterboots, the underarm of her blue and white short-sleeved t-shirt visibly wet as she lifts an arm again to steady the load on her head, turns to continue down the hillside. Maryam walks up the hill through the red bougainvillea she had planted on both sides of the stony path.

Her brain is at it again, not making her laugh out loud this time, just turning things over so she could read them inside her head and try to make out anything that might be wanting to hide in the

20

margins. *Lanng épi dan.* Hmm. Tongue and teeth. Yes. She know they dangerous. Anyway, she must go back inside. She just had to run down the hill and get some air. She like to look down at La Baye from the bend in the road, especially when the head feeling kinda full. Something about that particular bend-in-the-road view always make her feel better.

They will christen the little girl tomorrow in the church. The priest give them a date, so February twelfth it is. Just do it quick and quiet. Don't give tongue and teeth too much time to talk about what it don't know about.

Maryam is restless this morning. True it getting brighter and brighter and the sun starting to look at her as if it wondering if she waiting for it to get high, high in the sky, but she still not ready to go back inside. So she let her body down on to the wooden steps that Oba and Eero build for this little board house on the hill. *They work good together, those two.* And Oba knees not doing too well these days, so is a good thing Eero there to work with his father. Well, the father seventy. Seventy, yes. Old man she take put on her account. He wasn't old when they start out all those years ago. But... and Maryam sits there with her chin in her hand, leaning on the elbow pressed into her right thigh, thinking about this thing called her life. She must brush away these cocoa leaves, *wi.* Where they come from? No sound from inside, so the baby must be asleep still and Gerda probably sleeping too. She out of school – big lady, yes, twelve years already now – and she could help with the baby instead of looking for some kind of work in the big house and going and find trouble. Because is so these people stay. Those white man in these houses, their hand well fast. She know that from experience. You just have to be you and let them know what is what. And of course she will learn to sew. Girls must learn to sew.

Hard how things hard, she *had* to take this little baby from Ernestine, yes, because that girl can't cope. She really can't cope. She was always like that, worried about everything, but is like this thing with baby take the energy and the fight out of her. And look she close sheself up now and only staying on her own there, not even eating the little bit she could get, down there on the hillside in Richmond. I don't know what to tell this child... well, not child any more at eighteen – but she have to learn how to handle sheself in the world with these men. They don't care nothing about nobody, especially when dey not black like us, and dey skin clear, or dey white, and the world belong to them, but you have to know how to handle things when you is woman.

She say he force her, and I believe her, but Lord! Is like that child is a magnet for trouble! It hurt me heart, in truth. That same man, big official with white skin, the talk is that he get Miss Evangeline eleven-year-old little girl pregnant now. These white people, when they in position – well, not when they in position, *non*, because their skin itself is the position! So they always in position once they white. So is just to avoid them because sometimes they have you in a situation as if you, as woman, you can't say no. Is just to avoid them. I tell the child that. Is not her fault, *non*, is not her fault. So I don't want to sound – I don't want to feel – as if is her fault. Is so the world is already, but I tired telling her. Don't grin, grin with these men; make them think you want nothing from them. Because dem don't care! I tell the child. *Mwen di timamay-la. Mwen di'y.*

Maryam sits on the steps with her head down. Is to avoid them. Don't put yourself in a position where they could see you and corner you. Maryam rustles the skirt of her dress, trying to brush away the sandflies that waking up already to bother people this early morning. She sits back, elbows on the wooden steps, looking up at the trees – the *bwa kano* marking the boundary with Joseph down the hill, the mango tree over there, and a set of bush she not even sure what is what. This granddaughter of hers will have a good life if she Maryam have anything to do with it. This child will make it. She going make it. She going make it, for sure.

Maryam watched the world around her getting brighter. But look at me, eh, sitting down here like lady of leisure, as if I have nothing to do. Dolly must be reach home and forget. Let me get up, eh! Let me get up and go inside.

CHAPTER TWO

1895-1896. *I té la pou tout moun wè.* It was there for everybody to see.

By about June that year, 1895, *i té la pou tout moun wè*, it was there for everybody to see. The bad-mouth people in the area had enough to say. Maryam was right there to hear because she had decided to do a few days in the cocoa, carrying the heavy cocoa basket to bring in some extra so that she could help out Ernestine because she thought the child wasn't eating as she should at this particular time, and she seemed to be struggling on her own. It was there, when she was settling the *kata* on her head so she could lift up the cocoa basket, that Isidora whisper to Maryam that she didn't like to talk behind people back, so she would tell her what she hearing. And though Maryam knew that mouth was all over her business, she said nothing. She just listened as if she was hearing it for the first time, lifting up more worry same time with the cocoa basket.

She had always been worried about the way men – white, black and in-between – used to watch that child. And she always worried, too, about the way the girl responded, not really encouraging them but not pushing them away as Maryam thought she should. And when you hear people whispering like that under the cocoa is usually some talk about woman or about a high-up man. She didn't like it that this time again it was her Ernestine.

So here it was now, reach under the cocoa in June, in the middle of mango season, tongue and teeth – *lanng épi dan* – looking for another kind of juice, gossiping about what they didn't know about. June – just around the time when you could find the *pwa dou* that the two younger girls, Faith and Amèlie, liked so much that any time you miss them you could be sure they

23

under the tree up on the hill cracking the long black pods and sucking on the white pulp inside. The talk reach under the cocoa in June but inside the house Maryam had sensed something before that. April. About middle of April. The child was staying over a few nights, wanting to keep close to them, although her little one-room house wasn't far away, almost as if she was afraid. She was keeping her head down a lot, rushing outside early in the morning. Clinging around her a lot, but not saying much, her eyes looking dark and weepy and heavy. Maryam gave a deep, knowing sigh. Ah-h-h Lord! And then she could see the little girl vomiting her liver out, behind the cactus, on the other side of the walkway Oba had carved out in their spot there on top of the hill.

Non, Sènyè Jézi, non. Not again. It hit her already once and the Lord put a stop to it. Not again. *No, Lord Jesus, no!*

And as she walking under the cocoa basket, with her back straight and her hips moving like load is no stranger, is that she thinking about, not tongue and teeth and their *komès,* but what she remembering. Strange how the body and the mind could be shouting a thing and mouth just keep its own counsel, grim and closed and quiet, like nothing happening – or perhaps as if what happening so worrying that mouth think it better to keep its own counsel. *Non, Sènyè Jézi.* She not the youngest, Lord, but she have so much trouble in her life already with good-for-nothing people, and she young still, and although people might say well, at eighteen, nineteen she big enough, me, she mother, I know she not big enough, and she don't have a penny to she name, Lord, and things hard. She just drink water and she struggling to be who she is. Don't give her this tribulation now, Lord. Spare her, Lord. *Bondyé, otjipé-i.*

And because Maryam and the Lord had that kind of relationship, she could hear him and see him answering her with his head to one side, looking sideways at her. "Well is not me, *non.* She have to know to spare herself. *I ni pou konnèt pou otjipé kò'i.*"

Oba, meanwhile, didn't say anything. She wondered if he had noticed. He moving in and out of the house, doing his work as usual, saying nothing, and even in the night when they in bed together, nothing. Turning his back on her as if she do him something.

And then one morning they heard a golden-apple fall – rustling down through the leaves and then *boop* on the ground. Right after that movement, another kind of rustling. Somebody get up, rush through the hall outside, fumble and pull at the door. That was how Maryam remembered it – the sound of the golden apple falling from the tree outside, and then her little girl – well, they always little, even when other people think dey big – rushing outside from the hall. She couldn't help thinking about the tall woman over the hill on the other side of Grand Bras – Miss Mooma, everybody called her – Miss Mooma, tall and a very dark, striking black. Just the other day they were saying in the corner shop that Miss Mooma little girl was pregnant by one of those reprobates. Only ten or eleven years old the child was, and instead of picking up cutlass and going and look for the man and give him a good planass, people talking about how at least the child would have some good colour if that is the father in truth. And she think about it now because she hear that that same reprobate was sniffing around her little girl. In fact, his name call for the one the Lord take back. He not one of those big planters, but is their family, and the big *jèwè* in town had him managing and doing what he doing on the estate up the hill there. And she had warn the child as she always do.

Sènyè Jézi, tjébé lanmen mwen pou mwen pa sèvi yon koutla anlè yon moun. Lord Jesus, hold me hand so I won't use a cutlass on somebody.

Maryam knew that Oba was awake in the bed next to her. She held her breath. *I hope is the latrine she gone to, just to pee, and perhaps she gone to pick up the golden apple.* She had to think that. But she knew. Near her, lying facing the board partition on the other side, Oba took a deep breath. And Maryam found herself listening for the breath to come out, but it was like he would never let that breath go. Then he said simply, tonelessly, without turning in the bed, *Mwen asiwé mwen kay tjwé yon moun tan sala… I'm sure I will kill somebody this time.*

Maryam got up, put her feet down on her side of the bed that her carpenter husband made – *di Bondyé mèsi* – and she sat there for a moment moving her toes on the bedside straw mat that she had bought at the store in La Baye. She made the sign of the cross sitting there. She prayed, sitting down there. This is April Fool's day, yes, Lord. The month just start. My little girl eighteen, but she is a child without a penny to she name. Save her, Lord. She had warned the child: *Be careful. Man always watching you on the estate there, but the watching could be dangerous and could spoil you life. Be careful.* Well, what she want to save her from there, it happen already. But better not to think too much. Maryam stood up, dragged a breath from deep inside her and let it go out into the world. Papa God don't give you more than you could handle, they say. So Papa God, why you thinking I could handle this? *Poutji ou pansé mwen sa sipòté sa?*

Maryam felt she would always remember every detail from that morning. She picked up the checkered dressing gown, the one she had made. She moved the chamber-pot over to one side – she will empty it later. She looked across at her baby girl, Amèlie, asleep in the cradle, the sleeping space that Oba had built with his own hands for his youngest. She would even remember afterward that she took a deep breath before telling her feet that they should move and keep her going.

And for years afterward, Maryam will move her feet when her thoughts reach this place, an involuntary movement, taking the step nobody could take for her. Life had been good to her, she would remember thinking, almost as a prayer, as if insisting that it continue to be good. And she counted off the good things on the fingers of her thoughts. One, since she knew herself as a child, she had food to eat – mango to suck, governor plum, sapodilla, yam on the land where the estate let her mammie make provision grounds, green fig from that same land, ripe fig – so really she always had food. Just in that one thought there were six, seven good things. And she could add a second thing that made her know she was lucky. Even after her mother died, she had another mammie to take care of her. And once you could add one plus one, you lucky. So with two things, she didn't even have to find more, but she could remember all that laughter growing up and she had children to play games with. So she could stop now. Life had been good to her, and she hadn't even started counting Oba and the children yet. She put on her dressing gown, tied the two ends of the band at the front, walked to the door over the creaking floor, creaking so damn much that she feared it would wake the children, and then she turned the knob of the door that Oba had put up to give them a bedroom space, and walked out into the hall.

She wasn't really surprised to see Gerda sitting up in her nightie, crouched on the floor to the right of the bedroom door, looking as if something frighten her. Gerda would be eleven in just a couple of months. She had just started to see her monthly blood. *Sènyè, pwotéjé-i. Lord, protect her.* Where was Beatrice? Perhaps she had run outside to help her sister.

She must talk to this little one, too, yes, although what to tell her was a question she didn't much like having to deal with. But they... well, think about it another time. She looked at her little girl and said, "Everything alright. *Tout bagay byen.* Go back to sleep. *Viwé dòmi.*"

The other little one, Faith, eight years, yes – and this morning Maryam is weepy as she thinks of the age of each one of her girls. It was as if suddenly she was realising that they were in a world that had no respect or love or consideration for their age, that did not really *value* them or think about them as people. Faith lay next to Gerda in the bright red nightie that was her favourite colour – this one is Sängo, Oba always says. The rumpled sheet on the other side of Gerda was evidence that Beatrice and Ernestine had been lying there before one or both of them rushed outside. One part of Maryam's mind took in all of this but still the main part was focused on her daughters outside. On one of them, mainly. He will take care of her. God will take care of her.

Maryam tried to walk carefully and not to brush her hand too hard against the green curtain on her left, separating the hall into two rooms. Rex slept there. Both boys used to be there, but now Eero had left the space to his six-year-old brother. Perhaps he might be at his cousin's house this early morning. But who know where he is? She can't worry about him now like she used to when he was younger. She was only thinking about him because while every instinct told her to run outside, her feet and her whole body were putting things off.

Oba would soon replace this curtain with a proper wooden partition. He just had to organise himself so that he was taking on less work outside to make ends meet and could spend time on the many building ideas he had for this precious living space they had at least been able to say was almost theirs.

Maryam walked to the door, held on to the doorknob, turned, pulled the door open, walked through the doorway, and down the steps to outside. Ernestine, her back to the house, her body outlined in the long grey cotton nightie, was just under the coconut tree, knees bent, hands just above them on her thighs. Instinctively, Maryam's eyes went to the branches of the tree. Don't stand under coconut tree, child, she cautioned in her mind.

Later, the story came out – more from Beatrice than from Ernestine. The person who had forced her daughter was one of the high-up people – a big shot not because he was rich, because he wasn't rich, really, but because he was white, and he knew of them there on the hill, while he was further up the hill on the estate. He didn't think much about them, of course, and what they might want, Maryam felt sure. If you white, you all right. She wouldn't tell the child anything, not now. It happen already. She heard that a woman up the road beat her little girl for being too forward. And was this the same man as before, she was wondering. She doesn't really want to know. And *tifi*, people said, should learn to keep their tail quiet – *Sipozé apwann tjenn latjé-yo twankil*. They should learn, people said, not to form fashion so much that they make man drag them in corner – *pou pòté kò-i a manyè pou nom pa halé-i a ti kwen*.

But Maryam couldn't blame her little girl. True, from time the child like to skip, to perform, to challenge big people, to form fashion. She is a child who like to see how far she could go. She is an inquisitive girlchild grown big in a world that does not respect girlchildren and definitely does not like inquisitive girlchildren.

The planter man, the sailor man, the insurance man, the high-up man, all man, and especially the high-up ones who had the say-so, they watched little girls, and you could see the big eyes saying, *This one ready already*, as if the girl had been put in their garden to grow and feed their hunger, and they just keep watching the fruit to see if it was ripe enough for their taste. Sometimes you could see their eyes thinking they could even eat it green. It's not as if man hiding.

What her girlchild is guilty of is being a girl in a world that does not think twice about shaming little girls. And Maryam knows that no one would forgive her girlchild for that – that even her own – the Africans and the Creoles – would be watching and blaming her, and whispering that you could see she like to take man. She had heard whispers like this too often not to know it would happen. Plain talk, bad manners. So the less said the better. Is okay. *Bondyé bon.* They would see after themselves.

Oba says quietly, "I am going to kill somebody." For days after this, he siddown on the step sharpening his cutlass with a file, moving the instrument with precision and intent. He stop going to sit in the corner shop on his way home the day the talk in the shop turn to the story of a little girl whose belly was swelling because a white planter or his relative… he or his brother, one of them high-up people – that's how the story went in the shop – one of them just throw her down in the boucan and pull her this way and dat, and had sex with her. And tongue and teeth started to create.

In the boucan? I thought I hear was under the cocoa? Miss Marjorie, give me two pound a flour dey please, Ma'am. The madam say she will pay you weekend.

Well, however it happen, it happen.

I not sure if is the man in the big house himself or if is one of his relative – you know how they stay! They can't keep their thing in their pants.

And is so people talking . And the laughter in the shop is long and loud. Somebody say *steupes* and shake head from side to side, but nobody take up cutlass to go up to the big house. They just mutter about how those white men like black meat. Somebody even say that the young white man is a relative and they hearing talk about perhaps he married one of those little black girls. And so the talk continue.

Perhaps he what?

Gason, ou fou? Boy, you mad? Sa épi yon bouwik vè.

That and a green donkey!

Woy! Tongue and teeth don't laugh at good ting, in truth.

Lanng épi dan pa ka wi bon bagay, pou vwé.

And of this eleven-year old little girl, Adolphus said, "You think that is child, then? Some of these little woman an dem act like big people, you know."

And Oba heard Jerome, who used to be his friend before that moment, announce, "Me self will take a piece if I get it. Those little woman fresh too much, you know." And on Jerome's face was the same look you could see on Boss face when he watched little girls on the estate.

Carlton said, "She get what she want. I sure they does see how the big man eyeing dem. Dose little girls not stupid, you know."

And Oba, wise because he is hurting for his own child, said in a quiet voice, "But is a child, man." And even as he says it he thinks he should say more, protest more. He remembered Maryam saying, "An eleven-year-old little girl is an eleven-year-old little girl, no matter how fresh you think she is. As the grown-up person, she can't put question to you, and if you think she putting question to you, tell her to go home. You-self, you not a child. And even if the girl is eighteen or more, if she tell you no, is no she mean, and you can't just decide that she pretending that. And if she just didn't say nothing because she realise you are a boss man and you powerful and could be the one to give her a work, you still not suppose to take advantage." Oba walks these days with Maryam's voice in his head, so he isn't afraid to say something.

But still, perhaps Maryam could say all of this better than he could. The words stuck in Oba's throat even as Jerome said, "Me, I not going to miss out. Leave all for the Boss? No sir! I have more sense than that."

Old Adolphus, silent until now, said, "That is just nastiness. All-you letting Bossman take all-you soul just because you hear how ting happen. And because that is what you have in your head already. That is just nastiness."

But the laughter echoed around them. Oba told Maryam later that he sat and listened, unable to join in the general laughter. And Maryam said nothing because she thought that when man get together she know for sure they does say things they wouldn't say in woman presence. Beg God pardon but she couldn't help wondering if Oba's reaction would have been different if he wasn't thinking that this was his daughter. He told her that in the rumshop a woman's voice from the doorway turned out to be that of Maisie, mother of Jerome's woman, Dolly. And Maisie said,

"What happen, Oba? How you looking downhearted so? You have a dog in the fight?" Oba didn't take the bait. That, he said, was when he got up and walked out of the shop, limping a little because these days the right knee was always swollen and hurting.

It was as if Oba retired from the village around this time. The house benefited, Maryam thought. You have to look for the silver lining. Oba finished all the work he had long been planning to do in his house. Sometimes she had to remind him that he had to go out, do like her, and get a few days work because bad how ting is, they have to eat.

He put a partition in the large hall so that now they had two proper bedrooms, like big shots. He said he would build a third. After he did some work on the house and some carpentry in the estate yard, and could put his hand on some money, he painted the house green to fit in with the surrounding vegetation and put edgings the colour of the purple bougainvillea, and he paid Vincent off for the piece of land. From the bottom of the road, as they walked up the hillside road everybody called Waterfall, people paused, standing arms akimbo and head back to look up at the special board house standing back from the green and settling there behind the purple bougainvillea. *Woy! Oba and Maryam is big shot these days, man! You doh see house! And that is not wall it have in the bottom down dey? Like they planning for the future? Well yes. Oba and Maryam well reach! They reach where they going, wi…*

CHAPTER THREE

1895-1900. The new arrival

Bush-gram busy shoo-shooing. All-you don't hear? A new baby in the Langdon house on the hill up there, yes.

Oba and Maryam didn't stop on the roadside to talk to people and hear what tongue and teeth had to say. If you don't wash your clothes in the open river, nobody could say they see the colour of the water that the river take away. Tongue and teeth eased aside the doors of their hideout up there in face-top, but nothing much they could wag and slobber-lick with each other about except what they imagine, or what fast people who know nothing at all present to ears sitting down on the corner.

And me, I could tell you because I am Spirit of the Place, hearing and seeing and knowing everything. You know how old people does say walls have ears? Well, I am the ears that walls have, and although they don't usually say it, walls have eyes too. When you think you see something, so you turn right around to find the something, but nothing there, is me, Spirit. I don't let nobody catch sight of me, but I witnesssing.

And yes, tongue and teeth shoo-shooing. Baby coming, they say. And those who know the names of the Langdon girls say is each one of them that mother this child.

E-heh? But the big one – what she name again? Beatrice! That little girl is only about 12 or 13, yes! And the one after her only about 10, 10 or 11, you know. And the other two girls – they little. Is four of them that there as girls. And then is the two boys – the big one – the one that does hold he head in the sky as if he is the governor, and the little one. So which one? And spit swish word around in mouth to see which one taste good enough to keep teasing tongue. And another one say, well, if it is *that one* is the mother, she lose the baby fat quick, but perhaps is not that one. Then which one, *non*? Well, perhaps is the other one that people say sitting down in Richmond round the corner down there watching through the bushes all day long trying to see the sea, as if she believe blue going out of style, and looking as if she have something heavy weighing down her spirit. But couldn't be she! That is their child, *non*? I thought I hear was a relative? *Non. Non. Non.* I hear they had a child before, you know. *Never!* How I don't know that? Or – well, it might well be the one that born just before the big fire in La Baye. I know them, you know. I know Maryam since she used to live with a relative in Grand Bras land for a little time, before she married and had children and everything. That little girl pass school age already, but not long, *non*, not much more than – twelve or thirteen. I hear she take off go in Trinidad – Beatrice or some other name they does call her. Or something else happen in the family, *non?* Perhaps. Nuff ting that get bury does happen in family when you see white people and man – whether black or white – involve.

They even say it might be the last little girl that is the mother – which goes to show how much some people know about the natural way of things – or perhaps is just that they don't know the age of the last little one. Because that little one is a baby, yes, about three years old. Is to tell you how *tongue* and *teeth* could be dangerous.

And all tongue and teeth could do was whisper, because neither Oba nor Maryam invited conversation or ventured explanation. It's not that they looked down at the ground as if they drop shame and had to find it to pick it up, *non,* but they just look a little bit above everybody head, as if they like the sight of the *bwa kano* growing in boundary line in the distance and waving to the sky up there. Or as if they wondering about that nutmeg tree over in the corner on the hill and how it looking as if it bearing already and thinking that it can't be true, that is anywhere from five to eight years these nutmeg trees take to bear and produce the tight yellow pod that will suddenly open one day to show fancy red and brown skinfit outfit. And when, their heads still high, Oba and Maryam wrinkled their nose a little bit, people had to wonder if they think they seeing thrips on the cocoa tree and trying to figure out if that little sucking insect really there to destroy the tree. Because Maryam and Oba had nothing to say to nobody. They just there looking like if they don't know that everybody shoo-shooing and trying to figure out what don't concern them.

The children from that Langdon house, too, kept their own counsel. The big boy keep his head high in the usual way, making people say that – ay ay! – is like he feel he is the governor in truth. But how he could be governor with nothing much in his pocket? Those Langdon people meet things hard like *gru-gru,* like everybody else on this hill. So what it is with this head high business? But some asked, So what? You can't hold you head high if things hard?

What people sure about, though, is that Oba and Maryam have a *chabin* grandchild. Anybody could see that later on when the family take the little bundle out to introduce crinkly face and tiny rolled-up light-skinned fists to the La Digue air, and they could see it even better a lot later, when the little girl with the long black plaits and the red skin start walking down through the bottom road there in Waterfall, holding on to her grandmother's hand or to the hand of one of the girls who may or may not have been her mother.

Then later on, they watched the little girl walk down the La Digue road to go in the shop like everybody else, and they marvelled at her *high colour.* Some said, *She pretty, eh? Whatever happen, the skin well pretty. Whatever you want to say, she raise their nose. She raise their chances in this world. Look how Maryam grand highcolour.* But when Maryam heard that kind of talk, she ready to cut neck.

She say, "She pretty, yes. She pretty because all my generation pretty, and that reprobate colour have nothing to do with it. Trying to spoil things, but it ain't succeeding. If it wasn't my child, I would say that colour is a evil mark, but is mine, so is just a stain we couldn't avoid, that is all it is."

And people watched the little light-skinned Langdon, not one that get the Langdon name and some of the skin colour from a white Langdon, but one that tongue say could get another white man name that staying secret for now, a name from another wandering white seed; and they marvelled that this new little Langdon so active already, and she so small that she just barely able to keep the little legs steady. They watched her hold a big person hand, the little blue skirt and white shirt neat on the near-white body, the little knife pleat of the blue school skirt sharp even when she a little thing – little, little. And they talked, of course. Ay! *Ma Maryam buying plenty starch boy, or is manioc she grating so?* They watched the child walk up the dirt road to that place the church say is a school – they put a roof on it and it looking well good dey – is not for style, is for the children to have some place to sit down and learn their lesson – one day they go make it a proper school. Ma Maryam taking in front. She starting early. Before time, everybody who want lesson had to go down to La Baye but the Archdeacon well trying in La Digue here! Ma Maryam start to send her grandchild to learn early early, as if, they murmured, to prove a point. And it was as though Maryam was the mother, because she was the one taking the child on Sunday mornings to the Anglican church in Holy Innocents, where the English school and the English church together on one long piece of land above the place the French people call La Digue when they were here, taking the child to church to give God thanks for letting eyes open up on a day of sunshine – or rain, if is rain *Papa Bondyé* choose to give; is Ma Maryam introducing the little girl to the market in La Baye; is from Ma Maryam she learn early to watch the eyes of the fish in the market and not to buy no fish with the eye too cloudy because that probably mean it there since Jesus was a little boy; is Ma Maryam dropping the little Langdon girl off to school most times. And so, time come and pass; one and one become two and two, become four, become eight and more.

CHAPTER FOUR

The times before. Earlier in the nineteenth century.

Sometimes when life hit you, you have to go back and trace the steps – see where you come from and remind yourself how many steps you take, even though you don't think you reach where you want to go yet.

Maryam couldn't remember much about her own childhood. It was right in this land, as far as she knew, but the grown-ups talked about capture and boats and the ocean, and when you hear their voice gone low is because they whispering about some kind of thing that seemed too terrible not to make it a secret. They frightened her, for sure, although they never explained anything much, as if either they didn't know too much, or as if it were something people shouldn't really talk about, especially when little children – *piti zanfan* – around.

There was something shadowy, something that her ma and aunties and the men didn't really want to talk about because, as they were always saying, sometimes through pipe smoke, sometimes straight so, with no smoke to cover it up, there are things you have to leave right where they are, and is not everything, everything you have to run your mouth about. So the – *Steupes, child, leave me alone*; or the – *What the eye don't see, don't hurt the heart*; or *Child, you don't know trouble; count your blessings – that is ask you have to ask!* Or – *alé asiz anba tab-la, go and sit down under the table, ka dammit* – these were answers to questions she couldn't even shape most times out of the shadows that framed her way of being.

She never saw the something shadowy but she could feel it, sometimes, even though she couldn't name it, as she lay at night with her mammie in the board house with the thick plaited straw roof in the place that the estate called Nigger Yard. She only thought about things like that later on. When she was growing up in Nigger Yard, it was their home space, and it was just the way things were.

Sometimes, when her mother and her aunts talked the past, about capture and a boat and the sea, she thought she was part of the story, and if they didn't look so sad, she would have thought it was exciting, and then they said it was her mother who would be able to remember a sea like a mountain it was impossible to climb, and who would even remember a night that had no beginning but had a part where they were in the bottom of a ship, like in the middle of the boat belly, her mother had said. The *idea* frightened her, and although she wanted to feel part of the story, she couldn't really imagine it – the ocean and the bodies and the shouting and the jumping, and the taking, and people fraid because they can't find their mother, can't find their father, can't find their child. And white sailor man just jumping on top of woman because they could and because African body belong to them they feel. That one does really tie up her inside. Boss people acting like African belong to them still, but in those times it was even worse. And who frightened jumping out in the ocean because they just can't take it, and… woy-o-yoy! It just sound like an impossible kind of story. But that's how they got here, yes, Maryam figuring out, her people and Oba people.

And to tell the truth, when Oba was telling her the story his father told him, he talk so fast that she could hardly understand, as if he anxious to leave one part of the telling and reach another part – like the part where his father and other Africans didn't have to be called slaves and they could learn a trade. They had to work on the estate but it was a little different. If they get tuppence, was theirs. And his father say he hear there was something some people called a contract but he didn't know too much about it. Oba told Maryam that he himself didn't know a lot, but to her it sounded like he knew a lot more than she knew.

Maryam knew nothing. She didn't even know who was the "family" that her mammie talked about when she said that all her family disappeared. But Oba now – Oba know his family – his father from Africa and then his mother's people on this side, although his mother, like a lot of other mothers, died when he was a baby.

From what they told her, she had been born on the estate, and her mother was the one in the boat with the sea mountain shaking it outside. And her mother didn't live long after she, her little girl, was born on the estate, but she left her ship sister to take care of her. And nobody ever talked about a father. But there was the woman she knew as Mammie.

Maryam's earliest memory is a wood-plank house on the estate in a place called Baillie's Bacolet that people say was the property of Mr Alexander Baillie, and then that same mister or his friend probably had a place in Boulogne, because she can't remember how, but she was working in cocoa there in Boulogne later, walking with Mammie and sitting down under the cocoa tree to pull slippery cocoa seeds out of the pods. And then she knew that the last name Sam was hers. Perhaps he, Mr Sam, owned or had some kind of interest in both of those estates – Boulogne and Baillie's Bacolet. She not sure how they divide up, who responsible for who, but she know that she get the last name Sam.

And the talk big people always talking, she couldn't really say that she pay attention to all of it. She would hear them say that things happen *just before the big rain*, or *the time God suddenly send a dark day and cover up his world* or *the year of the flood*, or something like that. And they always talking as if things happen yesterday, but sometimes when she figure it out, was even before she was born or when she was a little, little child. Always, there was some part of the story they told that wasn't very clear. In fact, no part of that story that had to do with a tumbling ocean and a place on the other side of it was clear.

Maryam knew mainly that she was born here in Grenada and she was a Sam – or at least she had the last name Sam when she met Oba. So Grenada, in a way, was a kind of beginning. And when Eero, her son, asked her later, she realised that she couldn't tell the child that she used to think of herself as unhappy. He was so vex for her that it was as if that was the answer he expected, but she couldn't really say that. Now she realise that she didn't know a lot because Mammie took a lot on her own shoulders. She take the brunt of things to protect Maryam, but she only figure out all of that later.

As she remembered it, her house was one of many just around the corner from the big estate house, and she used to go to work and clear the land like all the other children and then when they went home she played in the dirt in Nigger Yard with other children of the estate. And is only later she realise that her mammie sometimes would shout at her to stay in the yard and not follow her to the big house, although Maryam always wanted to go, and it was only something one of her aunties said long afterward that make her realise her mother was trying to shield her because she knew that, as her auntie said of the manager on the estate, *the man hand fast*. And although Eero face well make up and vex to beat a band when he even hear the name *Nigger Yard* – the child don't even want her say the name but that is what they calling it even now – but that is Eero.

The main game she remembers playing was *Up and down the deck*. Whoever was the captain would shout at all the other children to *Keep moving,* and when somebody didn't move fast enough, and the boom knocked into them and they fell overboard into the sea and out of the game, the whole yard would fall apart laughing. *Up and down the deck, keep moving. Up and down the deck, keep moving* – and then *Boom overhead!* And if you don't duck fast enough, you tumble down in the water. So then they fall on the ground, and that used to make them laugh. Sometimes they would stoop down laughing, the thing so sweet, and they only kept from rolling on the ground because they knew that some-body might take the opportunity to say that they out of the game because they fall into the sea. So you had to stand you ground. They used to enjoy that, but the big people sitting down in the doorway watching them would laugh a different kind of laugh, and say, *Yes, laugh! All-you don't know trouble in truth. Zò ba konnèt mizè pou vwé.*

So life around the estate was what Maryam knew growing up. Oba, now, was another case. From the beginning, Maryam wasn't sure about his story. He told her that he was from Africa, which seemed to mean that he hadn't been born in Grenada, like her, and so he was African, not Creole, like her. Those estate owner and overseer and manager and people like that used to call some of them *African* and some *Creole*. If you born here, they would call you *Creole*. They didn't think good about you once you black, but still is as if they think worse about those that they call African. At least *Creole* born here, so they acting like they think you a little bit more civilised because of that. She, Maryam, was Creole, as far as she know, because she born here, and Oba was African, as far as he say when she meet him.

But as time come and pass and as she talk more and more with people who work with him in St David's and other places, and as he himself open up and talk more, and as she hear about him working for a while on an estate called Tufton Hall, she gather that his father was the one who had been taken from a boat that another set of the slave traders were going with to some other country – a mix-up story about boat and sea and capturing – sometimes she can't even keep up. On the estate, though, they called him by the same name that they called his father. He was Oba Two and his father was Oba One. So she come to realise, when she put things together, that *really* his father was African and although on their papers they may have called Oba, the child, a Creole, he always knew himself as African with his father – so that is what he consider himself as and that is what he tell her. He tell her he was a liberated African working on the estate from long time.

Africa seemed to Maryam such a mystery. She had heard so much talk about the new free Africans they bringing in on boats now. Sometimes people said these new ones act as if they more important than those of them that had to work and be called slaves, but she was happy to be talking deep talk with this African man. Though even before Oba admit to her that really he born here, one of the women on the estate tell her that it wasn't true that he come from Africa, or that he come in many, many years ago; another one say that she think his father and perhaps Oba had just come in on the *Barbara Campbell* a few years ago, the same year that news come of slavery abolished in the United States. That Mr Langdon had taken them to Mirabeau estate first, and that they had brought Oba from there to here in Baillie's Bacolet; that he was a Langdon because he was one of those who Mr Langdon take from the boat. People was always *shooshooing* about who was who, and they say that Oba people was one of those new Africans that didn't know nothing, the last, last set that come in as liberated Africans. It was all so confusing. When Maryam tell Oba this story, he say they could call him what name they want, that he was his own African man and he have nothing to explain. The other people in Baillie's Bacolet stand around listening when Oba talking, and they say that African just like to talk and pretend he know thing. Well, Maryam didn't know, but she liked him anyway. She liked the way he could stand up for Africa. Nobody could say a bad thing about Africa; Oba would just spit sideways and look at everybody under his eyebrow. Whether he was pretending or not, whether he come in early or late, he don't plan to say and she don't think it important. She liked that he was standing up for himself and for Africa.

So when Oba talked about being African, Maryam agreed. She was African. Even if she was born in Grenada, she was African. And Oba liked that. He was from the Yoruba kingdom, he told her. He talked about a people called the Ebira. When Maryam agreed to be with him and him alone and to marry him – because he ask and because he promising that he would be with her and her alone – she reminded him that their children would be Creole *and* African. Oba said they would have to make sure that their children did not become like Creoles could be, laughing at Africa as a slave place. We have to be proud of Africa, he said. We have to know the Yoruba, and the Fon. She and Oba agreed about this. He told her he liked that she was a good woman. He taste her hand and he know she could cook. He watch her and he like how she handle herself, not like some of those crazy woman he see about the place. In those early days, when they were together but not yet married and she was young girl just learning things, she like how he talk. Even when those who knew him told her that you could see that man eye bright with woman, she say, well, he is man, and people does have history. As far as she was concerned, he was a good man to her.

Because right from the start of knowing him, Maryam was thinking about a time when they would promise themselves to each other alone, even though Mildred, who she would always tell her little story, Mildred steups and say, Poor *djab* you. *Ki nonm ou konnèt ki pwonmèt i kay wété èvèk yon sèl fanm èk y ka tjen pwomèt-*

41

li? What man you know promising to be with one woman and meaning it? But she always tell Mildred, and she would say that same thing again, you don't start off expecting the worst. Mildred just say that she don't like surprises, and where that concerned no man would surprise her. Well, whatever Mildred say, this Oba was a good man. That is what Maryam guts tell her. And she not swearing nothing for him because it not wise to swear for nobody, but when they make that early promise, she believe in him. And as if he had already started being severe with the children even before they have them, Oba opened wide the eyes that she always think look so small in his big face, and he say, "The two of us will not have a child who will laugh at Africa."

At the time, Maryam couldn't help wondering if he had another child somewhere who did laugh at Africa, because she can't believe is theirs to come he getting so vex with, but she tell her mind to shut up, put that aside, and she listen to him. "Our children will remember Yoruba and Fon. They will remember that place that is Africa, whether they go there or not." And Maryam just had to laugh, and she touch his face and tell him stop get so vex about things that not happening or might never happen.

CHAPTER FIVE

Unravelling the story. The children asking questions.

And then, there they were, the two of them, having children and with their boy Eero, a child who seem to have come out of her belly asking question. He always serious – too serious, Maryam thinking – frowning as if he vex with the world he in and mourning the loss of... well, something that she was sure he never knew. Because she didn't know it... That nice time before that he was mourning the loss of... she didn't know it, except from whispers and some broken-off stories and – really – she didn't mourn the loss like her son mourned it. Perhaps he was like that because his father told him what he could remember from *his* father. And that was a lot for Eero's father to do because Oba was not much of a talker, but perhaps there was a thing that made him talk because this was his first son. Maryam keep telling the child that she know nothing, but Eero keep asking.

"You remember Africa, Mammie? Tell me what you remember your Mammie saying about Africa."

"Well..."

"You must remember something."

"It was a long time ago, Eero."

He ask and he ask and he ask and she tell him that she didn't know.

"My mind is like the sea, Eero. Always rolling. Sometimes I just feel it rough and rolling around inside there."

"So you remember *lanmè*, Mammie, the ocean?"

"No. Is my mammie that really remember the ocean. I don't know the ocean that way except here. Except the sea that I see getting on bad down there by La Baye sometimes."

She didn't tell him that she didn't know it in the sense of being able to name its streets, although she knew from what big people whispered there were streets and caves and valleys and tracks in the ocean, and hidden places, and an ocean bottom with a world of things that could just get you frightened. She was sure of that because of the way big people talked about what they had lived through and those they had lost to the ocean. She told her son that she knew the ocean, but not well enough to be able to give names to its secrets. She watched his face, though, and she could see that he understood something of how her mind rolled. Some children were like that. Elders had told her that some children came with their knowing. Mammie used to say that you could see it on their face from the time they born. When that happened, people said, *This one was here before – sala té isi avan.* And perhaps, Mammie said, there were those who knew more when they just arrived, and forgot as they became older, so that a lot of the anxiety in their life was about something they knew they had forgotten. They could feel the knowledge of something else just there, and they kept straining forward to catch it. Maryam saw this something on her Eero's face. So much so that she nearly asked him to explain to her. Because, perhaps, inside of her belly, before he came out, he absorbed stories that she – and now he – had forgotten. Perhaps he might still remember something, though. She wanted to ask him but she didn't know the words to use to help him remember. Maryam wasn't the kind to hug and kiss a lot but Eero seemed to sense that he was loved without his mother having to physically pull him close. It was as if because he knew how much *he* was loved, in spite of the threat of something else all around him, in spite of the fact that of course they – both his mother and his father – throw some licks in he tail when he growing up and he wouldn't listen to what they said, in spite of the fact that neither she, his mother, nor his father, Oba, *talked* a lot about love, he sensed it was there. He wanted to find that lost memory of something more than a rolling past and recover something beautiful, especially for his mother. For his father, too, but Poopa was older, and somehow he looked as if he could manage. Maryam tried to dredge up something to tell her son, but what she remembered was the estate, pulling aside cane straw, but mostly cocoa straw, then picking up nutmeg, pulling dry pieces down in the banana plot, planting yam, ochroe, tannia, picking callaloo – not hard work, really, and she told him, "The work wasn't really hard, you know. Was just work, that is all."

And Maryam keep thinking that she did not have an awful childhood. She knew that her last name, Sam, was the same as Mammie's and the same as that of one of the big planter men who was a friend of the Mr Wells who had an estate that they worked on further down in St David's and later on in that other part, Belle Vue. And as Eero keep asking her, she figuring she could trace some of the story through the white people and their names and the estates that they owned. But it hard to know what is what with these white people. In fact, one of them who was high up in the Council and had the same last name as her husband – or, or – well, perhaps Oba had *his* last name – died the year before Eero was born. And she tell Eero that. That Langdon man and a Mr Shears from up this side too, both of them were high-up men on the Council in town and both died the year before Eero was born. She knew, too, that the Langdon name was the same as that of the man who had taken people from the ships that liberated Africans came in on. And perhaps, in truth as people say, Oba got his name from working on the estate that the Langdon man took liberated Africans to. But those white Langdon people, as far as Eero said, weren't in Grenada before that time around the 1850s and 60s, so if Oba… When she tried to talk to Oba about it, all he said was, "Why you worrying up yourself about their name? All these name is theirs, not ours. Forget that. No sense trying to trace your story through those white people name. They bestow name on you when they feel like it." And Maryam thinking, look at what Eero had told her about a 11-year-old little boy that get some Graham merchant man name. So perhaps Oba and other Langdons were related either by blood or by ship or by the white Langdon man name. Nothing to worry about, as Oba said. And again, some people didn't really need a last name when they were on the estate, so is really when people come to need a last name to pass on that they begin to use one from one of those white people they work for. Women, children, men, taken by one set of white people and rescued by another set who needed people to work for next to nothing on plantations that they were trying their best to keep going; it was such a huge, confusing story that sometimes she just sat thinking not so much about that place they were calling Africa or about England or about France which had left its language so strong in this island, but just about the ocean. Fancy just taking away a whole set of names from people and giving them one because you think your name more important. And then the evidence there for people to discover that donkey not wrong when he say the world not level. *Bouwik dit latée-a pa plat, pou vwé.*

So, as Maryam tell it – only to close people like Mildred, who will always listen even though she not always too believing, one thing become another. She and Oba come and have children, and the son Eero, when he hear the story, because as he grow up he was a child that always finding some kind of book to read and some kinda people to talk to that know ting, he tell us, Maryam say, that from the things we say, he realise that his grandfather, Oba One, or even if not him, some of those people called liberated Africans, reach Grenada after the slave trade end in 1807, but before Emancipation reach in 1838 and some even come after 1838. Sometimes you have to wonder where these children get all this information. Eero even name a ship that some of those Africans from early come in on. He say that there were African names for people on that ship, that it was one of the ships captured by the British. He didn't see an Oba on whatever list he see, but if it was a ship with liberated Africans, it could be a ship called *Negrinha* – so people who hear their family say they are liberated Africans could find out about that ship – or another one like it. Eero say, "Youall lucky yes, Poopa. For those they bring as slaves, they don't even know what the African name was and they don't have it on paper. For some of those ships with liberated Africans, they had the African names on paper. You lucky, Poopa." And his father say, "*Ah wi? Sé konsa? mwen chansé?* Oh yes? So I am lucky?" And Eero realize where Oba coming from – the child not stupid – if you escape slavery in one country to work like slave in another, you lucky? Okay! Perhaps – so Eero just say, "Well, you know what I mean!"

The story, as Eero tell them, was that after things not so profitable as in the beginning, and Britain starting to see the writing on the wall, it decide to listen to all those who rebelling and complaining and agitating and end the trade, and apparently it was just after people like Maryam mother so reach Grenada that Britain decide that if it not getting profit from the trade, nobody else among its *patizan* out there in Europe must continue making profit, so everybody must stop this trade. And Spain and the others, who Dutch and French and Portuguese and so, they say *Non, misyé – no, sir!* So they continue going and picking up people in Africa to be slave. And then Britain would stop them on the high seas, chase them down and capture their ship, and is so one of these ships that get captured was the one that Africans like Oba father was on. One like the *Negrinha* that Eero say get captured in 1830-something. Thirty-six, I think he say. And so, that is the boat that my big son Eero say he see list for, with African names and European names. And was a Portuguese ship, Eero say. So look how, if it was really that ship Oba father was on, he nearly end up in Brazil or somewhere and it coulda been a whole different story. Who know? So Eero see African names like… like what again? I will have to ask him… but what I remember… is … yes … name like Oussa and Mya and Kyma. So Eero see all these names; that is why he telling his father that those who could see their names from before lucky, even though they write down the African name and then they just give them another name. So that is how we even know the name Oba, Eero sayin. And I remember that the example he give from the list was that there was a child called Bipi, who was eleven years old, and on the list they give Bipi to a merchant named Mr Rob Graham – uh huh! That was it, and Bipi's European name become Hannah Graham. I keep that in me head because that was the example my son give. And it make me wonder where Bipi children and grandchildren today, and if they know that they nearly end up on a estate in Brazil some-where, and that the name they have is from Mr Rob Graham, a white man merchant. That their mother real name, Bipi, just get crossed off and buried one lick, and she become a Graham, so that now today all of them are something Graham, and it have a set of people with the last name Graham in Grenada, just as it have people with other last name, like Sam and Langdon and so. What a ting! An it really make you think how all of us Africans in this world out here is one people, and we end up anywhere and everywhere – and sometimes nowhere, and how the name we have is not ours at all, but white people name. So we might as well X it out and call weself X, because when we proud of name, is them we proud of.

What a cuffufflement!

And Maryam wondering how to think about Africa. She could more easily think about the sea, the Atlantic that draining into the Caribbean sea that she could see from the bend in the road along Waterfall, that she could stand up and watch all the time when she go into La Baye. The Atlantic, that was what they crossed and what was still crossing them here and that they had to look at with wonder, especially during hurricane season. The sea. *Lanmè.* That sea and its hills and curves – like a rock ocean – that was definitely something to marvel at, *wi*. A world of tumbling blue rocks that is something they call an ocean.

CHAPTER SIX

Maryam's Musings. 1895/1896 – and after.

Sometimes you just have to keep walking back and looking again to see how the story stitch together. You have to remind yourself and to arm yourself for what and what will happen whether you like it or not. And Maryam could stitch. She not backward with the sewing.

That time, when she first, first meet Oba, in the early days, she was only around nineteen or twenty – nineteen, in fact. And he was a tough, strong man in the field, almost the age she is now, twice her age that time, but he didn't look it. Afterwards, she thought that she believed all kinda thing he tell her, perhaps because, to her, he was big and experienced. Yes, Oba was old enough when he and she start up, but he didn't look it, in truth, as far as she could see, especially those times. Or perhaps people does see what they want to see! She don't know. *Time and tide, eh! Huh!* Ah well! The years catching up with him now, though.

These last six children come after she married Oba, before she could think too much about it. Six more of them, and now you could say seven. Three years ago, Amèlie was her belly-wash child – the last one, the one that empty out the belly. After the last set – Gerda, Faith and then Rex, she thought she was done, and then it was as if Amèlie appear when they weren't looking. And that was the problem. They weren't looking. But then with Amèlie, *Kaput*, she told everybody who wanted to hear, and even if they didn't want to hear. *Kaput. Done. That is it.*

And her Eero, know-it-all even at fourteen years at the time, born 1879, as he always telling her, so that sometimes she just let him interfere in big people talk even though she know she should shut him up, he tell her, "Mammie, kaput is a word that come from so many different places, and I think it mean broken, not done." Well, she say to him, "Is awright. Let it come from where it want to come from, is Grenadian now, and whether you think is broken, done, or whatever, is finish. *Kaput. Fini. No more.*" That child, Eero – in fact, all her children, yes – when they talk, *how* they talk – it remind you about what is possible when you could read book in addition to listening to story. And he always find people who like to talk so he could listen. She hope they telling him sense. Huh! Is like these children get to know things.

The years going. She'd been surprised that at the age she was, Amèlie had come. Middle of those years after forty at the time, yes, that's what they tell her, climbing up the last hill to go down the other side, and baby appear. By that time, Mammie gone and meet she maker, Oba father gone, and is them figuring out what is what. But now Amèlie had company, and yes, *Papa Bondyé*, you know what you know.

And anyway, they going make it. *Papa Bondyé* don't give you more than you can handle. Perhaps Papa God decide there must always be children in the house. After they married, 1879 – that is the year Eero tell her he find when he go and look for his birth paper in the registry office – and then one born in the year people say they have something they call an Ordinance – so people children will get schooling in primary school and Eero see it write down. That was 1882, and then 1884, 1885 – beginning and end of 1884 – so you might as well say 1884, the year they start to build the new Courthouse in Grenville, and 1885, the year that big man, Governor Sendall, become Governor – then 1886 with Faith she thought they were done – until Miss Amèlie, Miss *Matwité* – like Eero, grownup since before she born. She see they not looking and she sneak in to appear at the end of 1892. And don't talk about before they married – those that their church divide into two with different name for one side of the blessing and another name for after the blessing. *Ill* legitimate and then legitimate. What a church! Because that can't be God idea. It must be church own! So now – 1895, they calling this year. Ah! Take a deep breath! Ah wa! The year gone wasn't a bad year when you think about everything, they say, but when things rough it hard to think about what they call everything. It didn't start off so bad but in the end was a really hard year, though. Cocoa price was way down, so there wasn't much work on the estate. Not only that, the cocoa crop wasn't as big as usual but the price low. Is like the trees know the market not giving much. Nutmeg bear, though, and nutmeg price was good, so people who had their little piece of land with a nutmeg tree or two could make tuppence. And ground provision bear like it going out of style, so that help no end. And road work did good. So all in all, you have to say one thing balance out the other. Lord, what a life!

And the little ones help out with the work too, digging yam hole, picking peas, picking callaloo, going and get bush for the cold and the fever and cooling – things like the sugar dish, the coraile, the ven ven, the shado beni, the soursop leaf – picking up the one-one cocoa when the ripe ones get left on the ground, cracking the yellow cocoa pod and putting those wet, wet seeds in bucket, putting the cocoa out to dry on crocus bag in the yard, picking up the nutmegs and peeling off the mace. Lord! Land have work, yes. Ay-a-yay! *Wi,* land have good work, though cocoa not doing well these days so work on the cocoa estate scarce. Some people don't mind, really, because it mean more time to work on this hillside land – the hillside lots, as they call them, that they carve out of the mountain to make sure people have to break their back to make it produce. But we doing it. We going do it. Just now dem self – *yo menm,* the high-up ones – *moun ki ni lajan*, they will want mountain land when they see what we could make it do. Because we know how to work and make land talk.

Anyway, it just don't make sense doing the break-back work that Mammie and dem had to do for so long on the white man estate. I doing it still sometimes, but not my grandchildren. Not them – *pa yo*. I don't want that for them. Anyway, it sensible to make use of this year, because for ground provisions, if not for a lot else, is a good year. Kitchen garden with yam, tannia, manioc, and things of the sort give good food to eat and you could even sell some. So that is that. That is that.

Though, come to think of it, I not glad that estates weren't doing well because that is where the work for poor people is, but

I can't say I sorry either. Those people high up know how to get butter for their bread. I glad that those like Vincent and Garraway and who not else deciding to let go some of the land in La Digue and those places around so that we getting a piece, though I have no idea why people think everything perfect when you could get land for *next to nothing*. If they pay you *nothing* to work, then it have to be *nothing at all* to pay if they serious about you getting a piece for yourself. Hmm! It had better be for nothing. It was good that Oba had a mind for the future, too, yes, so that we could get a good piece on the hillside here in La Digue. Papa God know what he know. *Papa Bondye konnèt sa i konnèt.*

Thank God this was a good year for the government work on the roads. *The colony is making strides* is the way the Administrator, Mr Drayton, say the word, and really it is true that people could find work to put some money in their pocket. The government fixing road all over the place. For herself, she felt better sending her young ones to do a few days on the estate *lè glo plis pasé fawin* – when water more than flour – but she could understand why some people preferred to make a few shillings in *twaveau – twavay nan chimen-a* – work on the road. What a life!

Really, a lot of things happened last year and still happening this year. Of course, the biggest one – the biggest one – was Ernestine getting pregnant and having big belly early in the year. And as if to mark the year, lots of other things were happening. Last September, half of Grenville was under water, in fact, *oui*.

The children tell me I always talking to meself, but in this life you have to talk to yourself to remind yourself what and what happening. And Eero telling me I don't even know which language I talking in, French or English, but is neither one, *non*. As he father say, is the one we make for weself out of all of them. *Wi*, is that one.

And they were doing some work up there in St Patrick's, too, after the flood. I didn't see it, but people say that Belmont bridge collapse. When I hear about things like that, I think is a good thing we on the hill up here in La Digue, *wi*. Hill could slide, is true, but sometimes they make so much fuss about land in the flat and when thing like the flood happen, you have to wonder if is worth the trouble. Hillside land could slide down, yes. And is a lot of mud until you could fix it. But God is good.

So, well, work going on in the country if you could get it, and to top it off, Eero tell me that, down in St George's, that miracle joining one side of *Town* to the other, Sendall Tunnel, the idea of Governor Sendall from long ago, is at last finally done. They stop work on it for nearly two years, but they say it finish now. So perhaps the Administrator right and the Colony looking up! I hope when it look up it see everybody – all of us black hen chicken on the hill here – struggling. But that Governor Sendall was one of a kind in truth, yes. He do a lot of things for the country, and is good that they having a street right down there in La Baye – Sendall Street – name after him. He work for the country, even if country is theirs, not mine. All of them in whiskey company together, but he well work for the pounds, shilling and pence that they paying him. So let's see how things will go.

And thinking and thinking every day, Maryam turns away from her usual spot at the bend of the road in Waterfall, from where she would look down toward the sea in La Baye. Standing with her back to the sea now, she looks down to the left, where, under the road, as they call it, she and Oba decide to get a spot cleared for Eero, now that they know Vincent the boss-man would let them keep this land and not make it too hard for them to buy. They will have that spot so Eero could put up a little house. Not a bad spot, and after the children drink water already, is time for them to secure themself in their own little spot. She liked the hilltop, where Oba had built their house, because the estate and the high-up people tell them it would be okay to put down a little board something – doing most of it himself, yes, she thought proudly; her husband is a good man.

And it is literally true – he himself put up the house with the help of those who learning from him how to do this carpentry business that always seem to come out right for him. It don't provide them with enough money to make a living, but is definitely a help for everything. And Eero have the same gift, God be praised. Give him hammer and nail and he could help himself. Uh-huh! Maryam stands looking down into the land, past the two mango tree, just behind the cow pen. Down there under the road is a nice little spot, and you could still get a glimpse of the sea from there if you twist you head, or come up in the road, and you would see it better. And anyway, you could see, over on the other side, the cocoa trees the Government planting these days, all over the place. Eero might well like the spot, even though she knows that his independent streak – and almost in spite of herself Maryam purse her lips and the sound of a steupes push itself from between her teeth – is another story.

Up there on the hill near the house, the trees took away a little from the sea view but, as Oba always says, they need the trees for windbreak if a hurricane were to hit the country. But no thinking about hurricane now. February is not hurricane season, though in this life all season is hurricane season, *wi*. Ay-a-yay! All season is hurricane season.

Time will tell.

Tan kay di.

Oh yes, time will tell. Ah, *wi*.

And so, as is the way of things, time come and pass – sometimes it feel like it walking slow and sometimes it running, but it passing, making its way to tomorrow. 1895 pass, 1896 gone, baby born and baby christen, and sometimes the less said the better. That is how Maryam thinking in this moment about the crying and the not eating and the way her child don't seem to have no friends, and the way her daughter walk unhappy in the world heavy like a hammer in the mother's soul. And the father, too. It seem to settle across his shoulders more than anywhere else, and more and more it pushing his back to the ground. But time don't care; it just moving on like is nobody business what it do. And while she thinking about what going on inside her family, Maryam listening, too, to what happening around.

She knows that while Eero likes to tell her how things are going in the country, she is sure he doesn't tell her everything, but he is always stopping by to talk. Once, when Mildred was there, Eero called out from the yard: "Mam! I just passing to see how you do," and then, because he realised Mildred was there, he said, "I going pass back and check you out later, okay?" And Mildred say, "Even though that boy big now and he going other place, he always checking on you and talking to you like is people." Maryam laughed. "How you mean he checking on me and talking like is people? So I is not people then?" Mildred say, "Girl, that is gold, yes, when they talking, is gold. Is like you win a sweepstake. Sometimes I wonder if mine know how to string words together." And although Maryam laughed at that, she is thinking, *I don't think I could stand it if he was like his father. So yes. Mèsi, Jézi!*

Now, Maryam sitting under the house. Oba and Eero had put it up on tall pillars so there would be space at the bottom where they could hang clothes to dry and get some breeze, and not be in the hot sun while they worked. Maryam sits there on a chair that they call the old chair because it has seen better days. It is sturdy, but the wood is dull and marked, not as pretty as it was in the days when its name was *the new chair*. Going the way of all of us, is what Maryam says of the chair when it wobbles a little bit under her. She sits there grating coconut for the peas soup she plans to cook and in her head she turns over the happenings.

Eero told her that just earlier this month there was a boat in St George's, a boat named something like Lou … Lou … Louisi … well, something or the other – a boat with people – tourists, Eero said, coming for the races that the high-up people now starting to have at the race track down there in Grand Anse, down by *Town* side, and Eero say they even going to have horses from Trinidad, and they having all kind of picnic down there at the place called Quarantine Station in South St George. Good for them. Their bread well butter. *Pen-yo ni bè.* And Trinidad getting bigger and bigger these days, since they take Tobago away from us, the Windwards, and join it up with them. Just now people would have to say Mister Trinidad. About ten years or a little more since that happen. Is like Trinidad get bigger in its boots, *wi.* Not ten years yet, *non,* about seven, perhaps, because Eero was a little boy, about ten years old according to what he say he see on his birth paper – ten years old when it happened.

And now she wondering what it is Eero always doing and why he trying to catch the mailboat in La Baye every other week to send letter go in Trinidad. Who he know there? And now every minute he want to be in St George's town to talk to people. Quite down in St. George's. What it is he have to say to people so much? Maryam hoping he not in no confusion.

Eero doesn't tell her a lot about his doings, except when he go to political meeting, because he knows she wouldn't mind. He like the political talk, and is sheself he take it from – she and his father – so she expect he would be into all kinds of things, listening at least. She don't want to guess what, though, and anyway, Eero is a good child. The younger ones don't come and talk so much about what and what happening, but she know Eero nurse from sheself this interest in *politics and history*, as he self say the thing, in what and what going on, and he always ready to question what it is the high-up people doing. Is so she used to be in all talk about which estate striking, and which overseer doing what not right. He get it from her, no doubt about it.

Oh gosh! Look how ah grating me hand, *non*! Where the pancup? Let me dip it in the bucket of water in the corner there and rinse out this hand. It don't look as if it bleeding, but this damn grater scrape me hand. You can't be too careful!

Well, he get the politics thing from his father, too, but he wouldn't even know that, perhaps, except when I tell him about Oba, because Oba don't bother to talk to the children, really.

Maryam looks out into the sunshine and up at the white clouds hovering just below a pretty, pretty blue in the sky. *Pwotèjé li, Jézi. Keep him safe, Jesus.*

CHAPTER SEVEN

1900s. Maryam: Still a lot on her mind.

Looking down at the sea and the town today, now that another little one come to bless the generations, Maryam remembering those early days, the talk about Creole and African and how they would like to see the children think, even though the children life is theirs, of course. And she thinking, too, about all the things Eero telling her, and how the country going as a country for itself, not thinking about Creole or African or anything but figuring out this place they calling Grenada.

Where Eero does get his information, Maryam cannot say. Perhaps in one of those youth meetings he always going to. She hope he not planning anything that would get him in trouble, *wi*. She had enough to cope with already. He telling her thing like, *La Baye is like all over the country, Mammie*. The names of different places, he tell her, they don't let us forget our history; it's as if they trap us, although they – well, we looking at that. So he say it, *wi*. And that is the thing that keep making her wonder. *We* looking at that? *Who is we? He and who?* "La Baye for the French," he tell her, "because they were here, too, you remember, Ma? That is why we had the Fedon rebellion long ago in the hills on the other side – you know Fedon's Camp in Grand Etang around there, and through Gouyave and so, with people fighting against the British for what they want? That is why we speak this other language. *É sé pou sa nou ka palé lòt lanng sala.* You know that, Mammie?"

And she just watch her boy, because these young people have a way of talking these days as if they invent things and is dem alone that know. So she had to tell him, where the language concern, the French had a part in it, but is us, the Yoruba and the Asante and the Igbo and the Wolof and other African people and our way of figuring the language, that make it like it is. So sometimes we use their word, *oui,* but sometimes we just use ours and we say it like how we say things. And in the way that these young people have, that could really make you want to say long,long steupes, this boy, her son, he kind of shrug his shoulders and lean his head to one side and act as if he mean *Of course I know that!* These children could make you want to heave them somewhere far, where nobody can't find them! And then she said to herself, not really, *non,* we going find them, because they belong to us, but they could try your patience. And Eero explain to her that he think the name Grenville is to remember those like Lord Grenville and high-up people over there in England. *What a thing if that is true!*

We African and Carib people, her son Eero say, we have to look out for what is ours. *Nou menm moun Afwitjen é moun kwayib, nou ni pou gadé pou sa ki sa nou.* And is that same one little word, *we,* that still have her worried, although she glad is not just African and Creole he thinking about, but Carib too.

Imelda from up in La Poterie tell her that is the way some of the young people talking nowadays, as if they in secret society together, but it just mean that they going to meeting and talking about things and studying, and that not bad. Remember how we used to talk and plan thing? Imelda say. And is true, she and Imelda were two of the workers long time ago who didn't use to take no nonsense. But still that *we* word worry her, because she know that when you decide to look for what you think is yours, and is not you alone but is group that you calling *we,* is there trouble does start. *Jan mennen'w alé, wi. Yé pa mennen'w viwé.* Friend bring you go, yes. They don't bring you back.

And what on her mind too is her daughter Ernestine and this little grandchild that twisting her inside every time she look at her. And she remembering that day in 1895 when she and Oba had to take stock that having children meant having to go through a lot of the same things again and again. She wonders now if her Mammie used to feel like that. She glad that little girl is part of her life but it had not been easy to watch her child struggle with life and with man and with trying to figure out what is what. Her Ernestine take on things and look what happen! That child wasn't for this world. She just couldn't cope. Was a thing to see her whole body shake like that. *Eclampsia,* or how the doctor say the word. The body couldn't take and the mind couldn't take, is how Maryam think about it, so is as if Papa God clamp down and decide to take back his creation. But this child that come like a gift to her will survive. She, Maryam, will see to that. That little girl will make it in this world.

CHAPTER EIGHT

Oseyan. 1896 to early 1900s.

And so now, this little girl child! Her name, the one they put first
on her birth paper in the church that February day in the year
1896, comes from ancient times. Her uncle Eero says so, and he
is the one who talks to the little girl about the name. According to
him – and soon the little girl is looking up at her uncle and asking
him about many things that happen in books and newspapers –
there are stories like that about an ancient city called Troy. She
learns that hers was the name of a woman who had a face that
launched a thousand ships – *non sala sé sa yon vijay ki lansé yon mil
bato.* Her face launched the boats, caused them to sail out there,
because of its beauty. "Myth-o-lo-gi-cal," he tells her. Sound out
the word. That is what my teacher used to tell me. "Myth is like
a story in history that help to explain things and that everybody
talk about and shout about." And then he said, "Ask your teachers
when you go to school. They will tell you more." He tells her that
the word sounds big, but when you break it up, it's just a lot of
small parts. Eero talks about the name and says it with so much
wonder in his voice that the little girl comes to think that this
name is one that shouldn't be said just any and everywhere. A
complex figure was this Helen of Troy, her Uncle Eero told her.
"I know you are not a simple person yourself. I could see it in your
face," he said, smiling and putting a finger on her nose. "You are
a young lady of great beauty and deep, deep thought, like Helen
of Troy." And the child grinned up at him, pleased to be like
Helen of Troy. But she came to feel that this name was like the
good clothes you put away – the going-out clothes you would
wear on a Sunday for church, or on a Saturday, depending on if

you're going to the church Ma goes to sometimes on the Holy Innocents strip, or on a Saturday to the church of one of her aunties. Hers, she thinks, is a name special like good clothes. Or even more special. A name to keep secret because is like the thing inside you that her grandmother calls the spirit. When people speak her name out loud, or sound forceful with it, the little girl holds her breath. You don't just handle things like that anyhow. She knows that without anyone having to tell her, so that she is relieved when, through her grandmother, she begins to use another name that she thinks of more like home clothes – a home name, one you could use every day.

The little girl always seems thoughtful. Perhaps it is because of the stories about Helen of the sea that her uncle told her when she was little. Or perhaps she just come with her knowing. Sometimes, frightened by the idea that she might launch a thousand ships and then not know what to do, or have to wait until those who have sailed away come back, she turns her back on the sea down there in La Baye and stands staring into the La Digue bush, as if looking for something in the green that would not remind her of the sea's churning blue. Sometimes her face is a cloud as thoughts chase one another inside her head. Then Ma, her grandmother, would be thinking, *Don't tell me is another one that was here before!* On one such day, Ma says, "*Wanjé fidji'w tifi*. Fix your face, little girl child. You are just one little boat on a big ocean. *Ou sé yon ti bato sou yon gwo lanmè.* Try not to worry about the whole ocean."

And Ma, her granmama, would sing her the song that she said her own mother, the woman who took care of her, used to sing to her when she was little, because, her mother told her, she heard the white people singing it:

Oh carry me over the ocean
Oh carry me over the sea
My Bonnie lies over the ocean
Oh, bring back my Bonnie to me..

Bring Back
Bring Back

And by the time they got to that part of the song, the child would be laughing and asking, "Ma, who is Bonnie?"

"Well what kinda question you asking me dey, chile? I never think to ask that. I just know it over the ocean. Ask Uncle Eero when he come."

Uncle Eero said that the song was a Scottish song and he had heard it said that *bonnie* had something to do with Scotland and England and how some people thought about *Bonnie* (meaning the nice) Prince Charlie, over the ocean. The prince had to leave Scotland because he was one of the Stuart kings, Uncle said, fighting to keep the throne of England and Scotland, but he didn't succeed.

It was confusing. When they were talking about the song in school one day, one of the children whispered that she, Oseyan, was from those terrible Scots because people said her white father was a Scotsman. Oseyan didn't know, but that was what people said. So was Bonnie Prince Charlie her friend? Was he her father's friend? She didn't want to think about it, so she just asked the question in her mind, and she sang along with Ma.

My Bonnie lies over the ocean
My Bonnie lies over the sea.

And sometimes Gerda, her aunt, passing by the house as she always did, walking down to visit her mother from her own place now higher up in La Digue, past the turning going toward Holy Innocents, Gerda would look at them together there and smile.

Today the child asks, "Ma, *ou kwèyè mwen pé sé tout oseyan-a?* You think I could be the whole ocean?"

Ma straightens her body, takes a deep breath, holds her frame straight and her shoulders back, her head with the black plaits almost circling it, looking near to the open rafters up there as the child put her head back to look up at this most important person in her world. Eh, Ma? Ma puts out her hand briefly to touch the hair. The wedding ring circling her slim finger looks gold and pretty to the little girl. And Ma stands looking down in wonder at this little person who had come from unimagined places to bless her understanding. "*Tout lanmè-a? Tout oseyan-a? Ou sèl?* The whole ocean? You alone?" The word ocean that the child used made Ma think of more than *lanmè* in La Baye, made her think of *oseyan Atlantik-la – the whole Atlantic Ocean.*

The child's eyes fill with tears. Ma bends to tickle her and chase away the watery shadows, so that for a long time the little girl can't stop laughing. Ma settles her down and sings other songs, keeping the child smiling.

Alouette, gentille alouette
Alouette, je te plumerai
Je te plumerai la tête
Je te plumerai la tête
Et la tête, et la tête

Ma touches the little girl's head. Repeats – *la tête, la tête, la tête*. Oseyan repeats, laughing, *la tête, la tête, la tête*. Oh, how she loves her grandma.

Alouette, gentille alouette
Alouette, je te plumerai
Je te plumerai le bec
Je te plumerai le bec

And Ma pushes her lips out to try to make them look like a bird's beak.

Et le bec, et le bec – pulling gently at her lips with her fingers and then touching the little girl's mouth, then touching her head. *Et la tête, et la tête.*

They move their shoulders side to side, smiling, laughing, put arms akimbo and sing:

Alouette, gentille alouette
Alouette, je te plumerai
Je te plumerai le cou

Putting a finger to her own neck and the child imitates, touching her neck. *Le cou.*

Je te plumerai le cou
Et le cou, et le cou
Et le bec, et le bec
Et la tête, et la tête

Alouette, gentille alouette
Alouette, je te plumerai
Je te plumerai les ailes
Je te plumerai les ailes
Et les ailes, et les ailes

And Ma stretches her arms wide, flapping them like *les ailes* – the wings –

Et le cou, et le cou
Et le bec, et le bec
Et la tête, et la tête
Alouette, Alouette

Ma laughs and laughs and Oseyan giggles with her and together they sink on to the bench. Ma takes some deep breaths – in, out, in, out. "*Bondyé, mwen las.* Oh Lord, I tired." Giggling, the child puts her head back like Ma, pushing herself back into the tall chair behind her. The child says, "Me, too."

Ma says, "Chile, you tire me out." Tickling her. Giggling with her.

"Let's do it again, Ma. Let's do it again."

"*Non Non Non.* Enough. Enough for me."

"I could do it, you know, Ma. I not too tired."

"Poor *djab mwen.* Poor me. *Sé mwen. Mwen las.* I tired. Rest, child. Rest."

Then Ma, taking in a deep breath, releasing it, and closing her eyes, puts her hands down on either side of her on this bench that she told Oseyan Poopa made long ago – in a time the little girl can't remember, the time, Ma said, that was before *yon lanné tounen kwen-a* – one year turned the corner, and it became *yon syèk totalman diféwan,* a whole different century, not eighteen hundred and anything, but nineteen hundred. Poopa didn't too like all this change, Ma said, so when nineteen hundred showed its face – *a whole one thousand, nine hundred, imagine* – Poopa only waited to see what it looked like after we buried our daughter, your mother, and when one year of the century had gone by so that he knew it was real and that his family could cope and would manage to live and survive in it, Poopa said, "Okay, enough for me. *Okay, asé pou mwen.*" Then he turned his back, put what remained of their generation's time in Ma's hands, because she had less years on this place called Earth than he, and so he went to meet the ancestors. And that is how Ma tells the story. When Oseyan hears this story, she stands looking at Ma, wondering if there is more. Had Ma just said that Poopa Oba waited to bury their daughter before he died? Our daughter, *your mother?* Nobody told her anything. Did that really mean her mother?

"Ma, did my mother die when *yon lanné tounè kwen-a*, and it became *yon syèk totalman diféwan?*"

Ma pats a spot next to her on the bench and says, "Come and sit here next to me, Ocean. *Vini asiz koté mwen, Oseyan.* The answer is yes. Your mother went to meet her Maker and she left you with me because I had you with me already and she left you to keep on living with me because she know I was very happy to have you with me. But come. Come. Come. Tell me what happen in school today. *Di mwen,* Oseyan" – and Ma smiled. "*Di mwen, Ki sa ki wivé'w an lékòl jòdi.* Oseyan." The child smiled, too, because Ma was calling her Oseyan all the time now, and she liked the home name.

The girl who wants to be the whole ocean. Oseyan. That is what the wind calls her now when it moves whispering in the trees on the La Digue hillside. And the drizzle that she won't leave sometimes even when Ma shouts to her to *Come inside child, you can't see it raining?* The drizzle says Oseyan against her face as she looks up to the blue skies. Oseyan, her home name, is the name everyone begins to call her. Tongue can't trace how the name moved from the mouth of her grandmother to the ears and then the mouth of the whole of La Digue and then La Baye and then the island, but that is what happened. Oseyan, the little girl who looks at *lanmè* down in La Baye, listens to stories about the *oseyan Atlantik-la, and* wonders if she can be the whole ocean.

Oseyan tells her grandmother why she is sad. When they went into the school yard for break today, the children teased her. It was not the first time they had done that but today they really teased her a lot. They called her *chabin* and *tifi wouj* – red girl. Little Man, the boy who lived under the cocoa in the straw house with his mother, the woman who had come to La Digue from Mirabeau…

Her grandmother stopped her. "Eh? Little Man in your class? I thought Little Man was older than you?"

"No. He not in my class, but sometimes the teacher does bring him in to be with us. I don't know why. But Gwen say she believe he have some things to catch up on. He in Standard Two, but he was in my class today, and it was breaktime."

"Okay. But is not a lot of all-you. How much of them in this Standard Two?"

Oseyan seems to be counting in her head. Ma says, "Is okay. Is okay. It don't matter. Tell me what happen."

Little Man, her grandmother knew, was the son of Ezra, their Cousin Julius's daughter – Ezra whose mother was from Mirabeau although her father was La Digue people. They weren't close cousins, more like *pumpkin vine* cousin. Ezra's mother was a Sam, too, because at one point she worked on a Sam estate, but as far as Maryam knew there was no blood relation. Or perhaps she might be a cousin of a cousin of a cousin somewhere along the line. Of course, they knew each other well because they were people who lived in La Digue together, but they weren't close. Sometimes Ezra would pass by, stopping on her way down the hill through Waterfall, and Maryam would give her a few coconuts, or some soursop, a hand of fig, or mangoes from the land around their house that she and Oba had planted there on the hillside, and they would always give somebody – well, less fortunate, let's call it – although they themselves not *too* fortunate – but they could give a hand of fig, a bunch of bluggoe, a yam, or something like that. Most people had their little estate garden these days, but not everybody could plant everything. Eero said that as bad as things were, Grenada was plenty better than some of those other countries around that were tied to the sugarcane and didn't turn also to cocoa and things like yam and plantain and eddoes and so. Bad as things were, Eero said, they could be a lot worse. And his mother said, *Amen. Amen to that. That is the way to think, chile. Amen.*

Maryam remembers that she was there in Misyé Jerome's shop at the junction one day when the little boy walked up from La Digue road, from the Richmond direction, and turned right into the Holy Innocents Road with a little swagger, walking and dancing across the road like he owned it. It was Jessie, Cousin Gerald's wife, who said, "That is Julius gran. A real little man. And is so the mother say he stubborn!" The name had stuck. It wasn't clear how the name Little Man had moved from the mouth of adults to the ears of children, but perhaps only his teachers now knew that, on paper, the child was Adolphus Leconte, though some knew that his grandfather called him Dolphie.

Now Maryam asks, "So tell me, what Little Man do you?"

"He ask me if is true my father is a good-for-nothing white man," Oseyan says tearfully. "And he ask me if… if… if…" and at each pause the child sobs shakily, "if I like white man too like my mother. And everybody in the yard laugh. All those children laugh, Ma." Now Oseyan is really sobbing. She doesn't see Maryam's jaw clench and she is crying too much to see her grandmother's lips tremble, but she does hear her say, "*Lanng épi dan*. Tongue and teeth."

"What you mean, Ma?

"We have a saying, *doudou mwen*, that *lanng épi dan pa ka wi bon bagay*. Tongue and teeth don't laugh at good thing. People like to talk, my dear, but they like best to talk about things that they think of as good gossip, and most times these are not things they think are good or nice. You understand? Try not to let it make you unhappy. Don't give them the satisfaction. They know nothing about your mother. And they definitely don't know anything about you."

The child put out her arms as if she wanted to wrap them around her grandmother although she couldn't reach around. She put her thumb in her mouth as she leaned against Maryam. Maryam looked down at the top of the head with the long dark plaits and thought of the big skirts of her own Auntie whom she called Mammie. When she herself was a little girl, she would pull the bunchy part of Mammie's big frock over her head. But Maryam's body was different from her mother's and she liked these long slim skirts – big, but not bunchy enough for a child to pull over her head and wrap herself the way she remembered she used to do. She should get a big bunchy skirt. She was old enough. Fifty-a-lot was plenty age to be a proper grandmother. *Gadé mizè mwen*. Look my trouble. And the trouble is mine, and I have to say she is my very own child. She touch my heart – right inside.

Oseyan didn't tell Ma that Little Man had also said, "You grandmother not so old, but because she take old man put on her account she only dressing like if she old." Because children hear their own mothers and grandmothers and fathers and uncles and grandfathers and aunts speak, Oseyan knew that although this came from Little Man's mouth, it had come from a big person's mouth first. She knew it was one of those things about which Ma said, *Bouch ouvè. Mo sòti.* Mouth open. Word jump out. *Ba'y lè. Kité'y pasé.* Give it room. Let it pass. *Pa kité'i touché ou.* Don't let it touch you.

"I know you're not a suck finger," Ma says now, "so don't let anybody make you suck your finger and be sad."

"All right, Ma."

"Listen, my dear," her grandmother says as she passes her hand over her grandchild's long dark plaits. She unplaits one down to the end, silent as her hands move, then she runs her fingers through the hair and begins to plait again. Oseyan quietens. Ma's fingers in her hair soothe her. Ma moves Oseyan's head so that it bends and curves, massaging the little nerves at the back of the child's neck. "That little scamp know nothing about you or your mother or your family. You cry when they tease you?"

"No, Ma. I didn't cry in school. I pick up a stone to buss his head but Mr. Ansel come and tell me to drop the stone." Oseyan doesn't see Ma nod and smile.

"So you get in trouble in school?" Even though Ma had just heard the story and was nodding when she heard that her granddaughter had thought of defending herself – although, well, not buss head, *non,* but they must stop teasing the child – and Ma was sympathetic, but now that Oseyan had mentioned the teacher, Ma's voice became severe. She pulled herself up, pushed back her shoulders, turned her grandaughter to face her, and looked down into the child's face with a frown. One thing you don't do is get in trouble and give your teachers cause to complain. You could defend yourself with children but rudeness to teacher is another thing entirely. "The teacher beat you?"

"No, Ma. Mr. Ansel know they always teasing me, so when somebody go and tell him, he just come and talk to me."

"He come out on the playground?"

"Yes."

"Hold your head up. Yes, who?"

"Yes, Ma."

"What he tell you?"

"He tell me not to let anybody make me do anything foolish. He say children could talk if they want, but they can't take away what's inside my head, so I just have to focus and make sure there's something inside there."

"Good, good," Ma said, smiling. She pushed the child away gently, stood up, turned the bench so that it was near the board partition, sat down, leaned back against the partition, and put her hand out to lift Oseyan's chin. "I tell you to learn from that Carib man. Hold your head up. Your mother had a lot of spunk. In spite of how and how ting go, she had gumption. Hold your head up. That Mr. Ansel have good sense, like his people before him – well, not before him, *non*. They there still. Like his people. The mammie apple don't fall far from the tree. That man have something upstairs, and he giving you good advice. Listen to that Carib man!"

"*Wi*, Ma. Yes, Ma."

CHAPTER NINE

1903/1904. Carib Stones.

There are about forty of them in the school, though some children, especially the girls, don't come every day. On Monday morning, though, Sir gathers them all together in the room before they divide up into different classes. Sir calls it Assembly and that is where he tells them about different happenings. He tells them that week about some people from Germany who are going through the river in Mt Rich, up in St Patrick's Parish, and finding what they call Carib Stones. These are drawings done on stone in the Mt Rich river by people who were there long before Columbus or the French or the British had come out to these places. Sir tells them about it and then Mr Ansel, their teacher, talks about it when they break into groups and go to his Standard One class. Mr Ansel says it is a really important thing that is happening on the island – not only for Mt Rich but for the whole island and even for the West Indies. Remember this year and this month, he says. February 1903.

The people working up there in Mt Rich are finding all kinds of images, Mr Ansel says. Sir must have heard him from where he was on the other side of the room, because he comes into their class just after Mr Ansel says that, and he tells them they call what the researchers are finding "petroglyphs". He makes them sound the word out in syllables – three syllables – and spell it. The archaeologists – Sir and Mr Ansel say that is how you call people who do things like that – they are looking for remains from way, way in the past and studying them like science. These archaeologists said those carvings and then some pottery that they found in Montreuil, a place not so far from Mt Rich, could have been

70

carved by people like the Caribs – if not the Caribs themselves –
around the year 700.

Think about that! That's what they keep saying to one another
in the class after Sir and Mr Ansel tell them that. Woy! Think
about that! The year 700! That was long, long before anybody
from Europe even had a dream about coming out here, yes.
Oseyan had heard her uncle advise that you should be careful
what you say, but she had also heard her uncle say the same thing,
so she looked up at Mr Ansel and Sir after Matthias said that, and
she saw what looked like a smile pass between them. Mr Ansel
tells them they must say what they think and even disagree with
one another; it's okay, he says, although some other people might
have a different idea. After they discuss these things in class, they
talk to each other about a time before England came, or before
Britain came, and then one day in class Mr Ansel tells them it isn't
just before England came, it is before Europe came. In fact, Mr
Ansel says, as far as Grenada is concerned, Britain wasn't the first
of the Europeans who came. That sounds like the kind of thing
Ma would say, but it isn't the kind of thing that you could talk
about, Oseyan thinks. Anyway, this is her teacher, not Uncle
Eero, who is always explaining things to her, and who, Cousin
Mildred says, is becoming a dangerous *gason*. Now her teacher
also saying England was not the first. If they hear him in what
Uncle Eero calls the Legislative Council! That could be confusion, from how Uncle Eero talks about such things.

Spain, through Columbus, was the first from Europe – after
the Arawaks and then the Caribs – to set eyes on Grenada, and
because they weren't educated about the area – that's what Mr
Ansel said – and when she told Cousin Mildred afterward she said
it in a low voice, because she knew it was a dangerous kind of thing
to say – and then, he said that like most people who plan to take
what is not theirs, they didn't really want to know anything about
the people who were there before. So Columbus just pointed at
this little island as if it was his, and he named it *Concepción*.

"What kinda name is that, Sir?"

Before Mr Ansel could answer, Cosmos, Miss Imelda son –
Miss Imelda from La Poterie who now living down round the
corner by Richmond side – says, irritably, "Is Spanish, boy. That

71

is what Columbus called Grenada." And Mr Ansel added that Columbus never even landed back then when he saw it in 1498. A voice from the bench behind Oseyan says, "Wo-o-y! Fourteen ninety… It had people living then, Sir?"

And Julien, from the other end of her bench, says, "Dotish boy! The Caribs were there. You just like Columbus!"

"Mr Ansel, he call me dotish, Sir."

"Now please, gentlemen, you are young men pursuing an education. You respect each other and you know that no question is unimportant. Mr Bonaparte, there are no dotish people in my class."

"Yes, Mr Ansel. No, Sir, Mr Ansel. Sorry, Sir."

Mr Ansel is very proud of the Caribs and he says everyone should be proud of self and origins. This is why, although the school is in La Baye and there is no big school up here yet, we are making sure you put something in your head because we know that those of us who know a little bit have to share it in spite of everything. That is what Mr Ansel said.

When Oseyan told Ma that the other children were saying that Mr Ansel, who came from Dominica, might not be full Carib, Ma said, "People know too much. Full or not full, he is Carib." Being Carib was something to be really proud of. In the playground, Little Man said that Mr Ansel was really kind of *dougla*, and when some children say that Sir had some Carib in him too, although you couldn't really see it, Little Man say that mean that both of them savage.

Oseyan didn't tell Ma that. Gwenevieve say she had heard her mother say that Ma probably had something like Carib in her, too, and Oseyan wondering, *Ay ay! So everybody have Carib in them!* She didn't know if it was true and she wasn't going to bother to ask Ma for her to say that she listening to every little nonsense she hear on the street. She knew that Ma didn't want people to say anything bad about the Caribs, and that she was friends with Kalinya and the Carib people living higher up the hill there along Waterfall.

Gwenevieve is Oseyan's friend, and she is a little girl who people say has a mother who disappear but who is Miss Dolly's grandchild from the other side of La Digue, one of the few girls who always attended school, like Oseyan, so that tongue and teeth saying their family making sure the Anglican school get the shilling the government giving if a child attend school for at least one hundred days in the year. Anyway, Gwenevieve get really vex when Little Man talk about Carib and savage, and she shout out to Little Man, "Savage, you mudder!" Some of the other children marvel, *Woy! You don't hear what that girl say?* And Oseyan know Ma always say people mustn't curse about people mother. Is to leave people mother alone. Little Man say he would go and tell Mr Ansel, or even Sir, what Gwenevieve said. And Gwenevieve shout, "Well go, *non*. I will just tell Sir why I say that." Little Man just look at her as if he think looks could kill and then he say, "You say *non*, so you don't really want me to do it, otherwise I do it for sure. But you say *non*, so I could hear that you frighten." And he run away before Gwenevieve could answer him.

Oseyan thought about what she wanted to say when that little boy troubled her or her friends. She could never tell Ma the way she thinking in those times. Ma would *probably* be ashamed of her, but only probably, because sometimes when she get really mad about things, Ma not easy. But the things that little boy do and say, Oseyan feel she have to say like Faith does say sometimes, *You will get your comeuppance.* She thought about how Faith so think she big that she trying to insist that Oseyan call her Auntie, although she only just turned sixteen, so she not no big person. When she tell Faith that, Faith say, "You better hush you mouth and call me Auntie. Is me that going in sewing and working for me money, so you better call me Auntie if you know what good for you." Oseyan just look at Faith crosseye and fold up she mouth like how she see Ma does do.

Another thing Little Man said was, "You don't hear the name of that German man they say working in Mt Rich and finding Carib Stone? *Sap!* Who does call people *sap?* That man is a *sap.*" He said that because Sir had told them in assembly that the name of the man from Germany was Sapper. When Oseyan hear Little Man say that, she know she should *keep her own counsel*, as Ma would say, but she couldn't help it. She whisper to Gwenevieve about how Little Man must get his *comeuppance*. After they whisper to each other behind Mr Ansel's back in class when he was writing on the board, they look at Little Man and laugh. He didn't know what it was about, so *he* watch them crosseye and he mouth form the word *paipsy*, a name he often used to tease Oseyan with on the playground. *You don't see how you yellow and paipsy!* And then he push his hand high up as if he want to say something to Sir, but that must have been only to frighten them, because he put his hand down quick as soon as Sir let the chalk rest in the ridge at the bottom part of the blackboard and his body moved as if he was going to look around and face the class seated on the two benches in front of him – three, really, but when some children absent, they push the other one aside because they could fit on two.

Oseyan told Ma about the Germans finding markings and *doing their do* to decide that these were markings left there by the Caribs. She told Ma and Auntie Gerda that you could tell from the way Mr Ansel talked about them that the Caribs were a really bright set of people. But Auntie Gerda wasn't so happy to hear how Oseyan said they talked about Columbus. She said they should at least make sure all-you know he was a great navigator, so I hope they telling you that. And she added, "If those people down in the Legislative Council hear about the things these two teachers saying, is real confusion." Oseyan didn't say anything, and Ma didn't seem to be too worried about Columbus. The only thing Ma said was, "They good, but they better be careful and remember that is the Archdeacon letting them use that space there. But they good!" Ma was pleased to hear how her grandchild was learning about the people who were there before Columbus.

CHAPTER TEN

1903. Remember Baptism Day.

February twelfth. February twelfth. *Ting ting! February twelfth!*
Oseyan is running around and around the big bed in Ma's room,
the high bed they say Poopa Oba built. She singing, "*Twe-e-lve go-
o-lden rings*", a somersault and back up on her feet. Dancing
around the bed.

Four collie birds
Three French hens

"Girl, hush you mouth. What you making all that noise for?
And is four *calling* birds, not *collie* birds." It's big-mouth Amèlie,
and Oseyan ignores her. Amèlie and her friends are the big
children in Mr Harvey's class. The girls in the class walk down to
the big school in La Baye for sewing some days, and they always
act like they think they important. They have to leave school just
now, because they nearly twelve, and perhaps if they were in the
big school they would have had to leave already, because at least
one of them must be more than twelve. Amèlie comes closer and
puts her hand out, trying to grab her niece.

"Ma-a-a."

"What happen to all-you inside there? You not getting ready
for school this morning? Amèlie, make sure you sweep down the
step before you go. Don't waste your time and then tell me you
going be late."

Amèlie takes the opportunity to stamp her foot, looking
daggers at her little sister, in fact, not sister, *non* – niece.

"Amèlie! Ma, look Amèlie stamping her foot at you, yes, Ma."

"You little devil!" Amèlie hissed. "And you better say Auntie."

Oseyan puts her hands up to her mouth, puts her fingers on

the two sides, pulls her mouth wide in a grimace at this annoying aunt-sister. Amèlie dashes forward and Oseyan screams.

From the room next door comes Faith's voice. "Stop it! What is wrong with all-you children? Every damn morning is the same blasted…"

The little board house on the hill falls silent.

Faith say *damn* out loud, big and broad, in Ma house. Not only damn, but damn and blasted! Ay ay!

The house waits. Even the rain, that had made a sudden big noise on the galvanize as if it planned to fall all day, has given up.

The house waits.

Then Oseyan can hear Ma walking across to the door that opens into the room that used to be for Uncle Eero and Rex, the one Faith uses now. If Amèlie weren't there, Oseyan would go and lean against the partition near the door, but Amèlie is standing right there. They watch each other waiting.

"Madam, when you get big and you powerful like boss, and you have to use big word like *chèf twavay*, find you own place for me please. If I hear you say anything like that again, is feel you going to feel me hand turning you face wrongside. You won't hear me mouth. You powerful! Well walk to you powerful lodgings any time you ready. Okay, Madam?"

The door is pulled shut. They hear the click. The sound from the galvanize tells them that the house has released the breath it has been holding. But that is all? Ma in a good mood this morning? Faith don't feel her hand? Oseyan and Amèlie listen, wondering if it is all over; they don't even hear a suppressed *steupes* from next door, and if it happen they would hear it, because they listening. The fury from that room has been warned into silence. Keeping her eye on Amèlie, Oseyan pulls up the drooping sleeve of her yellow nightie and drops to her knees, quickly making the sign of the cross to say her morning prayers. She is safe. In this house, people don't attack others when they are at prayer. Not if they want to face Ma and hope to live to tell any kind of tale. And especially not when they know that there is anger in that pressure cooker waiting for somebody to take off the cover. Arms akimbo, Amèlie looks down at Oseyan for a moment, and then, frustrated, she walks out of the room.

Oseyan says her prayers, going through the *Our Father* so fast this morning that if Ma was watching she would have been sure to ask if Oseyan and God have some special kind of shortcut language nobody else don't know. Oseyan gets up and does a kind of dance, winding her body up and down because the day feels so good, even with grumpy Faith in the next room, even with Amèlie awful as usual.

Oseyan composes her face and goes out to the hall. She says a proper *Good morning, Ma,* trying not to giggle or to look too self-satisfied because of the tantalizing smell of fried bakes. There are several little rolls of flour near Ma in a pan on the table and she is standing over the kerosene stove – the *primus,* as Uncle Eero called it when he brought it to the house – with a long fork in her hand to turn the bakes in the frying pan. Oseyan wants to say, *It smell good, Ma*, but you never know how Ma would react to *anything* and no sense trying to spoil this wonderful fried-bakes-smell morning. Oseyan takes the long broom from the corner on the other side of the stove, watching the bakes and the frying pan and the stove out of the corners of her eyes. She turns to walk through the hall. Then she remembers that, *if she know what good for her*, she shouldn't sweep while Ma is cooking and things are open there on the table, so she goes with the broom to start in the other room instead.

The house smells so good. It was the early morning smell that made Oseyan's spirits lift and sent her dancing around the bed. Ma's face this morning, though, is like the face that isn't always happy to have children in big people business even when the big people business is really for the children. Ma is definitely not in the best mood, although she missed an opportunity to *really* give Faith what is what. Ma and Faith had been arguing last night because Faith now has *a little hold-on* and is earning her own money and she is planning to move out and take a *live-in* job doing housework for a high-up family in Grand Bras, so she *think she is big people.* That is what you can catch Ma muttering to herself if you are near enough. But however things are, Oseyan knows that this fry bakes morning is for her. So nobody better spoil it. And then, as she pauses at the room door, Ma starts to talk, slow and soft, and with the sound of the voice, now everything is alright.

"I know you like fry bakes and saltfish. I make that for you today so you could eat it and drink some cocoa tea before you go to school."

"Yes, Ma!" Oseyan is smiling broadly now. Is alright if Ma see. Ma talking.

Ma says, "I thought that would make you happy. You just like your mother and your aunts and your uncle. You couldn't give them enough bakes and saltfish. Especially Gerda."

Oseyan leans the broom against the room door and stands looking at Ma. It isn't often that Ma says it like that – "your mother" – as if it is a very natural thing and her mother is there like all other mothers. Most times, not only Ma but everybody seems to avoid saying "your mother" to her. Oseyan holds her breath in case Faith isn't too vexed from all the arguing and might even come out and say something, because this mention of her mother is a super special thing – must be so for everybody, Oseyan thinks. For Faith and all of them, she was their sister. And they keeping quiet about her as if they don't know that was her mother. She waits, but nothing.

Sometimes she asks Auntie Gerda about her mother. Auntie Gerda doesn't hug a lot, but sometimes when Oseyan asks that question, Auntie Gerda would grab her and hug her. Sudden so. And now – just that – "your mother," Ma had said. Oseyan stands watching her, waiting for more. *Tell me more about my mother,* she says aloud inside her head. She keeps looking at her grandmother, willing her to hear what has not been spoken, but Ma must have forgotten how to look up. And perhaps it's because she is chopping the onions into fine pieces so they would mesh well into the saltfish and the tangy juice from the onions is making her eyes water. So Ma doesn't look up, only lifts her right hand a little bit, raising the arm with the shortsleeve white shirt so she could wipe away with her sleeve the tears caused by the onion juice.

"Today is a special day," Ma says after a while. Oseyan has put the broom in a corner and she stands there, settling into silence and into conversation with Ma. "Today is seven years since we take you, this little little baby, to the Anglican Church – the Church of England – to baptize you. When they ask us, we give your mother's name as Ella, and they put it in the book, and we didn't put that reprobate name when the priest ask us if we have a father name, because you don't have to wash no dirty linen in public... and... well, anyway, the church when they ask for a name is a married name they want. If you not married, they don't want man name like that, and anyway that man is dirty linen if linen was ever dirty."

Oseyan hears a scrambling sound, then the door of the other bedroom opens, and Faith – Faith who just a few minutes ago say bad word in Ma house – is standing there in her blue curlers and a long red nightie. She is just standing there looking at Ma as if the other thing hadn't just happened. Ma doesn't say anything more for a while. Faith turns her head a little bit to the left and looks at Oseyan and Oseyan just has the feeling that Faith's eyes are like Ma's, as if she, too, wants to cry, even though she not near the onion. What is going on this morning? Is she right that there are tears around? But nobody cries. And just like that, Oseyan is smiling a little kind of eager smile because somehow she knows that her mother is there with them, and her mother is not crying. Faith looks at Oseyan, crinkling up her long face and narrowing her eyes, as if she is wondering what wrong with that little girl and what she smiling about. That child strange!

Ma says, continuing as if she hadn't paused, "And because we is black hen chicken and the church know black people living on the estate is labourer, they write down for your mother's occupation: labourer. They didn't even ask us anything." Then she says, "She would get one-one day working as domestic, when people want somebody to wash or iron or something, so they coulda put domestic, but they always hurry to put people in dey place and write labourer. Perhaps, when you really think about it, she a labourer in truth – working in their damn blasted land." And Oseyan thinks, look how Ma could say damn and blasted easy! Ma continues, "And labourer is what they like to mark us down as – to make sure they divide us properly from them and tell us where we belong. Labourer, they write on the paper. Your uncle see it when he go for the baptism paper. Labourer." Oseyan stands frozen. She says nothing. She is not smiling any more. A lot of people, including Ma, work in the *damn blasted* land, so this is not a surprise. But something tells her that Ma is more vexed about the *damn blasted land* and the way they work in it for nothing than about the word *labourer.* Is not the work, she had heard Ma say once, is the labouring for other people pocket.

Ma is putting some saltfish in a white bowl. She stands there for a moment just looking down at the bowl. Then she reaches with her hand, opens the safe, puts the bowl inside so flies can't get at it, closes it back, and turns around to look at Oseyan.

"But that is not what we talking about today," she says. "And don't wipe you hand on the tablecloth like that, child. Straighten yourself up." Ma's tone settles everything, even things that don't have to be settled. Faith pulls her body back inside her room and pushes the room door closed. Ma continues, "Look how I bring out white tablecloth to celebrate you. We giving thanks that seven years after that day when we lift we head and bring you in the church, three months after you born, you right here – a big, beautiful, bright little girl. Seven years old. And study your head like I always telling you. You have a bright future in front of you if you put something in your head. A bright future."

Then Ma takes a deep, deep breath and says, as if she is saying it to herself and Oseyan is not there, "Every cloud have a silver lining, and the Lord don't give you more than you can handle." From her room Faith says, "Amen." Oseyan, sitting now at the table, bites into the brown fry bakes and wishes Ma would say more. Should she ask her? But little children don't just ask big people question like that. But all of them talking and acting as if is them alone her mother belong to!

"Ma, what is the cloud with the silver lining?"

And when Ma gives no answer but only looks briefly sideways at her from that great height up there, with her head almost near the rafters, Oseyan hears her voice asking, gently, "My reprobate father?"

The potspoon falls out of Ma's hands onto the wooden floor boards. The bedroom door is pulled open, and Faith stands there again, mouth open. Right then, the person who is always saying things inside Oseyan's head admonishes, "Close you mouth, girl. Don't leave it open to catch fly."

Ma picks up the potspoon, leans against the kitchen counter, rubs one knuckle against her forehead, and stands looking at the child. "What wrong with you this morning?"

"Nothing, Ma."

"You got the devil with you this morning?"

Oseyan freezes, stops licking her finger and sits there with it in her mouth. That is the kind of question that might come just before the peas whip, and Oseyan glances quickly at the corner by the pan where they put the rubbish, but there is no peas whip stripped of its green. She keeps looking at the corner, even feeling Ma's anger, because somehow she can imagine her mother standing right there, dressed all in white, smiling at her.

"No, Ma. Not the devil, *non*, Ma. Nothing, Ma," she says, anxious now.

"It better be *nothing Ma* for true. I don't know what happening in this house this morning."

But Ma doesn't say it harshly. Her tone is almost questioning. Not like when she means *You little children like to interfere in big people business; keep yourself quiet.* More like, *It look like it have a spirit around this morning controlling things?* And if this is the conclusion, there won't be too much questioning of a spirit that makes its appearance from a world not much understood.

Oseyan wants Ma to say more, to explain exactly why her father is a reprobate, or what her mother was really like, and if her father forced her mother under the cocoa, like some people say, and why the church doesn't put man name down on the certificate, or if her mother was *forward*, as Little Man say, and that was why she, Oseyan, was *chabin*, or if it was true what the children whispered and Gwenevieve told her about – that her grandmother and grandfather had so wanted to cut neck when her mother became pregnant by the reprobate white man that he, the reprobate, run back to the people in St George's who send him up to work managing estate in Grenville, and then he take boat and run back to his England or his Scotland or one of those places until things cool down. Even if he white, he run, people say, because her grandmother and grandfather don't make joke. She hear all of this in the school yard. The reprobate come back afterwards, was the story, but he had to run because her grandparents were ready to cut neck. And even Uncle Eero, who was big enough even then as uncle, he wanted to cut neck too, schoolroad said. And in schoolroad, just because she wanted to sound as if she knew something, Oseyan had said, yes, that happen in truth. So the next time the story was told, it included that even Oseyan say so, so is true.

One day, when the feeling in the house is different, perhaps she will tell Ma that when Little Man is teasing, he says to her, *At least you get the colour!* And she might tell Ma, too, that she wished she didn't have so much of the reprobate's colour and could be the same as the other children in school. Perhaps they wouldn't tease her so much then. She wonders about her mother. She looks over by where the peas whip is usually kept, but there isn't one there. Her other aunties didn't seem as bothered by the whole thing as Auntie Gerda and Ma. And sometimes Faith. And of course Amèlie isn't a real *Auntie*, because she in school like her, only in a higher standard, and she just noisy and talking too much. Not like a real auntie at all. A good thing that Amèlie stays by Cousin Mildred sometimes because when Faith is at home she is in the bedroom usually. So Oseyan thinks of herself as really the child always in the house with Ma. Is a good thing.

Sometimes, Oseyan could hear Auntie Gerda and Ma talking quietly, and something about the way they talked would tell her it was about her mother or perhaps about Auntie who was in Trinidad from long time ago, but they always stopped when they knew she was nearby. Did her mother really die when she was just a baby? If her mother died when she was four years old, she should remember, but she remembered nothing. Sometimes she imagined that her mother had sailed off somewhere to catch herself after the reprobate did his do, and that one day she would just reappear on the La Digue hillside and claim her daughter – not that Oseyan wanted to leave her grandmother! But nobody said anything that she could really make sense of. She thought she heard Auntie Gerda tell Ma something about Dr Lang, who was the doctor at the time, signing some paper. She wondered if Dr Lang had anything to do with the black Langdon name, because his people used to own a lot of land in La Digue. But it had other white people in Grenada with the full Langdon name, so perhaps not him. But he was white La Digue people, so who know? Perhaps one day, when she got big and important, she could ask the high-up doctor if he knew her mother. Was that the doctor they were talking about, the one Ma said was in the surgery in La Baye sometimes?

Anyway, the bakes and saltfish really nice, so when she and Ma and Amèlie were done eating, Oseyan say, "I really like the bakes and saltfish, Ma."

"I could see that. You licking you finger like food going out of style. Drink you cocoa tea. And don't be late for school. Leave the sweeping. I will do it this morning."

And suddenly, ignoring Amèlie who sat there looking superior, Oseyan was on her feet and throwing her arms as far around her grandmother as they could go, which was not very far. Her head only reached Ma's waist, although they said she was tall, and Ma had a biggish bottom that she was proud of, even though she tall and thin with the long face she had given to most of the family, and definitely to Faith. She had the bottom that she said was a gift from her people. And Ma always said, as if she was disapproving, that Oseyan didn't have much bottom, and Oseyan couldn't help thinking that it was probably the reprobate's fault.

Ma said, "Okay, *doudou* darling. Okay, sweetness."

And Amèlie said, "Which *sweetness* dat? Dat is *sweetness* too, then?"

Ma said nothing. Perhaps she knew Amèlie was her last child who would ordinarily be getting for herself alone any sweetness her mother could squeeze out after sifting through sour and bitter and other things. You could see on Maryam's face that she didn't know if the child felt she was missing something, but she hoped not. She put her hand out and rubbed Amèlie's back, a sign of affection that Ma didn't give anybody too often. In fact, Amèlie made a movement that was more like a flinch than a response to affection. Perhaps it was a movement of surprise.

"Okay," Ma said. "Both of you. Time to go. I have to go in the shop so I will walk down the hill with you. You have your bag? Your slate in the bag? Your slate and your exercise? You too big for slate now, but I know you still like it. You have your exercise, Amèlie? Wash all-you face and let's go."

This was a special day. Oseyan walked down the hill smiling. Ma had given her bakes and saltfish for her special baptism day on this 12th day of February.

CHAPTER ELEVEN

1903. The Royal Readers: The Storm.[1]

The class read a lesson in the *Royal Reader Book One* with Mr Ansel.

There has been a wild storm, and the good ship is a wreck.

Do you see how the men cling to the mast of the ship? The life-boat has been sent out to save them: and some of them are in it. They try to reach the shore. Row, men; Row for your lives.

See, the boat seems to sink in the waves!

Down, down it goes. Oh, the poor men!

But see, there it is once more! It is on the top of a wave. Now it comes near the shore. Pull, men, pull!

Here it comes! The boat is on the shore, and the men are safe! The boat goes out once more to the wreck. And at last all the poor men are saved.

Kneel down, men, and thank God, who has saved you in the storm.

Mr Ansel told them to notice that the story was told using words of one syllable. Oseyan acted out the lesson in the road on the way home – the school road, as everybody called it. *See, the boat seems to sink in the waves! Down, down it goes. Oh, the poor men!* And because there was no adult around, they stretched out on the hot ground, going down, stirring up brown dust as they flailed around in the ground ocean. They would brush it off afterwards so the big people wouldn't know. When Oseyan got home, her grandmother listened to her recite the lesson in the way they had done it in class.

"You are a good little actor," Ma said, "although I don't know why walking from round the corner in Holy Innocents there to here would make your skin so dirty, and your ribbon untie and everything. No. No No. *Non.* Don't bother try and explain. Let me hear about the lesson."

Ma listened to Oseyan explain the lesson and then she said, "You have a good voice, and you know how to tell a story. Just like your grandpa. And then she said, "Let me tell you a story your grandfather tell me about another storm and about the ocean."

In her grandfather's story, some people drowned and some people were taken by British sailors to Grenada… this same Grenada where they were – *menm Lagwinad*.

Oseyan wasn't sure how to feel at the end of the story. Ma said that on estates like La Digue, *menm koté sala nou ka viv*, this very place where we live now – except that where we live is not an estate any more – a white planter paid people to bring us here – *yon nonm blan péyé moun lajan pou mennen nou isit*.

Oseyan looked at her grandmother and her mouth stayed open as she waited. *Nou? Us?* Ma had said, *Pou mennen nou isit, to bring us here.* Was Ma one of the people from the ocean? *Nou? Ma? Grandpa? Who is nou?* But Ma had stopped talking and was now knitting and murmuring, *Knit one, purl one, knit one, purl one,* holding up the pattern and looking at it, making a white runner for the dressing table that Poopa Oba had made for her before he left to cross over to the other side. *Nou?* Was Ma really one of the people on the boat? No. She had said it was a story Poopa told. But she said *nou*. And Ma's face was suddenly set up like the rain over La Digue hills, and her forehead pleat up, pleat up, and when Ma put her face like that, Oseyan didn't know how to ask questions. Ma had folded her lips and the two black plaits that made a circle around her head looked like a crown, and the part in the middle, starting from just over her nose going back, looked almost as if it had been made with the sharp kitchen knife that could cut right through a carrot like is butter, and she was humming a tune that sounded like a constant groan. Oseyan couldn't ask her anything. Little children did not push big people to talk – or at least they had to know when to do it.

At the end of the story she told, her grandmother hadn't said what they said in the book, that the people were *saved*. She said they were *alive*, and yet she sounded sad. Mr Ansel told them, and Sir said the same thing too one day when he came to teach for Mr Ansel, that they should think about *tone* when they read and listened to stories. Mr Ansel had explained it to them and although she couldn't remember everything, Oseyan thought about that now as her grandmother's story settled itself – settled and still kept flowing through her mind – flowing, flowing, as if it were a restless settling.

CHAPTER TWELVE

1903-1904. The Royal Readers: The Moments.[2]

Mr Ansel made the class look at what he called *how the book is structured*. "These things are important," he said, "and you're not too young to pay attention. That includes you, Mr Leconte." Nobody giggled, of course, because this was Mr Ansel in the early morning, and everyone knew better than to test him early in the morning. They had learned that. All heads turned, though, to look at Little Man, who was really a regular part of the class now, squirming in his seat on the back bench on the right side of the class. He used to sit on the left side, where it was easiest to dash outside quick when the bell rang but Mr Ansel had moved him to the right when you facing the board, so everybody had to look over their left shoulder to see Mr Leconte squirming, and to save up the image in their heads for when he tried to play big during the break. Nobody would forget the long face. Nobody would forget the white shirt suddenly looking rumpled halfway out of the khaki pants at the back, visible when he squirmed in his seat. Nobody would forget the half-opened mouth, the watery eyes, the sweating forehead, the hunched shoulders. Nobody – not one of them – would forget what Mr Leconte looked like when Mr Ansel's eyes pinned him to the end of the bench.

Mr Ansel pointed out that at the beginning of the Royal Reader No. 1, in Part 1, there were words of one syllable. In Part II, there were words of two syllables. In Part III, there were more words – one syllable, two syllables, and sometimes even three, and there were lots of illustrations in the book. There were questions to help them put together ideas based on the illustrations. Mr Ansel took his time explaining all of that. He pointed out that on page roman numeral four (iv) of the "Preface" was written, *"By being made to frame each answer in the form of a sentence, the child thus unconsciously produces a little composition exercise."*[3] Mr Ansel made them read that again and again and he said that they were reading enough in his class to be able to produce a composition exercise.

One story in the First Book was about how God takes care of everything. Oseyan knew it by heart, almost, because they had to learn it. In fact, they had to learn nearly everything in the book. It wasn't so hard because they recited it when they were walking home, or when they were skipping in the school yard.

> *Who taught the bird to build her nest*
> *Of wool, and hay, and moss?*
> *Who taught her how to weave it best*
> *And lay the twigs across?*

Oseyan and Gwenevieve said it over and over again in the school road. Then there was one that was about Time, and Oseyan thought of that as a poem-story. It was a nice little story, but it had rhythm like a poem, too. She always whispered the title to herself: "The Moments". It was a sad poem. She put her hand up in class when Mr Ansel said he wanted "discussion" about it. Oseyan said that she thought it a sad poem. Mr Ansel asked her why. Oseyan said, "Because." Her voice put a full stop after "because", as if it were the end of a sentence. There were titters. Everyone knew you didn't do that. It was afternoon and the class knew it could take at least some chances with Mr Ansel then. He was more relaxed. Mr Ansel said, "We did punctuation in extra lessons last week, so I know you realize that is not an answer. 'Because' begins an explanation, so what is the explanation? It can be used as a conjunction," he said, "joining two parts of a sentence. I think the poem 'The Moments' is sad because…" The class waited. Mr Ansel was waiting, too, for Oseyan's answer. With Mr Ansel, it was always better to attempt an explanation than to say nothing. Oseyan said, "Sir, it makes me sad because…" Another hand went up, its owner straining upward with the extended limb, but Mr Ansel waited.

"Mr Ansel, because all the moments are flying, Sir, just going away and not coming back."

Eyes looked up at Mr Ansel. Was this a good answer? Mr Ansel said, "Yes. I can see why that would make you sad. Time goes. We'd better use it wisely, not so, class, because we don't get the moments back."

"Yes, Sir. No, Sir."

Mr Ansel asked the class to read the poem out aloud, together. "The Moments" was right at the bottom of the page.

The moments fly, – a minute's gone;
The minutes fly, – an hour is run;
The day is fled, – the night is here;
Thus flies a week, – a month, a year.

When Oseyan went home that afternoon, she didn't read that poem to Ma. She thought it would make Ma sad. Her grandmother was not so well these days. Her back was always hurting. And even Amèlie was nicer these days. Amèlie poured some methylated spirits from the bottle into her hand, and she sopped Ma's forehead. Ma breathed deeply and put her head back against the bedhead.

Oseyan didn't like to see Ma like this. It made her think of people who had gone away, never to come back, like her mother, although she wasn't sure that her mother was really gone, never to come back. It just seemed like the kind of thing that wouldn't happen.

Something Ma often said was, "When I come back next time", as if it were a given that she would die and that after she died she would come back into this world. This frightened Oseyan. She didn't like to think about things like that. She didn't like to think about dying. For one thing, she couldn't imagine playing with a little girl who was Ma because she had just come back from the other side, and she didn't want to think about Ma going anywhere and not knowing when she would come back or if she would come back and start again as a little child in ABC class.

Sometimes, while Ma is knitting, she says, "Knit one, purl one; knit one, purl one." And Ma has given Oseyan two coconut flex and a small ball of thread of her own so she could begin to do her own knitting. "Little girl suppose to learn to do these things," Ma says. And she adds, "When you finish in that school there, I will ask the sewing teacher in La Baye to give you lessons sometimes. She does even give them exam in the big school down there. I will ask her to teach you."

And sometimes, in the middle of knitting or ironing or anything, Ma suddenly says, as if she is thinking about it, "The Atlantic Ocean this time. I wonder what next time?" Then she would sigh and say, "What is to be will be. Let tomorrow take care of itself. Today have enough trouble all its own. *Papa Bondyé konnèt pli mèyè.* Papa God knows best." And then she would be quiet for a while, whispering to herself, and afterward she would begin again, "Knit one, purl one." And if Oseyan wasn't doing homework or something else, she would pick up her coconut flex knitting pins and whisper along with Ma, "Knit one, purl one; knit one, purl one; knit one, purl one."

CHAPTER THIRTEEN

1903-1904. The Royal Readers: Facts for Little Folks.

There is a lesson entitled "Facts for Little Folks" in Part II of the First book. Oseyan likes it.

> *Butter is made from the milk of the cow;*
> *Pork is the flesh of the pig or the sow.*
> *Worsted is made from wool soft and warm;*
> *Silk is prepared and spun by a worm.*[3]

When she reads that lesson out loud at home, Amèlie rushes to stand near her, and stays watching her mother's face, as if she expects her to say something. Ma runs a palm along the length of the slim grey skirt she likes to wear. She pats the bench and says, "Come, sit down next to me, both of you." Amèlie sits on her right hand side and leans against her mother. Ma looks down and says, "Look at you, my big little girl. I remember when you read that story in school, Amèlie. And you like that one, too." She turned to her left where Oseyan is leaning against her. "I like the beat of the story, Oseyan. I like how it rhyme. It have rhythm," she said. "*I ni riddim.* Nothing to say. Is a good poem." And then Ma says, "Let them tell you what pork made from, but don't you put that thing in your mouth, little one! Remember that! Don't eat pork. Is not a thing you eat here, and don't eat it anywhere else. It is not good for you."

"Yes, Ma. Why, Ma?"

"Ay!" Amèlie sounds scandalized. "You asking Ma why?"

Ma says, "Just hear what I say. You little children like to ask too much question as if you think you big… What is the lesson you read out to me? Facts for Little Folks. *Ou sé yon ti moun.* You are a little folk. I am the big folk. I have plenty more years than you. Listen to what I tell you."

"Yes, Ma." Oseyan still has questions, but she knows when it is best to keep her own counsel – *I konnèt ki lè sé pli mèyè pa di ayen.* And too, besides, Amèlie there, and she only interrupting.

As they move away to their room, Amèlie mutters, "Just because you fair skin, you feel you could ask anything."

"Ma! Hear what Amèlie telling me."

"Sh-h-h! Sh-h-h!" Amèlie says urgently. She knows this was one line of argument Ma didn't like. "Sh-h-h!"

"What?" Ma questions.

Oseyan looks at Amèlie's pleading face. "Nothing, Ma."

She wouldn't want Ma to beat Amèlie for talking about colour. She just don't like the reprobate's colour. She don't like the way that people act as if it makes her different. But she don't want confusion this morning. "Nothing, Ma."

And perhaps it is because she didn't get her in trouble that Amèlie sounds like a not-annoying aunt when she says, gently, as if giving good advice, "Remember what Ma say, eh. She remind me of that when I do that lesson in class, too, you know. We don't eat the flesh of the pig or the sow. Ma tell me is because our people didn't eat it from time. Her own Mammie say that they don't eat it where they come from in Africa. And they don't eat it here."

"Okay," Oseyan says. "Okay, Amèlie."

CHAPTER FOURTEEN

1903-1904. The Royal Readers. Nursery Rhymes.

At the end of Part 1 of the first book, they read nursery rhymes and Mr Ansel doesn't even have to tell the class to learn them. They say them over and over in class and everybody really likes them. By the time they leave the class, they already know the rhymes without having to sit down and learn them at home – especially the one about the old woman in the shoe. And later, in Standard Five, sometimes when they hear the little ones behind them in Standard One saying those rhymes, they would look back and smile. When Oseyan recites for Ma the one about the woman in the shoe, she explains that the class really enjoyed that one and that Sir, who taught them that day, told them yes, it was comical.

Ma said, "Yes, it nice. Nice rhyme. And I guess it comical depending on how you look at it – *èspwèsman ba moun ki pa oblijé viv an soulyé.* Especially for those who don't have to live in shoe."

There was an old woman
Who lived in a shoe;
She had so many children,
She didn't know what to do;
She gave them some broth
Without any bread;
She whipped them all soundly,
And sent them to bed.

What her grandmother said made Oseyan begin to wonder why the old woman was living in that shoe. *Pòv sé ti zanfan-la!*

Poor little children.

Her grandmother says, "Is to tell you how people make the

world. *Sé sa ki moutwé'w kouman moun fè latè-a.* Some have, a lot don't have, and who to suffer with the children in the shoe is the women. *Sé fanm-la ki ka soufè.* Is the women who suffer. I sure all those children have father, but is this poor woman living in shoe alone with the children. And is white woman they showing us there in that book, you know. But she poor for sure. You show me the picture and I see she white. So confusion all over the place – with white, with black. And woman carrying it on their shoulder, in shoe, all about."

When Ma says things like that, she makes Oseyan think. "Is Papa God make the world, Ma, not so?"

Ma considers. "Papa God give us the world and is man that think he powerful, putting thing in place as he want and doing what and what happening in the world. Is not Papa God fault that the old woman living in the shoe."

Oseyan thinks about this. She asks, "Ma, where is the children father in truth? He not living in the shoe with them? So he somewhere else? And he have more children somewhere else?"

Ma looks up from picking at the rice, taking out the ones that look faded and bad. She looks at Oseyan. "*Sa ou dit?*" Then she makes a short sound in her throat, "Huh!" After a moment or two she says, "*Sé vwé, wi: hòd bouch ti bébé.* Is true, yes. Out of the mouth of babes, in truth. Say your rhyme and go to bed! *Ou menm ti zanfan enmen pozé gran moun kèstyon.* You little children like to ask big people question! Go to bed!"

Oseyan went. That night she dreamt that her father was living in a shoe, but she couldn't see his face. He had a lot of children but they were scattered around the shoe and he was sitting down inside it looking out at them. She kept trying to see more but when she leaned forward, the sea came rushing toward her. She was afraid she would drown, so she turned over in her bed, came awake, and lay for a long time in this bed that Ma told her Poopa built long ago for Amèlie. Still remembering the sea, like a mountain in her dream rushing at her, Oseyan lies looking into the darkness.

CHAPTER FIFTEEN

1903-1904. The Royal Readers. Skipping.

They read a story called "Skipping". The girl in the story, Mary, is learning a lot from her mother. Yes, Mr Ansel says, there is a big lesson there about learning. "Be conscientious," Mr Ansel says. "Put your mind to the things you have to do." He tells them, "Learn from your parents. Tell them about this lesson. Your mother and your grandmother and your aunt and whoever are the people taking care of you, they are older than you and they can teach you a lot." He stops for a few moments and then says, "or your father, or your uncle, or your grandfather. Listen to your parents and to older people," Mr Ansel says, "as this little girl listens to her mother."

Mariella in the corner on the back bench doesn't usually talk much in class, and she doesn't come to school often, but when she comes, if she arrives early enough, she always takes Little Man's seat at the end of the bench and then ignores his elbow jamming into her side because she has his seat. Mariella puts up her hand and Mr Ansel looks pleased. He says, "Good, Mariella. Yes. Tell us."

"I think is not usually father or uncle or the man teaching children at home, Sir. Ent is usually the mother or grandmother or aunt or somebody like that?" Mariella sits biting her lip, and everybody could see one tooth bigger than the others in the top part of her mouth. She is pulling at one of the plaid ribbons hanging down from a plait and looking earnestly at Mr Ansel.

Jerome's hand goes up in one push, and he says, "But in class is Sir."

Jessie says, "But in the house, to teach people how to do things and so, is a different thing."

Mr Ansel thinks for a while, puts a hand up to the plaid tie that Oseyan and Gwenevieve tell each other later looks really good on that kinda cream colour shirt he wearing. He says, "Yes. Yes."

That was all. "Yes. Yes."

Ma tells Oseyan that she should learn about the people they talk about in books and then one day she could write about a little girl she knows and about that little girl's mother. "You don't have to write about this Mary in the lesson, 'Skipping', and her mother," Ma says. "I sure Mary white. You could write about a little girl like you, you know. You could write about a little girl in La Digue. You could write about me, your Ma."

This is such an amazing idea that Oseyan giggles. But Ma does not laugh. She continues sweeping the yard as if she hasn't heard Oseyan laugh. Oseyan takes another bush broom and helps gather the leaves into a bundle on the side. "You could write about skipping if you want to," her grandmother says, "because you could skip, too. Or you could write about how your grandmother could always turn her hand to something. How she could plant cabbage and carrots and yams and have little kitchen garden around the house. You could write about that. Or about planting sugar dish for the cold, and about how the sugar dish leaf rough, about picking soursop leaf for cooling. All of that is the kind of thing you could tell a special story about."

Oseyan is not sure that is something she could write about, but Ma isn't laughing, so she says nothing. Oseyan knows you don't see things like that in the books. Later, when she told Gwenevieve about this conversation, Gwenevieve says, "You grandmother strange, girl. My aunt doesn't tell me nothing like that." Yes, Ma has some strange ideas about things sometimes and Oseyan is not sure how much Ma knows about the kind of things people could write in books. In fact, Mr Ansel had told the class that they should make all use possible of their education and be sure to come to school, because, he said, at the time that you were born, in eighteen ninety five or eighteen nineteen six or thereabouts – that's how he said it, *or thereabouts* – there wasn't even a school in Holy Innocents in this area here, although there was the Anglican School in Grenville. That's what Mr Ansel said, and he said that all over Grenada there are more schools now than back then, so most likely, Oseyan thinks, Ma didn't even… Ma couldn't know, really. And then, as Ma opens the mouth of a crocus bag so that Oseyan could pick up the leaves and start putting them inside there, Ma says, "I well know that is not what you reading in book now. The people who write your book don't know anything about all that, and they don't think it is important, but *you* know. So don't think I don't know what I saying."

Oseyan says, "Ma, I didn't…"

Ma makes a gesture of dismissal with her right hand, lifting the hand and bringing it back down in the way people do when they say *steupes*, although Ma doesn't say *steupes* this time. Just the hand talking this time. The gesture stops Oseyan in the track of her thought. *Like Ma could read mind sometimes!*

"Don't mind what you didn't," Ma says. "I know what I saying. How many of the little girls around here you see going to school? Miss Moira daughter Antoinetta, you see her in school? And Mr Antoine little girl, she in school? Or even if she go, she going regular like you? They home taking care of other little ones and they going to help in the garden with their mother, or they doing work in the house to help their mother in her job if she have a live-in job. Even Antoine – the one in the Grand Bras junction there – he son not in school. So I well know what I doing and what I saying. I think school important and I know that school in the future will be different because *you* learning now and people like you learning, so all-you will make it different. So I not stupid. You going to school for a reason."

"Yes, Ma. But I didn't think you… you …" – how could she even say that word? "I know you not foolish, Ma."

"Huh."

They went inside. Oseyan starts helping Ma prepare something to eat. Ma hums one of those tunes that don't seem to have a name or any real *tune* – just going up and down like – uuum oo uuum uuum – and then Ma stops a little bit as she peels the thread from the dasheen bush. She plans to make callaloo soup tomorrow. And she has to go to La Baye to get a pair of shoes for Amèlie so she trying to advance the work. Ma is thinking, *That little girl want to wear shoes, because she have high mind from she big brother, but she foot turning shoes because it shape just like the father own. Children could really take funny things from their parents. These days that child always some place with Gerda. Well, that good. Is good that there is a togetherness with these children.*

"Help me peel the callaloo," she says to Oseyan. "And you can't feel that dress-band dragging, child? Tie up your dressband." Then she continues as if she hadn't changed the subject already. "And perhaps you could even find a father or an uncle who paying attention to children. Write about them, too. They really teaching all-you in that school that is woman to take care of children. I could hear the lessons you reading out to me, so I know. When you could write, write about man taking care of children, too, and when the boys read what you write, your lesson might give them a different idea. But regardless how they say it and what they say, learn, learn all the same. Read the book and learn how they do this thing that is telling story in book. Listen to their story. Read and learn." And then she says again, as if she wants to be sure Oseyan is listening, "Read, you hear me? And learn."

CHAPTER SIXTEEN

1904-1908. Extra Lessons.

Ma tells every teacher at Holy Innocents School that if they had any time after school to explain things to her granddaughter, Oseyan, and give her extra lessons, she would pay, because, she said, education is important and she wants her granddaughter to start early. The teachers knew that for up to two hours after school, Oseyan could stay back and get extra time to have things explained to her because her grandmother would pay, even up to sixpence altogether, during the term, for the extra lessons. She would have money from the tuppence that Oba had put aside from doing all the carpentry for himself, and from what Eero would give her sometimes now because he was doing carpentry just like his father, and because she worked in the garden in their own piece of land and could sometimes bring corn and peas and yams and things like that to sell in the market in La Baye. And, of course, whoever was teaching her granddaughter would get something when peas in season or when Julie mango bear or when French cashew in season and she had something to give. And sometimes the chickens would lay, so they could get two egg or even a chicken self, or something to keep the body going. Mr Ansel was in charge of giving lessons himself and of talking to other teachers to see if one of them thought it would help to have an extra lesson with Oseyan. Sometimes they would tell Oseyan to go home, because she had done enough for the day.

The teachers marvelled that Ma Maryam was one of the main parents in the area pushing for her child – or her grandchild – to get an education. They were the ones who had to take attendance, so they knew that for many parents Monday and Friday were not real schooldays. If she hadn't sent her own children to school, people would say she only doing that because the granddaughter have little colour, because some people are like that, you know – taking on the children with light skin more than the others. But Ma Maryam – not she! She believed in education from time. You could see that. All the children went to school, even when the school was quite down in La Baye. Perhaps the little ones didn't go as regular when the school was far away and they had to walk down there and the ground hot, but they go, so they could read and write. But still people couldn't help thinking she had a special spot for this little one. And although people would want to put colour in front, they couldn't honestly say that for Ma Maryam, so they thinking is how the child come into the world, and how Ma Maryam want to make sure that her grand make it in spite of everything. Sir knew that Oseyan had to be really sick for Ma to let her miss one day. You could depend on seeing that little girl there on the front bench. Ma had walked Oseyan to school herself that first day, although she had a bigger sister or aunt or whatever in the school. It was Ma who put her to sit down on the bench, and who announced – to Oseyan and to Mr Ansel, the teacher, "That is your seat." And that seat at the front of a class had lasted for other classes. Oseyan's class remained mostly the small group she had started with, though more children were coming into the school now as younger ones. But even with the few of them, she was getting really tall for the front.

For some children, Monday was the beginning of the working week and parents and aunties and uncles and grandmas say sometimes that they need the boys in the land to help. *Strike while the iron is hot*, a father once told Sir, who was acting headmaster that time, when Sir asked why the child was not in school. Sir was taken aback because it was the saying he might have used to urge the parent to let the child get an education when the opportunity was there. But the father take the saying first. As the father saw it, that saying had nothing to do with school and everything to do with getting the land prepared so the family could have enough to eat and the family would be ready when they had to send things to the cocoa dealer or the spice dealer. So – *strike while the iron is hot*. And then, of course, Friday was the wrapping up of the week, and if there was a maroon or some other collective work to build a house or to pick cocoa or something, Friday was usually the day people would reach out. You couldn't expect others to help you, some parents felt, if you had your own child wasting time in school. Then there was the question of the girls. For some parents, sending girls to school was even more of a waste of time. The girls grow up, they start to have children, and that is the end of that, as far as they could tell. You waste all your time for somebody else's household because the girls usually follow the man – if they get a good man, that is – to a house somewhere. And though people in the area had asked the church to open a school near them and, because church is church, they try to help out even if people can't pay, though some who didn't have a lot put their little shilling and tuppence into it, when the men talking in the shop, they generally agreed that this thing about educating girls is a waste of time and money.

Ma Maryam didn't hold back when she heard them. She told Mr Jeffrey in the shop once that if he find a mirror he would see *who* is a waste of time, but she say she wouldn't waste her time to see if he going to find one. She going buy she two pound a sugar and go home and do she work.

So, because of the ideas Ma had, in Standard Three, Oseyan started taking private lessons from Mr Ansel every afternoon. He was no longer her teacher, but Ma believed in him. Although she liked Miss Pierre, who taught Standard Three, she was a woman and is mostly sewing women does teach, though Miss Pierre used to teach other things; still Ma stuck with Mr Ansel for extra lessons. No sense changing the recipe, Ma said, if the cooking good. Then later Oseyan was taking lessons from Teacher Denison, and then Mr Ansel again. Sometimes she had a friend, the little boy named Cosmos who took private lessons too, and then she might have company to walk some of the distance home, before she turned right to walk up Waterfall to her house while Cosmos kept walking down the road toward Richmond.

One afternoon, on her way home from school, walking alone because her friends had turned up the La Digue hill, while she self turned the other way, Oseyan met Miss Paterson in the road.

"Good afternoon, Miss Paterson."

Miss Paterson was wearing black waterboots and she had on a

straw hat with two plaits sticking out at the sides of her head, and a band of rolled bluggoe straw tied around her waist, as if she had just come from the garden. She had a small crocus bag on her head. Oseyan had seen her grandmother, and sometimes people like Miss Dolly, walking down the hill, carrying a crocus bag just like that and she imagined that the bag contained a few hands of green bananas and probably some bluggoes. Perhaps a breadfruit, too. Not that it was any of her business. She just liked to guess.

"Good afternoon, dear. How your mammie?" The question seemed automatic, as if Miss Paterson wasn't really seeing her but was answering the greeting of a child with manners who knew not to pass a big person in the road without saying howdy. Then Miss Paterson, her face streaming with sweat, turned her head to the right and focused from under the *kata* holding up the crocus bag. Miss Paterson was light-skinned, but not as light as Oseyan. She looked as if she had white in her somewhere, but it could have been a grandfather or great-grandmother or something. One never knew, because Papa God doesn't say how he divide up the genes and is not every family story you know. Oseyan had heard Cousin Mildred and Ma talking about these things, so she knew that people could have all kinds of mixture in them, whether it show or not.

"Oh Miss Langdon gran'! How you do, chile? How your grandmother?"

"She well thanks, Miss Paterson."

"And how you uncle? He alright, too?" Oseyan didn't know if Miss Paterson was trying to find out if was true that Uncle Eero had gone away, but she knew better than to say that Ma had told her he gone for a while in some place *Away – like Panama or Venezuela or Maracaibo or one of those places. Children like to ask too much question*, is what her grandmother had said when she tried to find out. So Oseyan just said, "Yes, Miss Paterson. He well thanks, yes, Miss Paterson."

"*Bon.* Nice. Tell you ma howdie for me, eh! You are a nice little girl and your grandmother well taking good care of you. Don't lose road, you know, child. Be a nice child, you hear?"

"Yes, Miss Paterson."

Josephus, who usually walked fast and talked just as fast, had come up behind Miss Paterson just in time to hear the end of this exchange. As he raced past, he said, "Good afternoon. Good afternoon." And as he moved away with his bare back and his three-quarter khaki pants, he added, "The Grannie so want she child to be big shot that she spending all money she don't have sending her to school. I hope it work. I hope it work."

Miss Paterson stood up in the road, put her hands on her waist, and said indignantly, "Of course it will work. Go home, you hear, child. Your grandmother well right. Education is the future." Miss Paterson turned, put one arm down and kept the other one up to balance the *kata*, and continued up the road, shouting out to the disappearing back of Josephus. "*Malkasé* – Fresh! *Mal lévé*. If you sorry tail want to walk the road with you three-quarter khaki pants and don't study book is you business, but leave the child alone! Is covetous you covetous! Leave the child alone, Ah say! Of course it will work. It working already! You too fast with youself. Ay-y!"

Josephus had already walked fast out of range of her words, but Miss Paterson didn't care. She was having her say.

Oseyan told Ma about the exchange, and Ma said, "Ma Paterson know what is what. Don't take on that *mouth open word jump out* man who only speeding back and forth up and down La Digue road to deal with the confusion in his head. Just study you head and don't let no confusion get into yours. Study your head; you hear me? Study you head."

CHAPTER SEVENTEEN

1906-1907. Pick sense from nonsense.

When Oseyan reached Standard Five, some things were different. Uncle Eero had suddenly appeared, back from Panama after only a few months. He told her it was Panama he went to, and he said she was really doing well. For poor people children, he told her, the Legislative Council say Standard Four is the test, so if you go past Standard Four you really good, he said. He was proud of her. He told her to keep her mind on her books, because things *hard like grugru* in this country. Is not that they better other place, *non*, but at least you get a little more money. That is all. She wondered if he had picked up a little more money in Panama. He told her that more than one thousand of them went to Panama, but the work is *back-breaking,* that is what her Uncle Eero said – *back-breaking* – so some of them decided to come back after a few months. He didn't stay long, and though he said he was mostly with other people speaking English like him – from Grenada and Barbados and Jamaica and places like that – he brought back words that Oseyan could use in school – on the playground if not in class.

He brought words like *jefe* and *papeles* and *desayuno* and *hombre* – although Faith said that *hombre* wasn't a real Spanish word because it was one she had heard before and she and her friends used it all the time, long before anybody think to go to Panama. But Oseyan gave Uncle Eero the benefit of the doubt, and in her mind she asked Faith, *What you know?* and filed away *hombre* as a Spanish word from Panama. Now, after Uncle Eero came back from Panama, she knew that Poopa wasn't just bald when he got old but he was *cocobolo*; that sometimes when Ma cooked the food it was not just salty but a little *salada*. When she stood watching her friends using chalk to draw hopscotch lines in the road, she said *dale pues*. She wanted to tell Ma *buen provecho*, so she would know she wanted her to have a good appetite and enjoy her breakfast, but she only said it in her head. You didn't show off like that with Ma unless you wanted to get your *comeuppance;* she knew that especially from hearing Amèlie and her friends talk. And she didn't say these Spanish things in class, of course, or when she knew a teacher might be around, because she didn't know if the Legislative Council would like it and if her teachers would have to punish her. She knew she was safe with real English – the King's English – so in class she tried to stick to that, although sometimes all of them forgot and talked ordinary talk as if they were in the street. The worst thing was to speak Patwa in class, because their teachers would have to answer to the Legislative Council and she didn't know if the Spanish from Panama was in the same category as Patwa, so she wouldn't risk it. They knew English was the real thing for what Sir called *the halls of learning.*

The extra lessons from Teacher Ansel really helped Oseyan understand many of the things in Book V. Ma said she was not a little girl any more, so she needed to settle down and think about the future. "I want you to be prepared for life," Ma said, and she added, "Education is the thing."

Sometimes, if you were just listening to the sound of Ma's voice and not hearing what she was saying, you might think that she was quarrelling. In fact, sometimes even if you could hear what she was saying you might think that, but Oseyan knew that Ma wasn't quarrelling when she talked to her. You could hear in Ma's voice – what Sir called the *tone* – that she was just anxious for Oseyan and wanted to be sure she was listening. When Ma talked to herself, though, most times it really did seem that she was quarrelling.

They make us fight the ocean and then they put us on these rocks in the sea and give us their books to twist up the mind. Well, give us the books. We will pick sense from nonsense, because it have a lot of sense in there too. Open your head and put everything you get in the school into it. Open your head! And when you find somebody like Teacher Ansel – or even Sir in Standard Five now – who will help you pick sense from nonsense, listen.

Even when Ma was talking to herself, while she was cooking

or sweeping under the house, or planting cabbage or cleaning up a banana stool on the hill, she would sound as if she was talking to Oseyan.

Oseyan didn't know yet exactly what was sense and what was nonsense, but she was learning, and she was always trying to recognise which was which. Sometimes she felt as if she wanted to open her head in truth, yes, to see where the different things were sitting down inside there, because she pictured the different lessons sitting down around a table in her head, reasoning. She would point at one and say, "sense"; at another and think, "nonsense". But sometimes she saw sense in a lesson she had thought of as nonsense, and she realised that picking sense from nonsense was not going to be an easy matter.

Uncle Eero helped when he came back from Panama. One day, when they were sitting under the house and he told her he could see she had a great *desayuno* and that Ma's bakes and saltfish really making her face bright, she suddenly asked him, "Uncle Eero, tell me about my mother. How my mother die?" Eero was silent. He looked down at the dust there under the house, his face even more serious than usual. He hadn't shaved this morning! Or was he growing a beard? From the kitchen above, they could hear Ma calling out to the chickens: *Ke-e-ep! Ke-e-e-p! Ke-e-ep.* They knew without having to look that she would be throwing corn out the window.

"I'm a big girl now, Uncle Eero, and nobody will tell me. Don't tell me to ask Ma. She won't tell me."

Uncle Eero looked up. She could see what she thought of as a *small* Panama gold chain around his neck. Small because there was another man people said had come from Panama or from Maracaibo or somewhere and *his* gold chain was huge! Uncle Eero sat back on the *ole chair*. He said, "Yes. You getting big, and children must know some things. "Your grandmother still hurting because – not only one of the girls, non…" He shifted his body on the chair, lifted his head, pushed his body back and sat looking up at the brown rafters he and the other carpenters had helped his father fit up there. He said, "Your mother, she didn't have it easy." He sat up, leaned forward, looking down at the ground again.

"Mammie say some things not good to talk."

Inside her head, Oseyan shouted, "Talk about it, Uncle Eero! Talk!"

Still watching the dust as if he could read something there, Uncle Eero said slowly, "That sister of mine, her body was tired and her mind was tired."

Oseyan asked without speaking, "And? And?"

Eero, still looking down, rubbing his palms against each other slowly now, said, "Mammie and Gerda say – they say – the men she –" he looked up, lifted one hand, and passed it across the back of his head. "The men she – men – didn't treat her good all the time." He stopped.

Oseyan waited. Uncle Eero seemed to be choosing his words carefully.

He said, "She was really a little –"

He seemed to stop himself, cleared his throat the way she had heard Uncle Rex do. Oseyan watched him. She shouted silently, Uncle Eero! Tell me!

As if he had made up his mind, Uncle Eero turned and looked at Oseyan. He said quickly, "Your mother's body was tired and her mind was tired." He stopped as if he were done.

Oseyan wanted to ask, "So that kill her?" As he sat there watching her, as if considering, she wanted to say, Talk fast, Uncle Eero. You know Ma doesn't leave people alone for long without checking, especially if is boy and girl or man and woman, even if is family. Talk fast!

As if he had made up his mind, Uncle Eero sat up straight and said quickly. "Her body was tired and her mind was tired."

Yes? Yes?

"She was twenty-three years old when she died. Dr. Lang write on the death certificate 'puerperal convulsions'. That was it. She was having a baby."

Watching him open mouthed, Oseyan thought, *A baby?*

"And her body and her mind couldn't take the pressure. Her body give up. It decide to go back and start again."

And start again? Oseyan could hear Ma moving upstairs. "When that happen, Uncle Eero?" she asked urgently.

Uncle Eero said quickly, "April 19, 1900. You were four years old. She was really pretty. And she was in pain. God took that

107

sister of mine because he was – compassionate. She is at rest, O," he said quietly. Ma was coming down the steps. Uncle Eero raised his voice a little higher and said aloud, "So I see you still like Ma bakes and saltfish? It all round you mouth still."

Another date to remember – *the nineteenth of April.* You have to pick sense from nonsense in the book you reading in school and in the things that happen in this life you living. Pick sense from nonsense.

CHAPTER EIGHTEEN

1907-1908. Royal Reader Book V. An Indian's Traps.

In her Royal Reader, the Indians were called savages. Sir told them this meant people like the Caribs, and others like them and not the Indians that came into the country on ships around the same time as their grandmothers and grandfathers. Several heads turned to see if Tim was not in class that day. When she was in Standard One, reading a lesson that said the same thing, her grandmother's comment was, *Those that writing that dey, they more savage than the Caribs.* She thought about her grandmother when she read the part about savages in *The Royal Readers, No. 5*.

> *Suppose yourself, gentle reader, standing at the gate of one of the forts in Hudson Bay, watching a savage arranging his snow-shoes, preparatory to entering the gloomy forest. Let us walk with this Indian on a visit to his traps.*[4]

When Oseyan read that, she couldn't imagine the savage. She thought about Kalinya, tall, thin Kalinya with the long hair and always wearing a long dress, Kalinya, Ma's friend who lived further up the hill from them. She thought about Kalinya's mother whom she could sometimes see sitting smoking a pipe outside the house, just like how Ma said her mother used to smoke a pipe sometimes. Up to now, Ma still grew a little tobacco in the back, so she could give smokers a few leaves. Later, she read the lesson to Ma and her grandmother said, "Remember what I tell you about picking sense from nonsense. Because book could have nonsense too, you know. Don't think book can't have nonsense." And then she asked, "Anything more in this book of yours about this place they call Hudson Bay?"

109

In Book V there was a lot about Hudson Bay, not just about a savage near a gate in Hudson Bay but about its discovery. And because of Sir, who was teaching her now in Standard Five, and because of lessons before that with Mr Ansel, Hudson Bay made Oseyan think more and more about the Caribs.

Even before Sir and Mr Ansel talked about them, Oseyan's grandmother told her that a long time ago, Sauteurs, the capital of the parish of St Patrick, up there at the top part of Grenada, was named for the Caribs. Her grandmother said, "You hear how they call it? Sauteurs. In St Patrick's parish. In the language of the French people Sauteurs means jumpers – people who jumped. Because when they were running from these French soldiers, they jump over a high hill to escape and some of them die on the rocks below. So they start to talk about them as *moun ki soté* – people who jumped. Because of that, there is even a place in Sauteurs called Leapers' Hill, *ti mòn-an koté yé soté*. The French call them savage, too, because is so these people stay when they take other people place. Is so they stay – *Sé konsa yo yé*. But every time we say *Sauteurs*," Ma said, "we should remember those from Europe who kill off a set of brave people – *moun bwav* – after taking over their place. They were living here," her grandmother said, "right here, you know, in their place, doing what people in their time do, and then these strangers from a whole other world come in skinning their teeth – *gwiyen dan-yo* – pretending they want to be friends, and then they kill them off. You hear me? – *ou tan mwen?*" Ma continued muttering to herself for a while, then suddenly she said, "So you see, child?"

Oseyan was almost surprised that Ma remembered she was still there, because when Ma start to tell a story, you can't stop her. She could talk and talk and talk – *palé épi palé épi palé* – to herself. "So you see? They could well twist a story! So study your head and pick sense from nonsense – *étidyé tèt-ou épi fè sans hòd sòt.*"

Once, Ma had told her a story, almost like a nanci story, and Ma made her say *crick crack*, but it was a story about a dream and about Poopa. In fact, it was about Ma meeting somebody who spoke another language the person in the dream was surprised Ma couldn't understand. It was a dream that frightened Oseyan, especially when Ma said Poopa Oba thought the dream was a visitation, and he dropped some rum on the ground as a libation to the ancestors who visited. Oseyan made the sign of the cross that time because she didn't think she wanted to see an ancestor in any dream. She didn't want dead people visiting her from any other world.

Listening to Ma, Oseyan decided that if one day she went to Hudson Bay, she would remember that there were people there like the Caribs. But that Ballantyne man in the Royal Reader – the one who wrote about an Indian's traps – he knew how to tell a story. He was nearly as good as her grandmother, who was a storyteller, too. And Ballantyne – Sir said his full name was Robert Michael Ballantyne – he was a Scottish author of stories for children. He is good. *I bon.* He good.

Sir said that R.M. Ballantyne died in 1894. That was more than a whole year before she was born. When Sir told them about Ballantyne's date of death, he said, "He is going out. Or he has gone out. You are coming in." That sounded like her grandmother. *I ka sòti; ou ka viwé,* her grandmother would say. *He is going out. You are coming in.*

Étidyé tèt ou.

Study your head.

R.M. Ballantyne was a good storyteller, though. Oseyan liked *how* he told the story. Sir told the class to notice the *how*. He introduced the Indian at the beginning of the story, showed what he looked like, how he communicated with his squaw, which is what they called the woman who was his wife, and then made them walk with the Indian in the story so they could see all his movements and how he killed the animal in his trap, and then at the end he, Mr Ballantyne, left them with a sense of the Indian, the wolf – the animal in his trap – and the walk the Indian would have to take back to his home. When they read the story in class, Oseyan thought about her grandmother and she said to herself, *Don't study him and if he call people savage or not, study how he get you to like the story.* She put up her hand and asked Sir questions. That Ballantyne man could tell a story.

He was almost as good as her grandmother.

I té pwès bon kon gwanmanman'y.

111

CHAPTER NINETEEN

1907-1908. Royal Reader Book V. Sir. Mr Ansel, Columbus and the Atlantic Ocean.

Oseyan told her grandmother all the things she was learning about the Atlantic in Standard Five.

> *The Atlantic Ocean lies between the Old World and the New. On the one side are Europe and Africa, on the other side North and South America, a distance of about 9000 miles. The waters of the Atlantic extend from Greenland to the southern extremities of Africa and South America, a distance of about 9000 miles. At the north it unites with the Arctic Ocean, between Norway and Greenland. At the south it joins the Pacific, the Indian, and the Antarctic Oceans. The Atlantic Ocean exceeds all the other oceans in the number of its seas and gulfs.*

In the *Royal Reader,* the Fifth Book, the story of the Atlantic Ocean is one part of a long lesson called *The Five Great Oceans.* Sir said that they were reading and studying the whole lesson but he wanted them to learn the part about the Atlantic Ocean by heart. She told Ma that Sir put up a map in front of the class, across a blackboard that was held up by the two stands that Uncle Eero built in the yard right outside there. "You remember, Ma? That was the day when the rain come and Uncle Eero say he must really put down some concrete so it won't have so much mud in the yard." Ma remembers. She had told him to do just a little part, because she didn't want too much concrete in the place. "Okay. So they using the stands in truth? That good to know."

Oseyan said that Sir put up the map, and he made them study

it – *Read it like a book*, he said – so that they could understand what the words they were reading in the lesson meant. He made them open out the atlases he passed out in class. John, Miss Johnson boy from Grand Bras, didn't have somebody to hold on with, because nearly everybody came to school that day and Sir only had six to pass out. So John jam up on the bench with Oseyan and Gwenevieve. John keep his head down the whole time and Oseyan feel sorry for him because he couldn't see everything they were watching in the Atlas, so she pushed it more in front of Gwenevieve, who was in the middle, and Gwenevieve said, "*Ou sòt?* You stupid? What happen? You like him? Why you giving him all the atlas?" And before Oseyan could answer, Sir was standing right over them and he said, "Young lady, you know it is forbidden to speak that language inside the school room. You are here to be educated. Speak English."

When Oseyan told Uncle Eero, he said, "He sensible. He watching his job."

Sir was like Mr Ansel used to be in Standard One. He always asked them to say what they thought and to ask questions. Nothing is "wrong" when you are learning, Sir said. If you have something that is not true in your head, and you keep it there, how will anyone know to correct it? Or to challenge you so you can defend and explain it? If you want to be a good debater, and to argue your points properly, Sir said, you have to test your ideas. Learning is about finding out and discussing your ideas, so he wanted them to feel able to make mistakes. Sir said that if you hear people say that they never made a mistake, they are not sensible people because to learn in this world, you have to know that you could make mistakes. That is what Sir said. When they started to talk about the map, Oseyan told Ma that Jonas – from right up the hill straight through La Digue and then going round the other side on the left, along the road that people say you could take to come out all by Mirabeau and Nianganfoix and places like that – Jonas, Miss Johnson boy, put up his hand and said that he was wondering if the people who drew the map had made a mistake. Sir said, "Say more, to help me understand. What about the map makes you wonder that?"

Jonas said, "We know that Europe, the part of Europe with England and France and Spain and so, is big, sir, but the map draw it smaller than Africa and smaller than North and South America. Why is that, Sir? Is a mistake, Sir?"

Sir said, "Good question. Tell me, how do you know that Europe – the part with Spain and England and France – that is Western Europe – is big?"

Jonas said, "Sir, Europe discover us, Sir, and although we smaller than Europe just in Grenada here, the map have the whole area that Europe discover – us, all the Caribbean islands, and North and South America – bigger than Europe and…"

Ann put up her hand and said, "The continent. I see what he saying, Sir. The continent… yes, the continent of America…"

Ann? I didn't even know that girl in my class, Oseyan thought. *What make her come to school today? What! She not coming to school and she know all that? She probably have a uncle like Uncle Eero!*

Cosmos, Marjorie and Lionel put up their hands, too. And then, watching them, Oseyan put up her hand. They sat up on the edges of benches, hands stretched into the air. And just how it happen, so Oseyan describe it to Ma, acting out the whole story.

Sir said, "Good. This is excellent…"

Cosmos said, without even putting up his hand like Sir had told them to do, so that they all turned their heads in his direction and looked at him *bad eye*, "And Africa! Africa! Look at Africa! They even draw Africa bigger than Europe…"

Sir said, "Remember to wait your turn, Cosmos."

And some voice muttered, "He so push-up with heself!"

Jonas, with his hand still in the air, said, "So is a mistake, Sir?" He sounded excited, "I discover a mistake, Sir?"

Sir smiled.

"Okay. Okay. You could put your hand down now, Jonas. Let's talk about it. I'm so glad all of you want to talk, but let me say a few things. What you are telling me is that Europe has a lot of power. It has different things that made it powerful. Look, we are here reading this book that they produced in England and most of the writers in this book come from there, and, as you say, Europe tells us that it discovered America, although we know the Caribs were here long before Europeans came, and Europe took Africans from Africa to be slaves over here. So you automatically think that Europe is bigger than Africa. It isn't. The map has its own problems that we can talk about in another class, but it isn't wrong on that."

Johnson giggled, and continued giggling behind his hand.

Sir asked, "Are you okay, Johnson? What is the matter?"

Constance, who sat near to Johnson, put up her hand and said, "As you say 'slave', sir. He laugh because you say 'slave'."

Johnson said, "My father say 'slave' is stupid people."

When Oseyan was telling Ma the story, she said, "Ma you shoulda hear him, wi." She didn't tell Ma that when Johnson said that she, Oseyan, thought, *Study your head.*

Sir said, "Okay. We have a lot to think about today. We will talk about it some more. But for tomorrow, I want us to take some time to think about the word 'slave' – and why 'slaves' are not stupid people – and I will ask you to write an essay about that."

And Constance moved her body so hard on the bench that she almost fell down. She pushed her book away from her in anger and she had to bend down to pick it up off the floor. She said, "You, Johnson! Look how you making us have essay to write! Just think what you want to think for yourself and hush up you mouth next time, eh?"

Johnson look well shame, but Constance was taking chances. Even if Sir might look mellow sometimes, you didn't do things like that with him unless the class was doing something like poetry. Sir walked across to Constance's bench, and took the strap from off his shoulder. "Young lady, do you understand what is manners?" He wrapped one part of the strap over the fingers of his right hand and he stand up there looking down at Constance, and Constance looking as if she want to cry now. And Sir had on his glasses. Lord, woy-o-yoy! He have on his glasses. The glasses does just stay on the table but when he put it on is trouble. He was wearing his glasses! And Constance look like she real fraid licks. She say, "Sir, no, Sir, I didn't mean it, Sir." And the class held its breath. Sir stood looking down at Constance for a moment… Well, it felt like a lotta moments. The class waited. Sir said, "Come to see me after class, young lady." And the class leggo the breath. Sir take off his glasses, press his mouth together with the lips in a thin line – a thin, thin line, vex like – and he turn away. So two children now, John and Constance, could taste Sir's belt after class. They lucky. If Sir get mad vex, he beating you right there in front of the whole school and making you shame. He not waiting till after school!

And then Sir said, "Okay. Okay. Okay." That is what Oseyan will never forget. Sir stood and watched the class, his eyes moving from one face to the other, as if he was waiting for the mood to change. Then he turned away and they watched his broad back, stretched out and looking strong in the blue cotton shirt. He walked to his desk, put down the glasses they didn't often see him wear, seemed to wipe them with his white kerchief, put the kerchief back in the pocket of his grey pants, put the glasses down on the table, and turned back to face them.

"I want you to understand that although, for reasons that we will talk about, Europe is large in power, it really is smaller in size than Africa and America – and Asia, too."

The class looked at him open-mouthed. How Europe could be smaller than Africa?

Sir was like her grandmother. And Oseyan knew her grandmother liked him almost as much as she liked Mr Ansel, not only because people said he had some pumpkin vine Carib family somewhere, but also because she thought he was a gentleman. A real gentle man – *yon vwé nom janti* and a real gentleman – *épi vwé misyé* – and of course she liked him best because he took no nonsense and kept the children in order.

Sir was more mixed with Black, and he didn't look Carib at all, really, so perhaps people just saying that, and he was from right here in Grenada, not from Dominica like Mr Ansel, where people said there were more Caribs. When Mr Ansel gave Oseyan extra lessons, he told her a lot about the Caribs and how the other indigenous – in-di-gen-ous – people, *moun endijèn*, from the area had moved from one country to the other because they actually came up from South America long before Columbus – from Brazil and British Guiana to Trinidad and Grenada and Dominica and right up the islands, and even up to Jamaica, and Haiti, where nowadays they spoke *pli Fwansé épi pli patwa pasé Lagwinad* – more French and more patwa than even here in Grenada because France colonised them, and they were even in the Dominican Republic, where now they spoke Spanish because the country that colonised them was Spain. The Caribs had come from South America and moved right up through the islands – at least, that is what they understand from what Sir tell them. So Oseyan tell Ma that is what she learning from Sir and she learn a lot of things like that too from Mr Ansel in extra lessons, how he said that although we use the word *dékouvè*, we should understand that the Caribs were here in America – and Mr Ansel said what Sir always said, too – in "America", as if he meant all over the continent of America including us here in Grenada. They were here in America long before any Columbus. That's what Mr Ansel said – before any Columbus, just like that, as if he didn't think too much about Columbus. Oseyan told Ma that, and she might tell Auntie Gerda again and she would definitely tell Uncle Eero and she knew she would see them as usual, especially because Ma wasn't doing too well these days. But she wouldn't tell Faith when she saw her, and, of course, she wouldn't tell Amèlie. Amèlie had left school now and she wasn't too interested in little children school problem. And sometimes when she told Faith about things Mr Ansel said about the Atlantic and things like that, Faith would say, "I not so sure about this man, *non*," as if there was something suspicious about the way Mr Ansel said things. Faith never had Sir as a teacher and she only had Mr Ansel for a short time because some other teacher was taking her class. But Ma didn't think Mr Ansel was suspicious so she could tell Ma and Uncle Eero and sometimes even Auntie Gerda about Sir and Mr Ansel and Columbus.

CHAPTER TWENTY

1907-1908. Royal Reader Book V. Speak the Truth and Speak it
Ever.

They read about the principal rivers and about the Mediterranean. Sir told them that in these Royal Readers they were
studying they might see stories and information about anything
in which Britain had an interest. Sir stopped a long time after he
said that, just looking off into the distance, watching through the
windows toward where the church was next to the school, even
though from where he was standing he couldn't even see the
church. They wondered what he was watching. Then he seemed
to turn slightly and look over their heads and they wondered if he
were focusing on the little Standard One children at the back of
the room, or even if he were looking to see if the rector might pass
by the school since he was in the church next door. Sir was an
Anglican like Oseyan's grandmother, and like most of the children in the class. Oseyan wondered if he went to church, too, like
her grandmother did sometimes, although Ma always said any
church is good church because *Is not the building is the spirit*. But if
Sir went to church, perhaps he went down in La Baye. She hadn't
seen him in the Holy Innocents church on a Sunday morning. Sir
shifted his head again and stood up there looking to the left, where
a thick piece of board was holding up the window so that it pushed
out into the yard, making a kind of rectangle of the board window
opening to the sun outside.

Sir stood looking for so long that Oseyan and the other children
were able to take in the sounds from throughout the school. From
Standard One came the sound of *Four ones are fou - our, four twos are
eigh-h-t, four threes are twelve, and four fours are sixteen*. And they could

hear Mr Patrick interrupting the third standard children to surprise them with a question: *Lazarus, four fours?* And the answer, quick as a flash, *Sixteen, Sir.* And into Oseyan's wandering thoughts came the sound of Ma's voice saying, *Well, that lady really dotish. I know it have other people with that name, but she really call her child Lazarus? Some people different in truth!* And from somewhere else – Standard Two? –

Speak the truth and speak it ever
Cost it what it will
He who hides the wrong he did
Does the wrong thing still.

Was it Standard Two? Book Two Royal Reader? That was the George Washington story. Oseyan couldn't remember...

And then she felt something like a sting across her back through the white cotton shirt and Sir was standing right at her bench, directly behind her. Oseyan jumped and bit down hard on the insides of her lip. *Ease up*, she shouted to herself inside her head. Sometimes when the teacher's whip made her bite down so she wouldn't cry, blood actually came into her mouth. But better that than they would see her cry. Already the children were turning to stare at her. They didn't look for long because if Sir was in a mood, the strap could land on any one of them, but she knew that afterward they would say, *Girl, if you see how you get red!* She would cuff up any of them who told her anything.

"Sir?"

"Did you hear what we were talking about? You weren't paying attention." Oseyan couldn't help thinking, *Well you weren't paying attention before, Sir!* And thinking, too, *It good that people could think things and nobody know, yes!*

"Sir," in a shaky voice, but she *would not cry*! "I was... yes, sir. I was hearing what the children were saying in the other class, Sir. *Speak the truth and speak it ever.* The George Washington story, Sir."

"You know you should be paying attention. But I'm glad you learned the lesson and you are speaking the truth." Sir moved away. Then he said, "We will read the rest of *The Principal Rivers and the Mediterranean* tomorrow. Make sure you read it at home." He wasn't in a good mood. Uncle Eero said that the governor and the whole Legislative Council were saying a lot of things about primary education and teachers were not happy – especially those like Sir who were thinking for themselves, and definitely had ideas different from those the governor wanted them to talk about.

CHAPTER TWENTY-ONE

1907-1908. Royal Reader Book V. The Principal Rivers and the Mediterranean.

Oseyan was a little uneasy. When she got home yesterday, her aunt had said that the talk was that Mr Ansel and Sir were both cosy with a group from St George's that was printing things in a newspaper, *The St George's Chronicle and Grenada Gazette*, about the West Indies not having to be so close to Britain and having to move on to think about governing itself. Big-mouth Faith said she heard that Sir was friending up with people like the newspaper editor, Mr Donovan, and a young one who was coming up in the paper, too, Mr Marryshow. People called him Teddy. Oseyan didn't tell Auntie that Mr Ansel had told a few of them who stayed on in the class afterward for a short while, just to ask some questions, that Mr Donovan and the young man that worked with the paper, Mr Marryshow, had some good ideas. That is what Sir said. She knew her grandmother would approve of Mr Donovan and Mr Marryshow but she knew when to keep her own counsel – *pou pé konsèy'i ba kò'i*, as her grandmother would say. So she just keep her mouth shut. And she didn't tell Ma either that one day Uncle Eero and another man walked all the way down to St George's to have a meeting with people down there who talking about things you could only say in whispers, Uncle said: *self-government*. They'd decided to walk overnight, Uncle said, because of the time the meeting was and because they didn't want too many people to know, and anyway they would be able to stop in places along the way in St David's and talk to people they wanted to see about different things. And Uncle Eero told her, you know is not everything I tell you that you have to talk about.

Sometimes Uncle Eero told her things because he said she should know, and she was sensible, but of this, he said, *Hush your mouth!*

He told her there was a lot of talk in the Legislative Council about education. He said that there was a plan and a lot of argument about how teachers should be paid, and if a school manager should be able to give teachers the shilling on top of their salary when children attended for 100 days and more, and all kinds of things. Uncle Eero said that the teachers and Mr Seton-Hall, who represented them there in Grenville on the Legislative Council, were very angry with the governor, Sir Ralph Williams, and with Mr Drayton, the Colonial Secretary, but more with the governor. Uncle Eero said that the Archdeacon was busy making sure that St Patrick got a good Anglican School, but next it should be Holy Innocents, so their school will hopefully get a proper building and soon be on the colony's list of schools as another Anglican school. He said that the governor didn't care about poor people children, that they want to educate people like us to be labourer and servant and things like that. They think only the people in town might be able to go far and do more in education, and is only one-one people even then. He told her all that in a low voice, as if is not thing to talk out loud. They were sitting down in front of the house, and Auntie Mildred was inside, so perhaps that was why he was keeping his voice low.

The class read about *The Principal Rivers and the Mediterranean.*

> *The principal rivers which flow into the Mediterranean are the* **Rhone**, *from France; the* **Po**, *from Italy; and the* **Nile**, *from Egypt. Besides these, the waters of the* **Danube**, *the* **Dnieper**, *and the* **Don**, *come to the Mediterranean from the Black Sea by the Sea of Marmora. The countries on the shores of the Mediterranean are:-*

SPAIN	opposite	MOROCCO
FRANCE	"	ALGERIA
ITALY	"	TUNIS
GREECE	"	TRIPOLI
ASIA MINOR	"	EGYPT

> *Syria and Palestine form the eastern shore of the Mediterranean.*

The principal islands in the Mediterranean are Corsica, Sardinia, Sicily, Crete and Cyprus. Besides these, there is a large number of small islands: one of which, Malta, to the south of Sicily, belongs to Britain. It lies about midway between Gibraltar and Egypt.

Sir showed them a map so that they would understand what the book said. They had to learn that whole thing by heart and recite the lesson in class. Going home in the afternoon after school, they sang, *Corsica, Sardinia, Sicily, Crete and Cyprus! Crete and Cyprus* sounded nice after you sent a stone away into the nutmeg – *vun-n-g*! The stone bit at the leaves of the nutmeg tree.

Crete and Cyprus!

Mostly the boys did that, and it really sound good. Oseyan and Gwenevieve did it, too, because they were daring girls. *V-u-u-n-n-g* with the stone, the leaves rustling or breaking or something, then you move your waist round and round to:

Crete and Cyprus.

And sometimes the girls jumped rope to:

Corsica, Sardinia, Sicily, Crete and Cyprus!

It sounded really good when their feet slapped the concrete and their voices sang out:

Corsica, Sardinia, Sicily, Crete and Cyprus!

with all those "s" sounds that Sir told them were sibilant sounds. What also sounded good was

Malta, to the south of Sicily, belongs to Britain.

It had a chanting sound that was so nice it made you dance.

Malta
To the south of Sicily
Belongs to Britain.

And it just felt great to know that Malta was like them, and *belongs to Britain* had a really claiming, familiar, sure ring to it. Malta was a nice country. Although that thought came into Oseyan's mind, she wondered if Ma would approve. For sure Ma would approve of Mr Ansel and Sir talking to Mr Donovan and Mr Marryshow and people like that about self-government, but she didn't feel sure what Ma would say, and she didn't think she should ask Mr Ansel about liking Malta. She wondered if she should say anything to Ma. Ma didn't read, but she knew many

123

things, and Oseyan wondered how come Ma was so smart. Gwenevieve wondered that, too, because she said to Oseyan, "You grandmother good, girl. All those things you say she tell you there – about Africa and about the British and about how to listen to things in school and so, how she know?" Oseyan shrugged. She was proud of Ma, too, but she didn't know how Ma knew things. How did people get smart if they didn't read? What she knew for sure was that Ma was smart. But now, there was just something about the *sound* of Malta that she liked, and she couldn't defend it, and she didn't want to talk to Ma about Malta and Britain. She didn't know why. She had better not say anything. She would content herself with whispering when she was on her knees to pray at night. After she asked Papa God to be sure, sure, sure, to bless Ma and never let her die please, she prayed for Malta, too, because Malta, to the south of Sicily, belongs to Britain. Belongs to Britain.

CHAPTER TWENTY-TWO

1907-1908. Royal Reader Book V. Synonyms and Antonyms.

One day when she told Ma and Auntie Gerda what she had learned in school, her auntie said, "In spite of everything, they could've give that man a job for his looks because he not badly off. He tall, the nose straight and the hair soft, although the skin little dark, but he not there for his looks at all. He well making all-you work. He doing a lot of work. *I ka fè an pil twavay.* I didn't have him as a teacher, is true, but I never learn nothing like all of that in school."

She knew Auntie was right – not about Sir's looks because she knew Ma would be vex like hell and have something to say to Auntie Gerda when she thought Oseyan couldn't hear. And she felt pleased that she could think *vex like hell* now because Ma wouldn't know to root the thought out of her head with just one look – but Ma would be well vexed to hear about soft hair and skin that not too dark. Just the other day Ma told her, "I wish you did take the family nice black skin and not that pale thing the reprobate give you, but God be praised, you beautiful in spite of it! Look at you!" And Ma lifted up her granddaughter's hands high in the air and looked admiringly down at her. "You pretty, pretty." And in spite of the reprobate, Ma does touch her hair as if she like how it feel. Then Ma said something different. She said, "Reprobate as he is, he have name, so we won't fraid to use his name when the time come, if it will help you out. We have to wait and see. If it come in handy, we won't fraid to use it." She stood leaning up against the kitchen counter, looking through the louvres toward the golden apple tree outside. Oseyan waited to hear more, but all Ma said was, "Well, we have to wait and see."

Anyway, whatever strange thing Ma might be thinking, Oseyan

knew that she would definitely stretch her mouth when she hear what Auntie Gerda had to say about Sir's looks. But she would agree that Sir was an excellent teacher. Although there was talk that some of the high-ups thought he was a dangerous example, plenty people said he was one of the best in the region, and that they were lucky to have him there in La Digue. Especially now they were planning to make the school bigger and everything. Uncle Eero, though, wondered if Sir would continue to have a job when everybody paying more attention, because the high-up people in charge, and they want to make sure everybody know it.

The next day, Sir turned to the back page of the book, although the class wasn't as far as that yet in the reading. Sir said they might not have time to do everything in the book because the year seemed to be speeding up, but, he said, there were some things he wanted to make sure they knew. He made them do the dictation exercises at the back of the book. He read out passages, made them write sentences and then exchange exercise books and correct each other's work. Not only that, he made them do the lesson at the back of the book and they had to learn it – all about synonyms and antonyms:

> *The plan adopted in the following exercises is to select a word representing a familiar idea, with its opposite – to place a few synonyms under each – and to follow these by short sentences, showing the proper use of each word. These sentences are to be used in Dictation Exercises.*[5]
>
> ***Synonyms*** *are words of similar meaning – as **joy, gladness; sorrow, grief**.*
>
> ***Antonyms*** *are words of opposite meaning: as **joy, sorrow; gladness, grief**. And for a word like **begin**, you could have synonyms like **commence, initiate, inaugurate**. And for **end** you could have **conclude, perfect, consummate**.*

Oseyan didn't know why an end would be perfect and not a beginning, but when she asked Sir he pronounced per**fect** in a different way, and said it is as if you work on a thing until you think it's perfect – so that perfection is the end result. So he pronounced the word "perfect" in that Synonyms and Antonyms part as if it came at the beginning of "perfection". So that's different from beginning. It's really what takes place at the end. That's how he explained it to them.

For one of the exercises, they worked from what was in the book and then Sir made up other things for them. The example in the book was:

> A river **begins** at its source. The year **begins** on the first of January, and **ends** on the last of December. An army **commences** operations in spring, and **concludes** them in autumn. We **initiate** a student in a certain study, but he must **perfect** himself. A great movement, such as the abolition of slavery, is **inaugurated** and **consummated.** A dignitary is **inaugurated** when he is inducted into office. Proceedings **commence** and **conclude.** A struggle **begins** and **ends.**

Oseyan told Auntie Gerda and Grandma how, although they were talking about antonyms and synonyms, Sir spent a lot of time talking about the information in the exercise, what he called the "subject", or the "theme". And she told Uncle Eero, too, when she saw him. Sir told them to note that the editor – he said that was the person who helped to choose the different poems and stories and other things in the book – the editor, even if he was English from the England that took African people from Africa and made them slaves, the editor did not hesitate to use an example that said right out, big and bold, that those working towards the abolition of slavery were part of "a great movement". So you have to read the book carefully to know that not everybody in the book think the same way like high-up people, and that not even all high-up people think the same way. Ideas are ideas, that is what Sir said, and they can be discussed. Sir said that the planters in Grenada might not have said that *then*… and that is how he said it; he emphasized *then*, and they might not say it *now*, but as readers, Sir said, and he pointed at them with his ruler – "readers – you" – he pointed at them one by one – "as readers, all of you, you should take note of that."

When Oseyan talked about it at home, Auntie Gerda said Sir and Mr Ansel were good teachers but she didn't like the way they were always criticising the planters. Ma just made a sound in her throat, like "Hmmm". Auntie Gerda didn't usually say things like this out straight, although sometimes you could tell she wasn't happy with what she heard about the teaching done by Sir and Mr Ansel. Today, though, she came straight out and said she didn't like how these teachers criticised the planters. Oseyan wondered if the way Auntie Gerda took the news had anything to do with what she had heard Ma saying in a low voice to Uncle Eero – something about *fooling around* and *people not serious* – and… it was the other word she heard that suddenly made her think … *planter.* Oh no! she thought. Oh not my aunt! But she didn't know, and anyway, proceedings *commence* and *conclude*. Whatever this was with Auntie Gerda and – a *planter?* Well, no, couldn't be. Perhaps she was wrong. And anyway, if it was something, perhaps it had *concluded*. She would keep her own counsel. And she wouldn't tell Gwenevieve. But – well, things commence and conclude.

CHAPTER TWENTY-THREE

1907-1908. Lessons from Ma in La Digue. *Kòrèk sé dwèt.* Correct is Right.

Ma came to kneel near Oseyan when she was praying. As she eased herself down, she said, "God self see my old knees not bending easy these days. But God is good." Oseyan pulled up the left shoulder of the long blue nightie Ma had made for her on the new sewing machine. She turned her head toward Ma and asked, "What you think about what Sir said about the planters, Ma?" And Ma said, "*Correct is right – kòrèk sé dwèt.*" That was all at first, "Correct is right." And then she listened to Oseyan saying a prayer:

> *Now I lay me down to sleep*
> *I pray the Lord my soul to keep.*

Oseyan always stopped there, because the next part of the prayer frightened her. She didn't want her soul going anywhere without her while she slept, so she didn't see how she could say the rest, which went:

> *If I should die before I wake*
> *I pray the Lord my soul to take.*

When she was really little, she used to think fearfully, "I am not dying before I wake. *Mwen pa ka mò avan mwen lévé.*"

Ma knew, and she didn't mind. She had told her granddaughter long ago, when she and Amèlie were little together and used to be praying together, "Is okay. That is a story between you and your spirit, between you and God. Nothing is written in stone, you know, child, or between stone walls. So if your spirit say so, follow your spirit." Another time Ma told her, "It have a lot of different religions and a lot of them saying different things. Listen to your spirit and know what is what." And she added, "Think about Caribs and the spirit. Those Carib people didn't have worse ideas about the spirit than those who come and call them savage. Listen to your spirit, child. It strong inside you."

Faith did not agree that Oseyan should say the prayer the way her spirit told her. When she was praying one night and Faith heard her, she said, "What kind of half prayer is that? Say the whole prayer as you know it." And when Ma said, "It's okay. Goodnight, my ocean," Faith said, "I swear you spoilin that child, Ma." And Ma used the quiet voice that said, without having to say it, *You better know who you talking to!* "I know you big now, young lady, but not big enough to swear in my presence. Watch yourself!"

Now, when her prayers were finished, Ma suddenly said again, "Correct is right. *Kòrèk sé dwèt*. Right up to the end those high-up people an dem – the ones I hear Eero, and you Sir and dem calling *the planters* – they were sure it was **not** a great movement. At least some of those people writing story in book have sense."

Oseyan said, "Goodnight, Ma." Then she pursed her lips and blew out the light.

CHAPTER TWENTY-FOUR

1907-1908. The Royal Readers. Fifth Reading Book. Miriam's Song.

On the first page of *The Royal Reader No. 5* are the words **Fifth Reading Book**. They are printed just over the first poem titled "Miriam's Song". The poet's name is Thomas Moore. Printed in brackets after Thomas Moore's name is "(1779 – 1852)". That was when Thomas Moore lived, Sir said, in that firm, quiet way in which he talked about everything. Thomas Moore lived during the time that Britain was taking Africans and transporting them from the west coast of Africa to make them slaves in the Americas. Then Sir said that Thomas Moore's country was actually Ireland and that he used songs in his writing. When the slave trade was stopped by Britain in 1807, Sir said, Thomas Moore was twenty-eight years old. In 1838, when Emancipation Day was celebrated in most of that part of the Caribbean claimed by Britain – and Sir said that the name Britain included Ireland and Scotland – Thomas Moore was fifty-nine years old.

As Oseyan listened, it occurred to her that when Thomas Moore died in 1852, Ma and Poopa must have been very young. Or Ma may have been a child and Poopa a very young man. And because listening to Sir and Mr Ansel always made her travel away in her head, not just to try and find her mother but sometimes just to think things, plenty things, Oseyan realised she was risking a sting from Sir's strap as, with her black plaits unmoving, she fixed her dark eyes on his face, while her thoughts moved off in all kinds of directions, drifting, drifting. It made her feel adventurous to think that she was fooling Sir, who thought she was in class while she was off traipsing all over the place in her head.

The story in her family was that one of her great-grandparents was an African captured by British ships from a slave ship taking Africans to be slaves in another country – like Brazil, or Cuba, or Puerto Rico or somewhere else. Although no one ever said anything, not to her, anyway, since she was a child, she felt sure that there were secrets about Ma's parents and grandparents too. The people around – and even Uncle Eero – said the Langdons did this and the Langdons did the other and talked about where the Langdons came from. But from what Mr Ansel and Sir told them in class, and from what Uncle Eero and even Ma herself said, Oseyan figured out that this thing about the Langdons wasn't always there from the beginning, so things didn't happen the same way for everybody in her family. Ma said she was a Sam, and that perhaps she was something else – some other name before that, and for sure *her* mother was something before that, in Africa somewhere and perhaps here in Grenada too. And even the Langdons, as they called them, they had to be something else before that, in Africa and perhaps even here in Grenada. When she thought about the things that Mr Ansel said in extra lessons, she knew there were a lot of things she didn't understand. One day she would do like Uncle Eero and Sir and Mr Ansel and *find out.* That's what her Uncle Eero was always saying. *Find out.*

Oseyan knew that Ma was good friends with Kalinya and the other Caribs in La Digue, and she wondered if Ma was related in some way to them. For sure, she liked the Caribs. But was there a family relationship? Oseyan didn't know. And then her mind, jumping from one thing to another, reminded her how Faith had said, *Me? I not no African. I am Grenadian.* That wasn't what Ma would say. And in fact Oseyan felt sure Faith wouldn't say something like that in front of Ma. She was just saying it to shock Oseyan because Ma wasn't there. And she, Oseyan, wouldn't tell Ma something like that, because she didn't want to know how vexed Ma would be. It was real mix-up – those who were brought as slaves and then those who came afterwards and worked like slaves. And then there were those like Poopa's father who were something called "liberated Africans". What about them? How could you be sure? You couldn't really *know,* could you? And sometimes you could see Ma had a lot of things on her mind, from long time, perhaps, and from now. Sometimes she would seem to forget Oseyan was there and would mutter for a long time about things Oseyan couldn't understand. Once, at a time like that, Oseyan hugged her grandmother because she looked so sad, and she sang the song Ma sang to her when she wanted to soothe her. She remembers it now – although she better don't sing in class if she know what good for her, especially not no patwa song. She going just think about it:

> *Dodo, petit popo*
> *Mama gone in La Baye*
> *Buy cake and sugar plum*
> *Give Granma some*
> *Give Granma some.*
>
> *Dodo piti popo*
> *Piti popo pa vlé dodo.*
> *Zambi a ke mange li*
> *Sukugnan ke suce san.*
> *Sleep, baby, sleep.*
> *Sleep, baby, sleep.*

Oseyan sits straight-backed on the school bench, staring with interest into Sir's face and thinking about Ma and Dodo Petit Popo, and why they patting baby's back and saying that baby should sleep when a *soucouyant* is sucking the baby's blood. And suddenly Sir is saying, "Okay, so now I've explained the *context* for the poem, and I know you know what *context* is, we will read it during the next class. As Oseyan pulls her books together, she knows she will have a lot of homework finding out as much as she could – from the book and from Uncle Eero if he came by the house – about the context for "Miriam's Song". But sometimes Sir repeated some of the things when they were actually going to read the lesson. "Fingers crossed" is what Ma would say.

CHAPTER TWENTY-FIVE

1907-1908. Royal Reader Book V. Fifth Book.

One day, Sir said they were big children in Standard Five and he wanted to spend some more time helping them think more about things like *tone*. "As I told you before," Sir said, "that is about how the story sounds." Oseyan was excited because she could well remember that years ago, when she was little, Mr Ansel talked to the Standard One class about the same *tone*. *Tone*, Sir said, what the writer put in the story to make it sound the way it sounds. Now Oseyan realises that she was probably thinking about *tone* a lot when her grandmother was telling her stories. She just didn't know that was what she was thinking about. When her grandmother's story about the ocean had a different end than the story about the ocean in the Royal Reader – when her grandmother's story said people were *alive* after they were pulled from the ocean. *Alive* – a different word from the one her teacher had used in class and Ma said it in a different tone. She had said, "*Ki* **alive** *sa?* What kind of alive that? Huh! *Ki alive sa?*"

Now, in Standard Five, Sir makes them learn a lot of things by heart. Their teacher in Standard Three used to do that, too, but he – well, she after a while – they had two teachers in Standard Three – and well, they didn't explain things so much. Oseyan liked to stand up in class and recite. In fact, all teachers liked to make you learn thing by heart but with Mr Ansel in Standard I and now Sir in Standard V, is learn and discuss. Sir finds all kinds of things in the lesson that Oseyan doesn't even see when she first reads the lesson on her own. And Sir says things like, *The writer has his view; the person who put this book together has a view, but you think for yourself, too.*

And Sir tells Oseyan that she writes sensibly. He says he wishes there were opportunities for her to go on and study further, even do a certificate of some kind. And, Sir says, things will change but not yet. Sir told them that they should know the governor was trying to close down the Victoria Girls' Secondary School in town. He just didn't think it worth educating girls, Sir said, so think of the things you will have to fight in your life. This is not one of their new *combined schools,* Sir said, so they don't expect you to go on and do more, but you could do more in spite of that.

When Oseyan tells her grandmother and her aunt this, Auntie says, "That man real ambitious! He have big ideas! Imagine he thinking about little girl on the hill in La Digue doing certificate! Mr Man with Big Ideas!"

Ma says, "Nothing is impossible." And then she says, "Your poor mother would be proud."

Auntie Gerda looks across at Ma as if she is shocked that Ma has said this, as if she wonders why Ma would say a thing like that. Ma says no more. For some reason, Oseyan thinks now of how she first started to get her periods only a few months ago. Ma said she was later than the other girls, but perhaps Papa God was protecting her. And she had warned Oseyan to watch herself with the little boys always wanting to stand up and talk to her in any corner. "And just don't look at man anyway," Ma said. "If you look at them, they think you inviting them. They don't know how to think about anything else." Auntie Gerda was there that time , and she said in a disapproving kind of voice, "Ma-a-a!" And Ma just settled the matter, as she did sometimes, by singing a hymn.

What a friend we have in Jesus
All our sins and griefs to bear
What a privilege to carry
Everything to God in prayer.

And then from there she started humming. Auntie Gerda just say steupes in a soft, quiet kind of way and went on drinking her cocoa tea.

After a while, Oseyan started writing notes in her exercise book about her lessons and the way Sir explained things. She told Sir she was doing that, and he said, "You are developing good habits. And make sure when you are writing, you write good grammar. Write the way we try to teach you to talk in school, not the way we speak at home or the home way that we talk in school sometimes. And don't talk that Creole talk," he told her. "It will keep you back in your education. We speak one way, especially when we are at home, and we write another way, so write with a rubber – an eraser – and don't be afraid to rub off – erase – and write things again if you make a mistake, because you must think as if you are writing for the world, not for us here alone. Think internationally. Sound it out, sound out the word, and make sure you know how to spell it." Then, after a pause, Sir said, "It's not that we speak badly, because we have lots of African languages that are a part of the grammar of what we say every day, but we have to write English because that is what we present to the world, so remember to write with an eraser in your hand and think about English grammar." When she told Auntie Gerda and Ma this, Auntie Gerda said, "What do im? We talk bad. Why he fraid to say we talk bad? Sometimes that man thinking too much for he own good, but he mustn't mislead people. We talk bad, we talk bad. Why he can't say that?" Ma said, "Well, is something to think about." Auntie Gerda disagreed. "Is nothing to think about. He wrong on this one."

When Oseyan saw Uncle Eero, she asked him what he thought. He frowned, as if he was thinking about it, and then he said, "Well, he has a point there. That is a point. Is a lot to think about. A lot to think about. Huh. And Sir has to think about his job." Then, as if he were really thinking about it, Uncle Eero said, "But still, don't dismiss your own. Our language… the way we talk… has a history." Nobody seemed to have an answer is what Oseyan was left thinking. Perhaps this was one of the things she would have to find out.

CHAPTER TWENTY-SIX

1908. The Assyrian Came Down.

Whenever he decides it is time for poetry, Sir is smiling, and the knot in his tie is not as tight as he usually has it. One day on the playground, Felicia tells them, "Watch good. Whenever Sir put on a white shirt and not a blue one with his grey pants, is poetry time." They weren't sure about this. It didn't seem to happen all the time, but they knew poetry time was a time you could take almost any kind of chances with Sir. It was almost as if he became a different somebody. He and their Standard One teacher Mr Ansel were alike in that. In fact, other teachers in the school relaxed with poetry, too. Sometimes, on the way to another lesson, Sir would even stop and point out a poem. Oseyan's bench companion now is Miranda. Gwenevieve is in class, too, but Sir, saying she talks too much, has moved her to sit at one of the new little wooden desks near the other end of the bench. So Oseyan and Miranda sit together on a nice strong bench her uncle had made. Miranda put up her hand and whispered from behind it, "He smiling. Poetry today." Oseyan answered, "Yes, and is Lord Byron. He like Lord Byron."

The poem has a nice, racy beat. Sir divided the class into two – girls against boys. Today, there are eight boys and five girls. Sir said that two of the boys could go over to the girls' side if they wanted to. The boys didn't want to go and the girls didn't want them, and it was poetry and Sir was not insistent, so it remained like that. Everyone said, out loud, **"The Destruction of Sennacherib's Army"**, in the deep, strong way that Sir had taught them (*nothing paipsy,* he always said, because Sir could talk natural talk when it was poetry. He just made sure not to put in *too* many natural words. *Sound as if you mean it*), so they recited the title good and strong: **The Destruction of Sennacherib's Army** and the girls started:

> *The Assyrian came down like the wolf on the fold,*
> *And his cohorts were gleaming with purple and gold,*
> *And the sheen of their spears was like stars on the sea,*
> *When the blue waves roll nightly on deep Galilee.*

And then, the boys, some of them with voices changing, so that they were sounding cranky:

> *Like the leaves of the forest when summer is green,*
> *That host with their banners at sunset were seen:*
> *Like the leaves of the forest when Autumn hath blown,*
> *That host on the morrow lay withered and strown.*

And the girls came back at them sure and strong, sounding more like fifteen girls than five, Oseyan thought:

> *For the Angel of Death spread his wings on the blast,*
> *And breathed in the face of the foe as he passed;*

(the girls leaned across and breathed long at the boys as they said it)

> *And the eyes of the sleepers waxed deadly and chill,*

(the girls' voices slowed down nice and chilly)

> *And their hearts but once heaved,*

(and they heaved. Marjorie "heaved" so hard that she fell off the bench)

> *and forever were still*

but Marjorie got up. And then the boys performed, dead serious, trying to outdo their rivals.

> *And there lay the steed with his nostrils all wide,*

(and Anthony made his nostrils tremble in the way he did for them at breaktime)

But through them there rolled not the breath of his pride
And the foam of his gasping lay white on the turf
And cold as the spray of the rock-beating surf.

(They slowed down and tried to sound cold and dead – and then came the girls, well dead)

And there lay the rider, distorted and pale,
With the dew on his brow and the rust on his mail:
And the tents were all silent,

(the girls said it slow, slow, slow, and dead, dead)

                              the banners alone,
The lances unlifted, the trumpets unblown.

(and the girls wished they had the next verse alone, because they knew they could blow the boys out of the competition, but Sir made the whole class say it, so the boys came in even though the girls said afterward they thought the boys "well spoil the thing.")

And the widows of Asshur are loud in their wail,

(the girls were loud in their wail. Jessie was so loud that Gertrude looked at her bad eye and found a space in the pause after the next line to mutter, "What do you? You mother dead?")

And the idols are broke in the temple of Baal;
And the might of the Gentile, unsmote by the sword,
Hath melted like snow in the glance of the Lord!

(Oseyan thought the boys were kind of raggedy but the girls said it slo-o-o-w and powerful and strong).[6] And Oseyan concluded, "That is the best poem ever! The best poem ever!"

At home, Oseyan told them that Sir said the poem was about a biblical story from the Old Testament. Auntie Gerda said, "Oh yes! Second Kings, Chapter 19." And Oseyan read Second Kings and she understood it better after she and Auntie Gerda talked about it. She explained it to others in the class next day. In the story, King Sennacherib's Assyrian army attacked the holy city of Jerusalem because they could, and kings like to think they are powerful and they could do whatever they want, attack whoever they want for whatever reason they want. But God is the man – or, well, God is the God. So God say, *Who you? You think you powerful?* And God destroyed the whole army, even while the army thought it was all-powerful and it could come down like a wolf on the fold. That was how Oseyan explained it. But to tell the truth, who Oseyan really liked, she told her friends, was Lord Byron, because he could take a story like that and give it that rhythm and make you see the battle in your head. "But look at that, eh!" she told Gwen – Gwenevieve said Gwen was more stylish so they should call her Gwen now – "Look at that, eh! Another Lord again in the Royal Reader." The earthly Lord, as her Ma would say. "That book royal in truth." Through that book, they were really getting to know the British lords of the eighteenth century and the century that Ma and Poopa and all of them were born in, the nineteenth century. They were really getting to know the lords who wrote poetry and those who just ruled and decided and commented on things like laws in the House of Lords but didn't write poetry.

Sir said Lord Byron was a baron, one of those British nobles. So perhaps barons weren't so bad, Oseyan thought. He lived from 1788 to 1824, so he died well young. He was about 36 when he died, a lot younger than Oseyan's Ma, although she didn't know Ma's age for sure. But for sure Ma is older than Lord Byron was when he died. Sir said Lord Byron was one of the Romantics, poets who wrote in a certain way together, so people come to think of them as a group. Sir reminded them that they had met another of the Romantics before, but perhaps they had done the poem in Standard Three without even realising that the poet was one of the Romantics. And when Sir said, "We are Seven", everyone knew immediately. Gwen said, "Oh yes! William Words-worth," and she started to recite:

I met a little cottage girl

And the whole class chimed in

She was eight years old, she said
Her hair was thick with many a curl
That clustered round her head.

140

"So you see?" Sir said, "you know the Romantics. Wordsworth was one of them." And he told them that Lord Byron inherited money and estates in the way that these people away, in places like England and so, inherit estates and money.

Joshua put up his hand and said, "And here too, Sir. My grandfather say that the Laws and the Wells people and the Langdons and the Shears and people like that – the white ones – they inherit estates – and sometimes *chabin* ones inherit too."

Oseyan felt uncomfortable, even though she knew she hadn't inherited anything. Some heads turned in her direction but Sir just said, "Yes. Here, too, you have people inheriting estates." And then he continued with the lesson, and he told them that the great King Henry VIII even gave Lord Byron's family a lot of estates and things like that. Lord Byron criticised all kinds of things in his writing, but, Sir said, he wasn't like them there in Grenada and Dominica and Tobago and places like that. He was criticising with money in his pocket, and he was able to sell big house and get estates. So that was Lord Byron who wrote "The Destruction of Sennacherib's Army" when he was twenty-six years old. Imagine that, Oseyan and her friends said. Sometimes people in Grenada started off with little or no money, and then they might go away and get a little *pankwai,* but when Lord Byron didn't have, it wasn't the kind of *didn't have* they knew about in Grenada. And anyway he was in big position in the land of *Away* already, and he didn't have to go any place.

Still, the class really liked Lord Byron's poem. Sir said the rhythm of that poem, like the gallop of a horse, is because it is in – Sir liked big words, poetry time or no poetry time, so it was a big word explanation – anapaestic tetrameter. To build the rhythm, Sir said, you had two unstressed syllables followed by a stressed syllable and each one of those – the two unstressed and the one stressed – is called a foot. And there were four feet on the line. That was how you got the tetrameter. Listen to that word, *tetra,* Sir said. It's a word that means four. The class looked bewildered. And because it was poetry time, Gwen knew she could mutter that the poem good in truth, but it just didn't seem sensible to have to sit down and count all this foot and dem just to write a poem. Sir said that the other poem by Wordsworth, "We are

Seven", was tetrameter too, four feet on the line, but that one was iambic. Little Man put his hand high up in the air and said that yes, yes, he remembered the *iamb*. He said it was one unstressed and one stressed syllable. And because it was poetry and the whole class knew that poetry meant a chance to see Sir smile, Gwen took a chance with Sir and she said, "Well, Mr. Leconte! Very good." There were giggles, and Sir looked at Gwen severely but all he said was, "No teasing in my class, please."

Sir is Sir, so of course they had to write a poem like that – in the form that was the long word with the tetrameter after it. The girls learned the words with a skipping rope during break:

a-na-paes-tic te-tra-me-ter

down 1 – 2 – 3

and swing the skipping rope round and round over the heads of the girls stooping down

me-oh my-oh ri-oh

and up
and skip

a-na-paes-tic te-tra-me-ter

and down 3 – 4 - 5

and swing the skipping rope again

me-oh my-oh re-oh

and up

and the boys learned it by pretending to tease the girls and moving their waists round and round and taking the opportunity to learn it while the girls skipped. But remembering what it meant was a different thing.

Oseyan liked what Lord Byron did, and she would try to write like him, of course, because she didn't have a choice, but she was not going to share *her* poem with anyone but Sir. She knew it could be not perfect for Sir because it was poetry and Sir was really in a good mood even when he wasn't in class if he was talking to you about poetry. In fact, other people in the class must have felt like Oseyan, because the class begged Sir, and so he did not give them an amount out of a hundred for writing that poem. And to make matters better, he told them that they could write the whole poem in rhyming couplets. They liked the sound of that, especially when Sir explained that he meant they could find end rhymes, like "fold" and "gold," and use two lines (couplets), repeating that form for the whole poem. Sir said do it for fun, and he would take a look at their poems. For fun! They exchanged looks under their brows, trying both to associate the word fun with this exercise and to think of who they would make an Assyrian come down on. But Oseyan was so glad! The *anapaestic* business would have been her destruction. Let them destroy Sennacherib's army, she thought, but please leave Oseyan alone!

CHAPTER TWENTY-SEVEN

1908. Henry, Lord Brougham at Holy Innocents School.

Now that was a man – another of those British lords they met in the Royal Readers. Henry, Lord Brougham, lived way back between 1778 and 1868, so from the 18th century to the 19th century. And for those days that man must have lived a very long time, because it look like he was ninety years old when he died. Oseyan was thinking about all this after the class. It was Sir who told them this story. Mr Ansel was meant to teach the class but then he had to go to Dominica since his mother was sick, and he would have to wait for the mailboat and all kinda ting, so Sir taught them and then he asked Oseyan to go and fill in for Mr Ansel and teach the little ones.

Imagine that, Ma, she said later, and Ma grinned one broad grin, so that you could see where she had two teeth missing, on the side where Oseyan remembered she used to say she had toothache once. Ma was so pleased! Sir had invited her child to teach a class! The years does pass in truth, yes! And God be praised!

So, anyway, about this Lord Brougham! He became Lord High Chancellor – one of those really high-up people in government, and Sir said that he played a big role in the passing of the 1833 act for the abolition of slavery. And so the class met Lord Brougham who, Sir said, was quite a character! And Sir was quite a character, too, Oseyan thought, even more of a character than she remembered from when Mr Ansel used to invite him to talk to the class when she was in Standard One. Now that he was teaching her, he was something else! When, this time, he held up the Fifth Book, he said, "Class, open your books to page four hundred and two!" – and then he said, "Class, meet Henry, Lord Brougham on his visit to Holy Innocents School."

Holy Innocents! Just a strip of land, Uncle Eero was always reminding them at home, in that area that France had called La Digue. But the British were the ones who brought enlightenment, or Sir said that was what they intended. They built a school, and a church that could say it was interested in wellbeing for all. That's what Sir told them, but when she told Faith that, Faith asked "What he mean 'that could *say* it was interested'? Of course the church was interested in wellbeing for all. That man better watch his mouth." And that is another story, Oseyan thought, saying it in her head, repeating the words she heard Uncle Eero say when he was talking about Holy Innocents. She knew she could think things like that because Ma was not half as strict about religion as her own children – as Faith and Gerda, anyway. Or at least, Ma like the praying and the talking to God but she don't like the confusion between religions. Eero was more like his mother. So Oseyan knew she could even *say* that is another story and get away with it in front of Ma. But anyway, it was that strip of land with a church and a school, right there in the middle of La Digue, you could say, that the British called Holy Innocents and they put down their church and their school.

So – this lesson in the *Royal Reader Book V* was "Lord Brougham on Negro Slavery". It was right there, on page four hundred and two, next to another lesson, "Chatham on the American War". One after the other. It was in a section of the book that both Sir and Mr Ansel said the class would have to learn and perform. Depending on who taught the class, sometimes children didn't have to learn it by heart and perform, but both Sir and Mr Ansel liked performance, so there was no escaping. Sir had, draped over his shoulder, the long, thin brown strap that some backs could tell was really fat with the pee that tongue say he soaked it in at night. Most times, he walked up and down and didn't have to use the strap, because he was pushing the lesson into their heads so much that they wanted to learn it, some because they liked it, and some because they were afraid that this strap would come down on their backs. When Sir walked about the school with the strap over his shoulder, he had a lot of room to walk, because nobody was foolish enough to want to be close to him or to look up into his face as he walked. Mr Ansel didn't have a strap, usually, but perhaps Sir needed it because sometimes he was acting head-master when the headmaster was away. The headmaster was a man who sometimes rode to school on a brown horse, but most times he was away at meetings in town, so people knew Sir as headmaster.

Anyway, most children were glad when Sir called on them to perform and show what they could do. Besides, although a strap soaked in pee was something of a tradition, Sir didn't use it in the class often, so that they came to think he didn't really like to beat – at least not in the classroom, because he would beat you when he ask you to stay back after school. But when Sir let go with that strap in his office, giving you ten hot ones in one hand and telling you to keep it steady, there was nothing like reason in sight. The hand burning you like crazy, because Sir is a big tall man, but he telling you to keep it steady. How you going keep you hand steady when it stinging already and the strap coming down on it with a whole two hundred and fifty pounds behind it? But it might be better to think of the other times, Oseyan decided, when her mind reach there in reasoning.

A whole section of the fifth book, from page three hundred and ninety five to page four hundred and four, had the title "Rhetori-cal Passages". The Introduction to that section was a passage with the title, "On Learning by Heart", and it was written by V. Lushington. That was the name in the book. And then there was "Pitt's Reply to Walpole", "Traces of Ocean", "The Hungarian Revolution", "Lord Brougham on Negro Slavery" on page four hundred and two, and then "Chatham on the American War" on page four hundred and four. All of this was toward the back of the book, a few pages before the end. And Oseyan flipping through the pages as she learning her lessons, because Sir could suddenly ask you all kinds of questions, down to page number and where a lesson is in the book and why you think the editor put it right there. Miranda might mutter, because they just like to give people trouble, but that is not a thing you could say to Sir, of course, so she better flip through and know what is what.

About Lord Brougham, Sir said, this man talks nonsense sometimes, but here he knows what he is saying. Learn it! And the next week he made three of them in the class recite it.

Oseyan's part from Lord Brougham on Negro Slavery was right at the beginning:

> *I trust that at length the time is come when Parliament will no longer bear to be told that slave-owners are the best law-givers on slavery – no longer suffer our voice to roll across the Atlantic in empty warnings and fruitless orders. Tell me not of rights – talk not of the property of planter in his slaves. I deny his right – I acknowledge not the property. The principles, the feelings of our common nature, rise in rebellion against it. Be the appeal made to the understanding or to the heart, the sentence that rejects it is the same.*

And in class, Oseyan, echoing Lord Brougham recited:

> *In vain you tell me of laws that sanction such a claim! There is a law above all the enactments of human codes – the same throughout the world – the same in all times. Such as it was before the daring genius of Columbus pierced the night of ages – opening to one world the sources of power, wealth and knowledge, to another all unutterable woes – such is it at this day. It is the law written by the finger of God on the heart of man; and by that law, unchangeable and eternal, while men despise fraud, and loathe rapine, and hate blood, they shall reject with indignation the wild and guilty phantasy, that man can hold property in man!*[7]

That was her part. That was the part Oseyan had to learn. And when she finish saying it in class, although she didn't understand everything, she knew from that property part especially that she had just said something really important, and the class knew it, too, not only because of Oseyan's tone as she recited but because Sir was quiet, just looking down at the book in his left hand, and his right hand was up, fingering his moustache. He looked up at them, and Standard Five was silent as they watched him and heard murmurs from other classes as if they came from a long way off. Sir said, "Yes, the wild and guilty fantasy." And some in the class shook their heads up and down, imitating Sir.

Marjorie – who lived further up the hill now, at the top of Waterfall – had to recite the other part. Gwen would have had that part, but Gwen didn't come because she was sick. Oseyan thought about the part that Sir had focused on, from the end of what she had recited:

> *While men despise fraud, and loathe rapine, and hate blood, they shall reject with indignation the wild and guilty phantasy, that man can hold property in man!*

And then Oseyan couldn't do anything about those thoughts that kept coming to her. Slavery was over, but her father, people were saying, thought her mother was his property! He didn't have a lot of money, people said, but he was white, so he was important. From what she heard her grandmother say, she couldn't help thinking that – whoever he was, because she had never seen him – he didn't *loathe rapine*… Sir told them that was a word that had to do with plunder, and Uncle Eero had told her one day when she made him talk that he couldn't help thinking that her father plundered the body of her mother. The wild and guilty phantasy… Well, that was long before the story of her mother. But was it, really?

This Lord Brougham, as Sir told them, said some sensible things, but Sir also warned the class not to expect sensible things all the time. When Oseyan met Lord Brougham, she was a little afraid of him. He was saying that one man should not have other men as property, and she didn't know what to think. All she could say when she, Marjorie, Gwen and the others were talking about it later, after Gwen had come to school and they were talking about it, was, "Hm! That Lord Brougham is a puzzle, *oui!* A real puzzle."

CHAPTER TWENTY-EIGHT

1908. Chatham on the American War.

After Lord Brougham, on the next page, the class met Chatham, who came to Holy Innocents in the Royal Reader to say what he thought about the American War. That passage was among those they had to learn for elocution, and that one got Sir all heated up. In fact, Edna, who was always hearing more than anybody, although she didn't come to school often because her parents needed her to help out with the little ones, felt sure she heard Sir mutter "*blasted*" or something or other when they were reading Chatham's speech. Nobody else heard it, so they couldn't be sure, but they knew that the Chatham story had Sir all heated up because more than once he said, "Imagine that! Imagine!" They spent a lot of time in class reading, reciting and discussing Chatham on the American War. Later, when they were in the schoolyard playing, and even on the way home, more than one person kept murmuring "Blasted!" They weren't sure why, but they had heard that this man Chatham had made Sir say "blasted" on a day that was not a poetry day, so is not that he was relaxed, but was just too worked up to care that children might overhear. Although they weren't sure if Edna had heard correctly, the story was a good one. That was a *blasted* powerful man!

This Chatham was in the British House of Lords – he was really Lord Pitt, William Pitt. Another lord – plenty British lords and la… well, come to think of it, not ladies so much, but lords. Perhaps not ladies at all, but plenty lords in the Royal Readers.

So this Chatham was a Whig. In England, their teachers told them, there were Whigs and Tories but exactly who was who was another story that Oseyan wasn't too sure about. Sir said that, at the time, the Tories were the ones who most openly supported the monarchy and the church. But anyway, in the class, they all knew that this Chatham was a real important person. There was William Pitt the older and his son, William Pitt the younger. This one, this Chatham in the *Royal Reader Book Five*, was William Pitt the Elder, and he was a different kind of lord – so the story went. Still with the lord name and privileges and so on, but Sir told them that *this* Lord Chatham didn't even like the *idea* of lord and title and things like that. In fact, since in Standard IV, when they first met Chatham, they heard that he had refused to accept a title at first. He was so down to earth – well, down to earth in his way, the way high-up people like that could be down to earth – so down to earth that people used to call him the Great Commoner. *Imagine that, eh!* That's what they kept saying when they were walking from school into La Digue and up the road to the other side and up to and through Waterfall because it even had some children going back over by Belle Vue Land and over on the road to St. James. *Imagine that*, they said, as they sent a stone *vu-u-n-g* into the cocoa and over by the lime trees on the hill and in the corner by the bougainvillaea. *Imagine that! The Great Commoner.* In fact, Chatham didn't accept the idea of a title until 1766. And he died in 1778. He was born in… in… something like 1708, they argued on the way home. The Great Commoner!

Pitt, Lord Chatham, made a speech in the House of Lords, a strong speech, and the speech was called Pitt's address to Walpole. They had to learn that, too. Oh yes! Pitt *dékatjé* Walpole. *I dékatjé'y byen. He mash up Walpole good. He tell that man – nonm sala – what is what – how he corrupt and how he good-for-nothing. Koumen I sé yon kòwonpi épi i bon pou anyen.* Pitt wasn't joking. And then there was the speech that this Lord of Chatham gave on the American War.

"Woy!" Gwenevieve said when they were going home that afternoon.

"You don't hear Chatham? *Zòt pa ka tann Chatham? Sa sé nonm!* That is man!"

And even Little Man sounded just straight admiring as he said, "Yes. He say his piece, boy!"

What Chatham really had them marvelling about was a powerful American War speech he gave in the British parliament in

1777. That was 1777, and he died in 1778. *Woy o yoy!* So by that time, even if he wasn't telling the truth about who he was before, by then he was ready to go, so what he said had more weight. Even Ma say, "*Lè ou konnèt ou ka alé jwenn Bondyé, lè sala ou ka di sa ou vwéman vlé di.* When you know you going and meet your maker, at least then you saying what you really think."

So! It's like that – *Eh bien! Sé konsa!* That is what he really think!

This was about the war with the American colonies that were going to become the United States of America. This is when they really get to know Chatham, *oui. Wi. Chatham not easy.* That is what Oseyan thought. *Them over there in the British House of Commons, but we quite over here, right here in Holy Innocents, this strip of land where the British put their church and the school to bring us light.* And Chatham make them see the kinda light. This is when we really meet Chatham, Oseyan told Gwen and the others. And in Standard Five there, they turn it round and round in school road, because although they meet Chatham for a little bit in Standard Four, Sir talked about him a lot more in the Standard Five lesson. And of course, the class had to learn his speech and act it out.

Chatham was really vexed about white people fighting white people and bringing in Indians to help. *Ay! Chatham say, what kind of thing is that?* Well, he didn't say it like that, Oseyan explained to her friends in school road, but he say it like how white people like Chatham in England and the House of Lords does say thing like that. Chatham thought it was a disgrace – white people fighting their white brothers and bringing Indians to help – a real disgrace – *yon vwé disgwas* – and he let them know it in that Parliament!

"I stand up in class," Oseyan said in the school road, "and hear me speak like Chatham, man! *Tann mwen!* Hear me!"

And in class she really tried to speak like Chatham, elocution and everything!

> *I cannot, my lords, I will not, join in congratulation on misfortune and disgrace. This, my lords, is a perilous and tremendous moment. It is not a time for adulation; the smoothness of flattery cannot save us in this rugged and awful crisis. It is now necessary to instruct the Throne in the language of truth. We must, if possible, dispel the illusion and darkness which envelop it, and*

display, in its full danger and genuine colours, the ruin which is brought to our doors. Can ministers still presume to expect support in their infatuation? Can Parliament be so dead to its dignity and duty as to give its support to measures thus obtruded and forced upon it, – measures, my lords, which have reduced this late flourishing Empire to scorn and contempt? But yesterday, and Britain might have stood against the world: now, none so poor as to do her reverence.[8]

And Oseyan looked round at the Parliament that was her class, that should be ashamed of itself because it was losing the reverence of its subjects in the school. She flung her hand out to take in the rest of the school, and some of the children in Standard Four just behind them turned their heads to take in the excellence of the oratory from Standard Five. And because it was truly excellent, the Standard Four teacher let his class listen.

The people whom we at first despised as rebels, but whom we now acknowledge as enemies, are abetted against us – supplied with every military store, have their interest consulted, and their ambassadors entertained – by our inveterate enemy; and ministers do not, and dare not, interpose with dignity or effect. The desperate state of our army abroad is in part known. No man more highly esteems and honours the British troops than I do. I know their virtues and their valour. I know they can achieve anything but impossibilities; and I know that the conquest of British America is an impossibility.

You cannot, my lords, you cannot conquer America.

And Sir's class and some of those who were paying attention from other classes, because their teachers thought it was important, were almost in tears because they, the British, had to acknowledge that they *could not conquer* America. And because of the things they were approving *to try to conquer America*, it was an indignity. Chatham – and Oseyan – were upset.

What is your present situation there? We do not know the worst; but we do know that in three campaigns we have done nothing, and suffered much. You may swell every expense, accumulate every assistance, and extend your traffic to the shambles of every German despot; your attempts will be forever vain and impotent: doubly so,

*indeed, from this mercenary aid on which you rely; for it irritates, to
an incurable resentment, the minds of your adversaries, to overrun
them with the mercenary sons of rapine and plunder, devoting them
and their possessions to the rapacity of hireling cruelty.*

Oh gosh, Oseyan thought, forgetting Chatham for a moment,
how awful. Hireling cruelty! And the mercenary sons of rapine.
People like the Caribs? But anyway, the class was listening, and
she was Chatham.

*If I were an American, as I am an Englishman, while a foreign
troop remained in my country I never would lay down my arms;
never! n e v e r! – **N E V E R!***

Some of the children jumped, and the whole school was listening.
Oseyan paused and looked around so that the school – or Parliament – could take in the enormity of what she was saying. And
children in Standard Five and even those in other classes stared at
her open-mouthed, appalled at what they perceived to be the
condition of things for them, for the British. And Oseyan well
give it to the class good, because Sir and the *Fifth Book* explain how
to read and speak to capture your audience. It was right there in
the section, "Rules for Good Reading",[9] that Sir tell them to
study: "Lay additional stress on an emphatic word or phrase when
it is repeated; as, – 'If I were an *American,* as I am an *Englishman,*
while a foreign troop remained in my country, I NEVER would
lay down my arms; *never,* NEVER, NEVER'."[7] So she knew how
to do it. But woy o yoy! They were fighting against these
Americans who were really the same British, and here Pitt –
Chatham – was saying that if it was he, *he* wouldn't put down arms
and stop fighting, and then, he say, especially when the British
using *savage Indians* – to help them win the war. Woy-o-yoy!
When they get to that part, Oseyan was all mixed up inside,
because she could understand Chatham's horror, but she couldn't
help thinking, too, about Ma and Kalinya and Mr Ansel.

*But, my lords, who is the man that, in addition to the disgraces
and mischiefs of the war, has dared to authorize and associate to our
arms the tomahawk and the scalping-knife of the savage? – to call
into civilized alliance the wild and inhuman inhabitant of the*

woods? – to delegate to the merciless Indian the defence of disputed
rights, and to wage the horrors of his barbarous war against our
brethren? My lords, these atrocities cry aloud for redress and
punishment.

And when Oseyan was performing the whole thing in class, she
couldn't help it, but the thought of Ma interrupted Chatham's
flow. As soon as she had to talk about the *savage Indian*, Oseyan
remembered that she was acting. And when you remember that,
something does change, and Oseyan felt it change. Chatham
could talk and the speech real good, but *inhuman?* She was kind
of ashamed for Kalinya but upset with Chatham, too. And as
thoughts do, ones about Ma and Mr Ansel and the Caribs and the
German… what was the word again… those Germans who found
the markings on the Carib Stone in 1903 – all of that flowed
through her mind so that her tone changed although she continued *acting out* Chatham's speech. And bit by bit, teachers throughout the school called their classes back to order.

Afterwards, Standard Five was erupting in questions. Oseyan
fired them up with her performance and Sir said he wanted
discussion not only about the acting out of the speech, which he
thought was frighteningly good – that's what Sir said, frighteningly good – but about what Chatham was saying.

"So Sir, he is saying that although Britain lose – lost – he could
understand why the Americans wouldn't give up, Sir? Because in
their place he wouldn't give up, Sir? Which side he on, Sir? Which
side is he on? And what he mean about the tomahawk and the
scalping-knife of the savage, Sir?"

"He find is bad – does he think it is bad – to take Indians to help
them fight the white Americans, Sir? He find that white people
from the same place shouldn't do that, Sir?"

"Is because he think the Indians less, Sir? He call them savage,
Sir! Indians like the Caribs he calling savage, Sir?"

Sir had made Oseyan perform Chatham's speech before they
discussed it in class. Perhaps this was a good thing, because
Oseyan didn't know if she would have been able to perform as
well afterward. After the discussion, she was sorry that she had
used Chatham's voice with such passion and conviction. But

then she remembered her grandmother had said she was a good little actor and she must know the difference between acting and really being somebody. And act it out, Grandma had said, act it out with conviction, but know what you know. So that wasn't bad, and to tell the truth, she liked Chatham's speech. He so emotional and he use words so good! And her friends in class said how brave she was when she performed Chatham's speech!

"You brave, girl!"

"You do it really good!"

"Real Chatham, yes. You don't hear her?"

Sir praised her. He looked straight at her as he said, "Excellent elocution. You have a good voice. You perform well." And Oseyan understood that Sir was telling her the same thing that her Ma said. She said, "Yes, Sir, I understand." And Oseyan was sure that Sir smiled – not a big and broad smile, but a smile in the Sir way.

The same Marjorie from up going through Waterfall, who was the only one who could act and perform and learn things and say speech like her, she looked at Oseyan up and down as if she wished she could perform like that, as if she was seeing something else happening these days in Oseyan as they reach Standard Five.

Later, as they were walking home after school, although Oseyan was sounding strong and bold, she was also remembering how she and Chatham asked, *Who is the man who has dared to authorize and associate to our arms the tomahawk and the scalping-knife of the savage?* It frightened her, in a way, that she had felt so deeply with this Pitt who was Chatham that she nearly cried, because she was so vexed and ashamed that they – all of them, the British people – would do such a thing – bringing the *savage* with his *tomahawk* to fight against their white – well, Chatham didn't say white, but after they talked about it in class, Oseyan could see that's what it was – white American brothers, even if they were then fighting them like the enemy. Although she knew it was people like the Caribs Chatham was talking about, she had felt kind of disappointed in her parliament, in truth.

And in spite of everything, Oseyan had to perform the speech for Ma. And sometimes when she told Gwen what Ma said about some things, Gwenevieve would say, *So you had to tell her that, then?*

155

Girl you does tell you grandmother too much thing! You must hold back some! It was hard. And this one made her feel so emotional that she knew it was a very important one. She had to tell Ma. Ma kept nodding while Oseyan talked. Sometimes she looked up and watched her granddaughter with the white ribbons in her hair, the blue skirt, the white shirt for school, hands lightly folded in front of her, big important words flowing effortlessly out of her mouth, as she performed for her grandmother. Sometimes Oseyan moved her head for emphasis and lifted one hand to gesture. Ma watched the fair skin that spoke to her of so much. Listening to the performance, Ma's eyes filled and she had to open them wide, then sit back in her chair and look up at the ceiling that Oba, who insisted he was a Liberated African, had put up there. She sat back and looked straight up at the white-painted ceiling – Eero had painted it white after his father died – just to keep the water steady in her eyes. Then she sat up, and opened her arms to the child. As Oseyan leaned against her, Ma spoke:

"I am very proud of you, my Oseyan. You getting big. You starting to know yourself, and you doing real good in school. I am proud of you. Especially because you could say it like that, and sound so much as if you want us to believe, when I know that you know you not no English lord."

And here Ma put her head back and held Oseyan a little away from her to look down into her face, as if she wanted confirmation that Oseyan knew she was not an English lord. Oseyan nodded vigorously. She knew. Ma relaxed and hugged her close again.

"You like to read and you like to learn poetry and story, and you like to perform. I like that. You take that talent from people you don't even know – and I hardly even think I remember their face myself, although I thinking of them now as I look at you, in another place and another time. You are a good, strong little actor. You have that in your blood, but remember that what you just finish do for the class today and for me now is act, you hear? You say it good – really good." And Ma murmured, "Who knows? – *Sa ki konnèt?* Perhaps you even say it better than the one they call Pitt or Lord whatever-he-be himself. *Mwen ni kwéyans, zanfan mwen.* I am proud of you, my child. *Mwen konnèt ou ké fè yon moun ki gwan.* I know you will be somebody big. *Mwen ba konnèt ki moun, mé yon moun*! I don't know who, but somebody! I could hear it in you, child. *Mwen konnèt.*"

And after a while, Ma talked again, as if she thought perhaps she hadn't said enough, and she wanted to be sure. "That is Pitt speech, all right, my child? Is not yours. I know you don't think the Carib people who living up the road in the crossing over the hill in the back savage. You don't think that, I know." And Oseyan shook her head from side to side, no, she didn't think that, and then up and down, yes, she knew. Usually you couldn't shake your head instead of speaking when you were in Ma's presence, but the emotion was obviously so high this evening, that both of them, Oseyan and Ma, knew it was all right to shake your head on this occasion. Ma hugged her again. And two, three hugs in one afternoon from Ma was really something to make you cry.

Oseyan was so tired, she didn't even have time to get up after she said her prayers in Ma's room and walk across to the room that was hers alone now, since all the others were off on their own and she was Ma's solace, as Ma said the word these days. She fell asleep right there, on her knees, with Ma talking to her. And while Oseyan knelt there in a half sleep, Ma prayed, her voice low and almost sad:

"*Papa bondyé pa kité'y, non.* Papa god, don't let her go, *non. Tjébé'y épi maché épi'y pou mwen, tanpwi souplé.* Hold on to her and walk with her for me please. *Mwen pa sa wété tout tan pou gadé'y, mé pa kité'y.* – I can't stay forever and watch her, but don't let her go." And she pleaded again, "*Papa bondyé, pa kité'y.* And don't take me before she finish drink water and could handle sheself. *Pa kité'y.*"

Ma had to wake Oseyan to tell her to go to sleep for real this time.

CHAPTER TWENTY-NINE

1908. Fifth Book: Hear Chatham to the end.

The next evening, Oseyan performed the last part of Pitt's speech for Ma, because somehow this was feeling really important, and she wanted Ma to know everything about it, and Ma would enjoy it even more now because she was sure her grandchild knew she was performing.

"I could say it for you while you ironing, Ma?"

"Yes. I will listen. But perhaps wait let me finish iron this bodice, because I don't want to burn the clothes and I want to hear you good. So just wait a little while."

"Okay, Ma. And Ma, you know, Sir said – he told us – that if you listen to what Chatham is saying, you understand the ties between the – white, yes, he say white – Americans and the white English people that they were fighting. Sir said that in the speech Chatham is repeating what some of the other Lords said and he is angry because they seem to be assuming that the savage Indian is a person like any other person. You hear that, Ma?"

"Yes, I hear, and I am not surprised. Okay. You could start now. You ready?"

"Yes. Yes, Ma. I will stand up here by the dining table and say it. So Chatham speaking, eh, Ma?"

Ma nodded.

> But, my lords, this barbarous measure has been defended, not only on the principles of policy and necessity, but also on those of morality; "for it is perfectly allowable," says Lord Suffolk, "to use all the means which God and nature have put into our hands." I am astonished, I am shocked, to hear such principles confessed, –

to hear them avowed in this house or in this country. My lords, I did not intend to encroach so much on your attention, but I cannot repress my indignation – I feel myself impelled to speak. My lords, we are called upon, as members of this House, as men, as Christians, to protest against this horrible barbarity. "That God and nature have put into our hands"! What ideas of God and nature that noble Lord may entertain, I know not; but I know that such detestable principles are equally abhorrent to religion and to humanity. What! To attribute the sacred sanction of God and nature to the massacres of the Indian scalping-knife! – to the cannibal, savage, torturing, murdering, devouring, drinking the blood of his mangled victims! Such notions shock every precept of morality, every feeling of humanity, every sentiment of honour.

Ma was watching her granddaughter's indignant face – the brows coming together, the hand gesturing in annoyance.

These abominable principles, and this more abominable avowal of them, deserve the most decisive indignation.

And, for her grandmother, Oseyan spoke the last few words of Chatham's speech:

I call upon the honour of your Lordships to reverence the dignity of your Ancestors, and to maintain your own. I call upon the spirit and humanity of my country to vindicate the national character. I invoke the genius of the constitution. To send forth the merciless cannibal, thirsting for blood! – Against whom?

Oseyan's voice rose as she contemplated the enormity of it. That was the word used in class – both of them, in fact – "enormity" and "contemplated" – and she was thinking of that as she spoke.

Our brethren! – To lay waste their country, to desolate their dwellings, and extirpate their race and name, by the aid and instrumentality of these hounds of war!

Oseyan's voice rose on the word "hounds" and her right hand went up for emphasis. Now her voice was lowered in disgust, but it lost none of its intensity.

Spain can no longer boast preeminence in barbarity. She armed
herself with blood-hounds to extirpate the wretched natives of
Mexico. We, more ruthless, loose those dogs of war against our
countrymen in America, endeared to us by every tie that can sanctify
humanity! I solemnly call upon your lordships, and upon every order
of men in the State, to stamp upon this infamous procedure the
indelible stigma of public abhorrence. More particularly, I call upon
the holy prelates of our religion to do away this iniquity: let them
perform a lustration, to purify the country from this deep and deadly
sin. My lords, I am old and weak, and at present unable to say more;
but my feelings of indignation were too strong to have said less. I could
not have slept this night in my bed nor even reposed my head upon
my pillow, without giving vent to my eternal abhorrence of such
enormous and preposterous principles.

Oseyan stopped.

Ma said, "My child!" And her voice was quiet with admiration.

"Yes, Ma, and you hear what he is saying? Sir called it almost frightening that all of that is there for us to read. Sir said it was a big war, the American Revolution, but it was a family quarrel. You don't find that is a big something, Ma? And Sir says that all the things they achieve are meant for the white brothers of the British people, not for the savage Indian, of course, and definitely not for those black like us in America."

Ma nodded, moving her head up and down.

"So Ma, he is saying – Chatham is saying he think they even worse than Spain, Ma – the British, his friends that he is quarrelling with inside there. He just don't like how they act, Ma. He say, Ma, that Spain use dogs against the Indians – he call them the wretched natives – in Mexico, and he say that was bad enough. But look at what them in England doing, he saying. They releasing these dogs of war, the savage Indian, against their own white countrymen in America. And to Chatham that is the worst thing ever, so they worse than Spain. Chatham say that is a real sin and that they should let the church pray for them and bless them and do something to purify the place from this sin, because it really bad. That is how Sir explain it to us, Ma."

Ma went to sit on the bench now, and Oseyan sat next to her, turning to her as she explained. "Ma, Sir say that when he calling for a *lustration* is like what Uncle Eero does talk about and what they does do in Sängo up in La Poterie and Paradise and other places. Sir say when he call for it in there in Parliament they think of it as a good thing, although people like Chatham and them there in the House of Lords wouldn't like libation."

Ma sat there watching her child. "I suppose," Ma said, "is like he calling for a blessing. You know?" And then she added, "Well, my child, that tell you everything you need to know. That Sir is a good teacher. He making you-all think. I so glad they open that school there and get a man like him and Mr Ansel, too, to teach."

Oseyan recalled that when they did the lesson in class, Sir stood at the front of the class for a long time, just looking at them. He loosened his blue and white tie, moved his head around as if his neck needed exercise and as if the blue cotton shirt was suddenly too tight for him, and then he put the *Royal Reader No. 5* down on his desk. He told them, in a quiet kinda voice, "Please read that lesson over and over. Understand what Chatham is saying – and I beg you not to think that you are either one of those people in the House of Lords or one of their countrymen in America. Have sympathy for those they call the savages and for yourselves, for the Black people like you they don't even bother to talk about in America because the slaves who fight are working for them and belong to them, as they see it." And Sir continued to stand in front of the class just staring at them as if he wasn't really seeing them. Then Sir said: "Good afternoon, Children!"

And they answered in unison, "Good afternoon, Sir!"

And somehow Oseyan couldn't explain all that she was feeling after that class to Ma, but she relived it now, as she sat leaning against her grandmother.

Sir had said, "Class dismissed." And he watched as they walked, slowly for a change, out of his class and out of the one room that was the whole school.

When Auntie Gerda heard about the lesson and how moved the class was, Auntie Gerda said, "That really not sounding like the same Royal Reader I learn from. That man well dangerous, yes. They better watch him."

Ma said, "Is a real teacher, that man."

CHAPTER THIRTY

1908/1909. Watch it with me, young lady.

Oseyan was thirteen years old. She had left Holy Innocents School behind her at the end of Standard Five. At first, she was going to go to the Anglican school down in La Baye so she could do Standard Six. Both Mr Ansel and Sir told her she should come back to the school to help teach the little ones. Her teachers all said she was excellent with children and really bright. Although she hadn't gone to one of the new First Division Combined Schools, as Sir advised, she should think about being a pupil teacher. The Governor and the others there in the Legislative Council don't know what they are talking about, Sir said. All children should be given an opportunity. Now that his Standard Five children had left school, Sir was more open with his critiques about the Legislative Council when talking to some of them. She should tell him if she wanted to become a pupil teacher, he said, and he would tell her what she would have to do to begin. Ma talked to some of the family to hear what they thought. Cousin Mildred said that for a girl Oseyan had done really well and it would probably be best for her to continue with sewing. She was showing promise there. It was better to encourage girls to think about marriage and family as the future, and not to behave like boys. Even though some girls as good as boys at everything. That's what Cousin Mildred said.

Sir told Oseyan's grandmother that she could help teach the little ones in school there in Holy Innocents. He said she had an excellent mind. But when Ma talked about it again to Gerda and Eero and they thought about everything, they decided that Oseyan should continue the sewing – with the lady who taught sewing at the Anglican School in Grenville. She already knew how to sew some things because Ma had taught her, and she could knit. They had already been thinking about what opportunities there were for girls, of course. They had saved her from labouring in the land and perhaps even from domestic work in one of the houses of these high-up people around. Teaching – they would have to think about that. It would mean more studying to get some kind of certificate, and although Ma liked the idea of her granddaughter as a teacher, she self wasn't getting any younger, and things were hard, and perhaps it was time for Oseyan to ease up the pressure and start helping herself. Auntie Gerda was helping Ma think it all through, but Auntie Gerda had her own things to think about these days. She herself was working domestic with a family. Ma thought this was a lot better than going to work under the cocoa on people's plantation. She was holding out for sewing for Oseyan, but meantime Oseyan could help out her aunt with things in the house and keep learning to sew.

Auntie Gerda said that with the knitting and now learning to sew, Oseyan could do better than she, Gerda, and one day make a good living. She could even crochet. Her aunt said that she could become a big-time seamstress if she put her mind to it. "We mustn't look back," Auntie Gerda said. "We have to keep improving. As a family we have to keep looking forward."

Nowadays, though, Oseyan and Ma didn't always see eye to eye. Sometimes, Oseyan thought, it was as if Ma couldn't see that she was now a big girl.

"Ma, you only want me to stay in the dark under the cocoa and in the track up here in Waterfall. I only going in Grenville with my friends. What's wrong with that?"

"I tell you already, friends bring you go; they don't bring you back. What you want to be going in La Baye all hours of the night for? When darkness fall, little girl should be in their house. What's wrong with you?"

"Ma – "

"'Ma' nothing! And another thing. I hear you standing up on corner talking to Mr Jeffrey's son. That boy is older than you. He didn't sit down on same school bench with you."

"Ma, he mother living in Tivoli and he went to school in

Grenville. He couldn't sit down on same school bench with me because he was up in Tivoli."

"Don't give me your sass and make me walk over there to meet you. Tall as you is, even if I have to get up on tiptoe to reach you, I will get up there. So watch it with me, young lady. Who you think you talking to?"

There are some questions Oseyan knew better than to try to answer.

"Because you big woman now, you figure you reach. But I reach long before you. Remember that! So watch it with me, young lady! *Gadé kò'w èpi mwen, jenn tifi!*" Ma stood looking at her granddaughter for a while, and then she said what Oseyan heard her muttering often these days. "*Fanm sé yon nasyon.* Woman is a nation. So you reach you nation! *Konsa ou wivé nasyon'w! Eh bien!*"

CHAPTER THIRTY-ONE

1908. Baby Malcolm.

Oseyan was now often away from the house on the hillside. As Ma said, she was big lady and always going one place or the other with her *string band* of friends – *épi bann li*. So she wasn't there sometimes when Auntie Gerda had time off and came to see Ma. The last time Auntie Gerda was at the house, Oseyan thought she had put on some weight, but she didn't put two and two together.

One day toward the end of September, when the rain kept drizzling so that she was running in and out from under the house, Oseyan sat on the steps thinking about all the things she was doing now that she was finished with Holy Innocents school. The main thing was sewing. She liked sewing and didn't mind the idea of being a seamstress. She was always excited to go to the classes with Miss Grant in La Baye and Miss Grant said she was doing well. She wasn't one of Miss Grant's students in the Anglican School down there, but Miss Grant worked with her after school on the days she had to teach sewing at the school – Monday, Wednesday and Friday. Miss Grant said she was following the class syllabus, and gave Oseyan things to make like those she gave to her class. Oseyan was well on the way because she had already done a lot of the basic stuff with her grandmother. She told Oseyan what she had to do on the syllabus for level 1: hemming on stripes, beginning with black thread, rising to red and going on to blue. Hemming, seaming, felling and fixing. Oseyan at first didn't know what Miss Grant meant when she said "felling", but she knew when Miss Grant showed her. Ma just used to say, *Fold that edge under the other one, turn it over and flatten it out, then sew up the side, on the wrong-side.* That was what Miss Grant called "felling", and Oseyan could do that.

She had to show that she could complete a child's pinafore with all those different stitches, and she had already done all of that with Ma, though Ma hadn't followed all the instructions about beginning with one kind of thread and moving on to the other – it was mainly black thread she used. Sometimes sleeves gave Oseyan trouble, but pinafore don't have sleeve, so that was easy – and she was working on sleeves, anyway. When Miss Grant gave her a test , she said she was satisfied that Oseyan had done all of the things for the first level, so she didn't have to do them again. She had even done part of the next level, sewing on strings and helping Ma make a pillowcase for the bed and even for the bedroom in Auntie Gerda's house later on. So Miss Grant started her off at the third level, where she had to make a shirt. It had to be a plain day shirt or night shirt, and she had to show that she could do things like gathering, setting in gathers, buttonholing, darning, patching, and herring-boning. Oseyan liked learning all these different things. Sometimes Miss Grant might say things in a way she didn't know, but once Miss Grant showed her, she realised that Ma had done a lot of the same things but didn't use the same words to explain things. Miss Grant told her that she was a real good beginning seamstress, and she would see if she could get a certificate somehow, even though she wasn't a Combined School student in the La Baye school. Oseyan was excited about the idea of getting a certificate. By that time she would be her own woman in sewing, and she would be able to make a whole frock, too, and do all those different stitches. She was still learning to knit and to crochet from Ma, so she was sure she would be able to be a good seamstress and get a certificate if the Legislative Council would let her get it – or perhaps Miss Grant mightn't tell the Legislative Council. She didn't know. Auntie Gerda said, "Don't make it difficult for the lady, eh. She just teaching you quiet on the side there private, so you getting the experience. If you start to ask about certificate, it might be hard for her and then you wouldn't get certificate and you wouldn't get the training. So take the training and hush you mouth."

Anyway, she would see how things go. Today was not one of

Miss Grant's class days, and Cousin Mildred was up here on the hill, and she and Ma eating coconut tart – is she Oseyan who make the coconut tart, Saturday – and they inside there drinking ginger beer like Christmas reach early. Was Ma decide to set ginger beer a few days ago because she had some ginger and she feel like it, she say. They were there making jokes and laughing out loud, and then suddenly the voices go down. Oseyan out there on the step and she realise that the sound gone way down, so although she wasn't really listening before, now she want to hear. She push aside the plimsolls Cousin Mildred leave on the steps and she lean nearer the doorway. There was an obvious *shoo-shooing* and so, of course, Oseyan's ears pricked up and stretched out to hear better. Ma was saying to Mildred, "Well, she of age. I wish she coulda settle down already, but this time she of age." Were they talking about her? Finish school so now she of age? Or perhaps Auntie Gerda! The *shooshooing* continued even lower and she couldn't really hear. She wouldn't risk going behind the door and leaning there. Cousin Mildred had a way of suddenly opening doors – just to see who listening – and Oseyan didn't fancy being discovered.

Time passed, and then one day later on, Oseyan saw her aunt – and it clicked. Auntie Gerda pregnant. That was it! Strange, but her mind kinda go there, too. *Well, she of age! Eh bien, I ni laj.* Of course Auntie Gerda was of age. She was about twenty-four years. Old already.

That December, Malcolm was born. But even before that, Ma was always by Auntie Gerda because, as Ma said, *she need the support.* Malcolm was a real cute baby. The three of them – Oseyan, Ma, and Auntie Gerda – stood one day in the hall that had become a living-room now, with the other side of it partitioned off by Uncle Eero as a dining-room. Auntie Gerda held little Malcolm out to Oseyan as Ma looked on.

"Hold him," Auntie Gerda said.

Ma said, "Be careful. Be careful. Make sure you put your hand on the back. Support the head. Careful. Careful. Is a little baby. He can't hold his back up. Careful."

"Is okay, Ma." Oseyan grinned. "Don't fraid. I have him." She looked into little Malcolm's face and she loved him immediately.

"You look like your mother!"

She looked toward Auntie Gerda with a smile of delight but Gerda was looking at Ma. Then Auntie Gerda and Ma were hugging one another and crying. Ma must have been really worried about Auntie Gerda, even though she was of age. Oseyan's eyes filled too, because the moment, this first meeting with her nephew – or, well, her cousin – was about family. Was like her brother, little how he was, or like her child. Oseyan looked at Malcolm. "You are so precious," she said. "Precious one." She patted him on the back, said *doudou,* held him back a little and looked into the face that he was squinging up for her and repeated, "Precious, precious one." Then she said, "My little son. *Chéwi! Doudou! Ti gason mwen!*"

Ma said, "What wrong with you at all? Give your aunt back the child."

Gerda laughed. "Leave her, Ma. She just excited."

Oseyan held baby Malcolm up against her shoulder and whispered, "My precious one."

Ma said, "You better keep your hand there. He not big enough to hold up on shoulder. Gerda, take your child, eh!"

"I watching her, Ma. I watching."

And then Oseyan said, "I not little girl any more, Ma. I could manage. I could manage now." And Ma eyes full up with water. And for sure Auntie Gerda was crying.

CHAPTER THIRTY-TWO

1909. Meetings.

Oseyan went to open-air political meetings with her uncle. Sometimes Uncle Eero said he was going to a meeting by the crossroads in La Digue, just up the track to the road junction at the top. Sometimes, he walked down to some kind of meeting in Grand Bras. Sometimes she followed him to La Baye, and stood with other people in the market area not far from the sea. Gwenevieve – Gwen – went with Oseyan to one meeting. It was mostly men at the meeting – same thing Ma said – *I want you to hear what they saying about the country, but little girls don't go running about to meeting. Is the men that going. I want you to hear, but careful, you know.* Oseyan and Gwenevieve didn't hear a lot of the meeting. They walked through the track to just behind the Anglican church. It was nice there because they could sit on a kind of stone bench and watch the sea.

"The Caribbean sea!" Gwenevieve shouted. Oseyan thought it was only because she wanted to shout, because there was nothing in that to shout about. Or perhaps there was. Perhaps there was something about that blue that just made you want to shout. As Oseyan watched the blue, she thought of something she had heard her grandmother say, "Seawater don't have branch."

Gwen said, "You remember Sir told us that the Pacific Ocean touches Grenada too?"

"No. I don't remember that. I don't think any Pacific in Grenada. I don't remember Sir saying that."

"Yes. One time when Mr Ansel went to Dominica and Sir was teaching us those Atlantic Ocean lessons."

"Yes, but I sure you don't remember that part right. I don't remember Sir saying that."

"Well, we could ask him. We might even see him tonight. You know he like these political meetings."

"Sir talk about the Caribbean Sea and the Atlantic Ocean. The Pacific is higher up, near North America and the other parts of America – Central America and so."

"Perhaps." Gwen shrugged. "But we could ask Sir if we see him. He will be glad to tell us. You know how Sir is."

"Okay. If we see him – "

"You know you wish you see him! You always sweet on Sir. That tall, firm body and the shoulders and the smooth black skin. He nice, eh! Don't think I don't see how you does watch him. You like the serious face and the gren-gren low down on the back of the head – by the neck down there, disappearing down the back. I see you! I see you watching him!"

"You too fas! What you saying! That is just nasty! Sir is my teacher!"

"Not any more. If you didn't like him when we little, you like him now! And in fact you like him since you in school! I see you, you know. And you were always his favourite!"

"Who say that? He beat me in class like any teacher beat children. And even if is true – which I don't believe! – so what? That don't say nothing. You mind in the drain! An who *you* like? Mr Ansel?"

"Well, nothing wrong with that. Is man. And is nice man to boot. Look at the little Carib hair, man, soft and nice and the skin have a little milk in it!"

"*Now* you talking stupidness. Mr Ansel nice but nobody hair nicer than any other person own."

"So *you* don't have nice hair? You don't know people like you hair and how you fair skin?"

"Look. That is stupidness. Let us go back to the meeting. I don't want to talk no dotish talk."

"Because you know is true! And don't call me stupid!"

Gwen had to run to catch up with Oseyan because the long skirt of her dress was hampering her, and those legs on Oseyan were now stretching in a run back through the tracks.

Dotishness, Oseyan pronounced as her friend caught up with her. Her face was thunder and they didn't talk anymore. One thing that could get Oseyan mad was talking about her skin colour. That was off-limits for *any*body – since school days. Well, not for Ma, but for anybody else. They listened at the meeting. A man was talking about how he was proud of the fact that he was not only a Grenadian but a West Indian too – and not no British person. A West Indian!

CHAPTER THIRTY-THREE

1910. A man named Marryshow.

Auntie Gerda, who mostly kept her opinions about Oseyan's upbringing to herself, especially as the little girl got older, although she kept a watchful eye on the goings-on and was always asking about what Oseyan was doing, was not so pleased about Oseyan's habit of accompanying her uncle to meetings. Ma was also cautious about a young girl running up and down to meetings at night. Man don't keep their eyes open, Ma felt – even her beloved son. He was a young man in his twenties and living wherever he living and that meant he was a young man with his eyes always open, looking around, according to Ma. She knew that he was watching out for Oseyan, but still, man is man, and woman had to know that and keep a lookout.

Oseyan and her grandmother could not see eye to eye on this subject. But in the end, because Ma wanted to hear from them what high-up people were doing, she would usually say, "Go and hear what they saying. We should know what and what those people in high places doing." Faith, though, said that her big brother had a rebellious streak and she didn't know where he got it from. Oseyan was sure he got it from his mother, but she knew better than to say anything. And anyway, sometimes Faith acted like she was older than Ma. Uncle didn't look rebellious at all. He looked like any other quiet black man in La Digue. He wasn't so tall, not to her anyway. He was about five-foot... just under five-foot-six perhaps. She had started to think in terms of exact measurements since she started sewing and measuring skirts and shirts and things like that and people were asking her where she going, shooting up to the sky. Uncle was even a little bit shorter than she was. People said she was tall for a woman. But Uncle had this not very wide smile whenever he smiled – quiet and serious, and perhaps that's where the rebellious streak was hidden – although to tell the truth it looked more like what Sir might call a surly streak – and in the big eyebrows that her grandmother said looked like his father's did. She thought of Sir and "surly" because that word came up in a lesson once and the way Sir explained it was like the look she saw on Uncle Eero's face sometimes. A kind of – arrogant? – threatening? serious? – she wasn't sure what the word was, but she remembers that Sir's explanation brought up Uncle's face – not when he looked at her or talked to her – but sometimes with other people. And even with her, he was more serious and distant now that she had grown up. Anyway, Uncle Eero liked to go to these meetings that talked about politics and Oseyan really liked to hear what people had to say. They sounded like Sir and Mr Ansel.

A few times, she went with Eero to meetings in Grenville when a man named Marryshow – Teddy Marryshow – was speaking. Mr. Marryshow said they had to fight for their rights in the West Indies. That's what he said – not only in Grenada but in the West Indies, because they were all together. They had the same kind of treatment from the British government ruling them, although they kept saying they were reforming the constitution. When she was in school, Sir had said something like that. What Mr Marryshow was saying was that they had to figure out how to get out from under the British. Her uncle told her he agreed completely. Oseyan could understand that. She knew that Ma would agree. Her friend Marjorie – with a short, compact body that Gwen said made her look well *matwité* – went to that meeting with them. These days, Marjorie was all into birth signs and she said that Marryshow was a firebrand. He was born 7th November 1887, and Marjorie said he was a typical Scorpio. Scorpio people bright, boy, Marjorie said, and they have a very strong sense of having to do things. She would have known Marryshow was a Scorpio even if he hadn't said so. With that round, dark face of hers, mischievous and ready with a smile, Marjorie was like that. When she decided on something, that was it. When Oseyan asked her if that meant all the other bright people in the country were Scorpio, Marjorie just said *steupes*.

Mr Marryshow was youngish, not thirty yet, her uncle said, and he was already a big man in town. He came from down in St George's town, and he was some kind of editor in the paper she used to see her uncle reading – the *St George's Chronicle and Gazette*. That was Mr Donovan's newspaper. Faith said that the man Donovan was a menace. She said it one day when Uncle passed by the house but Uncle didn't seem to have heard, not too obvious, but Oseyan could see him fold his lips a little bit. And don't let him unfold those lips and turn in your direction after he wrapped them up like that, because you wouldn't think it was the same quiet person who sat there acting as if he couldn't talk. When he unfold them, he could talk in a distant, harsh kind of way about foolish people and the need for people to get up off their behind and to think things through like if they have some sense. And of course Faith would know that. She would know that her brother could be like that. Perhaps that was why she didn't say any more.

Oseyan knew that Mr Marryshow was a *thinking being* because when she saw Sir at the same meeting she went to with her uncle, Sir had said, "Good! Good to see you here! Keep it up. That man is a thinking being!" Marjorie looked at her face that time, and afterward, when they were alone, she said, "I well glad I not red like you. You gone even more red because Sir talk to you. Me – I could think what I want and nobody will ever know!" Oseyan chased Marjorie round the pasture and Marjorie said, grinning, "Sir well old you know!" Oseyan didn't answer her, but she thought of how Ma was always warning her to keep away from man, how she used to say, *That red skin that you have is not a blessing, and man eyes does open because of that. Don't let them fool you.* Anyway, Marjorie was wrong. And Gwen was wrong! She didn't think of Sir like that. She liked him because he was her teacher and he was a – *thinking being.* And Oseyan agreed with Sir. Mr Marryshow was a thinking being. She even heard that with all that man Marryshow was doing, he hadn't gone much further in school than she had. Perhaps he had a *good* primary school education, and then he studied more afterwards. Her grandmother said that Sir was one of the few people in the place who had gone away – she didn't know where but in some place far away to do what they called teacher training. So Sir was an educated man and he said a *good* primary school education was a lot more than most people had. It was Sir that made her understand that because Mr Marryshow was from town, he probably had the opportunity to do more subjects. From the way the Legislative Council saw it – especially the governor, Sir said – there wasn't much need to educate people in the country. Sir said that was why they were trying to leave the education of infants mainly to the churches – because if people in rural areas want to start that early, it was up to the church to do what it could. And, Sir said, even now, although they were just done updating the system and establishing an Education Ordinance, they had put that about country people in their discussions and in writing. Aim high, Sir said, and forget about what the Legislative Council want. Even in the Legislative Council, the governor was talking about – and Sir said his exact words were – "the education that the vast number of our peasantry needed to qualify them for their lot in life." They were talking about making sure people remained labourers but he hoped that she, Oseyan, and other country people he taught were aiming higher. Don't take on the Legislative Council in that foolishness, he said. High-up people weren't necessarily right. In fact, Sir said, sometimes they were very wrong. It was she, Little Man, and Gwen he was talking to that time – one day just after they finish in Holy Innocents. The Council was talking about making most rural schools "Lower Division Schools", Sir said, and that meant they felt children should be trained in Reading, Writing, and Arithmetic, and not more. They also talked about having to give the attention to others, few in number, who had more intellect and could get more from education. It was somebody from the meeting right inside there self that told him that, Sir said, and he thought it was his duty to let some of his best students know. "You are from the country," Sir said. "They expect you to be labourers on their estates and they want you to be labourers. See if you could qualify yourself to do something else." Sir said he was telling them that in confidence; they were among his best students. Oseyan didn't know if she could even tell her grandmother about this because she didn't want her to let something slip to Cousin Mildred. She told Uncle Eero, though, and he said, "Don't tell anybody else that is where you get it from, you know. He could get in trouble for that. Keep that to yourself." Oseyan understood. She only told her uncle because she knew how he would feel.

The world was mixed up. She was starting to think it would be hard to be grown up.

CHAPTER THIRTY-FOUR

1912. Something in the mortar besides the pestle.

Uncle Eero came by the house one afternoon. He took off his shoes at the door and said, "What happenin, Mammie? O, how things?" He must be in a good mood. He hadn't called her "O" since she was a little, little girl. She could hardly remember when. He used to smile when he heard his mother call her "my ocean", and sometimes he asked her, "You remember the name I give you?" Of course she remembered it. She couldn't forget it, like she couldn't forget the spirit that was her essence. He lifted his eyebrows and smiled. "Okay, Miss Lady," he said. Uncle Eero acted as if he didn't hear things, and then when he talked to you, you realised that he was hearing everything going on around him. Perhaps Ma had told him a lot about the ocean, too, even before the other children came along.

Now, Uncle Eero said, "Mammie, let's talk." Straight so. Oseyan knew this meant she should go into the bedroom or better yet outside where she couldn't hear them. Uncle Eero knew he didn't have to say more for Oseyan to know what she had to do. Well, there was a lot she had to do outside. She had been putting off checking the fowl run for eggs and she had to sweep it out. She was surprised Ma hadn't yet said, "Madam Oseyan, you don't think fowls like to live in clean surroundings too? You would like to see everything you put in the pit latrine scattered around your bed?" Ma hadn't said it this time, but Oseyan smiled and wrinkled her nose at the very thought. She would clean out the fowl run now. The brown hen started cackling just as she went around the bend of the house. That probably meant it had just laid an egg. But then a shout from down the hill, on the road below, stopped Oseyan in her tracks.

"Mamay!" That was Auntie G for sure. Oseyan turned around and stood looking down the hill. She stooped down a little to see between the branches of the red and purple bougainvillea. Auntie always called from the road.

"Good evening, Auntie G. Mammie inside."

"*Kouman ou yé, oseyan mwen?* How you doing, my ocean? Where is your grandmother?"

"She inside," Oseyan said again. She had to walk back to hug Auntie Gerda. This was her special aunt.

"Auntie G, Malcolm with you? You didn't bring him?"

"No. Amèlie watching him and his little sister for me. I not staying long."

"Why you didn't bring them, Auntie G?"

Auntie Gerda laughed. "When I busy, I can't get everybody ready and run."

Last year, Auntie Gerda had had another baby – a girl this time. Not last year, *non* – the year before. Olive must be two by now, almost three. As usual, Auntie Gerda hugged her so tight that Oseyan had to pull her shoulders together and lean into her aunt to be comfortable. Auntie Gerda passed her hand over Oseyan's hair and then under her chin. She stayed for a moment looking into Oseyan's eyes. She bent and kissed her on the forehead. "My little girl," she said softly. Then she turned her around so that she faced the house. "Go! Tell your grandmother I'm here."

Auntie G could be well stylish when she ready. Today she seemed dressed for church, with a long yellow skirt and a tan shirt – and brown shoes with a little heel. And the hair was pressed and in a kind of little bob around her face. You never knew with Auntie G. She could be going to afternoon service but she could also be dressed up just because she felt like it. Auntie G walked up the steps and paused at the door.

Ma called out, "You reach?" So that meant they had been expecting her! Something was going on. Uncle had left his carpenter shop in high hot sun on a Saturday afternoon and Auntie G was dropping in on her day off from work in the white people's house. She had even had to call on Amèlie to watch the children – which made Oseyan wonder where the man of the house was, her fairly new uncle. Perhaps he was working at some odd job somewhere. People sometimes hired him to build things for them, though she knew he wasn't as good as Uncle Eero. This getting together sounded like something planned. Oseyan left them to their greetings and went back around the house to the fowl run. Then she heard another voice call out.

"Cuz!"

The fowl jumped cackling from its nest, and Oseyan stepped back. She glanced over her shoulder, then turned her attention back to picking up the egg the fowl had just left for her. She must clean up all this fowl mess. Cousin Mildred too? Oseyan looked around the fowl run and started to sweep with the bush broom as she heard Cousin Mildred walk up the steps, protesting loudly about knees not being what they used to be. Oseyan heard her voice at the door as she headed inside.

"Where your big girl? She there? Not no little girl again, non. I see her in La Baye the other day, I couldn't believe. If she didn't call out to me, I wouldn't even know that was the same child."

Ma said, "Big lady, my dear. Fifteen years she had last birthday, you know, so she heading for sixteen now."

Sounds of surprise from Cousin Mildred. "Woy! What you saying?"

"These children don't take time," was Auntie Gerda's comment. "Time pass before you know it."

Then voices were lowered. Oseyan heard one voice – Cousin Mildred? – say *Fifteen years pass already?* And then rumbling and low grumbling that sounded serious, intense.

Oseyan put the broom for the fowl run in the corner, picked up the pan with the rubbish and went with it to the garbage bag she had put over by the bougainvillea. Then she set about sweeping the yard. She would go out to the corn and pick two or three and roast for them. She didn't have to ask Ma because she had planted and nurtured these corn trees herself. Once Oseyan left school, Ma made her organise her own kitchen garden. *You have to learn to do these things.* And nobody would say no to roast corn. When she was finished sweeping, she would pull out the coal pot and set it up in the yard at the back.

What was going on? For sure there was something in the mortar besides the pestle. After she had made sure all the mess was out of the fowl run and the place looked and smelt better, from where she sat under the house, she could hear voices still rumbling, but she couldn't hear a thing even when she concentrated. Were they still in the hall? Had something happened? She put the coalpot outside in the yard near to the big stone where she could sit and stay there in the warm sunshine roasting the corn. She wondered if they were smelling it. Of course they would smell it! Corn not shy to present itself. Well, they would be pleased, anyway.

Oseyan took the steps two at a time. Her sandals made no sound on the wooden steps. The door to the small room was closed. They had actually gone inside there to talk. What was the big secret? Or was it just the usual big people habit of trying to keep everything a secret? They were still acting as if she was a little girl. She stood looking at the green-and-white door that Uncle had painted just a few weeks ago. Ma said that the new paint on the house made them look grand up there on the hill. Just as she was thinking of moving closer to the room door and leaning against it, the door opened and Cousin Mildred came out. Cousin Mildred went to the bucket of water in the corner, picked up the dipper, which was really a large pancup, poured herself a glass of water, and stood there drinking.

Oseyan thought, *Is not no water she want. She just come out because she hear me come inside and she want to see what I doing and if I near the door.* Cousin Mildred cleared her throat and went back in, closed the door softly, carefully, behind her, making sure there was a click, and the low rumbling of voices continued. Oseyan walked back across the hall and sat in the doorway, with her feet on the top step. Then suddenly she heard her grandmother's voice rise above the others. "Ah-h-h-h!" as if Ma was yawning and stretch-ing. She imagined Ma putting her hands down on the chair and pushing herself up. Ma said out loud, "All right, then. Correct is right. The Lord knows best." Ma came out into the hall. She sank down into one of the four armchairs. The room door opened and Uncle, Auntie, and Cousin Mildred came out of the small room. They, too, moved to the armchairs.

Oseyan said, "I roast some corn, Ma. Enough for everybody."

Cousin Mildred clapped her hands. "Child, you know how to take care of people."

Oseyan smiled, stood up, and walked down the steps. She returned and handed an ear of roasted corn to each of them.

Auntie G said, "Just what the doctor ordered. Thank you, my dear. You good, *doudou*."

Without preamble, Ma said, "Ocean, your uncle going away!"

Away! So Uncle was going to England? That was where people went, mostly. Two of her cousins had gone to England. And she had heard some whispered talk about Amèlie trying to go there. Uncle was going to England! Was he going to join the army? There had been another hush-hush signing up for the army in the family. People said England was looking to the colonies to help build the army. Would Uncle go into the army?

"He is going to Canada," her grandmother said. He made up his mind that Canada would be a good place for him to go. We have some family there already. And Canada is British, too."

"And ent it was French once, too?" from Auntie G.

"Yes," her uncle said. The part that I'm going to, Montreal, that was French. In fact, Montreal is a big city in the Canadian province of Quebec. They were both taken by Britain from France by the Treaty of Paris in 1763."

Oseyan said, "You know, I'm sure I remember Mr Ansel saying something like that."

Her uncle said, "Something like that – or that?"

Oseyan shrugged, smiling. "Okay, Uncle. That's what he said. I just forgot. I will look it up again. I have the book there."

Canada! Her uncle was going to Canada. Not to England where she knew they also had family. Canada! He was going to Hudson Bay. She should go back and read that lesson in the Royal Reader. When would he leave? What was he going to do in that place called Canada? Suddenly, Oseyan was awed by her uncle. She wondered if she would ever go – Away. Her grandmother said they really had to think about her future. You couldn't just leave school and sit down for ever. As a woman, you had to do domestic, or sewing, or something like that, or go away. Perhaps she would be the best seamstress that La Baye could ever have. Should she have gone to Standard VI and then tried to become a pupil teacher? Perhaps go away somewhere and train to become a teacher? Sir said town people had more opportunity to move up when they went to school.

"When you leaving, Uncle?"

Uncle Eero said he would probably leave sometime soon – in a month or two – so, March? April?

Before Uncle left the house, he told Oseyan that there was going to be a meeting in Grenville to talk about the British and the way they governed. He would pass and meet her so they could walk down there if she wanted to go. Of course, she wanted to go. She would enjoy the breeze right there by the sea – even though Uncle said that where they lived, up on the hill just over the sea, they were in the best place for the breeze. More to the point, though, she would be hearing all kinds of juicy political stories about planning to fight what Uncle called British occupation.

Uncle said, "You know, in that place in Canada where I'm going, they have people like the Caribs. People were in that area long before the Europeans." Oseyan nodded. She thought about the savage in Hudson Bay arranging his traps. His traps or his snow-shoes? One of them. Uncle said, "One set is the Sikanni. And it have a lot of other groups."

Standing in the doorway behind them, Cousin Mildred said scornfully, "Sikanni, Fulani! You always on about something."

Ma said, "You know better than that, Mildred. Fulani is some of our own people, so I don't know who and who you sounding scornful about, but watch your mouth!"

Mildred said, "You don't have to take everything so serious!"

Uncle said, "Yes we have to take it serious, Cousin Mildred."

"All right, all right. Leave me alone. Let me put foot to road and head for La Poterie. I have to go up there. All you take it easy. All is well with the world and King George is on the throne!"

Of its own volition, Oseyan's head turned so she could see Uncle's face. Uncle said, almost pleasantly, "Goodbye, Cousin Mildred."

Ma said, "You gone right past Governor Sadler and those white people on the Legislative Council and you reach King George! You not easy, Mildred."

Auntie said, "My dear brother would say there's nothing to joke about."

Her dear brother said nothing.

And time did not stop to wait for them to get used to the idea of Uncle Eero leaving. He didn't just disappear without saying anything to Oseyan, like the Panama time, but there were some people he can't have said anything to, and he must have been getting his business organised for a while now.

He said to Oseyan, "I know that I'm going to white man's country. That is what here is too, you know. We starting to forget because we more than them in numbers, and they will be gone one day. You could feel it already although it don't finish happen yet. Canada and the United States, now, it have a lot of them there. The Canada that I going to – I know that they want to keep it mainly white and with them in charge, although they took it from those they call the Indians. They bring all us here to these Americas and we spreading out. We have no place to go back to."

Oseyan said, "I know a little bit about it. I read a little bit about it in the Royal Reader."

"Yes. I read the Royal Reader before you and some of what I hear you saying I didn't even realise was in the Royal Reader. But you had some good teachers. Nothing to say. You had some very good teachers."

In April 1913, Uncle Eero left Grenada for The Dominion of Canada. It was just as if he was there one day and then suddenly he was gone.

King George was still on the throne, king to them there in Grenada and the Windward Islands and the West Indies and even king to the Dominion of Canada. Uncle Eero was going to another part of the Kingdom.

CHAPTER THIRTY-FIVE

1915. This Mr Marryshow.

Mr Marryshow started his own newspaper about two years after Uncle Eero left. It was called *The West Indian*. Mr Marryshow said that *The West Indies must be West Indian*. That was written on the paper. He was sure that the West Indies and West Indians would soon manage their own affairs – government and everything – and not always let England act as if it had a right to be in charge. He put it all in his newspaper, and Oseyan thought it was good to see the title, year and everything at the top. The first issue was published on January 1, 1915. Marryshow wrote that he wanted the paper to be *an immediate and accurate chronicler of current events, an untrammelled advocate of popular rights, unhampered by chains of party prejudice, an unswerving educator of the people in their duties as subjects of the state and citizens of the world*.[10] Oseyan read it all out for Ma and Ma said, "Word in place," as if just the sound of the words from Mr Marryshow, who belonged to them there in Grenada, made her feel that things were going in the right direction. She asked Oseyan to read again for her – the *un* that talked about "education". And when Oseyan read "unswerving educator of the people in their duties as subjects of the state and citizens of the world", Ma smiled, leaned forward and touched her granddaughter. She liked the "citizens of the world" part especially. "Word in place," she said again.

1915 started off really good – or so Oseyan and Gwen thought. In February, though, Uncle sent by the mail boat a letter in which he said that in the US they had voted against giving women the right to vote. Gwen said, "Well ay ay! If man could vote, why women can't vote?" But of course they couldn't vote – either man or woman in

Grenada, but it was good to hear them talking about it over there. When Oseyan told Ma what Uncle Eero said happened in the United States, she said, "Well, that is their business because this vote talk is high-up people thing, but *Fanm pa sa voté mé nonm sa voté*? So woman mustn't vote but man could vote? Dotishness! *Mi bagay sòt!*" Later with Gwen, Oseyan said, "Is really white women they concerned about giving the vote over there. They still trying to stop black hen chicken voting – man or woman." Gwen said, "What a thing! Mr Marryshow make me think things looking up, but is like January making yangoo, after all."

And then something really exciting happened. At least, Oseyan thought it was exciting because all those that Auntie called *sé menm sé moun-la ki mwen té kwè-a* – the usual suspects – Sir, Mr Ansel, Ma – couldn't stop talking about it. It wasn't anything much, just a beginning really, but Ma said that the man Marryshow really show people that *is not dotish people* that living in the West Indies. What happened was this: Mr Marryshow talked about a South African politician, General Smuts, who was giving a speech at the Savoy hotel in England. Mr Marryshow said it was worth waiting to hear what General Smuts would have to say. So people said *Uhm-hummm. Let's wait.* And they waited. And that was it, really. The exciting thing that happened was that when Mr Marryshow talk about this big man from South Africa it was news. Some people were asking "South Africa? When he talk about South Africa from here in Grenada, people will know what he say?" But Ma said, "Yes, is news, because when people talking about a thing, it mean they putting our attention on it. That is why I used to be so fraid when I hear me son say *we* when he planning things, as if he in secret society. Well, look me self how I become part of this *we* secret society. So through Mr Marryshow, people started to talk about this big General in South Africa who, Mr Marryshow told them, was talking as if he had a right to be in South Africa and to take African people's land from them." Ma said, "We have to keep listening to this Marryshow man. He telling us what is what. This man will do something big. I know this is the beginning and not the end of the story. Watch him! That is a man who will make a difference."

CHAPTER THIRTY-SIX

1915-1916. Garvey and Marryshow: A lot to think about.

At the same time as Mr Marryshow was emerging as a political figure people listened to, things were changing for Oseyan. In her family, Grandma, Auntie, relatives in England, those in Canada, cousins, aunts, uncles, everybody – people Oseyan didn't even know but who came to the house or who sent letters by the mailboat to say things that Ma told her about – seemed to agree that once you were finished with school, it was time to look around not only for sewing as a profession but to see what else you might do. Oseyan remembered how, even before she started to go and learn to sew, she heard Ma talking with Miss Grant who had taught her, and Miss Grant had asked, "I suppose you trying to get her to go away, though?" That time Ma had looked over by the door and seen Oseyan standing there. She looked back at the sewing teacher lady and she said, "Little pitchers." The pitcher wasn't so little now, and though it hadn't heard much, it could guess. If necessary to improve yourself, Ma and other big people always said, you should go somewhere, so we will see. We will see. Oseyan waited to see.

Uncle Eero sent to tell them about a man he said all the black people in Canada were talking about now. Uncle was always talking now about Black this and Black that. Black people in Canada, he said, were excited about a Jamaican man named Marcus Garvey who was beginning to preach in America. And, Uncle said, he knew him. He had known him in Panama, and they used to talk, even in that short time, about how it would be important to start some kind of organisation. This Marcus Garvey talked about people – the colonies and people who were colo- nised – in the way that Marryshow was talking in Grenada and the rest of the Caribbean. Except that Garvey was making sure to say white people and black people. The colour issue was important to Garvey, Uncle said, as it should be. And he, too, in Canada now, was getting together with some people to organise.

In Grenada, though, Oseyan was more excited about Marryshow. He definitely reminded her of Sir in the way he talked about things. He was able to say what he thought about the colonial people and how to fight for better conditions. Marryshow in Grenada and now Garvey in Canada and the whole of North America. Her uncle said that Garvey had talked about the West Indies in a speech in a place called Chicago in America. Her uncle said that some of the things Garvey talked about were hurtful for the West Indies, but they were true. He reminded her that Garvey was West Indian himself, and he was a working man who knew what it was to struggle to improve himself, so she shouldn't feel badly about the way he talked.

Uncle said that Garvey would visit Canada, and he would want to organise with him and even perhaps join his organisation. Garvey talks sense, her uncle said, and he is not afraid of the white people, in a way just like Marryshow. Oseyan told Marjorie about Garvey, and that he was born in the same year as Marryshow, only in August, not in November. Marjorie said, "August 17, you say? Well that one is a real lion! Leo the Lion is his sign. Don't play with him. And it sound like he could well roar. That is how Leos stay!"

"So Scorpio and now Leo? It sound like a lot of people could fight!"

"Okay. You don't have to be so smart." Marjorie smiled. She was always right, so Oseyan just told her what Uncle Eero said.

In the Chicago speech, Garvey told people that Negroes have a common cause, but that the Negroes of the West Indies and the Negroes of the American south had ideas that weren't always the same and did things in different ways because they had different experiences. Oseyan told Ma and Auntie Gerda about all this. Auntie Gerda yawned. She didn't like to talk too much about these things.

"Yes. He write me, too. He tell me. These political people – *You* political people – a little bit too much sometimes, though. Always going on and on about something or the other."

Ma said, "Yes. But that man Garvey smart. What he say is true.

Over there, they less in numbers so those high-ups doing them what they want. Here, even if they walking on you and pulling you here and there as they want, and making you work for next to nothing, you more than them, and they know that, so there are things they wouldn't do."

Auntie G said, "Yes, that makes sense." Then she added, "But the money is theirs, so you have to see with them."

Oseyan said, "But is where they get it, Auntie G? Where they get the money? How they come by it?"

Auntie G looked offended. "You, too? You-all must remember is not only white people. It have high-up people who not white. And you see, Ma, I tell you your son not that good a influence on this little girl, you know."

Ma said, "Leave the child alone! Nothing wrong with her. We have to think and talk."

Gerda looked for a long time at Ma, and then from Ma to Oseyan, but she said nothing more.

In the West Indies, Garvey said, people didn't have race consciousness like they did in the United States of America. And Garvey mentioned people like Frederick Douglass and Booker T. Washington. Oseyan didn't know too much about them. She would have to ask somebody – Sir, perhaps. She wondered if she should go to the library in Grenville and find out more about this Frederick Douglass and other people Uncle talked about. But they mightn't even have that there. Where would she find out? It wasn't as if this was Chatham or somebody like that.

In the West Indies, Garvey said, they didn't have to respond directly to white people all the time like they had to do in the American South. Her uncle seemed to agree but Oseyan wasn't so sure. Grenada white people and white people in the West Indies were not easy, either. It was a good thing there were people like Marryshow who was not afraid to talk back when the high-ups – and is true that here is not only white and black; you had brown-skin too – acted as if they were better. And Marryshow said in the last meeting that they had to work towards having more people to represent them in government. So even if Garvey didn't think so, and her uncle seemed to agree with him, they had people fighting in the West Indies, too.

Her uncle said that Garvey called the American Negro "the most progressive". Oseyan wasn't sure she liked that. Garvey said that it had nothing to do with people being different, but with people having different experiences. You had to understand, according to Uncle and Garvey, that when people got hit in the face with race in the way that they get hit in the American South, they *had* to be particularly race conscious. And so the way they responded in the US, her uncle said, and especially in the South where things were worse and you had the plantations and so, was because of how things were. People act according to what they face. Oseyan supposed he was right. They were getting it not from the lords and people like that in the *Royal Readers* but from face-to-face, and not from what people said long ago but from now – right now. In Grenada they were getting it from the Legislative Council and the high-up people, too, according to what Sir told them, but you could not know or not hear and only see what right around you. But she just didn't like the idea that somehow they weren't as progressive in the West Indies. She knew that was not true. But if to prove it you had to have the kind of treatment that Uncle Eero said they had in the South, and even not have much of an opportunity to go to school and so, well, okay, she wouldn't want that. You would have to stand up and fight that however you could.

But anyway, she find Marryshow well strong. And her uncle was supporting Marryshow too, even though he left before Marryshow really started to have a lot of meetings and before he and Renwick started their newspaper, *The West Indian*. For her uncle to spend time writing such long, long letter, something must be happen to make him so het up. He said that because slavery had come to an end for them in the West Indies before it ended in America, and because a lot of the white planters from the West Indies went back home to England, although race is important and people are still prejudiced, a lot of Black people and… well, *Black people who look white and who want to be white* – he write it just like that; not *her*, though! Not me, Oseyan thought! That is one thing I don't want. A lot of them were getting into high positions, so it was a different thing in the West Indies, as her uncle said. He wrote that only a few Black people could get into *any* position in America.

Over there, he said, they really treated all Black people like dirt. Oh Lord! He must be really struggling, even in Canada. And then, yes, he said it. They didn't treat them too good there in Canada either, but it was different. So yes, she could see the point. And when she really thought about it like that, it made America sound like a place you wouldn't want to go, as bad as the Legislative Council and high-up people and white estate owners and others might be here. Even so, she still didn't like that her uncle had said he agreed with Garvey that Black Americans were more progressive because of what they faced and how they had to fight more openly.

And when she read the leaflet about Garvey that her uncle sent, with things Garvey said and so, she saw that he said even more than that to criticise them there in the West Indies. Garvey said that *seventy-eight years of Emancipation* – now, in 1916, he mean – did not make the West Indian Negro more advanced than the American Negro even though the American Negro had a kind of Emancipation only since 1862, so *fifty-four years*. They had a lead in the West Indies, Garvey said, but he couldn't see that they had done much with it. Imagine that! Garvey gave the talk in Chicago earlier that year, 1916, and the letter from Uncle with a lot of things said directly by Garvey came down on the mailboat. He sent a letter to Mr Ansel too, and Sir, and one to Auntie Gerda. When Auntie Gerda heard how upset Oseyan was about what Garvey had to say, she said quietly, "I don't know if your uncle tell you about anything else, and about how he coming to realise, even in Canada and not in the American South, how they could make black people feel small – smaller than they even feeling here, just because it have more white people." Oseyan looked at her Aunt Gerda in surprise. This was not Auntie Gerda talking! She sounded sympathetic to the way Uncle was feeling. Auntie continued, "He not having it easy. It not so easy to get carpenter job even if you say you are a carpenter. It's easier for him to get jobs shining people shoes and things like that while he wait to get the job he want."

"Uncle Eero? Shining people shoes?"

"Keep that to yourself. People don't support you when they know you struggling – even people who struggling too. For some reason even you own people don't like to know you going out of your way to try and improve yourself. So I don't give you message for nobody. But it's not an easy thing to be what they call *a migrant.* My brother tell me that. So that could be why he understanding better how this race thing working in places with more white people. Who feels it, knows it. You have to feel these things to know them." And Auntie Gerda stood up and started to fold the cloth diapers she had just picked up from the line outside. You could see she put *blue* in them, Oseyan thought. They well white and pretty. And so, with Auntie Gerda, that part of the conversation, about Garvey and about Uncle Eero, was over.

Oseyan went to the school and showed Sir what her Uncle had written because she knew how pleased he would be to get that information. Garvey had used the word "stagnation", her uncle had written, stagnation in the West Indies, in spite of the fact that people get some education. Oseyan still really didn't like that, but it made her think, especially after Auntie Gerda told her how Uncle Eero was doing in other ways. As Sir used to say, she must think about it and see if there was any merit to the argument. Perhaps, in a way, Garvey was saying what her grandmother had said, that if you don't have your head on, with the kind of education they were getting in the West Indies, and the fact that most of the white people were gone and were there mainly as *part* of other people, just the way things were could make them... well, could make some people think they were British and that Africans and Caribs and others were savages in truth. Huh! Not she, though. Not me, this Oseyan! Uncle Eero's letter made her think about all of that. Perhaps Mr Garvey had a point, although she must confess that she still really didn't like *how* he was saying what he had to say.

She didn't focus on it before Sir pointed it out when she went to see him, but in that Chicago speech Garvey had said that some West Indians in America acted as if things were so much better in the West Indies where race was concerned. And Garvey said, *Don't believe them! There is a lot to change.* That was what Sir pointed out from the Garvey speech that Uncle Eero sent. Perhaps she hadn't really wanted to see that part because, even without it, Garvey was criticising so much already. Oseyan thought, *Imagine that! Imagine him saying that!* Her uncle, though, wasn't vexed at all, and as for Sir, he agreed with everything; he said that Garvey had courage. He agreed with Garvey that West Indians could be further ahead if they had the sense to agitate for better conditions. Oseyan still felt that Garvey was talking as if he didn't know Marryshow and people like Marryshow! It worried her a bit that both Sir and Uncle Eero agreed with Garvey. Well, Uncle Eero was over there in North America now and perhaps he was starting to see things differently. And that worried her too, but it didn't seem to worry Sir. And perhaps she was thinking like this because her auntie was saying now that they should send her to Canada soon. But the thing that really hurt in the pamphlet that Uncle Eero sent and that he said was in Garvey's speech was this:

> The educated men are immigrating to the United States, Canada, and Europe; the labouring element are to be found by the thousands in Central and South America. These people are leaving their homes simply because they haven't pride and courage enough to stay at home and combat the forces that make them exiles. If we had the spirit of self-consciousness and reliance, such as you have in America, we would have been ahead of you, and today the standard of Negro development in the West Indies would have been higher. We haven't the pluck in the West Indies to agitate for or demand a square deal and the blame can be attributed to no other source than indolence and lack of pride among ourselves.[11]

Imagine that! Oseyan read it to herself more than once. That almost made you not want to go anywhere. Although what about him? He over there! And Uncle Eero say he went to Central America, too. So what about him? So he must know is not as he say – is not lack of pride have people going. And deep down, although Oseyan was afraid with all this talking, she still wanted to go. Anyway, perhaps she was not as educated as some of those who were going who Garvey criticised. And perhaps Garvey didn't look at the fact that the white people in the West Indies had made them work for nothing and now the white people themselves were going back to where their ancestors came from and not giving anything for the countries to help themselves. The white people in America stay there with their money. At least they didn't make people work for them and then go back to England with everything.

When she talked to Sir about this, he said, "Well, Garvey has a point. In America they have all of the whites there in high places, so they could always reach out and have alliances. They could build because they are white and the things they do are not wrong but new. And they could make alliances with England, remember."

Oseyan thought, "Yes. All of Lord Chatham's friends." And she was quiet, thinking. But she wasn't Sir's student any more, so she said nothing about Chatham. Sir was more Uncle Eero's friend than her teacher, so she had better not try to start any big discussion about what she had learnt in his class. She was still in his class, in a way, because sometimes he suggested things for her to read, but she didn't know how to talk to him now, even though he would still tell her about books and things. One time he told her that it wasn't his usual kind of suggestion, but he thought she would like *Jane Eyre*. "And now that you have been thinking about race," he said, "watch the white Creole woman in there." Yes, Sir said, we have to think about whiteness in the Caribbean and in North America.

Sir was quiet for a while, moving around the ruler on his desk, and then he said, "I guess part of the problem is that their crumbs over there are bigger than those who are looking for high places in the West Indies could get here." Oseyan suddenly startled herself with the thought that perhaps Sir was planning to go away, too. Oh no! That would be awful! If Sir and others who could help teach people left, that wouldn't be good. A voice somewhere inside of her said, *But you going!* And she almost said aloud, *But I going to learn, I not going with no set of knowledge to teach.* But even this thought troubled her.

As she walked home that evening, Oseyan thought about what Marcus Garvey and Sir said. Anyway, Auntie said they had to seize opportunities, and if they were serious about her going to Canada to meet Uncle, that was an opportunity. Here they didn't think country people should get an education that didn't have to do with keeping them as labourers. So it sound like wherever you go, these people who come from Europe organize society how they want it, and they could travel wherever they want to go. She wanted to go, even though somebody inside of her was asking, *So you hear that it better over there?*

CHAPTER THIRTY-SEVEN

1916. Changes.

Lately, Ma hasn't been feeling very well. Oseyan is often at Auntie Gerda's place, helping out with the children. And she takes in sewing to help make ends meet. The people she sews for – making things like skirts, dresses – spread the word that *Miss Langdon gran, the chabin one, is a good little seamstress, yes.* Almost every time she goes by the house on the hill now, Ma answers her query with, "Well, I dey. I not feeling the best, but one day at a time. And what happenin with you, *doudou*? You hear from you uncle?"

"Don't worry about me, Ma. I alright. Where hurtin you? How you feeling?"

"Is really a weakness, you know. Like I tired all the time. And even when I climb up these steps outside there, is like I do a whole day's work. Is a tiredness."

Nearly every day now, Ma wears around her head a white band soaked with limacol. Sometimes she soaks the band in bay rum. She puts the bay rum on her knees too. The whole body, Ma says sometimes, is not hers any more.

One day, after stopping to leave the two bigger children, Malcolm, seven, and Olive, five, at the primary school and the other infant school in La Baye, Gerda walks up to La Digue to meet her mother and walk with her down to La Baye. Oseyan is in the house there in Grenville with the younger children – Wilfred, two and Thaddy, the baby, just one.

Maryam moves slowly, walking one today, one tomorrow, stopping often to breathe deeply on the hill. Gerda says, "Is awright, Mammie. Take your time. Take your time. No rush."

The people they meet on the road say:

Good morning, Miss Langdon. Miss Gerda, good morning. Then they turn back to look as they walk. *It don't look like Miss Langdon doing too good. I wonder what wrong with her?*

Must be the heart.

Yes. She holding she chest.

Take care she fall down, non.

Gerda takes her mother to see a doctor in the Grenville dispensary. He is there once a week on a Wednesday. Maryam looks at his face after she tells him about the shallow breathing, the pain all over her body, the tightness in her chest. The doctor tells her to breathe deeply, listens to her chest, in the area they think of as the heart area, with a stethoscope. They don't know what he hears but they watch his face as he nods and puts a finger on the pulse at her neck. He gives her a prescription. Will he work some magic? Ma Maryam doesn't ask questions. The doctor knows what he is doing. The dispenser takes the prescription and he gives her what looks like a clear-coloured medicine in a dark bottle. When they get back home, Rex, Faith and Amèlie are there. Faith puts some water on the coalpot because she doesn't want to touch Ma's stove and light it up; and she adds soursop leaves to the water. That would cool down her mother, she says, ease the rapid beating of the heart. Mammie looks ill and tired. She needs cooling. Rex says that her chest sounds rattly so perhaps she has a cold deep down. "You know how Mammie does want to drink corailie bush to take out cold, cold that is there deep down," he advises. "Let's give her some corailie later."

People pass by the house on the hill to see Ma – Mr Ansel, Sir, Miss Pierre, Teacher Lenorice, Auntie Mildred, Kalinya, everybody who knows her. Ma sits up in her bed. She looks alert but tired when Mr Ansel, Teacher Lenorice, Miss Pierre and Sir talk to her about education and how things are going not only at Holy Innocents School but in Grenada, in places where Teacher Lenorice, who it seems knew Ma a long time ago, has taught. Ma smiles when Kalinya touches her forehead with the back of her right hand. Ma asks how things are going in the country. When they say, *Okay, things alright*, Ma insists, "So some magic work? I sick but I not dotish." In what seems almost a whisper, she asks to know what the high-ups are doing. Mr Ansel says it seems sensible to hope that things will be changing soon. He says that Marryshow is still talking about the need to expand representation and some are saying that one day there will be people like him – with his ideas – on the Legislative Council. And perhaps the people in Government are listening, Sir says, because just this year in April, just last month, the Legislative Council had passed what they called "An Ordinance to provide for the establishment of the Scholarship." He tells Ma, "You see? Talk works. We have to struggle."

Faith explains, "He mean scholarship for poor people children to go to high school, Ma. They saying perhaps one scholarship to start, and then more and more over the years. So eventually poor people children will reach high school."

Maryam whispers, "It too late for you children, and is not plenty children they choosing as you say… and it go be a boy, so the girls have to wait till later, but now poor people children – and one-one girl too, between them – between the boys – will start to have a better chance. God be praised."

Sir says, "It's a beginning. It's not much, but it's a beginning."

"The way how they think," Ma pauses to breathe, "is much. Keep opening your mouth and talk." She breathes deep. She whispers, "Keep doing it. They in the middle of war now," she says, "but we self, we have to keep living." She adds, "Even if they talking about war in a place they call the world, and we not in the world, we have to try."

Sir touches her arm. He leans over her. "Mrs Langdon," he says, "I want you to know that you have been doing a wonderful job for the education of your children. And Helen is an excellent young lady. You should be proud of her." Ma smiles. Oseyan doesn't think she has ever heard Sir give a long speech like that that isn't about somebody in the Royal Readers. And he called her by the name on her baptism paper! She'd almost wondered who he was talking about. He formal today, yes. Oseyan feels all tied-up inside of her. Sir tells Ma he would leave now, give her a chance to rest.

They stand in the yard near the red and white roses. Sir is wearing a shirt the blue of the sea in La Baye and Oseyan thinks that his long legs look shapely in the khaki pants. She tries not to think of Gwen's mocking. Sir is a fine man in truth, a nice-looking man, and a bright man – her teacher.

196

Sir says to everyone, "Miss Langdon is a fighter. And she fights very hard for education, too, just from the way she has been sending you young ones to school. Miss Langdon – and people like her – are important in the country. You wouldn't imagine some of the things these people in the education department here say and do. They really don't think we are people, and when I say 'we', I mean not only black people, but people from the country generally. We just have to listen and learn." He pauses. Without details, and conscious that they don't have his education or his knowledge of things, the Langdon sisters and brothers nod. Sir says, as if he has to at least explain some things so they know what he means, "In those big offices in town, they have something called 'departmental leave' for the officers, and that is usually their people from England, but I was hearing that for what they call 'subordinate officers' in Education departments and other departments, they would give a certain amount of leave for those who are, and I quote 'black or at least coloured'. And they write that, you know, just like that 'black or at least coloured'. Imagine! So to get into these offices you are better off being *at least coloured* and not black. And they write it like that. They are not afraid to say it. I imagine they think we will never be able to read as a people." He sounds almost surprised, as if he had known it but is still a bit bemused to hear it directly from someone inside there, and to see it written. Oseyan thinks that he glances in her direction as he says this. Is he telling her that race is there although they don't shout about it like in Canada or America?

Faith says, "You might make it in a office, Oseyan. You have the colour."

Oseyan's face reddens. Sir says, "Oseyan has her head on, thanks to her grandmother, so she knows colour is not every-thing, and is only a thing here because of the way they make us think. Oseyan has her head on. And, you know, in this country it's colour and connections. A person from the country with colour and no connections still can't move through the ranks as fast as the town coloured. But I agree with you. They have a better chance, just because they have the colour. And you know that is not a comment about you, Oseyan. You know who you are."

Oseyan! Now he was calling her Oseyan! It suddenly occurs to her that they didn't call names much in school. In a small class, when the teacher is talking to you, you know. She frowns, trying to remember it all. It feels so far away already. He is talking to her almost like he might talk to a friend. It makes her feel odd.

Mr Ansel says, "This place is a mess."

Auntie Gerda says, "That is why you have to use what you have to show you have name and connection."

Silence greets this observation.

From the doorway where she is sitting, Oseyan thinks she can hear Ma whispering, "Those reprobates!" It's probably her imagination, but she gets up, pushes the door wider, and goes through to Ma's room. She stands watching her. Ma's eyes are closed. She seems to be asleep.

CHAPTER THIRTY-EIGHT

1916. Afterward.

They are sitting, leaning, standing near the front steps of the house. Gerda is inside with her mother, sitting on a chair near her bedside. Looking at the trees all around the house – a guava, two golden apple, a few soursop, a couple galba, the red and the purple bougainvillea somehow both droopy today – Rex, who lives with his family somewhere in St Patrick's parish, says, "We must cut down some of these trees so we get a better view of the sea." No one else says anything. Amèlie, on the bottom step, is leaning forward, arms on her knees, staring at the ground. She says, "We must go in La Baye by the telephone exchange and call Eero." She lifts her head, looks around. "And somebody should try to reach Beatrice in Trinidad." Faith's head turns sharply toward her and swivels back. Faith is sitting with her back against one of the pillars of the house, looking out toward the banana trees that she had helped Ma plant on that side of the house. Oseyan sits right in the doorway where she can hear if Auntie Gerda or Ma makes a sound or if they want something. Faith gets up and stands looking down the hill. She turns, stares toward Oseyan for a moment. Then abruptly, she swerves, moves toward the track downhill and says, "Coming back in a minute." Oseyan begins to get up. She is afraid. She doesn't want anyone to leave. Sensing the movement, Faith glances over her shoulder and says, "Just down the hill. I'm not going anywhere." She walks quickly down the track and stands there in the road at the bottom, where Ma used to stand sometimes, watching the sea. Oseyan can see the left side of her face as she seems to let her eyes feast on the sea. She can imagine that Faith is just looking at the blue coming in, soaking the sands of La Baye, and moving leisurely back out. The waters would be calm today. Rex walks to stand at the top of the hill, looking down at his sister. And now Faith walks slowly back up the hill. The long grey skirt on her slim body makes her look even more like her mother, Cousin Mildred would say.

Rex walks up the steps toward the door. In the doorway, he stands looking down at Oseyan, now sobbing quietly with her head down on her arms. Rex looks down at her, saying nothing. He never seems to know how to act with this – this sister-niece of his. Now he bends and puts a soothing hand on her hair, passes it over the long, soft plaits. Oseyan quietens. It's the first time ever she can remember Uncle Rex touching her hair. He makes a throat-clearing sound, says, "Hush now." She leans forward so that he could pass on the side and go into the house. After a few minutes, he comes to the door and stands just behind her. He clears his throat again. He says quietly, "Come and see Ma, Oseyan, and don't cry, now. We have to let her go in peace." Oseyan waits a while. Lifts her head slowly. Looking out at the others, Rex says, "She facing the partition – as if she turn her back on the world, now." He goes back inside. Oseyan follows him through the doorway. Rex and Gerda leave her alone with Ma.

Oseyan kneels at the bedside and leans her head on the bed near to Ma. She must not cry. She says, "Pray with you, Ma? We call the deacon. He coming to pray with you again."

Ma makes a sound in her throat that may have been yes. Oseyan leans her folded arms on her grandmother and puts her head down on them. She says, "The pastor coming too." She prays.

"Lord, treat my grandmother like she treat me, like there is no one else in the world and like even if there are other people, you love her plenty, plenty. Lord, treat my grandmother like she treat me."

Then she says, "When, when – if – my grandmother come to you to rest before she come back, let her meet Poopa Oba, and my mother because she over there already, I think, and all the people that over there already, and all our people from the ocean." She is silent a moment then she whispers again, "Lord, treat my grandmother like she treat me."

When the others come inside, Oseyan lifts her head. Gerda

puts a hand on her shoulder, then drops to her knees near the bed with her niece-daughter. Gerda begins to pray the Our Father and everyone joins in... *Our father, who art in heaven...*

Amèlie stays at her mother's bedside as the rest of them walk back into the hall and then outside again, as if the air is a tonic they need, as if standing with the trees around them is something they need.

Without preamble, Gerda says, "Oseyan will stay with me afterward. I know you big, O, but for a while anyway."

Quietly, Oseyan sobs. Rex speaks through his teeth in a low, tight voice. "Why would you say a stupid thing like that?" he asks his big sister. "What sense that make?"

No one else says anything.

CHAPTER THIRTY-NINE

1916. The Golden Apple. *Ponmsitè-a.*

Next morning, lying on a cot in Ma's room, Oseyan hears a golden apple fall. Not that she wants golden apple so much, but for some reason she gets up and walks outside. Everybody is here, staying in the house, sleeping in the two other rooms and in the hall. She walks on tiptoe so as not to wake up anyone.

When Oseyan comes back inside, Ma is standing at her room door in her long cream cotton nightdress, a tan headtie wrapped around her head. She looks feverish, tired.

"You burning up with fever, Mammie. Why you get up?" Rex and Gerda are fussing around their mother now. Rex makes a sound that his niece thinks is typical of him, a clearing of the throat.

Ma speaks hoarsely, weakly. She is looking at Gerda. "You alright, my child? What happen? Everything all right?"

"Yes, Mammie. Oseyan just went outside for a golden apple. *Ponmsitè-a tonbé*. You could go back and lie down."

Ma looks at Oseyan with something almost like surprise, Oseyan thinks. Then her eyes move from Oseyan to Gerda to Rex. "Amèlie gone?" she asks. "Beatrice gone?"

Gerda says, "Yes, Ma. They gone and they settling in. Not to worry."

Ma's hands reach out and touch Oseyan's face. Her hands are cold. She says, "Oh gosh! You face hot." Oseyan has put a yellow golden apple down on the plastic tablecloth. She stands near her grandmother. "Never mind," Ma says, touching the side of O's face again. "*Pa mélé*. Never mind."

"Come, let me help you back to bed, Ma."

Ma lies in bed muttering. She talks to Oseyan, and her words seem to be rambling. She talks about Oseyan. *A little girl ocean. Oseyan. I tell them. What you saying at all. Tell them it happening.* She speaks of things Oseyan is not sure she knows about. Ma talks.

"*Ponmsitè-a tonbé.*"

Oseyan's eyes follow Ma's thoughts – through the window to the golden apple tree outside.

"*Ponmsitè-a tonbé.*

"Just like that. *Memn kon sa.*

"*Sézon ponmsitè.*

"*Dyak-la batizé sé zanfan-a.* The deacon baptize the little child. *Non-i sé Gentle ék i dous pou vwé.* Gentle by name and gentle by nature. There must be a reason is a man named Gentle that baptize her. Archdeacon Gentle in the Anglican Church. God know what he know. *Ayen pa lèwè.* Nothing is a mistake.

"*Apwé yon fwa sé dé fwa.* After one time is two time.

"*Pa obliyé dat-la.* Don't forget the date.

"*Douzyenm fevwiyé dizwit san katwèven sez.* 12th of February 1896. *Wimèsyé Bondyé.* God be praised. *Ti, piti zanfan.*

"*Tout bayay a lanmen Papa Bondyé.* Everything in Papa God's hand."

CHAPTER FORTY

1916. Mourning Song. I must tell Mr. Dickens.

Her grandmother had made the world for her, had made her understand what it was to mean the world to someone. She turned to the lessons her grandmother had made possible to say something to honour the life she had lived. She whispered it as Sir had insisted they learn it.

> *She was dead. No sleep so beautiful and calm, so free from trace of pain, so fair to look upon. She seemed a creature fresh from the hand of God, and waiting for the breath of life; not one who had lived and suffered death.*

When she read that in class and then in extra lessons, Mr Ansel said it was from a Dickens story that was sentimental and sad. In the story, Dickens had written about using winterberries to – she must go back and read it – to sort of adorn the space afterward, perhaps. Mr Ansel had told her to learn this part that the person dying had said earlier:

> *When I die, put near me something that has loved the light, and had the sky above it always.*[12]

Dickens used winterberries in his story. Ma loved bougainvillea. The bougainvillea was pretty like Ma, and like Ma it had thorns that could *jook* you when you least expect it. The bougainvillea had needles to defend itself if you play stupid and just push your hand in the space that belong to it. Oseyan planted a sprig of purple bougainvillea around the place on the hill where they buried Ma.

Ma would like the Dickens story. She hoped her grandma

would say, *You listening, child. You well take the story and use it how you want.* And Ma being Ma, she might even laugh and say, *I must tell Mr Dickens.*

CHAPTER FORTY-ONE

1917. Going Away.

It was all arranged. Oseyan was going to meet her uncle. She hadn't seen him in four years, but it really didn't feel that long. Auntie Gerda said she hadn't heard from him this last time to confirm the time Oseyan should get there, but he had agreed before, so she was sure it was alright. They would just have to find him. His last long letter was about the Chicago speech and then he wrote about his mother, and he hadn't said much else. Gerda reminded Oseyan that he had his own life, said that she believed he was trying to get married and everything, and things were never easy for people when they settling into a place; so, she said, be patient and take it easy. During the time Uncle Eero was in that strange place called *Away*, he had sent things down by the steamship, and unless he was sending some speech or something, he had been in touch not so much with Oseyan as with his mother and his sister Gerda – with the family. When his mother died, it was a painful time. He couldn't come for Ma's burial, and you could hear the hurt in his letter when he said that. He had just found a carpenter job at last, although he was still shining people's shoes sometimes; things were hard, and he couldn't come. Sometimes people don't really tell you what they are doing *Away* to try and put two cents together, and they'd better keep to themselves what he was telling them, because people don't wish you well, all how they might pretend. Nobody really want you to do well, he said, if it don't mean something for them, and if they know you not doing well, they glad to laugh. So keep quiet. He is only telling them how things are going, he says, because he really wants to be there, but he can't come. He is barely making it as it is. To pay a passage to come home – he can't do it. They know he would be there if he could. It was almost as if he were pleading with them to understand. The few dollars he could scrape together, he was sending for them to spend on saying goodbye to his *precious mother*. Uncle Eero didn't say things like that easy, so you could tell he was hurting. It made Oseyan cry. But after all of that, it was easier to leave La Digue now that Ma gone to meet her Maker. She wondered if anyone would know Ma when she came back. She wondered how that worked. She had to keep it to herself because it just sounded so strange. Would Ma come to Canada or would she, Oseyan, have to come back? Better not to think about it. Uncle Eero sounded like he had a lot on his plate. Would things go alright with her being there?

Oseyan was excited about going away, meeting new people, setting up in her own sewing business, perhaps even finding a way to go to some kind of school again someday. What would she do? Perhaps she would do teacher training, study Education – that's what Sir said when she told him. In a school, she could do that. She might have to study other things first and qualify in their country, there in Canada, for her to be able to enter a university, but she could do it, Sir said. The enormity of the thought frightened Oseyan and made her smile at the same time. *She could do it.*

It had taken Uncle Eero a couple years to settle himself and it seemed he almost gave up the whole idea of being out there when his mother died. But Auntie Gerda wrote to him about what his mother would want, reminded him what Ma used to say, *If you do all the things you suppose to do before a person dead, no sense cutting you nose and spiting you face to prove anything when the person done gone already.*

Ma would be pleased that Oseyan was going to Canada where Uncle Eero was. Auntie Gerda said that Uncle Eero had to have fifty Canadian dollars on him when he was travelling. He said it was what Canada immigration required. Auntie Gerda and others within the family had helped him to scrape that amount together. It was what people always had to do when they were travelling, Auntie Gerda said. Scrape. People always thought you had money once you reach *Away*, but she knew her brother was still trying to settle himself and he couldn't help much even if he wanted to. They would have to see who in the family could help. Fifty Canadian dollars might not sound like a lot to some, but here in this grugru country is a lot. "And don't forget, Oseyan," she said, "when you go, at least remember anybody who help, and in the future when somebody reach out, help if you could. Is so we have to live as poor people. We have to help each other out." Oseyan understood. Ma had told her – it felt like a long time ago now – that Uncle Eero said if she came she would be able to find something to do, but she shouldn't expect that to happen right away. Things take time – always, but especially when you go to a new country and you trying to figure things out. You might have to struggle a bit in the beginning, he had told Ma to tell her, but *you are bright, and you will be able to settle yourself eventually. Things take time.*

Gwanmanman mwen mò. My grandmother dead. She whispered it to herself, letting the thought move slowly through her head. What will life be like? *Mò.* She had been staying with Auntie Gerda for the last year or so, and sometimes she had been in the house on the hill. Auntie G's house was a lot of work and Auntie G's temper could overflow sometimes, but Oseyan liked being with the children even if they were a handful – Malcolm, Olive, Wilfred, Thaddy and Lynn. At eight, Malcolm was the oldest and he knew it, always helping her by ordering the little ones about. He prepared his baby sister's bottle as if he had been born doing it. He insisted on organising them all – their clothes, their food. He would hold the baby bottle out to Oseyan and say, "I think this just warm enough, O, not so?" And looking at her anxiously, he would say, "We don't want it too hot, okay? Check it for me, O. Rest it on your hand to check it. Pour a little bit on the back of your hand." He rinsed a vest for his little brother to wear, held it up for Oseyan to see and said, "Check it for me, O. It's okay?" Malcolm was her darling from the beginning, although the little ones taking her heart now, too. Little Mr Wilfred is a wonder at four. And so is Olive, about six now… or perhaps not yet. So much already? And then the babies, Thaddy and Lyn, just two and one. She would miss them, although house work, with children, is a lot of work. "A damn lot of work – *yon lo twavay. Sakwé tonnè!*" She says it out loud to herself. She could say it out loud because not only is Ma gone but the children are in school and the other little one, Thaddy, is outside. "A damn lot of work. Ma, I miss you already."

Will she find work in Canada? Uncle is a carpenter and after what he called *a rough few years*, he had been able to find work installing doors, and he thought he had work to come laying roofs. That is what Auntie Gerda told her. He was still hopeful about making more use of his carpentry skills in the place called Montreal in Canada. He had told Ma that Oseyan would stay with him and his wife. She hoped that was still true but – she hadn't heard from him this last time. It's white people in charge, he had said, so of course they think we Black people are less. But they are British, like us, so the immigration part is not as bad as it could be. But don't let that make you think it's a breeze. "Tell her to study her head," he had written to Ma what seems long ago now, and that makes Oseyan want to cry as she thinks about it. Yes. Even remembering it now, she wants to cry. It sounds so much like Ma.

When she is about to leave Grenada, Oseyan decides that she won't tell too many people about this Canada travel. They had cleaned up Ma's house. The family would continue to stay in it. There were enough of them. She doesn't tell many people, but she tells Marjorie, and she tells Gwenevieve, and her friends say, "Girl, I jealous you, girl. I not lyin. I wish was me." Both of them say the same thing when she tells them, separately.

Oseyan tells them she is a bit nervous, if truth be told. Marjorie soothed her. "Girl, you have both the sun and the dark in your sign, and you just have to stay strong, keep the leadership thing that is yours, and don't let nobody run over you." For the first time, she wonders if Marjorie has dimples, or if her cheeks just so involved when she laughs that some sort of dip appears somewhere. Or perhaps it is because she, Oseyan, is crying and her eyes are full of water. She says, "So I'm a leader too?"

"Stop playing the fool. I tired tell you that. You going be alright, girl."

"But tell me about Scorpio too, again. I have two birthdays – one in November and one in January. How Scorpio go?"

"Oh you like me! I have two birthdays too. One on the paper, and one that they tell me is mine. They go and register me late, and because the people in the registry office so rude with deyself if they think people register late, my family just give them another date. So for you too?"

"Something so. I not even sure why, but I not worried. I celebrate November and my baptism day, and I know for sure that the baptism day is February. That is the one on paper that they sure the paper get correct. That is what Ma like to do."

"Anyway, Scorpio strong too. Independent. Okay, Oseyan? You know your way. You have nothing to worry about."

Auntie G said she had better make the best of her opportunities. You have a start already, Auntie told her, because you educated and you can sew. Those people in Holy Innocents give you a good education to start you off, and that will help you make something of yourself. She could knit, too, Auntie G said, so she shouldn't let anyone mess her about. Ma well set her up. Uncle Eero was beginning to settle down there in Montreal, and once she could find him he would show her the way.

As Oseyan waited for her departure day, she remembered her uncle saying that he had made sure that his name was entered on the ship's manifest as both West Indian and African. Nationality: West Indian. Race or People: African. "We have to be proud to be African," he had told her. Never forget that. But how had he made sure of the way they put him down on the paper? Just by telling them? She would see. Perhaps. As Ma always warned her, things were different for everybody.

Different for her, for sure. When they went to the registry office to get her birth paper, she stared at the name on the certificate. She remembered that first name, of course, but the last name, Norton, was a shock. Was this what her grandmother meant when she said you have to use the connections you have even if you didn't ask for them? Who registered her birth, she wondered. Her mother or her grandmother? Or her aunt? Most likely her grandmother. But she would put down the reprobate's name? For spite? Or because you have to use what you have and a name with connections is a name with connections? Anyway, she wouldn't bother to ask Auntie Gerda anything. Auntie Gerda didn't talk to her about things like that, and these days when they talked about Oseyan leaving, Auntie Gerda was always crying. But, how she could travel as this Norton person she didn't even know? At least the name her Uncle Eero had given her, that other name of a woman of the sea, and the name Oseyan, would go with her – in her purse, in her head, in her spirit! She would keep Oseyan close. "Okay, Oseyan," she whispered. Lewwe go. Let's go. *Annou alé.*"

PART TWO

LETTERS TO MA

1917-1919

Lèt ki di dédé. Goodbye letter.

Babay, Ma. Ma, I'm leaving, and sometimes I wonder where you are right now. If there really is a heaven – beg God pardon, Ma – but if there is one, I know you are there. And you said you would come back, so I don't know if you are on your way back in truth and if anyone will recognise you when you come. Ma, although I say *babay*, because I'm leaving this place where I know us together, if you could come with me, *vini èvè mwen*. Come with me, Ma. I miss you. Perhaps I will look into a baby's face and know that *this one was here before* and it might be you – imagine that! But how I going know is you?

Ma, I miss you. You remember I told you that I let Sir know I was starting to write in an exercise book and he told me yes, I should do it, and he warned me to remember my grammar? Well, Ma, I am writing to you in my notebook. And as I write, I want to talk to you, and remember at the same time the lessons for letter writing in *Royal Reader Book V*. I know I won't follow them exactly. I will do as you told me; I will try to pick sense from nonsense, do what works for me. The main thing I remember about that lesson on letter writing in the *Fifth Book,* page 141, a section with the heading *How to Write Letters,* is what they had right below the heading:

Write as you speak; say exactly what you feel; and in the same way as you would speak if your correspondent were beside you. Cowper, writing to Lady Hesketh, said that he liked talking letters, *such as hers, and her rule was to write what comes uppermost.*[13]

All of that, Ma, "talking letters" and everything, all of that was in Royal Reader Book V. And Sir told us that Cowper is talking about how they speak, so write as you speak means write something kind of British and, Ma, you know Sir. He said, don't write patwa because Cowper told Lady Hesketh he liked "talking

215

letters". Sir is something else! If I'm writing as I speak, sometimes I will write like Sir told us to – proper grammar, but sometimes I will just talk, Ma, as we talk, although I know you want me to talk proper grammar, too. But what I used to speak to you, Ma, was our proper Creole grammar, so is so we will talk sometimes, but I won't forget to do what you told me, because I know the world will look at me in a certain way. You know Sir used to make us learn nearly everything by heart. I don't know if you will remember I told you, Ma, that Cowper was a poet who died way back in 1800. He was an abolitionist. He spoke up about the evils of slavery – way back then, even before you were born. You making me laugh already, Ma, because I could hear you saying, *How you talking as if you think I born in the dark ages so?* Lady Hesketh was Cowper's cousin and his good friend. Sir told us about a poem that Cowper wrote when he was in his fifties. He told us Cowper was a man who used to be mentally ill, and Sir said that just as the body could get ill, the mind could get ill, so there's no shame there; we have to find out from those who know about such things what is the best thing to do about it. You know how Sir is. That was one of the poets he liked, so sometimes he just used to bring those poems to class and tell us about them. And that day when we did letter writing in the Royal Reader and they talked about Cowper and Lady Hesketh, he brought in some lines from a William Cowper poem called *The Task*. And of course he made us learn and recite it:

> Oh for a lodge in some vast wilderness,
> Some boundless contiguity of shade,
> Where rumour of oppression and deceit,
> Of unsuccessful or successful war,
> Might never reach me more! My ear is pained,
> My soul is sick with every day's report
> Of wrong and outrage with which earth is filled.[14]

I'm laughing now, Ma, because I'm remembering how Gwen used to say that all these poet and lords in the Royal Reader writing as if they swallow a damn dictionary. You know that is Gwen. I will miss her, too. And Cowper's poem reminds me, Ma, of how you say the Bible is a good history book. You remember how in Matthew there will be wars and rumours of wars, but we should not be alarmed because it is written, nation will rise against nation? I think of that and the poem now, Ma, when there are rumours of wars all around and people are saying we have to look out for German U-boats that on the sea – well, I guess is the captain and so that have to look out – but that frightens me, in a way. But *Papa Bondyé bon*.

Cowper, in those long-ago times, wrote about the black man as just another human. Imagine that. He wrote in the poem about other men – I guess the white people like him – that:

He finds his fellow guilty of a skin
Not coloured like his own, and having power
To enforce the wrong, for such a worthy cause
Dooms and devotes him as his lawful prey.

You hear, Ma? Cowper saying that he tired. He just tired of all the foolishness going on in the world. And not now, *non,* but way back then. So foolishness always going on. And you see, Ma, he talk about how them there in Europe – he don't say that but is them he mean, finding his "fellow" – black people Sir say he mean – guilty of a "skin" different from his. You hear that, Ma? And Mr Ansel used to say like you and Sir, too. Read and know what people think, and how they say what they think. And this Cowper, living long, long ago in England, you know! He thought people were just people, and he write that those around him in England and so should be ashamed to call themselves people if they could treat other people in such a terrible way. In that same poem, he wrote:

I would not have a slave to till my ground,
To carry me, to fan me while I sleep,
And tremble when I wake, for all the wealth
That sinews bought and sold have ever earned.
No: dear as freedom is, and in my heart's
Just estimation prized above all price,
I had much rather be myself the slave
And wear the bonds, than fasten them on him.

What a thing, eh, Ma. You see why Mr Ansel did that poem with me in extra lessons and why Sir read it with us in class, too? He was the kind of writer they would like. A good thing you let me have extra lessons. And I'm thinking that is true we were well lucky to have people like Sir and Mr Ansel teaching us. Cowper was what Sir would call a *thinking being*, and way back even before you and Poopa were born, you know, so there were *thinking beings* in Europe way back then. Awrite, Ma. Don't say *steupes*. You know what I mean.

Ma, in those Royal Reader instructions on letter-writing, they talk about form. And you know Sir would tell us pay attention to form, but me, I am picking sense from nonsense, and I don't think I have to follow the form exactly if I am writing you a *talking letter* – my kind of talking letter.

Ma, I know I'm thinking about all of that because I'm afraid. So now I write it down and I have to face it, so it not so bad as when I just keep it in my head. I am going to a place where there are more white people than us and I have to remember that some of them think like Cowper. Yes, I know not to expect too much, Ma, but it reminds me that there are *thinking beings* all over the world. Ma, I miss you in truth, but it will be all right.

I remember how the *Fifth Book* says, *Attend particularly to the form of the letter.*[15] And then they gave us an example of the form of the letter. I remember most of it, because Sir made us learn it and write it out in class. On the right hand side you have:

Eastbourne,
date-year

And then, on the left hand side, the greeting.

My dear Fred,
    Many thanks for your letter of the 24ᵗʰ August. I was much interested in your story of the faithful dog. We have no copy of "Wordsworth" here, but my father has shown me a poem by Sir Walter Scott on the same subject, which I like very much. It begins – "I climbed the dark brow of the mighty Helvellyn."
    We bathe every morning, and often go out for a row in the afternoon. We drove yesterday to Pevensey Castle – a fine old ruin.
    Hoping to meet you at the old Hall on the 15ᵗʰ. I am, my dear Fred,
YOURS TRULY,
Harry Lush
To: Fred Brown

I'm laughing as I remember the letter and write it down here. Imagine that whole letter in my head! And the way they write it – the paragraphs, the signature and everything. I have whole chunks of those Royal Reader books in my head yes, Ma. I hope they're good for something where I'm going. In fact, I shouldn't say that. I know they are good for something already, but I know all of that kind of thing is theirs. But it good to have something in your head that you could hold on to. Yes, I know, Ma. I know. And that form of the letter is what was in the book but I remember Sir told us that conventions change and that in a few years the letter-writing conventions might be very different. And Sir said, *They have us coming and going. Notice the kind of information about their literature and culture they are giving in their letter-writing example.* And I'm laughing, Ma, because that way of speaking – *they have us coming and going* – that wasn't Sir usually, unless he get really intense – and after we left Holy Innocents, when he used to speak more relaxed, like, with some of us.

"Form" was the last thing they explain in that section on letter writing. And I remember Sir told us, *Pay particular attention to the **first** instruction they give you* – and that is where Cowper comes in, Ma – the first thing in the instructions about letter writing – the same thing that I tell you there. *Write as you speak. Say exactly what you feel.* I won't use the form all the time, Ma, but I will write you *talking letters. Mama mwen*, I miss you.

Lèt ki mwen ékwi padan tan mwen ka voyagé. Letter en route.

Ma, I am on the boat – going to Canada. I know that is what you wanted, but I am scared, even though I'm excited, too. Auntie Gerda made sure I dress myself properly, and I remember you told me to always present a good face, because people react to what they see. Auntie Gerda even made sure I have gloves, just in case, and I have them in my purse. I made a nice blue dress, so that the sea would recognise me. I don't play with the sea. Yes, I know, Ma. June started with me here in Grenada, and now I'm leaving. St George's is pretty. This is Mr Marryshow's town, and it is really nice in the harbour. We are waiting to leave. My boat is called the *Chaleur.* By the end of the month, I'll be in Canada. Imagine that! *Sé mwen épi lanmè ankò* – is me and the sea again. *Mwen chanjé ki manyé ou té ka diskité lanmè-a.* Yes. I remember how you used to talk about the ocean. *Mwen tounen asou lanmè-a.* I turn to the ocean. I'm thinking, look how I turn again to this ocean that swallowed my ancestors. You told me the stories. When Uncle Eero was leaving I remember thinking, *He brave, boy. Me, I staying away from that sea.* Is like mouth open, word jump out. I turn right back to the ocean – but yes, I know, Ma. It have no branch.

Ma, you know, when I hear Mr Marryshow talk about the West Indies, I start to think that, well, even to know the rest of the West Indies, we have to brave the sea. I remember you always say how when I was a little girl I told you I wanted to be *tout lanmè-a, tout oseyan-a* – the whole ocean. I was a little child, then, and I don't even know what I meant, but in a way I still want to be the ocean. And still I'm not sure what I mean. I'm on deck, and the waves don't look so rough. Perhaps I can't be the whole ocean, Ma, but Oseyan *in* the ocean. Help me, eh, Ma. I have to watch the sea. It is really pretty, and it's telling me something. I want to watch it. *Lanmè.* I will talk to you again later.

Lèt mémwa. Memory Letter.

In school, Sir told us about Henry Hudson and his discovery of Hudson Bay. He told us about how really America divided Europe while Europe was dividing America. I know I'm not no English lord, but it is almost as if I'm going on an adventure through all these places I read about. Last night I was thinking about *The Siege of Quebec* in the *Royal Reader* – the *Fifth Book.*

> *The Siege of Quebec (A.D. 1759)*
> *The closing scenes of French Dominion in Canada were marked by circumstances of deep and peculiar interest. The pages of romance can furnish no more striking episode than the Battle of Quebec.* [16]

And that in my head, yes. Imagine! The Battle of Quebec in my head! I was thinking about that as I felt the boat moving, that I'm going to Quebec. Or at least to Montreal, which is a city in Quebec. I not no English lord, so perhaps it won't be so romantic. But still, Ma, the book in my head tell me that – *the pages of romance can furnish no more striking episodes than the battle of Quebec.* It makes you think, not so?

And I was thinking, too, Ma, about how the Englishman, Wolfe, recited from memory, just like us, Grey's "Elegy in a Country Churchyard". He loved that poem so much that he said he would rather be the poet who wrote that than the person who conquered Quebec. Fancy that, Ma! In the end, although we won and Quebec was English and not French, Wolfe died. I'm sure you remember I told you the story. Yes, yes, I know. Is not *we* that won. I know. I know. But it is kind of nice going to Quebec, Ma, after reading about it like that. Even though it now belongs to the white people who were the English ones, Chatham's friends and people like them, still… You know what I mean? It's kind of exciting to be going to Quebec.

I am glad I could write you a *talking letter*, Ma. I really need to talk, yes. Is just that I don't know what to say. I all mix up, Ma.

Lèt ki konsèné latè-a. Letter about the World.

Ma, on the boat, people are talking about the war. They say they hope the ship will be safe. They are saying that German U-boats are sinking passenger ships, but it's really ships out there near England and Ireland. A lot of Americans died on one ship but it still wasn't out here on this side, and Germany promised America not to sink their ships. That's what I heard somebody say. I don't know about the Dominion of Canada. Perhaps it's different. They were talking about that on the ship today. This war, Ma, is the one that had started already, while you were still here, the war that our cousin signed up for, so I guess we are involved? I hope we will be safe. I have to say that I hope our side wins, because it's the side our family is fighting on.

I hear your voice inside my head, Ma. *Is their world war.* That is what I hear you saying. *Their country – sa sé tè-yo. Their world.*

It's true, Ma, but we are so mixed up in their world. Sometimes I don't really know what to think. I remember the things you told me – *Mwen vlé touvé yon manyè pou wakonté listwa mwen.* I want to find a way to tell my story. *Listwa nou,* Ma – our story. You know, as I'm writing parts of this in *Patwa,* or *Patois,* or *Creole,* as Sir would say – I am remembering how we couldn't speak *Patwa* in school. Sir said the Legislative Council didn't allow it. Imagine that! *Patwa* is nonsense, they felt, and Cousin Mildred used to say that, too, when she heard me speaking it. *Is nonsense language, so when children going to school, they should know better and teach us the right way.* That is what Cousin Mildred used to say. I know you didn't agree, Ma, but I was thinking about that as I write you these *talking letters,* and remember that Sir told me to write good grammar, and I know that you would have wanted me to do that, too. But I also think it is important to talk to you as I would have talked to you if you were here. So I will do both. Things so mixed up in my head, Ma. I don't know what is what.

I remember that when we were talking about me taking boat to go away one day, you told me that just to say *I* would *take* the boat and decide where I want to go is something to think about. You said, *Yesterday they throw you on a boat and send the boat where they want.* That's what you said, Ma. I'm laughing as I remember you saying, *Now you, like moun ki ba lòd – high-up people – thinking about taking boat for yourself and standing up to watch sea as if you is tourist. After one time is two time in truth! Wi, Bondyé. Yes, Papa God!* That is what you said, and I have to laugh, remembering.

Manman Mwen, when I stand watching the sea in St George's, it was as if I was tourist, *wi.* The sea and the mountains so pretty! Grenada really nice, Ma, my country, the country that I'm leaving. *Ovwa* for now, Ma. I will write you again soon.

Lèt ki té ékwi adantan nous té asou lanmè-a. Sea Letter.

You know, Ma, every time I write I am talking the writing out aloud in my head, because I imagine you can hear me talking to you. I used to talk out to you all my Royal Reader lessons. I never see you sit down and read for yourself, but I was talking to you. So here I am, Ma, talking to you again. I know you're hearing me. That is why I'm in my room – my berth – by myself, so you could hear me. You're not like us now, having to sit down and read. You could talk to people when they talking to you in their head, not so, Ma?

Tonight, I'm thinking about things that I see and hear. I'm learning so much already. Our ship is the *SS Chaleur*, and I think it is part of the Royal Mail Steam Packet Company. So it is really *RMSP Chaleur*. Imagine that! It makes me feel like a letter on the sea but I don't know what is in this letter. I serious, Ma. I wonder what this body I have saying. More and more I wonder that. On this boat, there are sections where only white people or high-up people go, and one of the officers – at least, I think he was an officer – a white man all dressed up in a kind of official-looking uniform – full suit, with the buttoned-up vest inside, shirt and tie in there and everything – he pointed and told me I should go over to the other section – he didn't say white section, but I guess that was what he meant. They were the ones I saw in there. I just smile, yes, Ma, and I say no. Imagine that! I know you told me I should make use of what opportunities I have, Ma, and I don't know if *that* is an opportunity, but I know that I couldn't do it. I don't *want* to do it. I'm sure that is not that kind of opportunity you meant. Can you imagine! If you were travelling with me, we could be in different parts of the ship, and whether they allow it or not, you probably wouldn't want to come over to my side if I go over there! I don't want to go over there, but I can – because of the reprobate. And with this colour I can go on the white side because we bought a berth so that I don't have to travel on deck – that is what Auntie Gerda told me to do – and the berth make it look like I'm *moun ki ni lajan,* people who have money, and then I have the skin to boot! Or at least some people seem to think so. No thanks to him, but I have to think about that.

All the ship's officers are dressed up like the one I told you about. One of them even had a chain coming across from sort of inside the jacket, and I guess a watch hanging near to a button at the front. Watch it tomorrow, Ma, when I'm near them – if I see them again, you will know and see who I mean. All the ship's officers are well dressed up, and all of them are white men. I suppose is a good thing Auntie Gerda got a berth for me, but it's so fancy and there's no black people with berth this time, although Uncle Eero said it had one or two when he was travelling. I see a lot of black people – I mean, fair-skin too – out on deck. In fact, I see only one other black – she could be black – very light-skin lady in the section with berths, but we don't talk or anything. She really look like *moun ki ni lajan*. She might be white, I don't know. I can hardly understand what the white people say when they talk, but I heard one lady saying something about how she came on the ship from Canada and went down to Trinidad, and now she's going back up on it. So she and her group must be tourists. And they're in high-up company. I hear them call the name of one of the high-up people Uncle Eero tell us about – Geddes Grant. The lady was talking as if they met him in Trinidad and then he was with them in Grenada. I don't think he is on this boat, though. I just sit and listen as if I'm not there, and they not even seeing me. Perhaps I am like a OHMS letter – the one with the border. An *On His Majesty's Service* letter. You never know what's inside. What a thing! You're smiling. You smiling, Ma. I could feel you smiling at me. And I'm glad for that. I glad for that. I miss you, Ma. We could just travel together and watch them and hear what they saying. Stay with me, eh, Ma.

Lèt asou dwa plantè-a. Letter about the Right of the Lord.

SS Chaleur, 24 May, 1917

Dear Ma,

Okay. I know you are waiting to hear what I am doing this time. I am writing this in the form of a letter. Don't worry, Ma. I will read it to you.

For what I want to say now, it's almost as if I have to get a different kind of voice, to talk in a more formal kind of way to even broach the subject. I don't know how to talk to *you* about it anyway. Let me see if the Royal Reader formal writing, or a little bit of it, might help.

Ma, I went with Auntie Gerda to the District Office in La Baye to get my birth certificate and they told us we would have to wait or go down to the office in St George's. In the end, Ma, I don't know how Auntie Gerda worked it out, but we got it in the District Office in Grenville – La Baye. We had to pay a whole shilling for the certificate. I had it from money that people paid me for sewing – but that is not what I want to talk about. Ma, when I got the certificate I see that my last name is the name of the father I don't know. And Ma, because you never had a good word to say about him, I was really surprised to see that I had his name. Eventually, when I couldn't take it any more, I asked Auntie Gerda who registered me, and she just said *Is long time ting*. Ma, I wish I could know. I know I couldn't ask you even if you were here, but I wish I could know. And I wish I could know *why*. Is it because you think his name will help me? Because, when I think about it, I'm almost sure you are the one who registered me – from what I hear about my mother and her state of body and mind around that time. Was it because you think he was a big man with connections, so his name could help me even if he never did anything for me? I have a feeling that is it, Ma. I feel sure that is it, *wi*, but I wish I knew for sure. I just have to write it – but that has to be it. I always wonder why you told me to try to use what little name I have. Now I think you meant *name* in a special kind of way that I didn't really understand at the time. Even if is a dream, Ma, I wish you would come and tell me.

Anyway, Ma, I am travelling in the name of the father – with the last name Norton. I started thinking that the letter form would help me to talk to you about it, but I can't even sign off like how they sign off in those letters, because it just not feeling right to sign off like that with my name at the bottom. We talking, Ma, and you know me. I will figure out what to do with this name. I just thought I should talk to you, okay? I will just sit by you on the bed here and pretend is the bench in the house on La Digue hill and lean my shoulder where you would be. The formal letter wasn't so formal after all. I finish, Ma. Is okay. Is okay. Is okay.

Lèt pandantan mwen kouté. Listening Letter.

Ma, in one meeting I went to before I left La Digue – fancy that! I'm talking about *back then, before I left La Digue.* And now I'm in-between. On the ocean. Between one place and another. No-where and everywhere. That is so strange. Anyway, in this meeting I remembering, Mr Marryshow was talking about our neighbours. He said that here in the West Indies we are one people, divided by time and circumstance, but that our destiny is together even if we may have different ideas about some things. I've been thinking about that these last days, Ma, as the ship passed through St Vincent and then Barbados and St Lucia. They say it will take us two weeks to reach Canada, and they are not staying long anywhere, but it makes you think, Ma, as we pass through each place, and then sometimes get a glimpse of what happening. I just stay on the ship and watch but I'm remembering what Sir and Mr Ansel used to say – that everything is an education if you keep your eyes open. I believe some of the *moun ki ni lajan* get a chance to go different place for a little while, because I hear them talking.

Let me see what I remember – and I do like Sir said and make little notes, too, about the different things. Ma, I wrote down "Mule cars, Barbados", and that was because I was listening to the same lady I told you about – I was eavesdropping, I suppose you would call it, Ma, because you know my ears long from time – look how you laughing now, and you used to look like you so vex with me. That lady I telling you about, it look as if she really does think about things, even though she is a *moun ki ni lajan.* I heard her talking about mule cars, and Ma, the way she described them they sounded like carriages pulled by mules, taking people from place to place. She didn't say donkeys or horses, but mules. I was wondering if she was talking about the donkey-cart, because all of us know that, but then she said *not donkeys but mules.* So it sounds like she know what she talking about. I don't know if they had them in St George's or perhaps I just saw them and thought donkey or horse. I don't know. Anyway, she and her friends were saying that they saw mule-cars in Barbados. When we pass there, two hoity-toity ladies in their hats and dresses came on the ship. There were hoity toity ones here already, but there was just something about those two – perhaps the way they were holding their heads, as if they always listening for something that ordinary people might not hear. You know what I mean. Hoity-toity. To make it worse, there was a man walking in front of them with his suit and his cane, but he didn't make any sideways motion with his head, and I guess that made a difference for me. Those ladies have a good seamstress, though. Anyway, Ma, this world strange in truth. I could hear from what they were saying that when they went off the ship they saw people like you and Cousin Mildred and Auntie Gerda. I saying that because they talked about seeing women carrying cane-straw high on their heads, and you know Barbados has more cane than us in Grenada in some places. And they were talking about a woman looking so comfortable with a tray of hot cross buns high on her head, over her wide-brimmed straw hat. They talked about the long dresses women on the streets were wearing, how they have *something like an apron over them at the front*, and *a rolled cloth folded in a sort of circle on the head*. I was smiling to myself, Ma, because I believe they were describing the *kata* that everybody put on their head to carry load, so I suppose they saw the women caneworkers with that. They were talking about how the women walked so tall and so straight with that heavy load on their heads. The lady – the *moun ki ni lajan* I tell you about – she say that the apron over the dress was different from the long one that her cousin's servants wore in Trinidad, because that one went right down to the hem of the dress. She talked about how the men servants were wearing a vest but most times not the jacket with the pants. I guess that lady cousin in Trinidad must be real *moun ki ba lòd* and *moun ki ni lajan*. It's really interesting to listen to them, Ma. I didn't understand everything because they talk in a *speaky spokey* way, but I get most of it. And I don't know if is something I miss because I was somewhere else on the ship, but I hearing talk about the coaling women in St Lucia and the way they walk up the plank – and I don't know if they were talking about a plank up to the ship. I'm not sure, and if so, is something I didn't see. But they talk about these coaling women in St Lucia carrying baskets of coal on their heads, and how their clothes are different – they have long dresses, too, but not with the same long wide skirts. And the women, they say, have both hands up, holding these baskets of coal. I've seen people carry baskets of coal in LaBaye, so I don't know if is the same thing, but everything sound so strange when these people talk about it. I was wondering why that sound so strange to them, because people had to carry coals to the ship in St George's, too, for some sort of steam on the ship. I had to think, well, is really La Digue and La Baye I know, but everything everywhere seem so strange to them. I guess is how they talking about it that make it sound so strange and have me wondering sometimes what they describing. And the thing is, Ma, I kept thinking: *but that is us they talking about*. Is you and Cousin Mildred and Kalinya and Auntie Gerda and all the people we know doing their work and carrying their load for the *moun ki ni lajan* to live. It was just so strange hearing what they see and find so *charming*. They use that word, yes, Ma – charming. They are real tourists, Ma, always going out with their camera when the ship stop for a while, looking well fancy. And sometimes they take a small boat to go closer to the land. Perhaps one day I will see pictures somewhere of people like you, Ma, that tourists take. What a thing, eh! That is the world I see so far. For me is really on the boat, and listening to what people say when they come on.

We have a few days to go, Ma, but we will get there soon. Bermuda will be the last place – Hamilton, Bermuda – so St Lucia, then Dominica, Montserrat, Antigua and St Kitts, Hamilton, Bermuda, and then Port of St John's in Canada, where I will be getting off the ship. A lot of travelling, Ma, especially for those tourists who always going out with their cameras to see what they could find. And I hearing and learning a lot, too. And although I don't want to write it and so have to think about it, the weather not always so good to tell the truth. I'm looking forward to getting there, Ma, even though I have to tell you I feeling frighten. I wondering if Uncle Eero will be there to meet me even though we couldn't reach him these last days. Auntie Gerda said people living *Away* sometimes not as comfortable as we think, so I don't know. I hope he will be there to meet me. I really hope so. You can hear that I am getting kind of frightened now, the closer I get to this place I don't know. Because I didn't really get to know it in the Royal Reader. Only in a way. In their way. Yes, Ma. You warn me, and I really feeling it now. Stay with me, eh, Ma.

Lèt fanmi. Family Letter.

Ma, I know you are travelling with me. I know because I have you in my mind all the time. I'm thinking about Sir and a poet he told us about. James Montgomery, that was his name. Sentimental and religious, is what Sir said about him. He lived from 1771 to 1884. No. That doesn't sound right. He was 83 when he died, so 1771 to 1854. I remember Mr Montgomery now that I'm thinking about you, Ma, because he talked about a mother's love. He talked about how the mother – *ou menm, manman mwen* – marked the

> *child's growth from day to day,*
> *Its developing charms admire,*
> *Catch from its eye the earliest ray*
> *Of intellectual fire;*

Pick sense from nonsense (that's what I'm thinking, Ma, because of you – he didn't write that, but what he wrote makes me think about that):

> *listen while it talks*
> *And lend a finger when it walks:*
> *This is a Mother's Love.*

Even though we argued a lot just before you died, Ma, I know it's partly because I was getting big and want to do what I want to do. And you wanted to be in charge, as usual, Ma. Okay. Let's not quarrel. *Papa Bondyé konnèt sa i konnèt*, because perhaps if you weren't gone, Ma, I wouldn't be talking to you so nice now. Seriously. Really. So I'm thinking about that, too.

It's as if James Montgomery knew about you and how you would become my mother. Hear his poem:

> *Saw her daughter bring a helpless babe to light.*

No. That's not just him. I am putting myself into it, too, Ma.

> *Then, while it lay forlorn,*
> *The grandmother*

(I'm changing his idea to "grandmother", Ma, because is "mother" he talked about)

Gazed upon that sight
Felt herself new-born,
In this babe's existence she would lose her own,
Help her live and learn and breathe in it alone:
This is a (grand) mother's Love.[17]

Pardon me, Mr Montgomery. I hope you will excuse me for changing mother to grandmother, but my grandmother was my mother. Ma, if you see Mr Montgomery over there, tell him. Tell him I am borrowing from him to create something for you. And he was conscious about Africa too, you know. He wrote: *Africa; be free.* So, Ma, I'm using his words to talk about you. And I think about Auntie Gerda, too, and everybody who help you with me.

Mèsi, manman mwen. Ma, I miss you.

Lèt ékwi kon an poenm. Poetry Letter.

Ma, today I wrote a poem in my notebook. I was thinking about Sir and extra lessons with Mr Ansel and Standard Three and the *Third Book* and "We are Seven" and trying to write a poem with something like that rhyme scheme. This is it, Ma. I will read it for you so you can listen to what it says. You will hear how the lines rhyme, Ma. I'm using one of the styles Sir and Mr Ansel and the other teachers taught us in Holy Innocents – especially Sir and Mr Ansel. So you see, Ma? You make me go to school and I learn, you know, I learn. I am calling the poem "Twavèsé – Crossing Over".

Get a berth, they told me
Don't travel out in the open
Take a cabin, they advised me.
Be respectable. Be well spoken.

On the boat, people are polite; they smile,
They point me to the Whites-only section.
But I am your child, Ma, your *own own child.*
Never mind how they read a reprobate complexion

On this boat to the other side
If you're not riding in the white section
You're in the black; there's no in-between ride
And the black side is my natural selection.

Ma, it hurts my head that they read me white.
They send me where you would not be welcome.
They remind me of the school-yard fights:
Black where I'm going and Red where I come from.

Ma, you know why I travel with the name of a father
And I know that you too, you carried a white man's name
From work, from life, from all the things that came to matter.
Like my teachers say, it is not new, this naming game.

Ma, for now, I will hold on to what I can touch:
Handbag, wallet, this notebook and such.
I am a seamstress from Grenada
I paid for a berth and am going to Canada.

That is it. You like it, Ma? You see how I thinking about you
and me, and all my lessons. I hope you like this *lèt poenm*.

Lèt épi antjèt. Anxiety Letter.

We're almost there now, Ma. We're in Bermuda waters. This is
the last place we will stop at before we travel a long stretch of sea,
they say, and reach the Port of St John, New Brunswick, where
I'm getting off. Let me look at my ticket again. My ticket number
is 3336. I have 50 Canadian dollars in my purse, Ma. That is what
they told me I should have – Auntie Gerda was explaining it to me.
I believe she was talking to Uncle Eero, you know. And the family
help me… but… well, is not everything, everything people must
say. You always say that, Ma.
     I have a form to fill in. Let me fill it in with you. I am – Single.
I intend to reside in Canada. That's okay, because Canada allows

that for us. Of course I can read, so the answer to that is Yes. And I can write – so Yes. My profession is seamstress. You know I'm a good seamstress. And I am full twenty-one years old – *plen ventéyonn lanné sel.* And Ma, is as if I could hear you saying, *Mé ki sa ou konnèt a ventéyonn lanné?* What do you know at twenty-one? *Gwo fanm.* Big woman, eh! And Ma, I know you will say, *Bèl tifi mwen. My pretty little girl. My own own chile, wi.* I know you will say that. You're making me want to cry. But I'm laughing because I know you will warn me, *Don't smile too much. Mind your purse. Lift up your chin, child.* Ma, I crying just remembering. I hear you. *Tjébé tèt-ou ho lè'w ka palé. Okay ti fi? You're well read. Hold your head up, when you speak. Ti fi, jenn fanm. Fanm Norton nan Kanada.* Is that what you are saying now, Ma? Not *fanm Langdon? Fanm Norton?*

Ma, I frighten. I en lying. I well fraid. I have to stop now. It going have tears all over the paper. I miss you. But I sleep well every night on the boat, yes, what with the weather and the worry about the war and everything. That is one thing. And now I'm going on the last few days. We're getting there soon. I hope I could sleep good still. I hope everything will be alright, *wi. Papa Bondyé,* help me, make everything be alright.

Lèt na Kanada. Letter in Canada.

Ma, I haven't written in this notebook for a while. It has only been two years but so much has happened, Ma.

Well, in the beginning it was nothing but work. Work. Work. Work. Auntie Gerda was trying to warn me, I guess, when she told me that although Uncle Eero was a carpenter, he had to do all kinds of other jobs he didn't want to do before he could even get a job pounding a nail to make something as a carpenter. And then when he went to Panama that time, the work was so hard that he and others – they saved what they could and first chance they had they get out of there. And you know, Ma, Uncle Eero didn't turn up to meet me. But it's okay; he still made provision for me, and that's all over now, so I won't try to pick up spilled milk. He did the best he could; he was trying to pick up some money to live and see about himself and everything. I was upset, at first, and I didn't know what to do, but somebody he told I was coming looked out for me. So he did his best. I guess things were more up and down with Uncle Eero than even Auntie Gerda realised. Ma, this being away is not an easy thing. Anyway, I had his address, and things turned out alright. That is all that's to be said about that. When we at home, just wanting to go and look for opportunity, we have no idea how things are, and how people have to struggle to do even simple little things. How people could lose their job they just get if they take a few hours to do something important. If you not in charge, you are just not in charge. And then, I suppose, when people come back home they talk about the good, and act as if things were so wonderful, and they don't say a lot about the struggle. They send money, so people think things are good. I guess people don't want to hear about the struggle. You probably doing better than them, they feel, however hard you might say things are. Anyway, it's okay.

With one thing and another, I've been working, Ma. Working as a domestic, and that seems to be what most women do when they get here – whether they leave home as teacher, seamstress, labourer, or anything else. This place put you all in the same bracket. People have a way of looking at you as if, whatever you do before, it can't be good, because where you come from is not an important place. So domestic is the main thing women get into. Is mainly if people studying for Certificate or something it might be a little different. It was Uncle Eero who found me the job. He is struggling himself still and the other girls I meet here tell me that is what you have to do. I met one of them from up by Sauteurs side who has been here for a couple years now. She told me that the same day she reach, her aunt send her to work in a white lady's house. That is what we have to do. Get in quick to do something and support yourself because things are not easy. Nobody picking money up off the ground, and you can't be leaning on people who trying hard to make it for themselves. The people who are not immigrant, and never have to go through that, might watch and think your family not there for you, but you just have to keep your own counsel and know that life is different for those who come in from outside. People who belong don't really understand that kind of struggle. So that is it. I wash, I cook, I sew – in a big house here in Montreal. The people have two children, and I'm used to taking care of children from the time with Auntie Gerda, so that experience is paying off, although I wish I could just start with sewing right away.

They speak a lot of French here and I understand most of it because you know that our language is like French – *lanng nou sé kon fwansé*. And sometimes I say things in Creole. I even say things in French sometimes when they speak to me. I don't talk a lot of French, though. I listen to them, so it's not hard. They like that I can sew. I'm not their seamstress, so they don't have to pay me as seamstress; I'm their servant who can sew. I made something for the little girl, so that was like a bonus for them. Now a couple other members of their family want me to sew something for them. So that is somewhere to begin. Perhaps I could branch out into a sewing business from there. I will try to do that. And Ma, they thought I was white when they hired me – that is something else! But when I introduced them to my uncle, they knew. They asked me, and I told them. I don't think it mattered to them. They just looked surprised and asked me questions. I told them my father is white. They didn't ask more and I didn't say more – except that my last name is his. You could see them thinking, but they don't ask questions like people at home would ask, though home they don't so much ask as talk and whisper behind your back, because they know something, or because they figure they know something. The people here just stay quiet, watch me, and smile.

I sing songs to the little girl and the little boy. I sing *Alouette*. You remember that you taught me that song, Ma? I sing that song for them. And that one is all French, so they feel good with that. And it makes them think I can really speak French.

The way these people recognise me is as *migrant worker*. That's what I hear my employer's friends saying in that way high-up employers have of talking about those they see as servants. They talk as if you aren't very bright, and as if you can't really understand them. Worse yet, if you speak a French they think is not as polished as theirs. Or perhaps better yet, because they let you hear more, because they are sure you can't understand. They whisper,

Elle parle français. I know you understand that, Ma. What's in that not to understand? *I palé fransé.* And they whisper, *Elle est la travailleuse migrante.* You hear, Ma? *I sé twavayè migran.* That's me, Ma, a migrant worker. They have a way of making you feel small – or trying to – with their labels and their whispers. *Elle parle français. Ou elle le comprend.* Or she understands it. *Ébei li konpwann.*

Ce qu'elle parle est une sorte de français. You hear that, Ma? What she speaks is a sort of French. *C'est un drôle d'accent, mais français.* A strange accent they saying, but French. *Sé an aksan atwanj, men fwanse. Elle fait bien du crochet magnifiquement. Elle coud, elle fait le reccommodage. C'est parfait! Et elle travail bien avec les enfants.* You get it, Ma? They think I crochet beautifully, I could sew, I could mend.

They say all of that, Ma, talking in French. And they talk as if I'm not there. And I have to keep remembering, *Tjébé tèt-ou an-lè.* Hold your head up! I hear you, Ma. I hear you. I hear you talking to me still, you know! Although I haven't been writing in the book, I know you are there, Ma, and you know I talk to you.

Sometimes I'm there laying the table, and I'm watching them out of the corners of my eyes. Yes. I watch them, Ma. And sometimes I just look outside through the window over the kitchen sink and I could see the trees trembling. It reminds me of looking outside in La Digue – at least when it is summer here. When winter hit, I was so glad I reach here in the summer months. By October, I was just staying inside more, and at least I could just stay there in the servants' quarters when it was my off-time. It was really hard in the winter, though, because they not really nice. They act as if servant suppose to work but not to eat. They look close, close, Ma – the woman, she look close, close, at everything I put in my mouth. That first winter I wanted to say, just leave me in the kitchen, let me cook and bake and everything, and you'll wonder. And is not as if they don't have the thing for themselves. Is as if she didn't know I had to eat. You remember Auntie Gerda used to say she work with a woman like that right there in Grenada? And then one of our family in Trinidad – who was it? I don't remember who it was – and sometimes you-all didn't really say who was who – but she said she had that experience too. People who work in all different countries could tell you about this attitude. So I used to be hungry a lot in the beginning. And then I figure out how to move. So don't worry. I'm alright now. But this place is cold, Ma. Don't talk about January and February. That is shivering time. Even March and April. Is only in May the weather start to get civilised again.

Uncle Eero not doing too bad now. He is still an organiser, interested in politics like his mother. When he first tell me that the organisation he is trying to start will have *international outreach,* I used to think about how the attitude I tell you about from my employers exist in so many other places that it has *international outreach* too. I hope you laughing, Ma. It's a joke.

Ma, I miss home still. I watch the trees. I watch the trees a lot. Sometimes I see a tree far away and I remember the *bwa kano* we have on the boundary line. You remember? I know you remember. I think the trees know me, Ma. I look outside sometimes and I just talk to them. I remember the mango, the bougainvillea, the *bwa kano.* Here one thing I like in the winter is a tree they tell me is called the paper birch. That tree really likes the winter and it looks best then. It's long and skinny and tall and I think it thrives on hard times, though I don't understand why. From *Royal Reader Book II,* I know from long time ago that the winter here is very cold, with frost and snow, but Ma, it is a kind of cold I did not know existed in the world. And although I work things out and know more or less how to make it, the lady is really not nice. You remember Cousin Mildred said she'd rather work in the field than inside people house because she worked inside once and that lady was a *real devil* and that she used to watch her mouth as if she want to see if it greasy and it saying that she ate something? The lady here is like that, Ma. As if she doesn't think people need to eat. Like I say, it's better now because I figuring out how to manage but sometimes I just want to go back home.

I know you don't like nicey-nicey talk, Ma, but that birch tree reminds me of you. True, you know. Okay. I will look at it through the window again. And even if I don't write, you know I always talking to you. Things going alright, Ma. I'm really alright. Things going alright.

Lèt ki ka palé nomn-la. Letter about the man.

Ma, I met a man. I'd better tell you straight out. First of all, let me tell you that I go to meetings at a church sometimes with Uncle Eero, or sometimes on my own without him, but he was the one who introduced me to that place. The church is called the African Methodist Episcopal Church. They have all kinds of discussions about religion, of course, and about the struggle of black people, and black music that they play here in Montreal and other places, and about politics and about pan-Africanism – you know, Ma, talking about African independence and why African people must work together and things like that. I really like those meetings. I learn a lot, you know, about Africa at home and abroad. We talk about developing the organisation they have here in Montreal, a black organization that Uncle Eero and some others have, and we also talking about the UNIA, the organisation Mr Garvey is building. You would like the meetings, Ma. You would like to hear what they say. In fact, you *are* hearing. And it's *us,* Ma. *We* – we all work together. There is a thing Uncle Eero says: a struggle is never about one person, not me alone. To make sense, it has to be *we, us.* So we work together in this church.

And Ma, that is where I met this man. He is really tall, and very dark. Like – well, dark like Uncle Eero, but a lot taller, like Sir and even taller, and he look like any man in La Digue, except that he is from the American South that Garvey made us talk about after we got that letter from Uncle Eero. You remember? And Ma, he talks about things like Sir and Mr Ansel and Mr Marryshow used to talk about. He is what Sir would call a *thinking being.* And he's a preacher, Ma. Not a preacher like back home where it is only Jesus, but here it is about Jesus for poor people – for the downtrodden. And this man is particularly interested in what the churches could mean for Black people – or for Negro people, as they say. Ma, he was saying that we work good together in the cause – he and I. Right now, I sometimes write the minutes for a meeting, and then at the next meeting I read them out and ask if people want to add or correct anything. We have lots of discussions about this new organisation that is developing. This man that

I met – he is interested in it, too, and in fact all of us are. The organisation – the full name is the Universal Negro Improvement Association. Ma, remember Uncle Eero telling us about a Jamaican man called Marcus Garvey when he first came here and how he had met him before? Well it is this Marcus Garvey that is starting this organisation to talk about Africa and how we could develop a world organisation concerned with the interests of Africa at home and abroad. Ma, I have to tell you that I'm really excited and fired up to do this work. I will tell you more soon. Remember, though, Ma, I met this man. That is important. Okay? I met somebody I really like. I will talk to you again soon. Well, we talking all the time but in letter I mean, with me writing it down. But this is really exciting, Ma. You would like him. But wait, *non*. I didn't even tell you his name! Baron. His name is Baron.

Lèt. Letter.

I know you will tell me to take my time, Ma, and that if something is for me, it won't run away. I know you will tell me to watch man carefully, Ma, and not to be *soft head*. Uncle Eero said something like that, and I think that though Uncle Eero wants to push things ahead quickly when it comes to Black politics, for everything else he is always warning me to go slow. He thinks I am trying to do too much with the sewing, trying to set up something although I just reach. He keep saying, *You know how long I do all kind of nothing job before I find something in carpentry? Take it slow.* And, Ma, is so he is with this man too. *Take it slow.* But Ma, I know I like this man. We have the same interest in working for Black people's struggles. He preaches, Ma, in the way that the Black church preaches over here, taking the side of Black people and not afraid to say right out that is what they are doing. That's what he told me. I like him, Ma. I really like him. I don't have to wait, because I know, and we have work to do. We were talking about it – yes, Ma, I know that we just met – but we were talking about it and saying that we will work together and join up with Mr Garvey. And that will mean that I will go with him, Ma, to where he is from. And that is the USA. America, everybody calls it. America. We will work with Mr Garvey there and help him to open UNIA branches in different places. Uncle Eero likes that but he is still telling me that the political work is one thing and my personal life should be another thing and I should be careful. And you know Uncle Eero was always the person I followed to meetings and things. Anyway, I like the ideas Mr Garvey talking about too. So, me and Baron will set up in different parts of the country, and even travel and spread the word if necessary. And if we are doing that work in America, Ma, that is Baron's country, so I will be going with him. Yes, Ma, I know I just got here. I know that I'm here not a good two years yet. But I'm not setting myself up here in the way I want to, as a seamstress yet, so I could do it over there. I know it takes time, and anyway, things have changed because I met this man. I like him. I didn't foresee that that would happen. It's sudden, yes, and perhaps if he didn't have to go back – well, let me not even say that. It's sudden and I'm thinking about it. I wanted to tell you that – to write that down so we could talk about it together. I'm thinking, Ma. I'm thinking about what we will do. Well, *we* are thinking about what we will do – Baron and I. We're talking about it, Ma. I want you to know.

Lèt ki pwan disizyon. Decision letter.

Ma, I am marrying him. He is a few years older than me, Ma – about eight. He used to be married once, but he showed me his immigration card and it says "Widower". His wife died. The card says that. He is a widower. I will write more after the wedding – well, it won't be any big wedding – but I wanted to write this down at least before we do it, so you know. I'll write more afterward. And you know I'm always talking to you, but I wanted to put this down in writing. I'm excited – and kinda fraid. I guess I'm of age, Ma. 23 years I will be having this year. Ma, I have to laugh, because that reminds me of Auntie Gerda and what I know you said when she got pregnant. *She is of age!* I got a letter from Auntie Gerda, you know. She is getting old, she tells me. She will be thirty-five this year, so she say she will have to do something before something do her. That is what she said. And she say she miss me like if I am her own child. And I miss her, too, Ma. And Malcolm and Wilfred and Olive and Lyn and Thaddy. I miss Auntie Gerda. She is probably trying to go away, too. But I was telling you, Ma. I'm of age. Okay, Ma? I will talk again soon. Soon.

Lèt: Mwen mayé'y. Letter: I married him.

Ma, how will I tell you all of this? Let me start in La Digue at Holy Innocents' School – after I left school, really. One day, when I passed back there to see my teachers, Sir gave me a book called *Jane Eyre*. You know how he was always encouraging me to read and how you always told me to *pick sense from nonsense*. That book was like a love story, in a way, although it had lots of other things. But I remember the love story and how this rich man fell in love with this woman who was an orphan, and who got a lot of bad treatment in her young life and who eventually ended up in a boarding school because the people who had to take care of her didn't want her. Anyway, she ended up in this rich man's house and he was a really grumpy sort of person, but he loved her. So I like the story but her life wasn't like mine, because I wasn't an orphan. I always had you in my life. And Ma, as I'm telling you this, I remember so many other things about this book. Rich or poor – all of them were white people, and even the woman who was on the other side, not on their side, the first wife that he married – she caused major confusion so that this grumpy man come to lose his sight in the end – she was white too, but Sir tell me take a good look at her because she was a white *Creole* – from the Caribbean, Ma – from Dominica right by us there – the Dominica that Mr Ansel is from, except that he is *kawayib* and this Creole woman in the book is Dominican white, so she must have been like the estate owners and so and their family. Anyway, Ma, that is not what I started off meaning to tell you. Jane, the poor young woman in the story who was the servant – well, not servant but governess, a teacher like for a young child – well, she loved this grumpy man and when she got married to him, she said,

240

"Reader, I married him." Well, now, I'm saying like Jane, even though Jane was in England and white, although she poor: Ma, I married him. I can't believe it even as I'm writing it now. And I have to write fast because he gone out and I don't want him come and ask me what I'm writing.

Ma, we got married in a church called the Methodist High African-American Church. I told you about it already. A lot of things with Black people happen there. Uncle Eero was a witness. And when they ask me for father's name, I gave the reprobate's name. Is John, not so, Ma? I don't even know really what it is. I just wanted a father's name. I can't have no father, and I know I have one, reprobate or not. Anyway, I said John. And I gave my mother's name as Ella, although you never talk to me much about her. Why, Ma? But this is not the time. And both of us signed. So Ma, I am married, and we are leaving soon to go to his country – to go to the USA and to work supporting the UNIA and building the struggle. We're good together, Ma. From the things he told me, his father is just like you about Africa. Africa was big for him growing up and his father never felt he was less than anybody, although they tried to Jim Crow him – that is what they call how they treat Negro people living in the south of the country. Jim Crow is like a figure they laugh at and, you know, treat as less. His father was a preacher, too, Ma, and they were living in the South. He grew up in a place called Georgia, and that is the South where they treat black people like dirt. Ma, I hope I do the right thing. But it happen already. I have to say like the woman Jane said to her readers: *Reader, I married him. Moun la ki ka li sa, mwen mayé'y.* People who reading this, I married him. *Ma, mwen mayé'y.* Ma, I will go now, but I will write you when I can. Imagine, Oseyan is a married woman now. Ma, I hope I know how to be that person.

I didn't really talk to you any more about the organisation, so I'll just write this quickly. Think about the name of it – Universal Negro Improvement Association. That's ambitious, eh? Not just one *dèggè dèggè* part of the Negro world, but all over the world. *Universal!* Imagine that. I just think that is so ambitious, and so good. Garvey. That is man with a vision. *Sa sé nonm ki ni vizyon, Ma. Inivèsèl.* Universal! You don't find so, Ma? I think it is exciting, and really big! Okay? So *Ovwa* for now, Ma. Leaving soon for *Lamèwik*. I can't believe what is happening in my life, Ma. I don't even know what Uncle Eero thinks. He isn't saying much. And sometimes... well, I don't really know what he is thinking, but I know he thinks I too hurry hurry, because he tell me that. But Ma, I have to figure things out for myself, Ma, and I'm excited about this work we're doing. *Ovwa* for now, Ma. Wish me luck. Well, I know you wish me that. I don't have to ask you for that. Okay? *Ovwa*.

PART III

THE UNITED STATES OF AMERICA

1919-1931

1. Getting There.

She hasn't written to Ma. She is thinking this as she wakes up in the train. They seem to be travelling forever. She considers taking out her notebook to write but he will probably see it as an insult. *Ma,* she tells her grandmother quietly, *he sees so many things as an insult. If I take out my* Jane Eyre *that I got from Sir and start to read, he thinks it's an insult. If I write, it's an insult unless it's a UNIA report. If someone smiles and I smile back – although I don't think I smile at many people, Ma; I listen to you and I'm cautious – but if I do that, it's an insult.*

He asks if she is comfortable. In a low voice, he tells her that it would be much worse if they were on a train in his home state, Georgia. The Jim Crow cars there are so terrible that sometimes you have to wear overalls to keep the dirt off your clothes. White farmers use those cars for their chickens and for their luggage and they are filthy. And when they smoke, he says, they turn aside and spew out the tobacco spit right there on the floor in the Jim Crow cars. He tells her that a man just got lynched in his home state and that this is not unusual but this one made the news. The man had fought in the war and he came home to find that he was safer there because Black Americans could be more American in a war they were needed to fight. His home state doesn't sound like a place they should visit. And she is about to tell him that Uncle Eero had shown her a paper about it, but she decides not to do that. He doesn't always look happy when he hears Eero talking as if they had read things and knew things from the newspapers.

Ma – she turns to the grandmother who sits next to her, unseen, in a wide-brimmed hat for the sun, as if she is walking up Waterfall – *you with me, Ma?* Ma sits there, squeezing up in between the two of them. Oseyan rubs her hand lightly over the seat and he looks down, as if he is wondering what she is doing.

She removes the hand from the seat and places the two hands that are hers one inside the other, on her lap. *Ma, I will just talk to you in my head. Listen, eh, Ma; it has only been a couple months. I am pregnant. These last two months have been busy, Ma, really busy. We are working hard for the UNIA, me and my husband. My husband, yes, Ma! Gadé mwen! Look at me! Gwen would laugh to see me. My husband! Mr Garvey is trying to build the movement and he wants a Canada part of it. Uncle Eero is a main person in building the UNIA in Montreal. We had meetings all over the place these last couple months – Montreal, Toronto. I been on the road a lot. You should hear my husband preach, Ma. He's good, you know. I remember you used to talk about how man like to be in charge, so you just have to let them be that, and he really like this being-in-charge thing. But it will be alright. I love him, and we good together. He is really a strong preacher. And he doesn't take any of their nonsense. He gives them hell, all those who act like we are nothing. He is a thinker, Ma. Like Sir. Like Mr Ansel. Like Mr Marryshow. And I love that, Ma. When he preach, Ma, I really get excited. He is so good! And Mr Garvey started a newspaper. Just like Mr Marryshow started* The West Indian, *the Honourable Marcus Mosiah Garvey started* The Negro World. *So both of them are trying to educate and to get us all interested in what is happening to African people all over the world. I feel better than I was feeling before yes, Ma. True.*

Oseyan leans back against the seat. She is travelling in her husband's area now. It is three years since she has been in North America; now she in the *United States* of America. This part of it is not the America that Sir talked about, the whole continent of America. These are the States that use the name of the entire continent as theirs. She is in the United States. This is a place her new husband knows, and she doesn't know at all. She had been unlearning the Canada from the Royal Readers and finding the new one she was living in. She thinks of the Royal Readers and some of the ways they mentioned America. She turns over the pages of her thoughts: *Moose, or Elk, the largest species of deer; a native of the northern regions of Europe and America.* Or in Royal Reader Book III?: *A boy rambling in the woods many years ago, in a part of America where bears used to live, one day found the cub of a Black Bear* or, in another part, *the robin redbreast in Britain, the black and white snowbird in America.*[18] Each time the book mentioned America – well, most times – she had thought about a whole continent. Ah well. This place is not the whole continent, but it is big all on its own. And there are things they have to do.

The Honourable Marcus Mosiah Garvey and the Movement had just bought a building in Harlem, New York, a building to mark the birth and development of this new movement struggling for the liberty of Black people. He said that the building was to be called Liberty Hall, and that soon, all over America, there would be other Liberty Halls… or, and she pronounced it again in her head… halls, as her husband would say. She smiled to herself. There were meetings every night, the reports said, and thousands of people were going out to these meetings. She and Baron wanted to be part of it, so there had been no question about whether they would find their way to the USA after the Montreal and Toronto meetings. In fact, the Movement had invited them to do that because her husband is a master preacher in the Negro cause and she, Oseyan, is a good organiser and writer. Imagine that! That's what they said. Sir would be proud. They would go to Pennsylvania, where he had lived before he travelled to Canada and met her. Back then when, to her, America was America and not Georgia or Pennsylvania, or anywhere else, she had asked him if they would go to his first home in Butler, Georgia; he told her that it was easy to tell she was not from *here*. Butler, Georgia, or anywhere else in Jim Crow country, was not a place Negro folk that knew asked to visit. No, he said. They would go to Philadelphia to help build the movement.

She knows the organization is planning a big meeting in New York for next year. In August, they said. If her baby is on time, she could perhaps take her – or him – although she thinks it might be a little girl – to at least experience the meeting. Anyway, the future is God's plan. Imagine! She is going to have a baby – a little Malcolm, or a little Olive, or Wilfred – because she is going to call her children after her family.

Trains, it seems, are going to be in her life. So strange after La Digue. She was almost afraid of this long, big dirty thing when she first saw it in Canada. And then the land. Look at all this land! The land of the Cherokee and the Navajo and the Chippewa and… Wide, wide spaces. Nothing like the big hill up Waterfall or even like the high mountain up by Grand Etang. Oseyan looks through the window and marvels at the long, long, amount of land going nowhere here in *Lamèwik*. Empty land. Spaces disappearing into the distance. You can't believe how big this place is!

She looks at her husband, framed against the window as the trees amble past outside. This morning he was talking about someone being lynched in Georgia. He will preach about it, he says. You have to talk about these things, he says, his face harsh with the pain of not just hearing but also knowing. She cannot even imagine how they do that. She doesn't want to imagine, but that is part of the struggle. She looks beyond him. Outside is so pretty in spite of the evil. The scenes outside make her think of her grandmother's ginger lilies on the hill, just behind the bougainvillea. The trees make her think of home.

Her husband. He is tall. He is handsome. He is jet black, not no *paipsy* colour like her. She thinks about Gwen's teasing about the *gren-gren* disappearing below the neck-line. Better not think about all that now, but he does have those disappearing *gren-gren*. And he is bright. In the way that Ma was bright. She knows that bright could mean a lot of schooling but it could also mean a little bit of schooling, less than her, and a whole lot of sense. When he preaches about white evil it burns you up inside. And he is her husband; he makes parts of her – well, like – like – nothing to compare it with. She can hardly believe that this scrumptious man is her man. Ma used to tell her be careful and keep her legs together because that thing between there is all man want. But, she thinks with a grin, it is all legal, and then the grin spills over from her insides. She turns such a big broad smile his way that he swivels his head away from his Bible and looks at her with a curious frown. The eye nearest her is the good eye, not the one the accident took away so that he ended up not being able to go to the white man's war. God works in mysterious ways, she thinks. He thought that, too. He told her about his not being physically fit for war and of a song black men being recruited in the last days of the war were singing:

I ain't got no business in Germany
And I don't want to go to France.
Lawd, I want to go home, I want to go home.

Damn right, he says when he tells her about it. *Damn right.*

She leans against him, puts a protective hand on her belly, almost as if to remind him and to ensure that he isn't tempted to move away a little. She thinks that he does that sometimes, as if being touched worries him, but she might be wrong. In any case, touch worried even Ma sometimes, but that didn't mean she didn't love the person. He glances around almost guiltily, as if to make sure others are not watching this display. Then he relaxes back into his seat and lets her lean against him. No one would be interested anyway, she is thinking. There are two other Negroes in their second-class compartment, and they had also been sitting in the Colored waiting room; they look like a husband and wife. The white people, sitting further forward, would not be looking their way.

From somewhere in the car she hears a cough. Instinctively she closes her eyes and wrinkles her nose. These trains are closed up and germs spread. She hopes that coughing person used a handkerchief or something to cover his mouth. It sounds like something has settled on his chest. It sounds like the cough of a man. A real *coohoo, coohoo.* She remembers a poster she saw at the train station in Vermont. Lots of people died in Vermont, just last year, of the Spanish flu. And after people came back from the war, this thing spread even more. The poster in Vermont warned about the "Spanish Influenza". That should be gone now, she thinks, but who knows? The poster gave "Rules to Avoid Respiratory Diseases", by the "Surgeon General of the United States Army". It reminded people to avoid crowding, because influenza is a crowding disease; to smother coughs and sneezes, because other people "don't want the germs you're throwing away". The poster was funny. She remembers reading: "Your nose, not your mouth, was made to breathe through. Get the habit." Oseyan chuckles softly. Not that it is anything to chuckle about. The sound comes out, though, quietly, and although she doesn't look up, she can feel him looking down at her. She feels sure he is watching her with that one eye slanting down. Another thing she kept in her head from the poster: "Remember the three C's: a clean mouth, clean skin, and clean clothes." She hopes they have seen the last of this thing they call the "Spanish Influenza", though every so often you hear about someone having it. *Stay away!* she thinks. She drifts off to sleep, remembering that people in her age group seem to be dying a lot from this flu. *Stay away!* She remembers not to whisper, because what Sir called *sibilant sounds* travel, and she is awake enough to think that she doesn't want him to hear her and think that she is talking to him. Of course not!

2. A baby.

By the time the New York meeting takes place, things are becoming hard to manage. The new baby means a lot more work, but she had known that. She had seen it when Aunt Gerda's Malcolm arrived.

February is a cold month and they say the wind is biting in Philadelphia. Her baby Wilfred is precious. Yes. She decides to give him the name of Aunt Gerda's second boy. She remembers holding baby Malcolm and falling in love with the child. Then later she fell even more in love with her aunt's Wilfred. And she sees the look on her husband's face when the baby is put into his arms by Cassandra, the renter who shares the apartment. She is someone his brother knows and is a great help during this time; she even took her day off from her housework job so she could help. Baron is in love with their baby, too. He seems almost weepy as he looks down at his son. "Our little one," he says, as Wilfred screams to show that he can breathe. "Our son." And then he leans over and kisses his wife, and stays just watching her. She sees again that look he had on his face when they first met in Montreal. As if he can't believe she seems to be attracted to him. She loves her husband.

She knows that even before a baby is born you sometimes need more people around you; afterwards, you definitely need support. She remembers how somebody was always passing by Auntie Gerda to *make sure she okay,* and she wishes now that her family were around. She remembers Ma having to go and *keep Gerda company, to keep her spirits up.* She remembers that sometimes when a woman's spirits went down after the baby came, people just murmured, as if it was to be expected, *Is the baby. She*

250

just have baby, you know. And then somebody might ask the midwife to pass back by the house to help the mother settle down. She also remembers Lazarus in Mr Patrick's class – a little boy, because he was in Standard Two or Standard Three when she was in Standard Five – she remembers Lazarus saying on the playground one day when they were near the little children, that his mother said she didn't have time to sit down and cry after she have baby because she had to go back to work.

Cassandra had taken the day off from work to help Oseyan when the baby was born but of course she can't keep taking time off. She has to work. And so does Oseyan. They have to make ends meet. Baron is working as a day labourer, doing odd jobs around the place, but neither of them is earning a lot of money. They have to pay rent, they have to buy food; she has to keep her strength up because she is breast-feeding the baby, and sometimes they have to put infant formula in the icebox so he could get that, too. She tries to get sewing jobs from the few people who are beginning to know what she can do. She worries that money disappears before it well reach in their hand, not because they are over-spending but because they are living. She will go out to work as soon as she can find someone to stay with Wilfred; she has to take some work doing domestic so they could put a few cents together.

She used to think it was hard always having to do something for the baby when Auntie Gerda had her children, but she finds herself feeling weepy now in a way she did not feel weepy then. If the children were with her on the La Digue hillside, there came a time when they went home. Home was with their mother, with Gerda. Now she, Oseyan, is where home is. Even with Auntie Gerda's children, she'd felt just a little bit fed up sometimes, if she can remember well. She doesn't feel fed up now. She can't feel fed up. She just feels bewildered – as if she is in a new role that she had not quite expected. And she even feels sad sometimes because she wishes her family – the one back home in La Digue – were around to help out, to hold the baby, and just to make joke sometimes. She wishes she could send a message to up on the hillside in La Digue and tell – somebody – to come and help her out with the baby for a while. She feels happy with her new baby, but she feels alone.

251

3. Emancipation Day.

August 1st. Emancipation Day. The day that Ma and Sir said they must always remember because it was the day in 1838 when the white people in England agreed that, *legally,* according to them, okay, yes, you are free. And now Emancipation Day is also the day in 1920 that the Honorable Marcus Garvey decided on for an international convention – the first one, he says, because there are more to come – International Convention of the Negro Peoples of the World.

She can only go for a little while, she thinks, because Auntie Gerda is not there to help her, and the baby Wilfred is not yet even one year old. She has to take care of him and he can't be out there all that time. She will just go for a little while. In fact, her husband thinks she shouldn't go at all. She won't answer him on this one. She is going, and she will figure out how to get back to Philadelphia on the train. More and more people are bringing things for her to sew and paying her. She will go. Ma, not keeping her opinions to herself even though she is on the other side, says, *Remember not to be too own-way, eh.* And Oseyan answers, *I not own-way, Ma. Is me writing all kind of letters for the Association these days and helping out all the time. I want to go. I going.* Is true they planning to have meetings for the whole month of August and people coming from all over the world, but she wants to be there early on. She is celebrating Emancipation too. Then, when she hears that they will have a big parade on August 3, starting from outside the Liberty Hall on W135th street in Harlem, with regalia, and people looking *stoosh* in their uniforms, with the red, black and green flag, and the Black Cross nurses, and all of them, UNIA, dressed up in uniforms and everything, walking and parading through Harlem in New York, she thinks that she wants to be there then, too, for the march and the big meeting in Madison Square Garden. Perhaps she can stay in Harlem. But who does she know in Harlem? Uncle Eero is coming with the contingent from Canada, so perhaps she can find a way to get in touch with him and organise something. People are coming from Cuba and Jamaica and the Gold Coast and all over. She right here, and she in meeting and organising and writing letter for the organisation! So baby or no baby, she is going. Her husband talks as if, of course, he will be there in Harlem. He talks as if she knows she has to take care of the baby. Why? What about him? He doesn't say that, really, but everything he plans is for somebody called *I*. He talks as if he is big *jefe* at the centre of things and she doesn't have to be there. He gets a suit and a hat with a big band around it. It's for the parade, he tells her with pride. She doesn't ask if the organisation gave the money. She know what the funds are like, so perhaps not. People are donating but everything costs money. He and his *jefe* self. She is not going to ask him for any information. Let him keep it in his craw. She would know if she hadn't had to miss so many meetings because she was taking care of the baby and going out to work doing some house cleaning when she could. She will support him, yes, because he has to do his work as a preacher, but she is going to participate. It's a lot, yes, but she will be there.

Uncle Eero, in New York now for the event, tells her about some cousins they have in New York, right there in Harlem. Doris, their cousin, a woman Oseyan thinks looks just like Auntie Gerda, except that she keeps her hair natural and doesn't press it like Auntie Gerda, would take care of the baby for her, but Doris wants to be part of this big Negro celebration too. Everybody wants to go, Doris says, and she has two of her own she will drag behind her because *they drink water already*. Doris tells her it will be hard to find anybody to take the baby for these days just because of the celebration. This is a Negro celebration. This thing you-all doing big, you know! But Doris has an idea. The Quakers have just opened up a place right there in Harlem where they take care of children. They are white but it's a coloured mission and it's right there on 131st street. Okay. Perhaps she could decide which days she would go and since it's not as if she is leaving the baby there for days and days, during August month they should be able to do that. She should ask early, though, and she, Doris, knows a nurse who works there and, she says, she talk good with the lady. She could find out. And if Oseyan wanted to stay with her, Doris, a few days, they could work it out. Oseyan is not sure about leaving the baby because these Quakers are white people. But one thing becomes another, and Oseyan thinks she can get to be a part of the festivities. She has to give *him* every detail, of course, and he isn't happy when he hears about white Quakers. *His* little boy shouldn't start out by having white people taking care of him, no matter how they pretend to be nice. You can't trust these people. As Mr Garvey says, we can't have the enemy teaching our children in their schools and places like that. *So what? You will stay with the child?* She only asks him this in her head, so he doesn't get a chance to answer. Well, she won't leave him all the time, she explains and her cousin Doris has a friend – a Black friend – who works there, and she will be the one taking care of him. We don't get a chance to put a black teacher in their white schools, remember, and we have to know how to turn things to advantage. She tells him this quietly, putting in the white schools and black children business so he would see how it is, even with people that are not helpful like the Quakers. They have a coloured mission! The white schools are white schools! With white teachers! So Doris's black friend in the white place for coloured children takes care of their child.

Imagine if she had missed this! The parade, the meetings, the speeches! Especially hearing the Honourable Marcus Mosiah Garvey speaking right at the end of the month. *One God! One Aim! One Destiny!* And the Declaration that come out at the end there, for the Negro peoples the world over. And hear him talk!

> *Our children are forced to attend inferior and separate schools for shorter terms than white children, and the public school funds are unequally divided between the white children and the colored children.*[19]

That's what he said. Just the point! And, she thinks, *They won't play with my children's education. If I have to, I will shove my way into the schools where they send their children. I will let them know my children are here to stay.*

4. Widower.

They are talking now about opening a meeting hall in Philadelphia because the place is full of UNIA members. She sees the man in her building – the one whom she thinks is a West Indian because she heard him speak one time – with a copy of *The Negro World* – and they – she and Baron – weren't the ones who signed him up, and there are other members in their building. She and Baron will stay for a while in Philadelphia, and then they will go some other place to preach the gospel – well, both of them will talk and organise, but *he* will preach the gospel of Black excellence, and start another Liberty Hall.

With Wilfred it is becoming harder to manage, sewing for people or picking up a few days' domestic work to make ends meet, going to UNIA meetings and doing the work of organising people – knocking on doors sometimes or just telling people at work or in the street, and writing minutes of the meetings. Her husband's job in a store, cleaning and organising the place, is not bringing in a lot.

Now, they are going to Georgia to visit his parents. "My father must meet my son," he says, "and they have to meet you." She asks him, "What about your mother?" He says, "Well, yes. I mean, both of them." She doesn't pursue it. She is sure his mother would like to meet her grandson, too. She wishes she could take Wilfred to see Ma and Auntie Gerda. *Ma, I'm sure you're seeing him.* Uncle Eero saw him in New York at the Emancipation and the UNIA meeting. Truth to tell, she is a little nervous about meeting his family.

"I have something to tell you," he says, and *he* looks nervous. It is the first time she has seen this look on his face. He is actually *sweating*. Beads of perspiration appear on his forehead. *Fore-head* is how they say forehead here, she thinks as she watches him. He takes a deep breath. He lets the breath out with an obvious rush of sound.

"Your parents are alright? Have you heard something?" She remembers that he and his brother sat talking for a long time yesterday while she was in the room nursing Wilfred. This is not the brother he knew was in the area when he first decided they would come to Philadelphia. That one died before he even met her, he says. This is a younger brother.

Come to think of it, he was very quiet last night. Something happen? His brother give him bad news from home? He sits now looking down at his hands. He says, "Remember I told you that my children – from before – are with my parents?"

"Yes." Oseyan unties her apron. There is a sound at the door and he looks briefly over his shoulder. The two also living in the apartment, Cassandra, who looks like Auntie Gerda, and Benjamin, should both be at work. They time their hours so that when they are here, the others are working. With four of them and a baby living here, they have figured out how to give one another some privacy. They both watch the door. Nothing. Perhaps just someone passing or looking for another apartment. Baron makes a sound in his throat and she thinks of her uncle Rex, who was always making that throat-clearing sound. She folds the apron and waits. Pulls out one of the other three straight chairs at the dining table and sits down. "What's wrong?" He worries one side of his mouth with his teeth. She can see the folding, then the biting of the lip. "Everything okay? Your children? Your parents alright?"

"No. They are fine. My parents take good care of the children." He clears his throat again. "Their mother…"

Yes. She knows their mother died.

"She is with my parents sometimes, too."

"Who?"

"The children's mother."

Her brows come together. "She –" Her body rearranges itself slightly, and her right hand closes protectively over her left wrist. He lifts his head and sits watching her. Not so much his words, which she doesn't believe she really heard, as his steady stare, tells her there is an issue.

"What you mean?"

"We… broke up. She didn't die. She… her family is right there, too, so she is with them, but she is with my parents, too, sometimes… because of the children."

She stares at him, her mouth open in disbelief.

So what he saying? He not a widower? But she saw it written down. His ID – his document – what was it? It said he was a widower. She saw it in writing on one of those official documents. Perhaps the print-out from immigration when he enter Canada, or something? She doesn't remember what the document was. Anyway, he told her. That was the important thing. And yes, she saw it written down.

"So…" She takes a deep breath. Holds it. Pulls her shoulders back. Her head moves, tilts to the right. She watches him.

"I should have told you."

She lifts her hand to her cheek, remembering.

"Told me what? But you told me. Should have told me what?" Her voice is quiet. "When you told me your wife was dead – that wasn't true?"

"No. And I didn't tell you she was dead. I told you – I'm a widower."

"So that mean your wife dead!" Her voice goes up. Her left hand makes a quick unfolding gesture, opening itself out questioningly.

"We broke up. When we say widow or widower, it may not mean the person is dead. You're just not together any more."

"When *we* say? When who say?" Both hands make the opening out gesture now. "Everybody know widower mean your wife dead! So I have to get a special kind of dictionary to talk to you? Who is the *we* that know?"

We! Who is this WE *he suddenly talking about? He and his American Negro patisan? So now is* WE? *Papa Bondyé, what I get myself into?*

"Oseyan, I'm so sorry. I fell for you as soon as I met you."

So now he writing song!

"You're beautiful and you are especially beautiful when we talk about the black cause. I really fell for you."

"Look! Don't tell me no dotishness! You lied to me. If I stupid enough to pick up a married man on my own, that is my choice – and that is not what I plan for myself. You lied to me. You lie to me?"

"I'm not married. We divorce. When we go to my home in Georgia, you are my wife."

Well they better be divorced! She have his child and they well stand up in church and married.

"So you not married to somebody else?"

"We divorce."

She stares at him. Were they ever married in the first place, he and that woman, or had she been his common-law wife? And was "divorce" to be taken in the same way as "widower"? It have a story there that at this point she don't even want to know.

257

Gwen... suddenly she wishes she could talk to Gwen. But could she tell Gwen this? She can't tell anybody this! She doesn't even know what *this* is, and beg God pardon, but she don't want to know! Oseyan turns her head to the right, watching their room door and listening for the sound of Wilfred from the room, as if the sound would make a difference. She turns back to look at him.

"So you my husband?" she asks. "Am I your wife?"

"Come on, Oseyan. What..."

"I asked you a question."

"You are the only wife I have. I love you more than I can explain. When I met you in Montreal, I knew immediately that I would be happy with you in my life. You are my only wife. Me and Myra – we broke up a long time ago. We divorce."

So they were divorced! She is not even going to ask how or when and she don't want to see no paper, because she realise now that paper mean nothing. Paper could lie as much as mouth because paper take what mouth tell it and seal it in writing. So they divorce. They divorce. She has plenty questions about that but no use asking them to get some kind of *we* answer because she ent have no dictionary for this language. *Papa Bondyé*, this is where I find myself. Who to talk to? She must talk to somebody. Not Uncle Eero, even if she could reach him, because he already thought she was too *hurry hurry* with this married business. Their cousin in New York? She had helped a lot during the time of the convention, but she didn't know her well enough to talk about things like this. And Cassandra, who shared the rent, or Benjamin, their lodger – of course not. Suddenly she wonders if Benjamin, who must be about Baron's age, is a *widower*. Oh God! She needs to talk to somebody, somebody like Aunty Gerda. But she needs somebody here! Gwen! She needs to talk to somebody. Nobody. There is nobody. Well, she wouldn't even feel good talking to anybody but Ma. And Ma gone. *I'm on my own! Oh God, I on my own!*

He leans forward. He begins – in a voice so quiet it doesn't sound like his – "Oseyan..."

Oseyan stands up. "Don't talk to me," she says slowly, in a cold, detached voice. "You have nothing to say to me. The only reason I'm here still listening is because I am far from home. I far from me people. And because my grandmother is dead. I might as well say that, because you know that already. Just have nothing to say to me. Give me time, let me figure out what this is and what to do. And just leave me alone, you hear me? Just leave me alone." She begins to walk away and stops at the door to their bedroom. She turns to face him. "By the way, I miss my periods so I know I am pregnant again. Congratulations, Elder. Congratulations." She stands looking blankly, not so much at him as at the empty space in front of her. Then she turns, opens the room door, and goes inside, taking her thoughts with her, leaving him to his.

5. Butler, Georgia.

To her, the visit is a mixture of emotions. Nothing mixed in her responses to the place. That is all approval. She likes Butler, Georgia. She feels as if she recognises it. It reminds her of home. Not just La Digue, but home – La Baye.

Not the dirty train – well dirty and nasty in truth, and people – white people – looking at you as if you're from another planet. On that train journey into the south, she can see that people look, with a question in their eyes, from her – a woman looking white – to him, the black man with her. Now that she is here in this country, she begins to understand why people here and in Canada always talk about black this and white that. They make you see things in black and white just from the way people look at you. You see things in black and white at home, too, but is not a lot of white to see there, so here is a different, more hostile kind of seeing. She remembers Sir as she thinks *hostile*. She thinks *surly*, too, but is both. Is a *surly hostility*. She won't lower her head because it seems to be expected of black people. In a way, she thinks, she has seen this at home, too – the sideways way a worker – well, a black worker – might look at a white or high-up brown-skinned person when they're around. It's just that here they are everywhere, so if you are going to look down or away, you have to keep doing it. There are more of them. That is it. She tries to imagine a La Digue full of white people and only a few people looking like Ma and Cousin Mildred and Uncle Eero. It may have been so once, she thinks, but she hadn't grown up with that. She keeps her head at an angle that might not be considered offensive because she understands that that is its own kind of problem, and she doesn't look at anybody. *Don't engage!* That's what Uncle Eero said he had learned.

In Butler, where his people are from, she goes with Baron into a shop and it looks and feels like Mr Jeremiah's shop at the corner, just before you turn into Holy Innocents – the shop itself and the people in it. She smiles because the atmosphere makes her feel so at home. It is the most relaxed she has felt in her head since coming into America. The shopkeeper, who even looks like Mr Jeremiah – a tall, dark-skinned black man with his hair cut short – straightens up from leaning against the board counter, looks with what seems slight surprise and curiosity at her, turns and shouts, "Baron! That you?" He pushes up the board divider, comes out, his arms open in greeting. "Man, you a sight for sore eyes! Don't stand there like stranger. Y'all staying around for a while, or what? And this pretty lady your madam?" He turns right around and smiles broadly at Oseyan. He even tips an imaginary hat. "Ma'am, mighty pleased to meet you. Look at that smile! Pretty. Pretty." Turns back to Baron. "You looking good, man. You sure look like you living high on the hog. You a sight for sore eyes, Baron, you and your family. Your family, no? Is what I hear tell. Yes. Yes. Yes." He leans back against the counter, puts up his elbows, his eyes taking them in. Baron is smiling. "Yes," he says. "This is my wife, Oseyan. Our little son is back home with the folks. Oseyan, Jerome is the man I been telling you about."

Jerome walks forward, stretches out a hand toward Oseyan. "Very pleased to meet you," he says. "Welcome to these parts. Welcome." He steps back, turns his broad smile in Baron's direction again. "I won't even ask what you been saying about me." He laughs out loud.

Someone passing in the road outside calls out and Jerome lifts his voice in a shouted return greeting. This is home! She wants to stay. In her head she hears Baron caution, *Inside here is only a little part of the story.* Yes. He keeps telling her that in Georgia Negroes are killed simply because they are Negro. But it is so good to meet people like this. Not just the shopkeeper, but the two other people in the shop – two women, one about her age, one about Auntie Gerda's – she miss Auntie Gerda so much that she find everybody look like Auntie Gerda – buying what they're buying but openly interested, smiling, and looking as if they are part of the conversation. This is so good.

When she saw his parents' house – the house he had grown up in – she thought of Ma. It wasn't perched on a hillside like Ma's, but it was the same board house with different rooms that his father had added over the years. And in the little plot behind the house they grew not golden apples and green peas and soursop but soybeans, corn – yes, she recognises corn – and peanuts. Not in their yard, but in some big person's garden she also sees peaches growing on trees for the first time. Before that, she'd only seen them in stores in Montreal and Philadelphia. She noted that peaches seemed to have long leaves like the leaves of the soursop, and the flowers looked like those of a tree – she couldn't remember the name – up at the top of Waterfall. As she looks around, trying to find plants she recognises, she suddenly remembers the lady on the boat. *Wait non!* It looks like here she has the eye of a tourist! But she is more interested in the plants than the people. Well, not really. With all these things like lynching and such evil, when you know that people are trying to kill you and yours, you have to be interested in what they are doing. That's why she and Baron would have a lot of work to do. You can't forget that. They in this country to work, too.

From what Baron said about what she thought of as his parents' property, she discovers the land doesn't belong to them but to some big farmer whom they have to pay with part of what they get from the land.

Baron's father, tall and *londjè*, or *lenguè*, as her grandmother would say – bean stringy – asks about another son, Baron's younger brother, whom she had seen in Philadelphia. She hears Baron and his father talking about money, and his father complaining that that boy – the son – ain't got the sense that God gave a billygoat, that he was constantly moving about the place. Everybody is leaving, his mother says. Well, she thinks of Baron's mother as Ma, but she doesn't look anything like Ma. She is not as tall as Ma, and she doesn't have those cheekbones. Her face is fuller, softer. A smile comes when Oseyan puts Wilfred into her arms. She looks up at Oseyan and says, "He has his father's looks. He looks like his father. I'm happy you brought my grandson to see his people." She smiles again, turns away, holding her grandson, walking with him, patting him on the back. Baron's father is still complaining – or maybe just speaking in a complaining voice – and as she thinks this, she remembers how Ma always seemed to be quarrelling, although she was just talking. His father says that his children are like everybody else, going north to do something or the other. He wants to know – "So Baron, who all from here you see in those parts where you travel?"And Oseyan thinks of Ma saying, *Everybody going Away. Once you get big and leave school, you have to think of what is the next step. So yes – we going try to send you Away.*

Georgia has a familiar feeling. So perhaps she liked this man, her husband, because she recognised him? Perhaps she felt that her husband was home people even if he wasn't from home? But being in the house with his children is not at all comfortable. She has to keep an eye on the baby because these children of his are not too pleased to see this new baby that is their father's child but not their mother's. And she actually saw the mother – Myra she is called. Met her in a kind of way, because one day she was there with the children, distant, giving no greeting, so not a real meeting. She is a black woman, as tall as herself, with a face round like her friend Marjorie's, but she is not smiley like Marjorie. Of course not – there is no reason for her to smile, although she doesn't seem to be making any claim. She says nothing, except what she was saying to her children and Oseyan couldn't hear that. Later when Oseyan sees her through the window, she is leaving. She just made that quick pass, and then perhaps she went home to her people or to wherever it was she was living – or staying now that they are here. She seems to find it hard to look at Baron and Oseyan decides that she wouldn't wonder what they had to say to each other and if there are things about this widow/widower business she still doesn't know. What is clear is that she, Oseyan, is his wife, and his mother and father accepted her as such, although they didn't say a lot, and it seems clear that any wife from before is out of the picture. She isn't thinking that she has won some special prize, but it is clear that this is the way things are. His children with the woman aren't pleased that their father has a new wife and they show it. Well, they are children – seven? six? They can't be expected to feel good about not having their father around. And their attitude emphasised that their father was no longer in their mother's life. Oseyan said nothing to Baron about the situation while they were there. His parents accepted her as his wife; he introduced her as such to everyone, and that was it.

One day, when Wilfred is alone in the room with Baron's big daughter Ezra, seven years old or so, he suddenly starts screaming. Oseyan rushes into the room and she could swear, although she hasn't seen it happen, that the child pinched him or something. She would keep her son close to her while she is in this place. If the surroundings are like home, the atmosphere inside the house is definitely not like home. As far as she is concerned, the visit is over. It is time to go.

6. Leaving Philadelphia.

The family is growing. Wilfred is walking and pulling down everything he can put his hands on. His father shouts and scolds him as if the child is a big man. Oseyan was just having a few months of ease from the constant *yehyeh* that came with teething, and now there is another one on the way. It is as if, she thinks, her body was just waiting. It's true she can do without having those bloody cloths to wash all the time, but another little one now to take care of is a different thing. But family is like that. Is so Auntie Gerda had them, one after the other. Well, we will see what going happen now. Right now she still can't touch Baron for sure, but – anyway, things seem to have sorted themselves out to some extent, and here she is already set up with the second one inside. Time will tell. *Tan kay di.*

And they are moving soon. The Movement wants them to start a Liberty Hall in Nebraska. *Nebraska, capital Omaha.* She remembers that from extra lessons. She didn't reach Standard VI to use the *Sixth Book* but Mr Ansel had done some lessons from that book

263

with her, because, as he and her other teachers said, she was showing such promise. *Omaha is on the western bank of the Missouri river...* Then... what else? What is the next line? Something something. She tries to remember the rhythm, to see if the words will come. She is getting forgetful with age! Or perhaps it is something else. And then, quietly, she hums the remembered beat of the words she had recited in class – the beat established, the words come. *Omaha is another instance of the remarkable progress of American cities. Its origin dates only from 1854, yet it has now a population of 25,000. It is a great railway junction, northern and southern, as well as eastern and western trunk lines meeting there; and it bids fair to become, ere long, the chief inland city of the Western States.* [20]

Oh! She remember it, boy! They are going to set up a UNIA branch in Omaha. She wonders if the African people in Omaha shared in the "remarkable progress" of the city. Most likely not. The "Midwest", as they call it, is still in America, and it would be a miracle if it were all that different from other places. At least there she wouldn't expect the Jim Crow existence that Baron always talking about – but who knows!

In a trolley-car, she looks up at a fading poster: **Spit. Spread death.** That poster must have been there from the last two years, when the influenza epidemic was raging. What would it be like in Nebraska? Perhaps her next child would be born there. *A child is a child*, Ma said when Auntie Gerda was pregnant the second time and wishing for a girl. *Papa Bondyé konnèt sa ki bon. What God give, that is what you want and that is what you take.* That was Ma. Cousin Mildred had said, *Or if you don't want it, leave it there!* Cousin Mildred! Well, she want it, if that is what God decides.

Omaha is not going to be easy, but there is work to be done and it is where the Association thought her skills and Baron's could best be used. Just last year, right in that place she thinks is not Jim Crow place, there was that horrible thing Baron said his home state was famous for – a lynching. He told her that members of his own family had been lynched. Her mind went to Uncle Eero, to Auntie Gerda's boys... to... She didn't know what to say. It frightened her. They really roll things back in the South for Negroes after that period they call the Reconstruction, he explained to her. Perhaps his father was a little boy then, if he was even born, so that is only a thing he hear about. One day he will tell her some of the things he heard about the period. Ah well! Now they were going to Omaha, where this lynching had just happened, and where young white men back from the war were up in arms about everything – especially trying to make sure that Negroes know they don't belong in this country. They talked about that in the Movement, and Cassandra had slipped her a 1919 article that came from a newspaper, the *Springfield Republican*. She has it nearby.

Crowd Lynches Negro at Omaha after Long Riot: Sheriff and Deputies fight Immense Mob for Nine Hours From Top of Burning Courthouse – Then Flames Compel Relinquishment of Prisoner. Omaha, Sept. 28: William Brown, Negro, alleged to have assaulted a white girl, was dragged from the county jail at 11 o'clock to-night and hanged to an electric light-pole, following a struggle of nine hours by an immense mob to wrest him from the sheriff.

That was part of all these race riots that they call the *Red Summer,* happening the same year she came into this frightening country. And it sounded like the man wasn't guilty of whatever offence they said he had committed. But guilt was not the point. Being Black was the point. So they lynch this man in Omaha just – not last year – the year before last. And a lot of other things like that have happened in Omaha and other places since then. It seemed that those doing the lynching know they can get away with it – even take people out of the hands of the police. Well, it's their police. And that is where she and Baron going – Omaha. So, she tells herself, *Don't feel so good that you're not going to the South.*

"God don't like ugly," she said when she and Baron talked about it. "Perhaps they think they won some kind of victory but the race is not for the swiftest. Think about it," she says, "'Do to others as you would like them to do to you.' Matthew 7:12. Is that what they want to get from Negro people?"

"The problem," Baron says, "is that they don't even think we are people, so they owe us nothing. They do not think it is possible for anything to be done unto them, because those with whom they deal are, in their estimation, not people. But," he says, "they should

265

think of Galatians 5:13: 'You, my brothers and sisters, were called to be free.' And that," he says, "is what we must teach in Nebraska as in all other places. We were not made to be anybody's *Jim Crow*. We are called to be *free,* in every sense of the word."

"Amen," she says. "Amen!"

They are ready to fight. They are fired up each time they talk about Nebraska and about the struggle of Negroes in America and throughout America – Sir's America, the whole continent.

They leave Philadelphia later than they planned – they don't want to miss the thirty-one days and thirty-one nights of the Second International convention of the Negro Peoples of the World. Wilfred has won the heart of Cassandra and she said that since her little darling was deserting her, she will give him all her free time during the month of August. So between that and her cousin in New York, Oseyan is able to go to some of the celebration though she is in the last three months of her pregnancy and a little nervous about her health these days. In the end, they decide to wait to hear Mr Garvey's speech on the last day of the Convention. Oseyan always liked it when he linked the idea of the Convention with Emancipation; it emphasised that the Convention of the Negro Peoples of the World is happening during the month of August for a reason. Garvey says:

> *Some worked to bring about the emancipation, because they saw the danger of perpetual slavery. They brought about the liberation of 4,000,000 black people. They passed away, and the others started to work, but the opposition against them is too strong; the opposition against them is weighing them down.*

And then he says:

> *The world has gone mad; the world has become too material; the world has lost its spirit of kinship with God, and man can see nothing else but prejudice, avarice and greed. Avarice and greed will destroy the world and I am appealing to white, black and yellow whose hearts, whose souls are touched with the true spirit of humanity, with the true feeling of human brotherhood, to preach the doctrine of human love, more, to preach it louder, to preach it longer, because there is great need for it in the world at this time.*[21]

And now she is hearing about lynchings right where they are going. Just hearing about it from far, and then feeling it all around you – those are two different things. Garvey says:

> And we are the more aggrieved because of the lynch rope, because of segregation, because of the Jim Crowism that is used, practiced and exercised here in this country and in other parts of the world by the white nations of the earth, wherever Negroes happen accidentally or otherwise to find themselves. If there is no safety for Negroes in the white world, I cannot see what right they have to parcel out the homeland, the country of Negroes, without consulting Negroes and asking their permission so to do. Therefore, we are aggrieved. This question of prejudice will be the downfall of civilization, and I warn the white race of this, and of their doom. I hope they will take heed, because the handwriting is on the wall. No portion of humanity, no group of humanity, has an abiding right, an everlasting right, an eternal right to oppress other sections or portions of humanity. God never gave them the right, and if there is such a right, man arrogated it to himself, and God in all ages has been displeased with the arrogance of man. I warn those nations that believe themselves above human justice. You cannot long ignore the laws of God; you cannot long ignore the commandments of God; you cannot long ignore human justice, and exist. Your arrogance will destroy you, and I warn the races and the nations that have arrogated to themselves the right to oppress, the right to circumscribe, the right to keep down other races. I warn them that the hour is coming when the oppressed will rise in their might, in their majesty, and throw off the yoke of ages.

To Oseyan, Mr Garvey is as impressive as usual. Yes. Emancipation. She is ready, after this convention, to begin the UNIA work in Nebraska. When she turns to look at Baron she sees his face is eager. She sees the light, the enthusiasm she loves. After she tells him how much she admires Mr Garvey as a West Indian for making the date of the convention remember Emancipation, and they talk about how West Indian and North American experiences have been both the same and different, he asks, "Did you know that at one time there were Negro representatives in Congress from the South?"

"When?" It is clear from her smile that she doesn't believe him.

"Remember I said I would tell you more about Reconstruction, well that was it. After the civil war," he says, "when the North saw how bad things were, after southern Whites were killing Negro people openly, there was a lot of pressure on emancipationist whites to improve things. I think it was Grant, Ulysses Grant, right after the Civil War, who was campaigning to get rid of anything to do with slavery. Negro men got the vote. It was a period called Reconstruction. So you had a few Negro people – and it was men, so – you had a few Negro men in Congress."

"What! So what happened?"

"Politics. Eventually, white people north and south got to-gether and decide they have to assert white authority. So things get rolled back."

"Well, you-all were ahead of us on that one! We don't have the vote in the Caribbean yet, and is not about rolling back – we never had it! So you-all were ahead!"

"Remember the things we talk about. Is not that one set ahead –"

"True. True. Is about what white people in positions see as their interest at any particular time – they make the rules to suit!"

"Exactly."

It is so good when they can talk like this – and realise they have the same interests, the same wish to struggle for their people's advancement. Perhaps they can get past this rough part of their journey together. She can't act as if everything is suddenly good again, because she really cannot forget that he lied to her, but moments like this remind her that they think alike, and they work well together – from the Caribbean and the American South. Ah well! *Tan kay di. Time will tell.*

Perhaps Omaha will make it possible for them to live together, for her to touch him and let him touch her, not because he thinks he has rights as a husband – because that idea would just get her damn vex, especially after everything she knows now – but because she wants to be touched. Really, just talking about Omaha and the work there and Emancipation and the push for the freedom of Negro people… all of that helping to keep her eyes on what is perhaps – perhaps – more important for everybody. They both have serious work to do.

7. Thoughts about the Journey.

They decide that travelling by the train is their best bet for getting to Omaha. A trip by bus on the Lincoln Highway with the baby would take even longer and be more uncomfortable. They think about travelling by car with someone from the UNIA but that might be a risk. Besides, Baron isn't sure about this new Highway. The UNIA wants them in Nebraska and Baron says the officers would help plan the trip to get them there by train. Baron's younger brother is also now in Nebraska and he will help them settle in. Although they had travelled into the South on the train before, Wilfred was then a baby and not a curious little boy, and besides they had been in their own Jim Crow section. She surprised herself by thinking that this had its merits when the other section belonged to mad people. A baby on a train with mad people in it wasn't something to look forward to.

And travelling by train makes her see that *Jim Crow* is everywhere, because she is never sure what a look means. Well, sometimes you know. There are those who would actually spit when they passed anywhere near you. She has seen it happen. Then there are those who would say something, just in case you didn't know. She doesn't want to think about the words they say. White people back home let you know they don't think you are much, mainly because you work for them, or because they say things about you in their meetings and then you get to hear – like when Sir or some thinking person hear something and might pass it on. Or they pull you in bush on their estate and take what they want. So yes, things bad, but here is a different kind of bad.

Here they could do exactly what they want – like lynch you – and it doesn't matter. And the look on their faces is always there to show you that they think you are nothing. It's worse and it's different. She wonders if it is because back home was small, and although white English people in charge, you have other Grenada high-ups – some of them half white – in position saying what they want for the country, and you even have other people – Black people like Marryshow – writing things in newspapers – and saying what they think. Though, she thinks, here you have people too – Ida B. Wells, Frederick Douglass and others. Even so, the situation is different because the history has been different, as Baron said. There are loud black voices here, too, struggling in a very different situation, and this, where she is, is not even the south. Sometimes she is afraid that Baron is in more danger when he travels with her, because people might think she is white. She asked him about that.

He said, "There's no such thing. If you not white, you Negro."

"I know. *I* wasn't saying. I mean, how *they* would see it."

"They see it like that. Is white or Black. If they decide you white, I'm in trouble. If they think you are Negro, both of us in trouble. So let's just relax and be! Let who think it's their business to figure, go figure."

Mr Garvey was right. Nobody should fight in their own little corner. Though experiences were different and strategies might have to differ, as Negro people the fight is one big fight. People have to know that. She and Baron have to tell people that.

Afterward, when they reach Nebraska, Oseyan thinks again about her Royal Reader and the word *savage*. In fact, one thing that helps her get through the trip is constantly repeating in her head a sentence from that book: "*Suppose yourself, Gentle Reader, watching a savage arranging his snow-shoes, preparatory to entering the gloomy forest.*"[22]

She can't help it. She shouldn't let them enter her thoughts, but she keeps thinking about the savages who lynch people, and whom she would probably have to meet in this gloomy forest.

8. Girl Child in Nebraska.

She can't remember which was which. Gwen had told her. Pointy belly, so a girl? Pointy belly, so a boy? Anyway, she has a pointy belly, extending in a definite line out in front of her, and the baby is a girl who comes into the world in October. She names her Olive, after Aunty Gerda's first little girl.

Wilfred is one year and eight months old when his sister arrives. He looks at her and he gives a speech. That is how his mother explained it later. Wilfred stands looking at his baby sister with intensity and then embarks on a long series of sounds his mother does not understand. And as he speaks, he gestures with his hands, opening them, nodding his head, opening his eyes expressively, acting, she thinks, as if he is giving advice. *That child look like his father.* The thought comes again as she watches him. Finally, he stops, turns around and goes to sit on his chair and finish his porridge. He says one more thing, shrugging his shoulders and opening his right hand, as if he has to let them know he is serious, before putting a spoonful of porridge into his mouth. Seated on the couch with the baby, Oseyan chuckles, looks down at the little girl in her arms, and asks, "You understand that? You know what he say? Yes? Yes?" – smiling at her daughter – "You-all have a language together? Yes."

Olive frets, draws her legs up, bunches them close to her body, wrinkles her face, looks as if she might cry. Then she laughs. Her mother says, "I know! I know! He's so bossy, isn't he? That's right, girl. Sometimes you just have to laugh."

Omaha is what had been promised. Another of Baron's brothers, a younger one living in Omaha, had told them that this was no place to live, that he couldn't even do his little gambling business without having police dip into his affairs. Baron no doubt does not plan on getting into gambling. Still, he warns Oseyan that she must always be careful. Remember, he says, that you are a Negro in America. That means that you can be found dead any day. You and the children, be careful. Even when you go to work in white people's houses – and he hopes the sewing takes off so that she doesn't have to do that too much – be careful. She knows this. Ma, Cousin Mildred, Auntie Gerda, everyone had told her that. Just that here it is worse. Baron's face and her experiences on the train as well as in New York and Philadelphia told her this country was different. The people here have the same kind of madness they said the Grand Etang mongoose was getting in Grenada.

She has not found it easy to be intimate with Baron after the widower revelation. Her spirit took a knock at that betrayal and she has avoided his touch for a full year. When she thinks about it later, she figure that whenever they talk about their work for the movement, both of them get fired up, bodily, mentally. Well, that's how it started.

They are doing all they can at the Omaha Liberty Hall – and the government and their secret agencies are doing all they can to stop them. With the children and the UNIA work and the jobs she has to do to keep body and soul together, neither Oseyan nor Baron can go to the third UNIA convention, but they know they are doing all they can to support the success of the movement and the efforts of the Honourable Marcus Mosiah Garvey.

She hasn't spoken out loud to her grandmother for a while, but now she whispers, *Things are not better here, Ma. But I will be part of this struggle. All over the world, Ma, Black people in trouble. But I'm here.* As she kneads the flour to make the fried bake Baron has discovered he also likes, she says in a louder voice, *Is here they plant me. Is here I will grow.* And as Ma turns to face her, she says again emphatically, *Wi. Ye planté mwen isit. Mwen ka pofité isit.*

From behind her she hears, *Zafè zò. Zafè zò.*

Oseyan turns. Seated at the table on the chair where she has placed her, her little daughter is pouring much too much water into a small amount of play flour from the cup she has been given for that purpose. She is intent on making a mess obviously pleasing to her, if one is to judge by the laughing face she turns up to her mother. *Zafè zò, Mama,* she says. Oseyan doesn't know when the child picked up those words. But now she can say to her mother, *Zafè zò. That's your business* or, in the way that Ma meant it, *Do your do* or *let it be.* Oseyan grins, holds her flour-filled hands behind her so as not to put the mess on her daughter, leans down and nuzzles playfully at the child's cheek. *Zafè zò, tifi mwen. Do your do, my little girl. That's your business.* And then, to make her laugh, she sings softly a few bars of the song the child likes: *Alouette, gentile alouette; Alouette, je te plumerai.* The child giggles. She loves her Mom.

Around October 1922, when Olive is not much more than one year old, Oseyan misses her periods, and since they happen like clockwork, she knows a third child is on the way. She remembers how she and Gwen used to giggle about a woman and a man who lived at the top of Waterfall, and ask with delight and smug satisfaction, *That is all they doing?* She can't help wondering if people will say the same thing about her that she and Gwen used to say about this woman. *Like every Monday morning she pregnant!* In fact, with the special kind of sneaky cruelty of the young and

272

thoughtless, she and Gwen would hide at the top of the hill when they found out that the woman – Miss Clementine – was pregnant again, and when they saw her in front of the house washing her clothes at the jukking-board, they would amble along the road, and Oseyan would shout innocently, *Morning, Miss Clementine,* and then Gwen would say, *Ay! What day today is, girl? Oho! Is Monday.* And both of them would say, *Monday morning, wi.* Oseyan knew better than to say her part in this play with Gwen too loud, because even if Miss Clementine and Ma weren't friendsy friendsy, if she happened to understand what was going on and tell Ma, Oseyan knew that when Ma was angry, her *little red tail* would pay for it. So she kept her voice down.

Her second boy, Norton, is born in May. Oseyan wonders afterward if she should have given him that name to carry. When she was trying to understand the mystery of the birth certificate she uncovered when she had to travel, she had remembered that Ma said once, *He is a reprobate, but their name always good, no matter how much reprobate they might be. Is ours that bad. That's why they take away ours and give us theirs.* She knew that wasn't what Uncle Eero believed. When Ma said things like that, Uncle Eero would *steupes* and say, *Ma, I don't think I know you sometimes.* She thinks of all of that when she is deciding how to name her third child. And once she decided, she talked to the baby in her stomach. *Use it how you could, you hear, my son. It could be blessing and curse. Make it blessing. Se bènnédikssyon mwen vlé ba'w. Is blessing I want to give you.* The child must have understood something. From the first time she takes him to church, Norton loves the singing and he crows his delight when his father preach. He put his little hands together in approving applause and grin up at his mother and around at the congregation. This, his movements announce, is wonderful. His big brother Wilfred looks on with no expression and his big sister Olive looks disapproving. Norton ignores them and just shows his enjoyment, looking around for faces with which to share his approval of the singing and movement.

Oseyan thinks of the UNIA meetings, too, as "church". Like church, they make her continue to marvel at the difference between a person's public face and the private one. When she fell in love with that preaching man in Montreal, the tall, handsome black man whose words were inspirational fire, she would not have guessed that he was shy in company. In public, with other people, he seemed tongue-tied, unable to express himself. It was as if, when the spirit left him, he was a different person. But she knows him when the spirit is with him, so she loves him still – well, she loves him especially when she doesn't think too much about everything. And as Ma would say, *It happen already. And even if is only think you think till death do us part, you and God know, and he going help you make it possible.* That's how she thinks about it now.

It wasn't hard for them to get the seven people the UNIA officers said they needed to make it a Liberty Hall. In fact, it was that from the first meeting she had planned with Baron, just two weeks after Olive was born. There is no time to waste. They have to build the movement. The opening song, "From Greenland's icy mountains", always makes her think of The Royal Reader and the poem by Thomas Campbell about Greenland as *a cluster of islands perpetually joined together by ice.* She wonders if this song is from the Royal Reader, too, so she asks one of the officers in the Movement – a man with regalia and everything – and he tells her it is a real hymn, written by one of those 18th or 19th century Anglican bishops, a man called Reginald Heber. He was Bishop of Calcutta, he says. *I knew it*, she thinks. *He sound like one of those lords in the Royal Reader. 18th or 19th century.* She felt pleased that she had recognised his voice; *it good for while we are finding our struggle.* Ma had told her, *Learn it how they give you, and study so you could write your own thing. Yes, Ma.*

So their meetings always start with the Heber man's song, "From Greenland's icy mountains", and after that, Baron, as pastor, leads the group in prayer. Then there are words from the Honourable Marcus Mosiah Garvey, and even when the authorities are chasing him all over the place, the words are inspiring. In the discussion afterwards, Oseyan brings up the point that they should always remember that those were the words of the leader of the United Negro Improvement Association *and* African Communities League. Sometimes people forget the last part, but it is important to remember that he spoke remembering the league of African communities all over the world.

Some officers from the Movement visited their home in Nebraska to talk about the problems the leader was having and about how the Liberty Hall could support him. They congratulated both of them, Baron and Oseyan, for preaching and contributing to building the Omaha Liberty Hall: *a firm group you have, a really firm group*. And they thanked the Sister for writing such focused reports of the Omaha meetings. They want the family's help with some things they would have to discuss at length.

They sit and talk, tell them about issues within the Movement. In that part of the exchange, relaxed and informal, Oseyan can see how uncomfortable her husband is. He keeps his head down, mumbles as if he can't find words, looks miserable. She wonders if it is because so many of the UNIA people sound Caribbean? But no. He wasn't like that with other Caribbean people they had met in Philadelphia, and he certainly is not like that with his brothers and other people he knows. Well, family is family, so that is different. Perhaps it has something to do with those he thought of as authority figures? She doesn't know. When one of the UNIA officers asks, "So, Brother, how are things going?" Baron almost chokes. He smiles and says something incoherent.

"People coming out to your meetings? Are they well attended?"

Oh of course they are! she thinks. *You should hear him preach!* But he has to say it himself. His weak *Oh yes*, and his small, self-effacing smile makes Oseyan pleased that they have heard him preach in Montreal, Philadelphia and New York, so they know his strength.

She says, "He's being humble, but you know how powerful he is in the pulpit."

They laugh, agreeing.

Afterward, Baron is not happy. With her, he has a voice. "So when people are trying to talk to me, you feel you have to interrupt – cut across me – and say something!"

That is so unfair. Oseyan says nothing. The look on his face is not one she has seen before. He seems angry, tense, almost as if he doesn't know her. But sometimes people look like that when they get angry. It is still unsettling.

9. It hasn't happened.

Mr Garvey was arrested at the beginning of 1922. Now it is the middle of July, around the time they are working extra hard for the convention, even if this year they aren't going. Things are becoming more and more tense with the other Negro American organisations that don't like Mr Garvey's style and some of the things he says. But their organisation is still growing, and perhaps, Oseyan thinks, because the South of the country is like the West Indies – well, that is how she feels it – the Movement is really growing in the imagination of the people from there. People understand Mr Garvey's goals.

Oseyan is thinking about all she has to do for the convention – make sure she has a list of all the new members, write up minutes for the next meeting, continue the membership drive. She is standing in the kitchen, thinking, too, about what she must do before going out to the meeting tonight – stew some of the vegetables she has in this bowl, clean up the kitchen after preparing a meal – and work out how best to organise Norton, who is just over three months old. Should she go with formula? Will he have to be fed before they get back from this meeting? Should she nurse him before they go?

Baron has stopped asking her to cook him some of the things he likes to eat – like rabbit and pork. He knows she doesn't like to cook those. Sometimes he cooks for himself, and when he does that she stays out of the kitchen. She is not going to cook pork and rabbit. They have chickens, and they both like rearing and sometimes eating them. She keeps a clean chicken coop, just like at home with Ma. He likes that, and she makes sure to clean it out regularly and show the older children how to keep it clean, even though they don't like the job. Ma was particular about cleaning out the fowl run, but here you have to be even more so, because you are what they call Negro. As particular as she is, some neighbours still complain. Anyway, with the chickens, she and Baron could at least share a meal they love.

But today, something seems to have irritated him enough to make him remember what he wants to remember and forget what he choose to forget. He would be silent in company where perhaps he feel less than other people, but he is always ready to take things out on her and the children. He would shout at them for a slipper left here, a little book not put away, a shout too loud from outside the house. He have strength with them.

With all of that, though, he is a good provider. Nothing to say there. In that, he reminds her of Uncle Eero, and of what she heard about Poopa. Sometimes he goes out working, building people's fences, doing small carpentry jobs, and when he comes back, he is never too tired to do some kind of project, just to make living better – repairing, putting up something – he is like that. He has also started to grow broccoli and cauliflower, and sow eggplant indoors when it is too cold, and then plant them out later.

But his temper – woy! That is one thing she can't get used to. He isn't like Ma who would shout at you too much but whose angry face you knew somehow would never do you real damage. Well, perhaps she is excusing Ma, but there is something about Baron's anger she caan understand. When he vex, is like in his head he go some place that is his alone, and he shout at the children as if they don't belong to him – well, they are their own people, yes, but he helped bring them into the world. She remembers how, when Wilfred was born, he looked at that little boy as if he were his world. Not now. It really upsets her when he show that anger and harshness to the children.

As she is thinking this, he walks up behind her and tells her that he wants her to cook pork. Make a soup, he says, not a stew. Where, she wonders, has this come from? He had asked her to cook pork one day in Montreal, after they came back from a UNIA meeting, and she had explained her objections. After that, when they were in Philadelphia, he had come in with pork sometimes, and cooked it himself, and she didn't mind. It is what he likes. She doesn't eat it and doesn't think it is something that should be eaten, but they are different people. When he had asked her to cook it in Montreal, Uncle Eero was there – in fact, they were in Uncle Eero's flat and she was cooking for everybody that day. When she told him *No, I don't eat pork,* he had just looked from her to Eero and there was nothing else to say. Eero hadn't even looked up. And she had said something like, *but I'll do a nice little gravy for you with the beef and with garlic and everything.* He had smiled and seemed to accept that. He didn't say anything else. Later, she explained that pork was not something they ever eat in their house when she was growing up. Her grandmother had trained them that way, and they had just not eaten it – for religious reasons, her grandmother said; even though she was Anglican and not Seventh Day Adventist, she still didn't eat pork. In fact, Ma always said that they could go to any church. He had listened to all that, said nothing. Her no was the end of that conversation.

Now, here in Nebraska, when she tells him no, it hangs in the place like she remembers Faith's *damn* and *blasted* hanging in the house on the hill in La Digue all those years ago, while she and Amèlie waited to hear what Ma would do. This time she is not thinking about what would follow the *no;* she is just aware that it seems to have filled the room with tension. Perhaps he will sigh and then he cook his pork for himself if he want it so bad? What happens takes her completely by surprise. She cannot say she saw something coming because she was not looking. In the house in La Digue they had been listening for Ma, because they knew how angry she would be. Now, if she thinks anything at all, it is, well, she has answered and they will talk about something else. Perhaps he might even engage her in a conversation about pork and she will tell him about the lesson – *pork is the flesh of the pig or the sow* – or she might tell him that it just wasn't eaten in her family – on both sides as far as she knew – and that had probably started in Africa. He would try to persuade her, and they might not agree but they would talk – about things that had come with families from Africa, because Africa was itself such a mixture of cultures and countries – a continent, not a country – and they would talk about things they had picked up from the Americas, because, with white people from Europe like the French and the English, and people from Africa who were from the Yoruba and the Fon and the Asante, and the people who were already there like the Shawnee and the Chippewa and the Carib, and people from Asia like the Indians and the Chinese – she couldn't even finish counting them all – they were well mixed up over there, as they are here in this part of America, too. But she thinks all of this in a muddled kind of way afterwards, when she is asking herself how else it could have gone. She has said no and they would move on.

So she does not see the hand coming. It hits her hard in the face, a cuff really, smashing into her jaw, the right side of her face, as she is about to turn around, almost knocking her off her feet. She stumbles, both from the shock and from the force of the blow. It takes her by surprise, like a belt across her back that she hasn't been expecting in class. Only this is worse. She puts her right hand up to her face and stumbles forward to sink down on the dining room chair, turning back with her mouth open, to look up at him, eyes wide and unbelieving. The foolish question in her head is *What you do that for?* She cannot take in what has happened.

He says, "Never you tell me no when I ask you to do something!" He stands there suspended in the moment – blue shirt, grey pants, angry face. She notes these things as he looks down at her. Then, he turns, crosses the room and walks out through the front door.

For a while Oseyan just sits with her hand up to her face, watching the door. Then, with a bemused look, she turns and lets her eyes roam around the rented room – taking in the radio on a shelf, the doors to the other room where the children would normally sleep. She thinks, *They're outside, thank God.* She gets up and walks toward the door of the bedroom they share. She turns the knob, enters, walks to the crib where Norton lies asleep, on his stomach, his face turned to the side, his bottom in the air as he *cockup* (she thought the word in her head as Ma comes in to witness). *Look how the child just lie down there, cockup innocent as what!* She turns and sits on the bed with its white sheets. The bed they share. She remembers her friends teasing that her face gets red easily. She knows that his lash will leave a mark. She cannot even look into the mirror now. She must stay inside, because she doesn't want anybody to see her. She won't go out to the meeting tonight, so Norton can sleep on. She won't have to pack up the baby and go out. So, is she not going out because of Norton?

She thinks of Gwen seeing her face like this. This is not happening. She is alone in this country. Suddenly she thinks of the man in the apartment next door. She hear him speak and she wonders if he is West Indian. He work in a restaurant. But what does that mean? She doesn't know him. He is not her friend. Who can she talk to? And would knowing a West Indian do more than make her feel there are other people in this world who might know her, who might know her country? She can feel her face burn. She does not want to see it. It hurting and she know it red and bruised. *My husband hit me!* He just reach out and do something she didn't ever think could happen. Of course, she know that men beat women. She even hear that it happen to people she know well. Gwen said her uncle and aunt were always fighting, and sometimes the husband beat her in the road. But in her house, when she was growing up, this hadn't happened. Perhaps she doesn't know. She wonders now if Poopa did that, but she can't imagine it. Nobody could hit Ma – nobody could give Ma a slap – a box – like Baron had given her. Ma was too independent. She can't imagine it. But she is independent, too, isn't she? Before it happened, she would have been sure no man could hit her like that. She hadn't even thought about it, to tell the truth. She is independent. That's the word that keeps coming to mind. She walks quickly out to the kitchen, which is also their dining room, goes to the sink, bends to pick up the basket of clothes she had put on the floor. She had washed them after he left in the early morning. She glances quickly, fearfully, toward the door to outside the apartment. She hopes he doesn't come back. She cannot see him now. She walks hurriedly back to their room, sits on the bed. She begins to fold the clothes – his, hers, Wilfred's little shirts, Olive's. As she folds, she thinks of ordinary things – the blue in the water when she was washing, the clothes drying on a rack over the kitchen range. She washed today because she has to wash the baby's diapers every day, and she washed other things too because today is Monday and from since home she always thinks of Monday as washing day. She thinks, *I am not going out to the meeting tomorrow either. Vaseline should work. Let me put some vaseline on this bruise. He hit me!*

She finds herself kneeling – not crying or praying or anything. Just kneeling. She should get up and go warm the baby bottle and keep it inside here so she wouldn't have to go out there to get it when he wakes. She hurries out to the hall again, opens the cupboard. She goes back into the room when she is done, again glancing quickly at the green door.

Oh! The meeting. Perhaps he went to the meeting. Yes. That's the meeting she would have gone to, because they were planning to talk about the Madison Square Garden convention. He hit her! She knelt there and listened, as if she might hear something. For a long time she remains kneeling, just listening.

By the time he returns, the children have come back into the house; they have eaten and they are in bed. Three-year-old Wilfred had pointed toward her left cheek. "Mom, face red." Olive, not yet two, looked up, but seemed more worried about a scratch on her belly as she lifted her dress and leaned her body to one side, looking down at her belly, searching.

Focus, Oseyan tells herself. *Study the children.*

"Okay, so what's wrong with you? You hurt yourself?" she asks Olive, who is explaining something that she doesn't understand. She isn't really hearing.

"Okay," she says. "Come let me get you two washed up and in bed."

So by the time he comes back, they are in bed. She has nursed Norton, burped him, and settled him in, hoping he would do his usual – sleep contentedly for a few hours. She has put the stewed beef and some rice out onto a plate. Covered it for anyone who might want to eat. She has washed herself, put vaseline on her bruises. She is lying in the bed she has made. She even thinking, you make you bed; so now lie down in it!

10. So what do you plan to do?

It isn't happening. She and her husband are a team when they talk about the struggle, the Movement, the way forward. As the days pass she tries to reason. *He hit you and you staying with him?* It hasn't happened. She searches his face, covertly surveys his body, watching the tall, really tall, almost seven foot, blackness that she fell in love with. She isn't thinking love these days. She is thinking what she must do – how best she will survive with the children in this country. She remembers her excitement when she first saw him preach, how she really burned – she knows Gwen would say she can't hide nothing. She remembers that first time and she knows that her friend Gwen would say she get red when he looked at her. And was true. Her friend Gwen who had told her long ago, *You pretty, girl, and man like you.* At the time, she thought, if he like her because she red, she don't have a problem with that because he damn handsome. She liked his blackness, and he liked blackness, too, but if he liked her being red and tall and slim, she had no quarrel with that. If is the reprobate complexion that attract him, well, he was attracted. That was the main thing. *The man nice.* That was how she felt then. Now, she is just disappointed and she doesn't know what to think. She is really still a stranger here, and Uncle Eero, as distant as he could sometimes be, is in Montreal. Would it be different, would she feel different, if he were here, would she talk to him? Would she tell Uncle Eero anything? Perhaps not. Not nowadays.

Men beat women back in her country, too. She knew that. Some men did. In fact, many men did. It was not a secret. She had never *seen* it happen in her house. And she couldn't imagine being beaten. Well, perhaps now she doesn't have to imagine.

She can't just run, can she? Run with a parcel of children? And run in the middle of all the good work they are doing together in the movement? Yes. That might make it possible for her to stay, because it was something they shared. But it is wondering how to manage with the children in this place where she has no support that really makes it hard to run. That – and not the work they do – is what prevents her from going. To where? You can't go back to La Digue and say, *Look, I try, but I didn't succeed.* What would she do? Everybody life hard. Why you think you special? It would be like giving up. She can't give up.

What happens in the houses and bedrooms of people they know? The women in the meetings. Do other women have to deal with this? Who else hits their wife? Now, she watches people covertly, trying to look for signs. Her mind does a double take and she wonders suddenly – would Sir beat his wife? Come on. That is nonsense. Sir had whipped them in school, but that was different. Everybody beat children in school. And they use ruler and whip on the children here, too.

Now, they do not talk to each other because she does not know what to say. She is quiet. He is uncommunicative. She is careful not to cross him. She realises that. Does that mean he has won something? Well, she answers herself, yeah; he win because you here still. You could pick up your children and go, you know! But can she? Three of them? Can she run with all three? She remembers Ma and Cousin Mildred talking about a woman who had left her husband and Ma saying, *When you in it already you might as well stay, because you don't know what outside there and people won't let you live as always. The world think different about you as woman and is man people does stretch out their hand to. You might as well stay.* But Cousin Mildred had said, *Well papa, not me. Not me at all. I going make it on me own.* Should she try to make it on her own? Things wouldn't be easy, but she could make it. Should she leave him? Would he want to take the children? Take them to his parents, perhaps, maybe? No. She wants her children. But quite there she reach? What is going on with her life? Three children – can she run with all three? She can't tell Uncle Eero this. No. She can't. Well, can she stay without becoming a doormat, without laying down on the doorstep for people to wipe their foot on? But how will she stay and make sure she is not a doormat? How?

And as she thinks, life moves on, like it running, like it going fast so she don't have time to think. She never miss Ma and Auntie Gerda so much. Perhaps is a good thing that the Emancipation month this year meets them so distant and cold that their bodies feel no need to give to each other. At least, hers doesn't feel anything. Is her mind that mess up.

11. Life goes on.

Baron's younger brother, tall and dark and looking like him, although he talks more and is always ready with a story, asks them one day if they had heard about what is happening in Northern Indiana. It concerns one of the Catholic schools, Notre Dame, he says it is called. The students confronted the Klan, surprised them and pulled off their hoods and everything. The story makes Oseyan think of a lesson in her schoolbook – The Assyrian came down like a wolf on the fold. It isn't a funny story, really, but she laughs because it makes her think of that lesson. The students came down on the Klan like wolves on the fold. And their school colours are – something and gold, Baron's brother said. She smiles when she remembers that the Assyrians' "cohorts were … purple and gold." If she had kept reading her poetry – and if Baron didn't think she was trying to show off when she wrote things – she would try to write a poem about it, but, well, life catch up with you and you have to choose – or circumstances choose for you. The story his brother tells is that the Klan was trying to have a picnic and parade in South Bend, Indiana, and the students said *Oh no! Not one bit of it!* And the students chased them to their headquarters and even pelt them with potatoes from a vendor who was nearby. Oseyan thinks about that Assyrian poem and the blue and the gold. She really wants to write that poem when she hears that the student colours are actually blue and gold. Perhaps one day. One day. The Assyrian came down.

Meantime, her own children are growing up. Life just acted like nothing out of the ordinary has happened. Oseyan accepts that she hadn't known much about the man she married. She wonders if he felt the same – that he hadn't known much about her. At least, she thinks, he knew that, whatever she thought, she wouldn't just walk up behind him and order him to do something that he hated to do, and then hit him when he refused. But he is man. What experiences are other women in the movement having? Should she start having discussions with them to hear what their lives are like? She could do that – but that would be confusion in her house. She knows it.

Baron has said nothing either about his demand or the lash that bruised her face. They talk about little these days. She listens to him shouting at the children when he comes in. He doesn't seem to know how to talk to them in a soft voice. Who is he? What experiences has he had to make him so effective in the pulpit, so uncertain about himself in some situations, and so unable to communicate with the children he loves and who so admire their father and how he takes no nonsense from white people and doesn't act like a meek Negro with them? One day they must talk – one day. They sleep in the same bed but do not touch each other – for about a year – almost a year. And then, without explanations or discussion the body takes control and the old pattern reasserts itself.

Wilfred is about four and a half, Olive is three, and Norton is almost a year and a half, when Oseyan misses her periods again. *Damn!* Is there not some bush or something she can take? Perhaps – well, not to think about. It hadn't happened after the last Emancipation, but this time she has done it again. Well, not alone – she didn't do it alone – but right on schedule. Once they get to talking organisation, this August/September to May thing works like clockwork. She would have to stop it. If she is counting right, this one will be born either late April or May. She would really have to remember that when she is enjoying Emancipation she must do something different – or plan seriously for very extended post-Emancipation activities. And she has to plan for this one, especially here in Nebraska. Besides all of that, aside from growing responsibilities for Negro children coming into a frightening world, there are enough things happening around to keep them active with the work of the Universal Negro Improvement Association and African Communities League.

12. 1925: Take it easy inside there, little one.

Today Oseyan is remembering Ma, mostly because since morning she has been talking to herself. She pauses to listen for the children. Are they around? Are they hearing her and wondering why she is talking to herself? Or perhaps they are too little to wonder that.

All these big men in their long robes, black and white, and the flambeau. Riding their horses and shouting and knocking on the board window and breaking what they could break. Is a shame for big men to be so destructive and so full of hate. She can't believe what she hears, that there are high-up people and even some religious ministers in this dotishness. What kind of religious minister that could be? What God they serving? The little one, Norton, is sickly and all that noise and confusion has him so fretful. And Wilfred – that little boy so protective, especially when his father not there – pulling hard on her dress because he don't want her standing up in front of the door. But somebody had been knocking on the doors and windows, just rattling them to frighten them, perhaps, and she wanted whoever it was to see that she had nothing but her pregnant belly and her little children inside there. She was hoping that would help, and possibly it did, although who knows what will help with these savages. Perhaps they were looking for Baron. In the UNIA meeting, people were talking about last week's sermon, Psalm 46, Verse 1: *God is Our Refuge and Our strength, our ever-present help in trouble.* So, Baron had said to people in the meeting, when you see they come around with their horses and their crosses and march through the streets trying to intimidate you, talk to each other. Gather and discuss how you will face them, because in togetherness there's strength. Matthew 11:28. *Come to me, all ye that labour and are heavy laden, and I will give you rest.* This meeting place, he told them, is for you to gather and find solace and support now that the devil is rearing his ugly head again in this place. The people found the sermon uplifting. They told him, *Elder, you give them hell. You really helping to uplift the downtrodden – all of us, all of us. Thank you, Elder.*

The UNIA here is still doing well on recruitment, even if the central organisation is in trouble and being harassed by the police. The Klan, though, is also doing really well in Nebraska and, as white people, they could organise without the fears faced by Negro groups. Oseyan thinks about this organised hatred on the other side; people say this evil – at least in its organized form – started in 1865 or some time like that.

As she sweeps the room with the long broom, Oseyan is muttering and talking to herself like Ma used to do. Ma used to sound like she was quarrelling, but she wasn't really quarrelling. Now Oseyan wonders, *And me, is quarrel I quarrelling?* To tell the truth, she doesn't know. It feels like she should be quarrelling. How are people supposed to bring up children in this atmosphere?

1865. Not only right after the civil war in these parts but also just about the time that some of those Langdon ancestors of hers were settling and multiplying in the West Indies. As people say, the eighteen-sixties were a real funny time – all about – funny over there, and funny over here, too. Over there in her country, slavery was supposedly over by that time, but people were still tied to the land and Africans were still being brought in under all kinds of pretences. Yes – from what Ma told her, and from what she had learned in school, pretences is the word. It's hard to find a beginning at all because those reprobates put people to work on estates both here and there – and they didn't want to know anything because we were not people as far as they were concerned. And some came after Emancipation; it was six of one, half a dozen of the other.

Uncle Eero had told her that he found church records with all kinds of names given to children, just to take away their African or their Indian name – Indians who came after Emancipation – and in the surname column for some children, just the word "African". What a thing! When people think you are nothing, they don't even have to remember your name. *Lè moun kwè ou pa anyen, yé pa menm oblijé chonjé non'w.* Surname, they write, African. Or Surname: Coolie. Giving Indians a name that people who don't know better or who don't care that this last name marking them as labourer is a colonial insult, still giggle and use today to put Indians down. Perhaps one day in the future, people will just claim it if it's there still and let the shouters know what is what! What a thing! They well make sure when they move away they leave a house divided against itself.

And then, here, in 1865, some white people so vex that they lose the American Civil War that they start this organisation that wrap itself up in white to terrorize black people. That is how they say this nonsense start. Wrap themself up in white and ride on horse and carry cross and thing like that. What a world! *Ma, talk to the Lord up there for me, please. Help me help my family. You could see things not too good with me.*

This little one in my belly, I will call him Malcolm. My husband leave the naming to me and I plan to name him after my precious little Malcolm for Auntie Gerda. Of course, if is a girl, it will be another name. I wonder what this baby thinking inside my belly and seeing the world that is out there. My child, listen to your Mama and take it easy inside there, okay? Don't let them trouble your spirit inside there, whether you are a boy or a girl. And whichever one you are, I welcome you.

She thought the children were asleep. The three of them had been lying down there when last she looked at them. Then they were behind her in front of the door, eyes brighter than the flambeau and afraid because of the shouting and the pounding from outside. She tried to sound calm. *Just take it easy*, as Ma would say. *Don't make bad matters worse.* "Just take it easy," she told the little girl leaning against her, trying to circle her with her small armspan. "You wake up? The noise outside wake you up? Come. Come. Never mind. Come to your mother, you hear. *Wété pwé mwen.* Stay close to me." As her grandmother would say, *Ou kwè ou kayé jwenn djab-la a lòt koté-a sèlman si'w pa chansé.* You think you will meet the devil on the other side only if you're unlucky, and then you look around and realise that he here already, right on your doorstep.

But the children are still young, and if one of them remembers anything about these days in Nebraska, it will be Wilfred. He is five. Olive, not yet three, will have only what others remember. For Norton this won't be a memory at all. She hopes the little one inside her won't be marked by her fear for all of them. Because she fraid for them. She hopes he won't feel her rage. She hopes they won't know any of this until they can process it. Figure out what it mean and try to figure out what they could do about it. Perhaps she will tell them then. Who know? Perhaps this thing will go on for a long time, and they will be living with this kind of nonsense – so it won't be just about remembering. But she don't wish that for them. *Let me not even have that thought! You can't wish that on people! We here. We have to make sure it's different for the next generation.* And for her this wish is also a prayer.

Malcolm is born in May, as she projected – May 19th. Look at that! August to May. A memory again, a product again, of Emancipation celebration. Give thanks.

13. Working Woman.

Like her grandmother did, she digs, looks for things to plant around the house that her husband has built and is always building – adding a room, dividing a room, fixing the roof. She plants chives, sweet pepper, chillie peppers, tomatoes, green onions, thyme, parsley and oregano. She wishes the summer were long and hot enough for dasheen and yam, and she remembers longingly the *gwo michèl* back home in La Digue. She teaches the little ones to cook what they can grow. It is what the Movement encourages, too, and she agrees because that is what she learned growing up. She teaches the children to make their own gardens, to plant, to knit, to sew. She tells them, and especially she tells her little girl, Olive, what her grandmother used to say: "Take up sewing so you can be independent. You won't have to work in the white man's land or perhaps even in the white people's house. If you are a seamstress, they will come to your living room for their clothes." And, she tells Olive, "Take the knitting needles. Knit one, purl one. Learn the stitches. Knit one, purl one. You can learn to follow a pattern. You can learn to crochet. Listen to what I'm telling you now. Do the things that can make you independent of the white people's kitchens. Carpentry, sewing – and when the weather allows, plant. Clear, dig, plant your own gardens. And above all, education. Go to school. More and more, these days, there are things you can learn to pull yourself forward. Find out what these things are because I mightn't know enough to tell you. But I know you can be a teacher, in spite of what they telling you. And you see what your father and I doing, trying to be independent? We are doing that because we learn from life. Always try to figure out how you can be independent.

"Whether it is there where I come from, or here where we are, whites try to do things to keep us back as a people. That is why we work with a Negro association that is international. As my grandmother would say, the more things change, the more they remain the same. *Plis bagay chanjé, sé plis yo wété menm.*

"And there is always a way you could turn your hand to something. My grandmother taught me that. You hear your father talking about the parable of the loaves and the fish. That happens all the time in life, you know. People make something out of nothing at all. All of us working for next to nothing, but we make it something so that you children could live, could get an education, could have a vision. So sometimes the sea looks like there is no fish in it, but give some people two loaves and just one dèggè dèggè fish, you would be surprised to see how well they eat."

It is Wilfred who asks, "Mom, what is *dèggè dèggè?*" She tells him, "Small, inconsequential, looking as though it can't do much." He is already learning that the answer to most questions about words is: "I will get you a dictionary", so he asks, "When I can read more of the lessons you teach me, Mom, and write and spell more, I will see it in the dictionary?" Oseyan pauses to consider this question. "No," she finally says. "*Dèggè dèggè* is a word that is ours in Grenada and in some other parts of the Caribbean and they – the people who write the dictionary – don't know it. You won't find it in the dictionary. And when you start to go to the big school, don't use it there either because the teachers won't know it." He considers. He says, "Okay, Mom." I must be careful, she thinks. I have to teach them things that will help them, not things that will make the other children laugh at them. They have enough to deal with already. But still she smiles when she sees Norton pick up a flat bit of cardboard lying on the kitchen floor, toddle towards a chair, try to pull it away from the dining table his father made, and eventually give up, sinking to the floor to fan his face with the cardboard and saying, as he tries to simulate blowing air through his mouth as if he is tired, "*Mwen ka alé asiz. Mwen las.* Let me sit down. I am tired."

14. Reaching Back.

In those last years in Grenada, when Oseyan was mostly in Aunt Gerda's house with the children, Ma seemed to wait for the opportunity to talk to her when she passed by the house on the hill. She would whisper urgently, *When you see a money come in your hand, from sewing or a day's work that you get paid for, or anything, if is tuppence, put it away. Start to save for a rainy day. Even if you not making much, you always making enough to put by tuppence for a rainy day.* Oseyan knows that she grew fed up with Ma always whispering some urgent something to her; she remembers that she sometimes said *steupes* in her head, but she recalls the warnings now with gratitude.

She and Baron need to put by a few cents for a rainy day and also to be able to buy the things they can't just up and buy like that. Her work in the white people's homes – taking care of their children and cleaning their houses – was for money to spend on living and her own house and family. Baron put the money he earned into her hand with a tired, satisfied look, leaving it to her to, almost literally, put elastic around the edges of the notes and make ends meet – make the money stretch, as Ma used to say. She has heard women say that they don't know what their man doing with money – she had heard Auntie Gerda say that. She can't say that about Baron. He tells her how much he gets when he does a day's work and he gives her most of the money to take care of the family. He clearly feels he has a responsibility for them. She can't bad-talk him for that. And she manages with what they have. But always, if it is only two cents, she puts some little in a separate corner, keeping it aside. Whenever she takes in sewing, that is rainy day money. They try to grow as much as possible to eat, and not have to spend a lot on that.

One thing she and Baron talk about is the way they get treated on public transport, so they decide they will learn to drive – just in case one day they could see their way to do the impossible. Baron's brother, who gained his driving skills by some unknown means, is the teacher. Uncle Eero had also helped Oseyan a bit, teaching her to drive in Montreal. All that concern to do things that will help his family survive and push them forward is Baron's good side, she thinks, and – seeing that – it is more painful to her that when it comes to dealing with the children and showing them the love he has in his heart as a father, that is a different thing. But he does have love for them; she knows it. He shows it every day, just by the way he works and plans for them, that he is a good, loving person. One day, she must sit down and talk with him about who he is and how he is and how he might show that love she knows is in his heart. She will find a way. Something tells her he would listen and explain why he has these other ways of being some other somebody. Sir used to say if you never make a mistake, well, something wrong. He used to say it in the way of Sir, but that was the message. And she know she have ways that could be better, too. Well, some things she doesn't like, but they must talk. Although she can see that he gets angry when she tries to talk about some things, because he just don't think woman should know what is what, nor should she try to instruct – "instruct" – that is the word he uses when he wants to tell her to shut up – "Don't try to instruct me about how things should be!" When it comes to realising that she is a big woman and can have her own opinions, he can't see that. But truth to tell, as a man he not alone in that. But she don't want him to pass those kind of ideas on to the children.

"Wilfred! What are these tins out here in the yard? Get these damned things out of the way." He has just come back from some job in the neighbourhood, fixing a fence in some white folks' yard, and he is taking out the rage inside his head on the children. He always comes home with this rage. So, he don't think she finding rage in the road, too, every time she go outside?

Oseyan walks to the door. "Leave him alone," she says. "We don't have money to buy him fancy toys, so let him play with those paint tin covers – feel good that he enterprising enough to shape them into something that he could use."

He turns his rage on her. "You making that little boy into a real mama's boy. You won't even correct him when he's making a mess in the place. You're helping him defy my authority!"

"I'm not making him defy anything, Baron. I just saying that – "

Now, Norton walks up to his father and Baron gestures for the child to move away from him. "Step back!" Malcolm peeks from behind her, where he is taking refuge from his father's shouts. Baron pauses, seems to collect himself, turns to look at this other son.

"Come. Come little one" – and as if he hasn't just been shouting away the other one, the father asks, "What did you do today? You been behaving?" Then he looks around briefly, as if speaking not only to Malcolm. Perhaps because he has the good grace to realise he shouldn't be so blatant about favouring one child. She doesn't think it helps much. Malcolm stretches out to his father a bit of the biscuit he has in his hand. His father stoops, opens his mouth, and actually smiles as he nibbles on it.

The only child that fool think is child is that one! If he don't like white, it look like he sure like the red skin that white blood produce. She is sure that is it. Malcolm is the lightest child and is definitely the one the father show the most love. She always guessed that her very light skin was in his eyes her most attractive feature. *Damn fool! We going talk, though. We going talk one of these days.*

It isn't only *that* that has her angry. He is getting into the habit again of wanting her to cook him things he knows are against her way of being. She has told him again that she isn't cooking pork, and when he looked at her in that way he has, she hadn't stood up to say anything more – just walked away. Something is coming. She can feel it.

It happens one day when Wilfred and Olive are at school and the two little ones, Norton and Malcolm, are outside, playing. He has gone to fix some fencing for white people in the area. He walks inside with his face all rumpled up – *as if somebody siddown on it,* she thinks when she looks up from where she is scaling the fish at the kitchen sink. He mumbles something that must be a greeting. Then he says, "I don't want fish today. Cook some stew pork for me."

"The pork is still where you put it in the icebox in the corner there. Take it out, let it thaw and then you could cook it later."

"What you say to me?"

She looks up from the fish in the sink. *Handle the knife easy. Is only the fish head you chopping off.*

"I asked what you said to me?"

Oseyan puts down the knife, rinses her hands, turns around, bends down and pulls open a cupboard door to take out the bowl she had forgotten to line up before cleaning the fish. But she is watching. His hand on her shoulder does not startle her, because she is watching for him. She is aware of every inch of him. She shrugs his hand away. He shouts, "Look at me when I talk to you. I say I want you to cook me some pork."

"Baron, you know I don't cook pork. You cook it."

He lifts his hand and is bringing it down, but she fights him. Moves her head into his middle section as he puts his hands out to hold her.

"So you have a plan to fight?"

"I have no plan, dammit, but if you think you hitting me and I standing up there and take it, you have another think coming!"

He steps back because she has tried to sink her teeth into his hand with her teeth and has nipped him. He towers above her. "Well," he shouts, "if you want to fight." His tone almost makes her expect him to pull out the belt from around his waist. He holds her with one hand and the other hand, clenched, goes up. She shouts into his face.

"Is me. Is me, Baron. Is me. The woman you marry pretending to be some other person that you not." She has startled him. He lets go of her. Moves back. As if she needed to remind him that she is the woman he married, his wife, the woman he couldn't stop looking at because he found her so beautiful. "Is me, Baron," she says again, shouting it. Then, in a lower voice, "Is me. You lie to me, you hit me. What? You want to wipe me off the face of the earth?" He stands, watching her. She stands her ground, stares at him, taking in the anger in his face. "Is me," she says again in a quiet, insistent voice. He takes a step back, watching her. The muscles in his face tense, relax, tense again. She can see the slow tensing and unclenching. She holds his gaze, trying to bring him back from wherever he has gone in his mind. "Is me, you know," she says again. In her head, she tells him, *Perhaps you watch the skin and you think is the father I tell you about. But is me, you know. I don't even know him. Is me.* Perhaps hers is the skin he hates and loves, but she knows she is more than the reprobate's skin. "Is just me," she says. "Me. Oseyan. The whole damn ocean. And whatever right you think you have, you have no right to hit me and push me around." She is watching him. He steps back. The right sleeve of the blue worker's overall slips down his arm. He turns, walks to the door, opens it. He goes outside. He leaves the door ajar, in the way that she had it before, so the children can come in without having to push.

15. Housewife.

Right around the time that Malcolm is born, the authorities in the country put the Honourable Marcus Mosiah Garvey in jail. They say he has done all kinds of things – stolen money, used the mail for nefarious purposes, advertised for the steamship line using false information, taken people's money for the organisation by making false promises – everything. She still feels that every penny she has put into the organisation when she carved out a little bit of money was worth it, and she will continue doing what she can in spite of all the bad talk going on now. A Negro organisation – a Negro international organisation is a dream that might stumble, but it is more than ever needed. That last time when he visited them in Omaha, Mr Garvey asked her to write letters, and she wrote them. She typed them up on the old typewriter and put the letters in the mail for him. He was trying his best, but work for and with Negro people is never good work, the way that white people see it. But they – she and Baron and whoever else is willing –will continue the struggle.

It is not easy, but she writes the report for *The Negro World* so they will know that the work is continuing. In the morning, when the bigger children are gone to school, she has a little time to work on the membership cards. The work for the organisation is a lot, what with the children and trying to do some sewing when she could. Her grandmother used to say that work is work. It is not meant to be easy. *So how you mean work hard?* That's what she would ask Gerda, Eero, Amèlie, all of them. *Is work,* she used to say. *It not hard. Is just work.*

In addition to their political work, she has to make money so that her family can live. Baron works hard and she has to keep her end up. She sews for rich white women, or for women who can pay, and that, most times, is the same thing. When things are really rough, she even cleans their houses. And, of course, when she is not what white people and the government call *working*, she is at home washing, wiping noses, cleaning house, making a kitchen garden, cooking some meal her husband might love, sometimes some meal she hates. And she teaches the children when they get home. Those are some of the things she does. But white people seem to believe that only work for them is work. Both there and here, it seems that's what they believe. They don't know that when you are in your house, doing for your own, you're at work too. It's just that you are not working for them.

But 1925 is not just the year in which her fourth child, Malcolm, is born and Mr Garvey imprisoned. Uncle Eero sends word from Canada that their friend, the man they knew would do great things, Mr Marryshow, has won a seat in the Grenada legislature. He is now a member of the Grenada Legislative Council. We moving on, she thinking. Oh yes! We moving on as a people!

16. Teach the children. American Midwest 1920s and 30s. Memory from La Digue, 1902.

After a while, they know they will have to move. The Movement can no longer give much assistance to their local Liberty Hall, either with advice or occasional supportive visits. Now, they are supporting the Movement more than the Movement can support them. They are helping to figure out what can be done to build the organisation and to help the Honourable Marcus Mosiah Garvey with his and the organisation's political troubles.

But what really makes them decide they will soon have to move is that the white people in Omaha seem to have the same disease they say the mongoose have now in Grand Etang, so that you have to be afraid they bite a dog or another animal or even people. These people they call the Klan are getting worse and worse. They know they have no law to fear, so, she and Baron think, to really organise and raise a family they would have to get out of this place. Perhaps they could move to Milwaukee. But is Milwaukee any better? The mad people are on the rise there, too, but – as Ma would say – nothing beat a trial but a failure. People say there are opportunities there. And the good thing they hear is that there are more Negro people there. That counts for something. For that alone it could be a good idea to move. At least let's try it, they decide. And that is how life is. You go where you think it is possible to make a living, because a living is what God put you on this earth to find out how to make. Although things are bad with the Movement, they will work to develop it there. They will start a group anyway, and Baron will preach the word of God and the advancement of coloured peoples. Uncle Eero says that one of his friends is in Milwaukee; this one had been in Venezuela with him. So at least perhaps she would know somebody to start with, somebody who knows her family, someone she could call on if she happened to be in a jam. The thing is always to try and go where there is some possible support, or just where there are other people who look like you and your family. Is true that sometimes even the people you think you might know too busy making their own living to take time knowing you. And you busy too. But just knowing it have others like you around is a blessing. And those restaurants that they say coloured people have in Milwaukee, places like that would always need tablecloths and serviettes and things like that. She might even be able to develop her sewing business. Well, time will tell.

So they settle in Milwaukee – until another place calls. And meanwhile they work on all fronts. After they talk with UNIA leaders and some other members, her husband writes a petition and letter to those people in government circles up there, to the US president himself – President Calvin Coolidge. Oseyan is part of the discussion to write the letter and get it sent, but she knows she is tired – physically and mentally. She finds that she gets tired much more quickly these days. And she is pregnant. There is a weakness that overtakes her body and, just before Rex is born, Baron is concerned enough to get her medical attention. A nurse tells her that her body is not reacting well to all these babies. She is drained. Oseyan knows she is tired, but she also thinks, *She don't know my grandmother. We not weak people. I just need to rest little bit.* The young white woman who is the nurse says again, "Slow down. Your body is tired." It's true, but she must also let people know what she can do. Sometimes UNIA members come to her house. Oseyan makes sure there are things about that tell them this is the house of a seamstress – a magazine she finds, balls of crochet thread in a glass case, a couple doilies there too, a crocheted tablecloth that might be suitable in a restaurant.

Time goes, and life suggests other things. And soon, although they haven't been here a good two years, they will move. There is no longer a little money from the central UNIA organisation to help with things, because there is hardly a central organisation now. And now that the Milwaukee UNIA division is up and moving, and Milwaukee klan groups are on the rise, perhaps they should move. They are committed to building Negro meeting places wherever they are needed, even more so now that Mr. Garvey is in trouble, so they must go.

Just before they leave Milwaukee, Oseyan misses her periods again. She doesn't have to ask or wonder. Some people say it's not always that, but for her it's always that. And now they have broken the pattern. Now that the Movement is in trouble and August is not the Emancipation celebration it used to be, it looks like they have found Christmas as a base. Rex is born at the end of August. A Christmas celebration baby. Or a Christmas comfort baby, if comfort it is. Baron is very down in his spirits because his brother has been shot in a confrontation with the police. Of course, he says, we are always the ones to die or to suffer in these confrontations. He doesn't know the details, he says, but he is not surprised. I always tell you, he says to her. Expect anything! And – be careful. Be careful. Be careful, she thinks, with the children and with your body. She knows there is a law that says you will be jailed if you do anything to prevent the birth of a child, but sometimes… beg God pardon, she wonder. She wonder about bush that might help. But life goes on, and as soon as they move, John makes his appearance in the flesh. But they are a strong people. She didn't know her grandmother when she had to take care of her six children, but they are a strong people. And look how her grandmother took care of her!

And always you have to think of the children, their education and their future – whether you are in Philadelphia, Omaha or Milwaukee. And now that the family is getting bigger, it makes sense to use the rainy day money that both of them agreed they must have to get a car – some kind of vehicle that would carry the big family around so they wouldn't have to pay train fares, travel with Negro children on white trains, and – just generally try to live like human beings. But a Negro man driving even an old jalopy – careful! A woman who looks like she is white driving might not be in so much trouble. So perhaps that? Okay. They try to figure out what Oseyan thinks of as – this race thing. They discuss, negotiate and consider. They drive from Milwaukee to what turns out to be Lansing, Michigan. What turns out to be because – well, think about it. If you manage to get one of those white people vehicles to yourself and you are travelling from –

well, think about Grenada. She visualises it, remembering her own discoveries in the years after she left school – from Attaseat in the mountains way above Hermitage, going to Town, as they call St. George's, you expect to break down sometimes. You would expect to spend a night by your cousin in La Baye or St David's and they would let the children spread bedding on the floor and make it for a night, or perhaps even two, if you have to stretch to two. With children crying and getting tired and the road not of the best, you will expect to stop and get more steam for everybody and for the vehicle. And that is how she explains it later to the McGuire lady when they meet up with her in Lansing. And as they travel from Milwaukee to Lansing, one of the places where they have to stop and restore the spirit is Indiana, where another of Baron's relatives – who seem to turn up all over the place – lives. And as for Miss McGuire, Eero had told Oseyan there was this lady from Grenada living somewhere in Michigan and Oseyan was more glad than she could say to see her. Miss McGuire used to live in Grenville for a time, so look at that – somebody who actually knows La Baye – and there is another Grenada lady who grew up in Carriacou, which is where this lady's father was from, but her mother was from Byelands side. With all that, Oseyan begins to believe that Lansing, Michigan is a place where she could live. When you are trying to find a way, the track that your brothers and sisters and cousins and aunties and uncles and just people you know are from your part of the world, have made with machete, with cutlass, with rake, with whatever they could find, is a good place to venture to do some more clearing. She had heard Ma say this – although she was talking about La Baye and St David's and Sauteurs and Victoria. And it look as if just as Baron is finding those of his people the white man don't kill yet in places they travel, she is seeing some of her people, too.

So now they are in Lansing, Michigan. Everyone is so tired they could sleep for a whole month straight. But only people who have servants to get tired for them can take that kind of break. Baron's family – brother again, and really that's one reason he thought Lansing would be good – takes them to a place where they find rooms to stay. "Reasonable," he says, sounding worldly, as if he knows what is what. And it isn't bad. They get one big long room that they have to divide into two because it is big enough, and the place has a dining room, so they have somewhere to eat and they could wash and everything. It isn't bad for a short time. But it has to be for a short time because June is a month dry enough to travel, but because it hot you get tired quickly, and in the hot rooms the children get restless. They ask Baron's brother, Isaiah, whether they can find some place with a garden where they can work and plant things in the summer. He says, "Where our people have to live, there ain't no place to plant a thing. Don't plan on that."

Baron says, "I am planning. We want a piece of land where we can grow things for our family to eat." He looks from his brother to his wife, as if he is inviting her comment. *What!* She thinks. *He getting sense. He want me to talk!*

"Yes," she agrees. "We want to be able to plant our food and have some place, on a hill if possible, where the children can play."

Isaiah says slowly, "A hill where the children can play?" He turns on his seat to look at Baron. He looks back at the children playing on the floor in the corner of his small room. "My man," he says questioningly, turning to Baron again, "you got dough?"

Baron shakes his head. "Nope. Just getting by. But I have a family and we have to live."

Isaiah makes a sound that is a bit more than a sigh. "Downtown Lansing, easy to find a place. I check for you."

"No. Check where there's land."

"Okay. See what I can find out. But my brother, you know how these things be."

It turns out that there is a white woman in Westmont willing to sell her land to them, even if they are Negro. And they have enough put by to buy it. "You have to know where you want to go," Baron tells his brother. "Or you can't get there. Just the little add one and one."

"Two sixpence is one shilling," Oseyan murmurs.

On top of it all, it is important not only to send the children to school but also to find the energy to teach them at home, because school doesn't think it is important for these black children to learn.

So Oseyan will teach. She teaches.

"So, you say that today you had some difficult words," she says. "You can pronounce any word in the world. I remember a lesson from my *Royal Reader Book Two*, page roman numeral iv. When I got home after school, I would read it to my grandmother. It said:

"As a special lesson in Pronunciation, the more difficult words are divided into syllables. Great importance is attached to this exercise, and teachers are advised to make use of it sys-tem-a-ti-cal-ly. You hear the word? We will syllabize that – divide it into syllables – and you will spell and pronounce it for me. The book says, *They* (meaning the teachers like me who are teaching the children) *will find that when their pupils have learned to pronounce these words correctly in syllables, the difficulty of spelling them will have greatly reduced.*[23]

"Okay? So, I will help you to syllabize words and you can conquer any word in the world. Nothing they give you is too hard. Pick up the dictionary and start to read and syllabize. You go first, Olive. I'm listening. You're a big girl now. Seven whole years, so you're not an infant. If you learn all these things, you have a good foundation, whatever they teach you in school. So tell me. Read this word for me. With you, Rex, we're starting now with words of one syllable. Two years is not too soon. You're a big boy. Your sister did these already. And then later you will do like your big brother and your sister – two syllables and so on. You understand "sylla-ble?" The smaller words, like 'one', 'two', 'three' – all of those are words of one syllable. Let's go, Rex. One! Go-o-o-d! Hold up the finger!" She smiles at him and he repeats, "One!"

"Good. Good. Help him, Wilfred, and you, Olive, help him. And Wilfred, put that dictionary in the middle of the table there while you big ones do your homework. Any word you can't spell or you don't understand, look it up in the dictionary. Let me go and see how the pot doing. Malcolm and Norton, pay attention to what your sister is trying to show you."

17. Where is your boss?

In Michigan, they live up on the hill with land all around them. Their neigbours always appear to have a complaint, and they seem to be constantly trying to ensure that they are the only

301

family living there, but Oseyan and Baron try to make the best of the situation. They talk to the children, letting them know, as usual, that they are Negroes in America, so that means people will try to put obstacles in their way.

Baron says to his four boys, "Think for yourself as Negroes. Don't let anybody think for you. And always look around you and look behind you. No white person wanting to do you good. Keep your head on!"

One day, a white man – probably a neighbour – stops as he walks along the road. He looks at the children – Olive and Norton – planting flowers in the garden outside. "Ay!" he calls out. Olive and Norton look up.

"Where is your boss?"

Olive answers quickly. "He's not there. He'll be back soon."

They put their heads down and go back to work, looking out of the corners of their eyes until the man disappears along the road. Afterward, they tell their mother. She says, "Oh yes? Good. Always tell me what you hear, not only in that school they think you shouldn't be in, but out there on the road, and keep an eye out for yourself. White people don't wish us well, and they think we shouldn't be living here. This is why I have to keep talking to you about people who are struggling to make the world different for Negro people. So now that you've finished your homework and we talk about all the things you do in school today, I want you to sit down and read some of the things here in *The Negro World*.

"You see the date of the paper, Wilfred? You see it, Olive? August 11, 1928. You know that the Honorable Marcus Mosiah Garvey got kicked out of this country. He went back to Jamaica. That's where they deported him to, and now he is in France getting this written in his paper – in our UNIA paper, *The Negro World*. So sit up, sit up. You're a whole nine years old already, Wilfred. Stop slouching. And you a big girl, Olive. You have to start to think about these things from now, and then you could teach the little ones as they're coming up. You see the heading?

"Honorable Marcus Garvey, Writing from France, Discusses Treatment Accorded Negroes There and In Other Countries of the World.

"So you see? We have to be concerned not only about Negroes here. That is what Mr Garvey always used to say. What he is still saying, from over there. We have to think internationally. Understand the different experiences all over the world. Because one is not more important than the other. They are all just different, so we have different attitudes. Read it and then you can tell me what you think. We can talk about it. And that word "internationally" – Wilfred, Olive, after we talk a little bit, you will sit with your little brothers and tell them what the word means.

"Malcolm! Please stop that amount of noise with your pretend car and pay attention to the problem your brother is trying to work out with you. *With* him, Norton, not *for* him. Explain to him what it is you're so busy writing!

"Okay, you two? Let's leave them there sorting out that and see what's going on here. Let me talk to you two big ones alone for a little while. You're done reading that piece, not so? Good. Look at this paragraph here:

> *"The Negro I have observed here is living a carefree life, much to my regret. Because of the privileges allowed him, he has not developed a race consciousness in France as racially helpful as that which we have developed in America and other parts where we are struggling for Racial Nationalism.*

"What a thing, eh! Think of those two words, 'Racial nationalism.' Remember what we talked about? Talk about it when you have some time later and then come and tell me what you think he is saying there."

"Mom, why does he say 'much to my regret'?"

"Good question, Olive. What do you think about the tone of that?"

"The tone?"

"How does that sound? What does it make you think about the writer's – Mr Garvey's – way of thinking here?"

"It makes me – ," Olive pauses. She has changed from her school clothes to this blue cotton dress that her mother calls *home clothes,* and the blue ribbons are still in her hair. Oseyan looks at her daughter and remembers her seven-year-old self at Holy Innocents. She knows that children tease the child, but all Negro children get teased if they are in a school with whites. They get teased even when they are not in a school with whites. She must tell them that, too. She watches her daughter's face and wonders what about it makes children tease her – the mouth? The nose? The dark skin? They say they are getting teased. *She* got teased. All these thoughts run through her head in the seconds that she waits – but they are always in her head when her children come home and she tries to picture their day.

"Sort of anxious –," Wilfred says. He is nine, after all. He can't just wait on his seven-year-old sister.

"Wait, Wilfred. Let her finish and then you can tell me what you think. She started talking first. Don't interrupt her.

"Continue, Olive."

"The tone – how it sounds – it sounds as if he is – sort of sad. He is sad because –"

"Come on. That's a conjunction. What's the other part of the sentence?"

"He is sad because he would want to see the Negroes in France not seem to be so carefree."

"Good. Excellent. Wilfred, you agree?"

Wilfred hadn't been looking so pleased. His face, nearly as chubby as his sister's, looks alert as he sits up. He likes direct questions. "Yes, I agree," he says. "He thinks there are many things wrong with the situation of the Negroes in France, and he would like to see them seeming to care more. That is what his words tell me he thinks."

"Good. Okay! So I want you to write these words now in your notebooks: Privileges, race consciousness, racial nationalism. Take the dictionary here – one at a time! – you don't have to look for the word at the same time. You could be writing your word, Olive, while your brother start looking, and when he finds it, you could pull your chair over, near to him, and write down the meaning that you find in the dictionary. And then you look for the next one, Olive, and the two of you continue like that. Okay. I will leave you to it. How you two doing over here?"

She moves to look at the two children seated at the side table in the kitchen. Their heads are bent over the book. Six-year old Norton is trying to show his little brother how to form his letters.

"Did you write this word here – France? Did you write it, Malcolm, or did you write it for him, Norton?

"I showed him, Mom, and I watched to see that he was doing it properly."

"Good. You picked out the words of one syllable?"

"Yes, Ma. "Home", "much", "has" –

Malcolm adds "not".

Their mother smiles. "Excellent. Okay, Rex. Your brother coming to play with you now. Yes, Malcolm. Spend some time with him. He leaning against you there for the longest time. Don't rough him up like that! What you think it is at all?

"Okay. Take a break. Let me prepare your supper." Oseyan walks to the sideboard, picks up her apron, looks around. Bit by bit they are getting this place together. She reaches up, opens a kitchen cupboard. As she moves, she is talking to herself but to them. The thought flashes through her head that Ma used to do this. You could never be sure when Ma was talking to herself or to you. It seemed the same thing sometimes. Ma talking out loud to herself and to Oseyan.

"You children are Negroes in the United States of America. I am from the West Indies. And since before I came to this country – in both Canada and Grenada – I knew that Mr Garvey said that he thought the Negroes here in America had developed more of a race consciousness than West Indians, and I wasn't sure about that at all. So think about those words 'race consciousness' and what they might mean. I remember that my uncle, who had just reached Canada, agreed more with Mr Garvey than I did at the time, but sometimes it's what you experience – what you go through for yourself – that help you think about things. So okay.

"Okay. Let me get these things together. Reach the lettuce your father bring there for me, Norton. When you-all done all the work I give you, go outside, get some water, sort yourself out.

"I will put the next paragraph there so you could look at both of them for your homework, to do when you have some time before we meet tomorrow. Remember to look for the words of one syllable in both pieces, Norton, and help your brother find them. Wilfred and Olive, you know what you doing already. And you have the dictionary. You don't have to read it now, but it there for you for homework.

"While France, however, is accommodating to Negroes in France and treats them with courtesy and respect, it is quite different with her colonies in Africa.

"You see what he wrote there? You see what he wrote there? Yes, go ahead, Wilfred, read it while I prepare these things here..."

"In the French colonies, the Colonial Administrators adopt a different policy toward the native than is adopted in France, where he is regarded as a citizen. The usual method of exploiting the native African is the order of the day. This is purely a subtle economic policy which we very well understand and which we will ultimately take care of. This is the reason why the Universal Negro Improvement Association urges every black man, French, English, American, Italian, German or Belgian, to forget accidental Nationalism outside of his own race and to remember that the first appeal to us as black men is that we are black and because we are black we must have a common outlook economically, politically, socially, religiously and otherwise."

Wilfred has been reading it out aloud as his mother does her work in the kitchen. Now he says, "Mom! I think I see what he means."

"Good! Good, Wilfred. Any word you don't know, look it up, and then we will sit down tomorrow evening and you will tell me what Mr Garvey is saying there in *The Negro World*. Good, Wilfred. So you big ones, look up words like 'nationalism' and 'subtle' and 'exploiting'. Look up any words you don't know and we will talk about what he is saying. I have to look up words, sometimes, too, you know. That is what the dictionary is for.

"Okay? Olive, look. I iron that shirt over there for you to wear to school tomorrow. Move it from the clothes rack and put it where you will find it early in the morning. Okay. Sort yourselves out. Let me get this finished so you-all could eat."

18. More Lessons in the American Midwest 1920s and 1930s.

"Yes, Norton. I see you there making faces, but you'd better pay attention. What did you do in school today?"

"Mark was calling me rastus and the teacher heard him, and he laughed, and the other children started laughing too."

"Okay. So it was another one of those days. Let's forget about them. You're a big boy now, nearly seven, so it's time for you to recognise some of the words we were talking about. Okay? We will work on that later. And what is rastus, anyway?"

"Is something they call Negro people, Ma."

"Okay, you have your tasks to do while I'm doing mine. Olive, take over from me here and watch the porridge. Don't let it boil up and fall. Keep the fire where it is there and keep stirring every so often. It just waiting for you to turn away for it to fall, so keep your eye on it. Malcolm, sit over there and fold your clothes. They're in the basket. Fold them like we show you to do, then go and put them away in your drawer. Come on, come on, you're nearly five years old, not a baby. Only the little ones I excuse – Rex and the baby. The rest of you get to it and do what you know you have to do.

"When I was at school in La Digue – Olive, *doudou darling,* pass the bowl of salt for me, please – my teachers made me learn many things by heart. *Corsica, Sardinia, Sicily, Malta and the Lomen Islands.* These are things I remember. *Hudson Bay and the straits of Gibraltar.* And different stories about the Atlantic Ocean – one from my grandmother, your great-grandmother, and one from the Royal Readers.

"Yes, look up at the ceiling, Wilfred – I seeing you out of the corner of my eye. What you doing there? The Math homework that's giving you problem? If we're disturbing you, go and sit somewhere else. Oh, we not disturbing you; you want to stay here. Okay. But in fact self, better you go; go to your room and work. I don't understand how you could be trying to do sums in all this noise. Go and sit in your room.

"So you children, listen to what I telling you. Learning things by heart is good, and I want you to learn from two great teachers of the race – T.A. Marryshow and Marcus Garvey. Mr Marryshow has a newspaper called *The West Indian.* Mr Marryshow has ideas that make you realise you are part of a large, important race of people, living not just here in North America but in the world. An important race of people – yes, Rex, so don't take them on with their *rastus,* whatever that mean. Good, Olive. Good. Thanks. I will take over now.

"You will sort these out? Look how your sister sorting out the clothes you have to wear tomorrow! Take example. Thank you, *doudou.* Thank you, Olive. You are a real help to me.

"Rex, when I was washing this, there were so many stains on it. What were you doing? Rolling over the ground or something?" Olive asks.

"Answer your sister! What were you doing?"

"When I was chasing the squirrel…"

"Chasing the squirrel? You could run with squirrel? Look, child! Get away! Go to your sister! Look she handing you something to wipe your face."

"Mom, when we were outside playing today, they were talking about a lynching, and they looked at me and they laughed."

"Norton, sweetheart…" She stops because she really doesn't know what to say. That is not playground conversation! Well, it shouldn't be any conversation. So these children growing up knowing… And she tells herself, *That is not the end of a sentence. Knowing what?*

She can't even finish it. Sometimes it hard to cope – but, she tells herself, you have to cope.

"Children, hear what the Honorable Marcus Mosiah Garvey says. He wrote it, you know, the same thing you are hearing about and the same way you see these mad people around you are acting all the time:

> *In certain parts of the United States of America our race is denied the right of public trial accorded to other races when accused of crime, but are lynched and burned by mobs, and such brutal and inhuman treatment is even practiced upon our women.*[24]

"You hear that? Think about that! You children, we are always hearing about people getting lynched. And you, all of you, big and small, you know from how they treat you in school and when you go out that people can be wicked. But never let that make you think less of yourselves. Even if the children in school call you names and tell you you are not important, they are telling lies. Okay, Rex? Okay, Norton? Perhaps their mother and father didn't tell them not to tell lies. Don't let that make you feel bad. Don't let *them* make you feel bad. You are important and you are bright. Take what I tell you! I am your mother. I wouldn't lie to you. Hear what I tell you and make sure you put something in your head to help you live in this world. And I know you will stand up for yourself. But take care out there. Okay? Study your book and study your head! Olive? Olive, I didn't know you ironing right away already. I thought… Okay. One or two pieces for school? But that is a big job, Olive. Leave the ironing for tomorrow. I will see what there is for the two of them to wear. You will have to heat up the stove and all that; you know you don't do that just so. I know it a little rumpled but – we will see. When I finish here, I will check.

"Malcolm, you there yawning and scratching your stomach. You tired? You finish what you doing? You put them away? Let me see.

"So you children, think of what Mr Garvey saying there. As a race we don't get opportunities – and we should – so we should try to get the opportunities we know are ours by any means possible. I will give you a piece to read later.

"Look at that. Continue that there. Okay? Take a look at it:

"We assert that the Negro is entitled to even-handed justice before all courts of law and equity in whatever country he may be found, and when this is denied him on account of his race or color, such denial is an insult to the race as a whole and should be resented by the entire body of Negroes. [25]

"Okay? So he is always writing about race, about how the Negro people feel – and should feel – about how they are treated in the world. When they tease you in school, just shrug it off. I know it's not easy, but try.

"Okay. Okay. Okay. He tired, Olive. That's why he's crying. He asleep all the time. Mammie baby awake? Your sister making you cry? No. She just trying to make you hush! Is tired the baby tired, Olive. Mammy sweet one? Just put him to lie down on my bed inside there again. He will sleep. Both of them will sleep. But don't wake him up, you know. He self need sleep, too.

"So the Honorable Marcus Mosiah say:

"*Our struggle as Negro people is not domestic. It is not for any one nation. It is for the Negro peoples of the world. We have to think internationally.*

"So you-all must read it and see if you could learn it off like how I used to learn things by heart. It will take time, but when you read it, listen to each other say it. Okay, go on now. Everybody finish what they doing? Alright! Run outside for just a few minutes before the light disappear completely in this dark, dark place. Then wash your skin for the evening. Wash away all that dirt you collect all day. Relax little bit, but come when you hear I call you. Okay? Okay, I say! Go on now! Go on!"

19. The Midwest 1920s and 1930s. Memories from La Digue. Plants make me smile.

"You taking care of the plot your father cut out for you? Good. Look at these! I see these same herbs here – well, I think they call them herbs here too, is just that they take out the 'h' when they pronounce it… so their 'erbs' is the same as our 'herbs'. You see this? This is *shado beni*. Good for the cold. This one is cactus. Very good for the skin. Keep your skin nice and smooth – and clean. You know why this cactus grows here in these parts? Because it not far from the lakeshore. And cactus good for the hair, too, you know. Serious. Yes. Don't make up your face, Olive. It really good for the hair. I go wash my hair with it and you will see how it makes it smell clean and nice and keeps it full and good. And you see this little kind of vine here? That is periwinkle. In Grenada we call it Old Maid. Here they call it periwinkle, I think. You make a tea with it and that is very good for the sugar… or what they call diabetes. And this one here with the yellow flower – this is senna. Good clean out it give you. Clean you out through and through. Clean out your intestines. You children must know these things. Move over and dig in that corner, Wilfred. We have things here we used to grow at home in the garden. Smell this. It smell good, eh? Chives to use for seasoning, and the garlic; we grow them the same way as this on the hill in La Digue, where I come from in Grenada. I hope you-all could go to Grenada one day. Careful! Careful! Don't fall there. Pull out those weeds over there. You know, although *people* don't know they are like other people, *plants* know they have friends and family in other places. Same, same thing. Look at how the earth knows. The land not foolish. And this – this is sage; it grow in La Digue same way. And same so, we have this little leaf thyme that we use to season the meat and you could put a little in some food like in the cheese sauce and in the macaroni pie I always make for you. But look, look! We have here the big thyme – you see this big leaf? I think here they call it oregano – but it is the same big thyme. In fact, that West Indian lady over on the other side of town, Mrs Mc Guire, she tell me that they call this big thyme Cuban oregano, too. Smell it. It smell good, eh? Same so, same same thyme it have in La Digue. The earth push up these things the same way here and in La Digue. I have to smile when I see these plants. They make me happy. You children have to take note of these things and always come to the land – when the weather allow you to do it, because when the cold start in this Michigan here, sometimes is like life stop for me. I can't understand this cold. I don't know if I will live long enough to understand it, but that is Papa God secret. Visit the land. It hold some good secrets. See how the plants grow same way in Grand Rapids, in Lansing, in La Digue. And they don't even have to get visa. They here because land is here and land is there and land knows its own. Land is not like people. When I come up here and meet these plants that I know and that I could grow the same way as in La Digue when the weather change, I know that for sure there is something more powerful than mortal man. The plants remind me that this place belong not only to you children and your father but is mine, too.

"I grow where they plant me. Look how plants have sense! *Gadé.* They plant me here. I grow here. Careful. Careful."

20. Turn your hand to something.

"Let me try and get this pattern right for this pair of booties I making for the people over there on the High Road. I promised them that I would have it ready soon. And when I finish this pair, I have to make another one for another family. I knitting these booties but the other family want theirs crochet.

"Knit one, purl one, knit one, purl one, knit one…

"You know? There was this poem that we learned. I don't think it was in any of the Royal Readers, but our Standard Five teacher brought it in one day and he made us learn it. It was just before I left school. It was a nice nice poem, by a poet named Thomas Hood. We used those poems to think about how to write our own poetry. Sir used to say, 'Try to get the rhyme, but even if you don't get the rhyme all the time, get the rhythm of a poem.' Let me stop here for a minute and think about this and be sure not to mess up my knitting. I don't want to drop stitches. But is alright. I have the rhythm. Write something that you could feel the rhythm in, Sir used to say. The rhyme will come when you work on it. Even if you don't get the rhyme, feel the rhythm. Feel the rhythm. And sometimes we had to try to figure out – what he mean, the rhythm! Yes. I hear you asking me, Olive. Is like how you know a song, you don't know the words and the rhyme scheme and everything, perhaps, but you know how it go! You could move to it. You have the rhythm. Yes. I see you moving your body. Is alright. Move your body. You have the rhythm.

"Knit one, purl one, knit one, purl one…

"And then look around you, he would say, and try to re-create it from what you see around you. That was our Sir! He wasn't joking. He used to beat us with his strap sometimes. He did not make joke. But he was a good teacher. I remember the poem that he brought in that day.

> I remember, I remember,
> The house where I was born,
> The little window where the sun
> Came peeping in at morn;
> He never came a wink too soon,

Nor brought too long a day,
But now, I often (wish? Yes, I think it was 'wish')
I often wish the night
Had borne my breath away!

"That was the first verse. And the last one was

I remember, I remember,
The fir trees dark and high;
I used to think their slender tops
Were close against the sky;
It was a childish ignorance,
But now 'tis little joy
To know I'm farther off from heav'n
Than when I was a boy.[26]

"Well, *he* said when I was a boy. *He* was a boy. But I'm not a boy and as my grandmother used to tell me, let anybody talk about themself and say what they want. Listen and learn the essence of the thing, my grandmother would say – and then make the thing your own. So I am not like that poet, that Thomas Hood in England. I don't think that poem was in the fifth book. Perhaps it was in one of the others. No, I think Sir really bring it in like he used to sometimes. But anyway, the poet was from England. Or I think the teacher tell us he was a mixture of England and Scotland. He is not me. I remember when our teacher tell us he from England and Scotland, those children look back at me because people say my father was from Scotland. Ha! Who know? Well, I don't remember all those things Thomas Hood remember but I really like the rhythm of the poem. So – and you children will laugh – after we read that poem I start to think other things, putting in my own ideas. And that is another story.

"Knit one, purl one... Oh gosh! I nearly drop the stitch. Purl one... I told the lady on the High Road that I will have these baby socks ready by the weekend. Or booties, as they say. She ordered them specially, and we need these few cents. You have to know how to turn your hand to something to make a dollar sometimes.

"Wait! Wait wait wait! Don't lean on me like that. Stop! You'll make me lose the pattern! Okay, *doudou* darling, okay. Knit one, purl one, knit one, purl one, knit one... Just let me finish this and then I will come and give you something. Knit one, purl one..."

21. Lessons in the American Midwest circa 1929. Negroes in America

"Good morning, Olive. Yes. Yes. Since I come out here this early morning I talking to myself as usual, because my brain overflowing with all the things going on. And yes, the baby is sleeping. You could peep in on her make sure she's okay. I leave her in the middle of the bed with pillows all around her. Don't wake her, you know – but I know I don't have to tell you that. You are a whole eight years old, not no little child who don't know nothing. Big girl. Big, big girl. Yes. Your father is gone already this foreday morning. He trying to make the rounds to do some little carpentry people ask him to do for them. It so cold out there this October morning, but he say he has to go because they will pay him and we need the money.

"Good morning, son. You-all know what you have to do, so get on with it.

"Yes, Malcolm, good morning, baby. Why are you up so early, though? You could sleep a little bit longer. You up early, child! Don't make any noise, all of you, because the baby asleep. Yes, Olive, help him with all the things he have to do this early morning. I thought you-all would sleep a little bit longer. Let me finish with this oatmeal and everything. Go outside – go outside in the back there and brush your teeth. It cold. It well cold, but you have to go and brush your teeth. Wrap yourself up properly. You just wake up and it's cold out there. Sit down a little bit first and cool down from coming out of the bed after you *koubé* up all night. Or if it's too cold, you could go back in the room and take two cups and a basin with you and do what you have to do and then empty out all the water afterwards.

"Watch that porridge for me, eh, Olive? Just turn it little bit. Don't let it stick to the bottom of the pan.

"When they ready – when they all finish wash up, empty out

that water and come back inside, and when it ready, pour out some for them, okay? You going help me out?

"Yes, Mammie."

"You wash your hands outside there already, Rex? Well alright, then. Big one help little one and you-all make it! Where you big brother? Come, the three of you, as soon as you finish eating, go and take a proper wash and everything and get yourself ready for school.

"Olive, I know these last days I've been really upset – even more than usual because they trying to stop us from living in this area. Bringing lawsuit, saying that we know we are living in a white area, where we shouldn't be living. Only white people should live here in this part of Michigan. We should be down where all the other Negro people live. That's what they say. Can you imagine that? Olive, you telling me that you see people snooping around, from your room up there in the attic that your father make comfortable, to give you your own space as a growing young lady. God be praised! We trying, but at each turn, demself trying to put something in our way. Anyway, you growing up. And your father is a good provider. Careful! Careful! Careful how you moving that!

"You children are Negroes in America, so you have to know how things going for Negroes. You are growing up here different from the way I grow up in Grenada because you are American Negroes. But you are growing up different from your father, too, because he grew up in Georgia all those years ago and you are growing up here in Michigan. And times changing – or we hope times changing and we working to try and make sure times change. They say the South worse; well, I really don't understand what worse could mean. But although there is the Klan and the Black Legion and other white devils to try to make life miserable, we could still lift up our voice here in protest. Yes, yes, my child, Mama said white devils. You told me that they call you all kinds of names in school. And you see how they try to make us afraid here in our very own home. As we tell you children, you must always lift up your voice and fight for yourselves and for the race. And push back against this ignorance as much as we can. We don't want you-all to get hurt, so be careful. And think about it. Think about the way things are and I know you will want to make it different.

315

"I don't know what it is these people looking for, but I know they don't want us here. They want all Black people to stay together in the town down there, in one area where they could make us catch hell, and where there would be no danger of our children and their children mixing with each other. What a world! I know is early morning and you getting ready for school, but you know, it never have a proper time to say these things, and you not too young to know that now they are fighting really hard to get us out of this place where we living. Is all of that your uncle know why he tell us to be careful up on the hill here. It's your home, too, so you should know. You must know what is happening. This is what me and your father struggling against. They bring up a clause that is there on the land paper. It's there, so no sense doubting it. Right there on the land paper, but they should shame. The clause say that only people of the Caucasian race should live here. Pass that paper up on the shelf there for me, Olive. You-all see this? Good morning, Wilfred. I say you not getting up this morning. Come let me show you. All of you. The writing written big and bold that Negro people should not live here. You see it? But I want you – all of you – to know that that is wrong. That is crazy. People sign things fast when they have a whole lot of paper to sign for land and for house and things like that – or sometimes, even if you know the thing there, but you don't see why you shouldn't be living in a certain area like this one, so you just ignore them sometimes because you know their law have nothing to do with God and is the law of worthless man. Still, eh, when you are Negro, you have to make sure to read everything because is you and you alone – nobody there for you. But even when you read it, is another thing, because you have to decide what to do. Give in and let them push you in some area where you know you don't want to live because they make sure nothing there for your advancement and the advancement of your children, or fight? But I tell you children, remember that clause. Only people of the Caucasian race – they write that, big and bold – can live here legally! Imagine saying that! That is so backward and ignorant I can't believe they consider themselves sensible to put that down on paper for everybody to see. But they do it. I remember Sir, my teacher in Grenada all those years ago, saying that he was amazed at some of the things they actually put down on paper in the Legislative Council, the legal body in Grenada at the time. So is not just white people here, but is colonial people throughout this place we call America. This continent of America that Sir, my teacher, used to talk about. Is how they think of Black people here and back home in the Caribbean too. They do different things depending on how much of them, and if they coming or going or staying. But is the same thing they think of Black people. So here the law saying is we that wrong because we break the law. They set up things so that you always in the wrong! And the Honorable Marcus Mosiah Garvey talk about just that – the way their children are the ones to get the good schools, and I always know I would want you children to go to the schools theirs going to because those are the ones they spending money on. That is why they could tease you and nobody care – because as far as they are concerned, you not supposed to be in their school, but I don't want you to think we are doing anything wrong. *They* are not right. They are not better than you. Remember that! I'm not making you children go to schools they decide they are not putting money into! Go to their schools, get the knowledge, and then use it how we want as a people. *Gadé mizè mwen, non*! Look me trouble!

"They make me feel I always have to be talking to you children and telling you to watch the world and to walk carefully because you are Negroes in America. And you are Negroes that belong to the West Indies, too, because that is where I am from. And as Mr Garvey say, you belong to the world. You are international. And you are not backward. One set of Negroes have different opportunities from another set and so they think differently, but one set is not better than another set.

"Yes, Yes. Take that plate. Take that plate up there. I didn't mean to talk all this talk to you children this morning. I get up well early because a lot on my mind, but I didn't mean for you children to be up so early and hearing all of this. Anyway!

"Take your finger out of your nose, child. What you digging for inside there? Clean him up, Olive –

"The meeting I tell you I want us to go to is organised by the NAACP. And over the years some of their people don't too much like the UNIA and Mr Garvey, but look at this now. Look how the NAACP take up our cause and fighting to be sure we stay in the house and don't get kicked out of the area because we are black. Look at that! Learn from that, too. We have to stick together if we want to achieve something in this world. The UNIA weak these days but look how the NAACP standing up with us here in Michigan!

"Okay. Okay, Olive. I will take care of the others. They have me head confused this morning with this house business.

"But you-all go on, go and get ready. You have to leave for school just now. Go on! They have me so I can't stop talking about this, and you children need to know! You need to know!"

22. X-rated.

"You finish sweep around the house? Norton and Malcolm, come here. Your sister preparing your supper. Take the baby bottle from her for me."

"Mom, it might be a bit hot for the baby. It will burn her mouth." Norton speaks with a thumb in his mouth.

"Let me see... Your sister said it was hot but she put it to stand in a pan of water so I think ... Okay ... Okay. It feels... Alright ... Put it back for a little bit. I don't want her starting to cry... Put it back for a little bit. A little bit. Thanks, Norton. You taking good care of your sister."

"Mom..."

"Yes, Malcolm. You, too. I don't mean to ignore you. You're taking good care, too. Both of you, sit down. After you done eating the breakfast your sister prepare for you – Malcolm, why those hands looking like you didn't wash them? Go back and wash all up your arm at the back there where I can see all the dust. And after the two of you eat, before you do your homework, sit down and read this passage here from a speech by Mr Garvey. Sound out the words and then later we could talk about it. Okay. Yes. You can read some of it out loud, so I can hear it. Look at it carefully:

I was sold to some slave master in the island of Jamaica. Some Irish slavemaster who subsequently gave my great-grandfather his

name. Garvey is not an African name; it is an Irish name. As
Johnston is not an African name, Garcia is not an African name,
Thompson and Tobias are not African names. Where did we get
those names from? We inherited them from our slave masters,
English, French, Irish, or Scotch. So, if I was born in Jamaica, it
is no fault of mine. It was because that slave ship which took me
to Jamaica did not come to American ports.[27]

Okay. Sit there and read all of that about names."

23. The Fire.

One morning, Olive walks downstairs to say that from her attic
room window she saw a *soucouyant* sprinkling things around the
house. "I was frightened, Mom. I don't know if it was rice." She
wonders if it was rice because her mother had kept them spell-
bound with her stories of a scary creature from Grenada, a *soucouyant*,
a creature that flew about at night, sucking people's blood. To catch
it, people would have to sprinkle salt around the house so that it
wouldn't be able to get back into its skin. Their mother's stories did
not say what happened then, after the *soucouyant* was left unable to
fly, existing without a skin. Perhaps it just kept its head down and
found some way to merge back into the population, unknown and
somehow unseen. Anyway, because of those stories, Olive thought
they had been visited in the night by a *soucouyant*.

"You say your prayers?" her mother asks her. "That is what does
happen when children don't say their prayers. They think about all
kinds of foolishness and it scares them. That story I told you is an
Ananse story. Nancy story, we call it, thing that don't really happen.
Ananse is really a spider creature from the Akan people of West
Africa, but we call all kind of story, not only the ones about spider,
nancy story. Don't be afraid. Say your prayers tonight."

Olive is careful to say her prayers that night. She doesn't see
any *soucouyant*. In fact, she sleeps on a long bench in the hall
downstairs, just outside her parents' room and she doesn't look
outside. She knows that her father is out still – he is always

319

working or preaching – and this time he went to the Wisconsin UNIA Liberty Hall to preach and have meetings. She wishes he would come back quickly. Perhaps when he comes back she will go upstairs. She drifts off to sleep, thinking about that in the darkness and about her mother and brothers. She doesn't hear when her father comes in nor see him when he dashes out of the room and runs outside, carrying a gun. What wakes her is a loud explosion. Olive screams. She can see flames coming from the top part of the house. Oseyan rushes out of the room with the baby in her arms. The house is on fire. The boys tumble out of the room next to their parents' room. They can see the red-yellow flames seeming to encircle the house. Oseyan and Olive scream. "Come," Oseyan says. "Hold the baby. Malcolm! Rex! Where is John? Norton?"

Olive shouts, "Outside! The boys run out, Ma. Hurry!"

"You go with the baby. I'll see who else."

"That is everybody, Mom. Dad?"

"We heard a sound just before the explosion and he ran outside with the gun!"

"Come quick, Mom! Come quick!"

In a little while, they hear the sound of noise. Engines. Shouts. People are gathering, walking from all directions, moving toward the house. Oseyan and her children stand outside in their night clothes, in their bare feet, and in shock. They watch the flames lick and climb, devouring their house. Oseyan holds the baby close, letting the child hide her eyes by burrowing into her neck, her shoulder. She looks around and makes sure she sees all of them – Wilfred holding Rex by the hand, Malcolm holding onto Rex's other one, Olive holding one of John's hands, Norton holding the other. Her eyes rove over them again – bare feet, underpants, for Olive and herself a thin nightie. What was that scrambling sound that woke them up and where is Baron now? A man walks up to her. "Let me put the children to sit in my car," he says. "My wife will watch them. They will be safe there." Should she? She has seen him sometimes. His face always looks kind. He doesn't look like one of the mad ones. How should she –? He says, "Really, it's alright." He stretches his hand out toward Malcolm. Rex pulls at Malcolm's other hand, pulling in the other direction.

A woman walks up – white, of course. She puts her arm on the man's shoulder. He says, "This is my wife." The woman says, "Let us help you." Oseyan looks from the white woman to the black couple standing a few paces back. Even in this confusion, she can tell they seem to be friends of this couple, or at least to know them. She can't take in a lot at this point. She looks at Rex and Malcolm, says, "Boys, go with them." Olive says urgently, "Mom, you sure?" Oseyan says to her, "Go with them. See where they are going." Still holding on to John, who is holding on to Norton, Olive follows the couple and the two boys.

A white man, in a uniform that is either police or firefighter or something like that comes up to the white couple and asks, "Who lives here?"

Wilfred points, "That's our mother there, with the baby."

"The lady standing there in the long – ? That's your mother?"

"In the nightdress. Yes."

The questions begin. The main interest seems to be where their father is, and if there were any guns or anything that could explode in the house. What were they doing? What did they do? What dangerous things are in the house? The questions begin. Suddenly Oseyan thinks, perhaps Olive's soucouyant was a real live person. He was sprinkling something, and perhaps it wasn't salt. She feels and looks even more bewildered, more dazed. She turns and stares at her children walking away, at her daughter who is quickly following the couple and the boys. She tries to think a prayer. She wants Baron to be there but she almost wishes he would not come now. The questions are about what he had in the house. She can hear that they already know how they will investigate this. She is relieved when she sees Mrs McGuire's slight frame hurrying toward her.

PART IV

PREMONITIONS AND ENDINGS

1931-1939

24. 1931. Blood in the dream.

She is up at five as usual, just to make sure she'll be ready for the day when it comes creeping in. Last night hasn't helped. For once she wishes he had snored harder and perhaps that would have frightened away her dreams. Where they have moved to is decent enough, and as usual he has started to build up things so his family can be comfortable, but the downstairs is not quite finished. *One step at a time*, Ma says with her usual calm, as if trouble is to be expected, as if starting over is ordinary, as if the important thing is how you let trouble see who is in charge. They will be okay.

As she lies down there in the night, she is back in La Digue, walking up the hill past the house in Waterfall, in her school uniform. She reaches the top of the hill and suddenly he is with her – her husband. They are walking past the cricket field, past Upper Capitol, on a stony road, turning left and walking past the old Belle Vue estate – the house, cane fields, cocoa fields.

Then she is crying and he is walking ahead of her, turning back to shout something. She can't hear what he is saying but he is moving his hands up and down, agitated, angry. Instead of moving forward through St James and around to Birchgrove, they are at the hill again, walking back down, this time, toward the house and they are wet from the blood falling out of the sky, blood falling like rain. At first it falls on him and she is sobbing. But then she looks up and the blood is falling on her face. He is making a garbled sound and is covered with blood.

The sound of something garbled. That's when she is pulled awake by his snoring. She is crying as she wakes. She stifles her sobs, whisper-sobs because she knows that he will be angry if she wakes him. She is always on about something, he will say. Always with her dreams and her superstitions. She puts her hands to her face and sobs, shoulders shaking. She is always believing in foolishness, he will say. In her head, the blood is still falling.

She gets up and stands by the baby's crib he built. But no. She must not stand there with the blood in her memory. Little ones feel even more than big people. She cannot stand like this over her little two-year-old. That's what she thinks. She goes out to the hall. On her left is the room he partitioned off for the four boys. At least the boys are no longer bunched up, lying there all feet and arms and legs askew. Wilfred even has a little separate space partitioned off for himself. Five boys she and Baron have, yes. Five! And for some reason this morning it hits her particularly hard that they have the responsibility for five young Negro men in this America! The girls, too, yes, but this idea hits her harder this morning for some reason. It is not a thing that makes you want to smile. Their father works hard. He might be many things, but he is a worker. They can be comfortable without too many problems in there. Olive is in her room on the other side. Olive is good at taking care of her little sister, Inez, no longer a baby now, even though since the fire, Oseyan feels better still keeping Inez in her room. She's not even sure why, but she feels better. The fire rocked her and troubled her spirit even more than it was usually troubled by the goings-on. And also, perhaps she wants someone else in the room, however young, to remind her that their bodies still don't seem to know any way to respond to their passion for politics other than to bring another human into the world. She must really remember what the medical people said. Be careful with your body. Even more than the medical people, she must listen to what her body is telling her. And this year, even though Mr Garvey has gone, they celebrated Emancipation month. They had services; they talked about Emancipation. And she felt so proud of her husband, the Elder, preaching about Black excellence and how the African nations will survive in spite of every effort of the devil to rub them in the dirt! Last year, 1930, was a good Emancipation year and a year to talk up the UNIA, in spite of everything.

1930. Perhaps she was fired up because of the census and all the questions about their business. The last time they did that census and she was part of it, Wilfred was just born and they were in Philadelphia. Now they come back again asking people about their business. She took two years off her age for this census. It feels good because her body is so tired these days it needs the little encouragement to see written that she is 32 and not 34. It felt good seeing them write it down. Asking people question about their business! Making us remember all this thing about who born where – Georgia and Grenada, and Pennsylvania and Nebraska and Wisconsin and now here. After all of that remembering, I sure that is why we get so fired up and hold all that service and remembering for August Emancipation month. You need something to keep you going for yourself after they stir up so much thing! The things they have to write down: my husband is a labourer who does odd jobs and I am a Negro housewife born in the British West Indies, and I am not working. So they know now, if they did not know before! I not working although I am at work from dawn to dusk! I am not working, their paper will say. Huh! Let me go and start my not-working.

One thing she is proud of, the census takers say their house is worth six hundred dollars. Not a lot of Negro people with a house worth six hundred dollars. And for sure is the two of them do that. In spite of everything people do to keep them down. He doing the building, like Poopa used to do, and she doing all the up-keeping and putting aside and other things. Their house is worth six hundred dollars. That is something to be proud of. Every time those devils try to pull them down, they build, even though he has to do it with his own hands – and with his family helping! We will make it, she thinks. Watch us! We will make it!

The ups and downs of 1930 make them look for this Emancipation joy and so, in spite of everything, 1931 was going to present them with a May baby, but Papa God stepped in and she had to say *Mèsi, Papa Bondyé.* Youself could see the body can't take it.

Now she must get the older ones ready for school. Let her put on some water for the oatmeal. It will keep them – all of them. Wilfred is grown. He can take care of himself, but he like oatmeal too. Olive is old enough. She is a responsible child. That little girl put out her school clothes since last night. She is always concerned about order. That's how she herself was at nine years old? She can't remember.

Just the question in her head threatens to bring tears, because she thinks of Ma. She doesn't understand why the tears come so quickly these days. Her body is tired. The doctors told her she must make sure not to get pregnant again. Ma had many children herself, but when she, Oseyan, was nine or ten, she and Amèlie were the only children in the house. And Amèlie was often with one of her sisters. The others – her uncles and aunts – were big and gone, or mostly gone. She wonders how Ma dealt with it all – in the days with her, but in the days long before her – with her mother and the other children. Poor people don't have it easy with a lot of children. She moves to where her little girl had put her folded school dress across the ironing board. Olive will be up soon to help get breakfast ready for the little ones. She can depend on Olive for that. You don't have to be after her about things. And you can depend on Wilfred to remind Rex to take his medicine before he leaves the house. He is such a help to her, her big boy, her first born.

And then Malcolm – Malcolm. She would have to put out a clean pair of pants for him – that one she ironed last night and put over the screen – and remind him to make sure he doesn't go crawling around everywhere. He is a big boy, six years old, and there are three younger ones to be thinking about. Hopefully John and Inez won't get up before the others leave, though Rex would almost certainly be trying to get ready so he could go with Malcolm. But he is sickly, that one. She worries about his hernia condition. It makes him so sickly. If she knew those high-up doctors, she would see if one of them could do something for him. That little boy wants to do everything his brother does. Lord help! *It is not that it is too much with all of them, non, Ma, but sometimes I hardly have a minute to think. Tell me how it was for you, Ma. And Ma, I am tired. My body just tired.*

She thinks again of how she used to help out Auntie Gerda with Malcolm, Olive and Wilfred the last two years before she left Grenada. It was a lot, but that was the kind of "a lot" you could enjoy, in spite of everything. Now that life has arrived, she is even more sure that long-time helping out Auntie Gerda was small potatoes. Nothing at all to compare. People used to say that when you taking care of people children, at least you know they have to go home. Yes. Or at least that somebody else is responsible for them. More than she can explain, she understands the saying *Vini ou kai vini. Ou kai wè* – Come you coming. You going see. You will see. She not coming any more. She reach. So now she seeing for sure! It would really make a difference if she had somebody here, right here in Michigan with her. Anybody. Anybody. Her husband here, yes – and that good, but that is another story. Well, that's the way men are, they say. Children usually the woman problem. But he does work. She can't lie about that. He working hard. It's just that taking care of the children every day is always *her* worry. And if he have to act with them the way he acting – always shouting and beating – sometimes is best he leave them to her. But she can't finish say that he does work hard. He always out there, doing something, fixing something, trying to get money, and he bringing the money right to her. Well, she shouldn't complain. He does really put himself out to make sure they have somewhere to live and she very proud of that.

And besides odd-jobbing, he always out somewhere preaching. And the children proud of his preaching and of his teaching. That is one good thing. People respect him. And perhaps the preaching and the organising help him to respect himself. People know he not afraid of anybody, and that is a good quality for a Black man to have in a world that is always trying to push you down. It is a dangerous quality but it make you feel good, too. The children might be afraid of him when he shouting, but they are proud of him when he doesn't let the white men treat him like a boy – like a – nigger. Say it like it is. The children know that they don't have to be that.

But sometimes he so drastic with them – like they have to be on edge every time he around. Shouting at everybody. She can't even speak her Creole language in his presence because he think she's showing off with her French. *Oh Ma! You don't know.* That little Malcolm is the only one that could get on his good side. He like the fair skin, is what! Say the thing like it is. His father likes fair skin. That is why he spoil that little boy so much. *But not if I have anything to do with it*! That child will have to learn that light skin is no special kind of badge of honour. So much he have to learn! But he will learn! All of them will learn!

And this thing about how they were forced to move when

people burn down their last house is not something she want to think about. Is the wickedness of people in the world, white people who think Negro people shouldn't live next to them – and she just want to throw away that chapter and keep the key somewhere private. She will have to take it out from time to time and examine it, but not now. Not now.

25. Their mother's tears.

He is in one of his moods, fretting about everything, and she is getting the children ready so she just leave his breakfast out there on the kitchen table. The two big ones gone to school already, and she must settle the others. Today she will try to do a macaroni pie for lunch. He likes that, even if he say that her way – the way Ma used to make it – is different from how he know it. He like it, though, and that is the main thing. She will do some fried chicken with it and some gravy on the side with carrots in it. She hope she could get going before he come back in from outside because she don't want him to ask her to cook rabbit or something worse. He start that up again and the older she get the less she find she have the strength to deal with it. She not putting any of that pork knuckle or ham hock or whatever they call it in the black-eyed peas. He damn well know she don't like to cook pork but he still want her to put that foolishness in the peas. He'd better not ask her anything. If she put all the food on the fire quick quick, hopefully he won't come and open her pot and ask her any stupid question.

As if her thoughts have called him, he comes inside and walks up behind her. He says, "I will go get a rabbit in the pen. Cook that today."

"No, Baron. Not the rabbit. Please. You know I don't like to cook that. I can't bear to see how those animals look at you with the eyes so sad and so pleading. And rabbit meat is not good meat to eat. No, I'm not cooking rabbit today." Is not pork, so she won't shout too much, but what is it with him, anyway?

"What? And who are you telling you're not cooking rabbit? Woman, watch your mouth! Rabbit is what I'm eating today and

330

you'd better get used to the idea and cook it! You have so much damn foolishness in your head!" He is sounding almost conversational, but this is the conversation where he always has to be in charge.

"Baron!"

"Baron what?"

How had she found herself in this mess? They have been together, married, a whole twelve years. He know what she like and what she don't like. They've gone through this. He know what is against her belief – even if it's not one particular kind of religion – it's still against her belief and the way she grow up to eat pork and rabbit. In the beginning he had just looked at her as if he couldn't believe she meant it when she said she wouldn't cook pork, wouldn't put ham hock in the peas. She is remembering now that when they were there in Montreal and she said that, he even smiled afterward and passed his hand over her hair. He knew that was the way they grow up in her family. He even said once that she was fancy – "Real fancy, this my woman."

Now he says, "Look. Cook this rabbit for when I come back."

"Baron…"

"Baron nothing. Cook the damn rabbit."

He stands there now with the live rabbit in his hand. As she watches, he position his hands and twist the neck of the rabbit. She screams. Six-year-old Malcolm stands with his mouth open. She knows he has seen his father do this before, but perhaps with her standing there crying, this time seeing the rabbit killed, his pet – because Malcolm pets all the rabbits they have in the pen – hurts him more. And the special cruelty of doing it in the kitchen! He could have done it outside! What punishment he plan for her this morning? The child covers his eyes. As if sensing the tension, John, still a baby really, cries. Rex stands with one finger in his mouth, his eyes wide, his hand worrying his white vest. Two-year-old Inez sits on the floor, hand in her hair, finger in her mouth, looking up at them. Their father pulls a bucket from the corner and throws the bloody rabbit down into it.

Suddenly Oseyan shouts, "That is the blood, Baron. That is the blood I dream about. It's not good, Baron. That is the blood."

He frowns. "What nonsense are you talking about now?

331

Another one of your hoity toity fanciful imaginings. Woman, cook the damn rabbit and have it ready by the time I come back."

He turns and walks away. And suddenly her life is this moment: children crying, a bloody rabbit, a man walking away. Sobbing, she picks up the rabbit, her face twisted with a hurt too deep to name. There is some boundary that has been crossed here. She knows it. She can feel it. She just doesn't know how to place it. She feels totally unable to control whatever it is. It is not only that it all hurts her because he is so bossy but things are hurting somewhere else, hurting in her spirit in a way she cannot explain. It is all troubling her deep down. She picks up a knife from the rack near to the sink, a knife like the one Ma used to call the brown-handle kitchen knife, and, still crying, she begins to skin the rabbit. The front door slams. He is gone. She turns and looks through the kitchen window. She can see him walking up the road. She looks back down at the rabbit through her tears and, as she turns again, her hands still on the rabbit, she looks back up the road at him; it is as if she sees the rabbit walking out there, and both are covered in blood – her husband and the rabbit. She drops the knife, rushes to the window. Jesus! The blood from last night. He don't know what he doing. Blood calling him. She goes to the front door, rushes down the steps and outside. "Baron!" she screams. "Baron!" She mutters, "Is not his fault. He don't know. He can't see! He don't know!" The white apron bunched in her right hand, covered with the blood of the rabbit, she stands there. "Baron!"

He hears her. He turns around. He waves. He stops and looks at her. Perhaps he thinks she wants to talk. Perhaps he wonders why she is calling him so urgently, so – feelingly – right after she has been so angry with him about the rabbit. Perhaps he thinks he should have spoken more gently to her. Perhaps he sees back to the beginning with her twelve years ago. Perhaps he could see before that, to his days in Butler, Georgia, not far from that shop that is like a corner shop in La Digue. Perhaps he want to tell her a man has ways that he has to be. Perhaps he want to tell her that people history important, and that their histories cross, his and hers. Perhaps he want to tell her he glad she with him and he proud of her and happy they have children together. Perhaps he wants to tell her that times hard but they together, and that is good even if he doesn't always know how to say what he feel. Perhaps he want to tell her that life is rough but he glad he going through it with her and the children. Perhaps he wants to tell her that they must talk. Baron stands suspended there for long moments. He stand up there for so long that she know he want to say something. He stands until the blood stops falling. Then he turns and continues going. He just continue walking, she thinking. He gone! She shouts again: "Baron! Baron! Don't go! Don't go!" But he is gone.

Her feet feel like they are dragging heavy chains as she pulls herself back up the steps and through the doorway. In the kitchen, she stands with her back to the sink and her hand over her face. Her baby girl has fallen silent and is just staring. John is crying and the three bigger ones still at home – Malcolm, Rex, Norton – are watching it all and seeing their mother's tears.

26. The Body.

They give him some lines in the newspaper. They call him THE BODY. The body will be taken back to Georgia. He was forty-one years old, the report says. He lived at Jolly Corners, it informed. He died at the corner of Detroit and East Michigan.

Those left are a widow, ten children, his parents, siblings. He was running to catch a street car, the newspaper report says. The street car driver did not see the Negro. She wonders – *When do they see a Negro?*

The items found on the body were purse, street car check, overcoat. Interment will be in Georgia.

27. Passing?

Now she has to think of what else she can do, how she will manage. She can continue doing what she has always done – planting, sewing seeds, sewing dresses, darning, crocheting doilies, crocheting gloves, knitting socks, teaching the children, cooking, washing. She can continue as she has always done. But some of those things are the work for self, and, she thinks, society, and they don't bring in money. The washing, the cooking, the teaching, some of the sewing – those are for herself and for her family. So – what else? She is not a carpenter and the children must have some place to live. The downstairs is not quite finished. The work of one half of this partnership is gone. And the children have to go to school. Book learning is the future. It was true when Sir said it, when her Ma said it long ago, and, she thinks, it is still true now. The children must go to school. Book learning is the future.

Her big boy is eleven. He can't do the carpentry work his father did. He is not big enough, for one thing, and then his father didn't take him along to do those things. Books, they always told him, that is what he must stick to. Study your lessons. You are going to be an office man when you grow up. And Olive has to be in school. She teaches the little ones already, but she has to be in school too. And then she also works hard in the house. That helps, but it doesn't bring in money to buy food and clothes and other things. You will be a teacher, in spite of what your teachers say. That's what they told her. But what now? Should she sell the car? She thinks about that because it is one of the first things the social workers say when they visit the widow with seven children who needs assistance. *Sell the car*, as if the sight of the car offends them. It is what helps the family to move around for all the little things around here. They won't move again in a hurry, but it's a big family and she has to do things for and with them. She is not selling the car. Perhaps she will get some kind of pension. She doesn't know how that will go. She has to think what she can do.

She gets jobs in their houses, cleaning their spaces. But it's not easy. Some people really don't want Negroes right inside of their house working. Work outside. Work on the farm, yes, but some of them don't want you in their houses. At least in Grenada they take you quick to cook and clean for them. Perhaps some of them here, too, but others, no. They don't want Negro people around them who think they are somebody. And some don't want Negro people at all. Anyway, if they don't ask exactly who she is, she doesn't have to answer. But she realises that sometimes they see the children and pull back their job. She gets one job cleaning a house. One of the children comes by to ask her something in that house where she is working. The dirt asks no questions, and the cloths and cleaning agents she uses get rid of it. But those who have to pay her ask, "Is that your child?" And just like that, the job is no more. "Here. This is what I owe you for the days you worked. Don't come back." The good thing is that the woman doesn't say "Don't come back, Nigger." The children say they call them that in school all the time, but the woman doesn't say that. Just – *Don't come back!*

If she keeps them out of sight, she might get a job, but can she keep hiding her children? Should she keep quiet about who she is so her children can eat? If they think you are all right because they think you are white, then perhaps let them think what they want to think. Perhaps her children will eat if she hides them and claims the reprobate's complexion. She whispers, *I have met a truly savage people.* Her little girl, only three, tugs at her dress and says what she hears others saying, "Are you talking to yourself, Mom?" That's what they say – the social workers, and now her own children.

"No, sweetheart, I'm singing for you. *Alouette, gentille alouette; Alouette, je te plumerai.*" The child relaxes, leans against her mother as she sits on the chair in the kitchen.

28. Eating the bread that the devil knead.

This is what my grandmother mean. She used to say, *Bad how it is, we are not the worst. We have food, we have clothes. But some people – ye manjé pen ki dyab pentwi. They eat the bread that the devil knead. We not so bad, we have a place to stay.* That is what she used to say.

Well, Ma, now I eating the bread that the devil knead. Before, with the work that Baron used to do, with the things that we grow there in the place where we couldn't be because is not a Negro area, we could put food on the table, we could put clothes on our backs.

But they talking legal talk about rights. *Legal shenanigans*, you used to say, Ma. Here you should see how they use that word legal for all that we know is not legal. Couldn't be legal. They fight to take our land. They fight to move us out of the house, to pull the rug out from under us. And Ma, is not that I depend on man and forget meself, but for everything they looking to see who is the man behind you, if your children have father or if they don't; if you are what they think of as *djanmèt* or if you are proper Christian woman; if they want you around them or if they don't want you. And, Ma, these are the kind of people you have to depend on for money to live. Now that Baron gone is a lesson for me to see how it so hard for woman to live alone, not because she can't live alone, but because they won't let her live alone. Black woman, that is all I know about. And perhaps is that I did know when I didn't know how to leave him when he do the things I didn't want from a man. Is not a lesson I want, Ma. Is not a lesson I want at all. But woman alone is not something they want to see. Man could be alone but is like woman alone mean something not right. Perhaps I did know before but now that I am there, it so hard, Ma.

Now that my husband gone, Ma, I struggling to find the money to buy bread. I could work; you know that because you teach me well, but Ma, I black and in this country that is a special kind of disease. And if you trying to work, black and woman is worse. And it all worse than home, Ma. Plenty, plenty worse. I don't know if you are thinking that I have the reprobate colour so I could choose, but Ma, all my life I want to be me, and I want to be what you are, Ma. I Black. Or as they say here, I am Negro. And some people call me uppity. Those that coming around now to decide things because I am a widow with children, and they have to decide if I could get pension and what not, they think I am uppity. That is what they say. If they think of you as a *djanmèt* or loose woman, as they say, is one thing; if they think you uppity is another thing. The real problem is that you are a Negro. And when you a Negro woman without a man is easy for them to think you loose and no-good. So is like I have a mark on my back.

And besides, this is what they call a downtime where the economy is concerned; for everybody things bad. I not full of pride, Ma. I don't think so. You didn't bring me up as a tender lady of leisure. I could cook; I could clean, even in other people houses. I want a job, so I going out and look for it – jobs some people say are mean jobs. But Ma, I Black. I Black. I Black and I have children so even if I want to I can't pretend I anything but Black. And worse yet, in these parts, me and my husband have a reputation for thinking that with our Black self we just as good as any white, and not just thinking it but saying it and telling other Negroes in church that they are important, too. So Ma, they think we Black and we dangerous. Baron – and I crying now just to think his name – Baron, he was a good man, in spite of everything. Elder Baron preach and he tell people the truth.

Ma, I have no money to buy bread. The shopkeeper self sorry for my children now. I know that the little one who looks like me – you remember how the children used to call me red, Ma? I know he picks up food that is not his in the shops sometimes. I know. They tell me. I hear about it. And although I quarrel with him, I can't blame him because I know he hungry. My children hungry, Ma, and it hurt. It hurt. I don't even want to look at them because I know they hungry. And I don't have a mango tree for when things bad. Is not as if I could plant two banana tree, and still you would need more than that even self you could do that. Ma, what I going do? The shopkeeper gives them stale bread sometimes and although I thankful when it happens, it hurt my heart. I talking to you a lot of the time now, Ma, because I really don't know what to do. There is a West Indian lady I talk to sometimes, and sometimes she pass by just to see how I doing, but is not everything, everything you could say, and besides she have her own problems. She black in this country, too, and she and her husband and their children – I don't think they doing too bad, but they still struggling like me and Baron used to struggle together. You know? They not doing bad in the way that me and Baron wasn't doing bad even when things hard. So I know they have their own way to make. I can't lean too heavy and say everything. Ma, Ma, that is what I have come to now. Ma, look at me! I eating the bread that the devil knead.

29. 1936-37. After twenty years in North America.

I am forty-one years old. Twenty-one years in Grenada; twenty years and almost another one in North America. Equal amount of time, really, in both places. Ma, Olive telling me I always talking to myself these days, and I could see she worrying, so I have to keep my voice down not to put too much of a burden on her, but Ma, I have to talk to you. She don't know is you I talking to. She telling me I talk to myself too much.

My oldest child, Wilfred, he just over seventeen. Time passing fast in truth, because I can't even believe he seventeen and Olive nearly fifteen. That little boy really been a father since he eleven. He was eleven years the February and they kill his father that September of 1931. Is now I could look back and think about it because in those days I couldn't think anything. I couldn't think a thing. The year that child father die, he was 11 years, 8 months and 14 days. When his father die he become a man, not like his father, because his father was a harsh man, if truth be told – a harsh man in the way that he behave with his children. My big boy is not like that. He is a father those others could talk to, yes Ma. And where that is concerned, he like the father, too, because he end up leaving school early to go and work and help me out – help out the family, so that he really become a father. My big boy is a big little man, and it hurt me that these days I see he looking at me with a look in his face as if he don't approve when he see me talking to somebody. He big enough now to cast judgement. Imagine that! And I could see it in his face even though, so far, he don't say nothing. They grow up hard, because is only the two of them, I sure – he and Olive – who could really remember much about the times before their father dead, when, bad how it is, they had enough food to eat.

When the father dead, Olive was nine. Nine or ten. Nine, and then she make ten the month after her father die. She nearly fifteen now. Fifteen, yes. Full lady. So they big now. Norton was eight when they kill Baron. Malcolm was six the May of that year. That little boy was the apple of his father's eye, as they say. Rex was four. John was three. And my baby girl was two years old. And I never forget how those little ones cry when they see me bawling that day when their father walked out, not knowing that he walking to his death. And… and… all the blood around and me feeling it in my spirit that he gone. I close it out because I have to, but I never forget. And you know, it getting harder and harder to live, Ma. I can't manage. It hurt my heart to say it, but those people that say they does help people – they suppose to be what they call social workers or whatever – but they not helping me because I not people, and I could hear it in the questions they ask me. They digging me and trying to get in my inside as if is mud they digging. And from what they saying they want to take my Malcolm away. Yes, Ma. I know I am people. I have to start to dress myself up again and keep looking like I feel proud of me, just so that I feel better. But it hard to put on clothes and fix yourself when things so bad. Let me fix my hair. Yes, I starting now self. Brush back the hair, Oseyan. You can't let them pull you down. I know, Ma. I know. And I so afraid that they going take that little boy away. He is the one that always in trouble for something. They could see it hard to control him, and it have nobody up the road like in La Digue – nobody that I could call and say I going leave him by you sometimes. Ma, I writing in the notebook again, yes. I writing. I did put that notebook away far, but it there. So, Ma, I not only talking to you. I talking to myself too. I know. Is that Olive saying, but she don't understand trouble, although she understand it a lot better than I understand it at her age. A lot of time pass, yes, and things different, and to tell you the truth sometimes I don't know what to say, but just doing this – talking to you and writing to you – this feel good, Ma. I know it make me feel better. I didn't know I still had that old notebook there, because I did hide it away. Thank God I does keep things, even if I forget where I put them. Thank God I find this when I digging to find old paper. And thank God for Olive, yes, Ma, thank God for that child. I know I leaving more and more to her these days, but to tell God truth, my heart and my head hurting me. My body tired. My spirit tired. The truth is, Ma, that I don't know what to do.

Twenty years in North America. My husband was a blessing I didn't know was a blessing. So much things he do upset me that it was hard to know. He gone now. And here I am. Here I am. I know I could manage if it wasn't this kind of world that don't care about little people – or those they see as little people. And definitely don't care about Negro people. And don't care about Negro woman. Truth to tell, Ma, I don't know what to do.

30. Reasonings in the dark.

Ma, help me. Auntie Gerda, tell me how to get through this. They will not touch my children. I will not let them hurt my children. They want to take them away. They want to have power over them so they could teach them. I know that. But you can't let your enemy have the responsibility for teaching your children. They show me that they are enemies. So I know. Me and Baron know. Ain't you know, Baron? He is not there any more. He is not here. They don't want Black people to have anything. They will not touch my children. They will not take my children away.

My big boy Wilfred look as if he don't approve from the time he see that man coming around, but me is woman. My body is still woman. And they giving me such a hard time. They – the people that in charge – they does feel better about woman when an upstanding man is around, and I hope this one is upstanding. Perhaps he can help me save my children from those devils. He look like a good strong black man. I surprise when he arrive right on my doorstep. Miss McGuire tell me to be careful of him when I tell her. But he look alright. She don't really know him either, although she say she hear that he come into the area not long ago. She tell me she heard that he saw me go into the shop, and people tell him I does drive the old car there sometimes. Even though they insisting I get rid of it, I keeping it. They don't want to see you have anything. If you in need as a Negro, they want you to look needy so they can crow. And I try to keep myself looking good, especially when I go out. You can't let people think you are the worst. Ma used to say that. And is true. They even threatening to take away the little bit of pension money, as if it's not what my husband work for in his time. And it's nothing much, but I glad I have it now. And those insurance people giving me beans. They pay out the smaller insurance, the little insurance that he had, but not the bigger one that could help us out. They say we can't get the insurance money because he committed suicide. That's what they're saying now. First they report that he fell and street car driver didn't see him. Now they saying he committed suicide. All of that help make us sure that they lie and they kill him, in truth, as people saying. So everything is pure nonsense and I won't even try to reason about it because I know they not serious. I saying I won't try to reason with them about the insurance, but I tried, and even Wilfred, my big boy, tried to state the case. But they keeping my money from me. When is not one thing is another. The one thing that make me proud is the fact that he had insurance because he did want to provide for his family in case anything happened. He was a man like that, and I am so proud of him, even as they making sure they pursue him even after death. Think about that. A Negro man without the means try to make sure he pay an insurance so he could provide for his family because he know how easy it is for them to kill black people. And after they kill him, they will not pay out the insurance. My husband. He was a good man in spite of everything. Whatever it is was eating him as a person, those are things you have to work out, you know, and we never get to talk about them. So now I have it to bear! Land, house, children, insurance. When is not one thing is another. I hope this one – this man that coming around now – I hope is not another one that the skin colour is what make his eyes catch fire. I think it was more than that with my husband, though. It had to be more than that. He was a good man. This one, I like what he look like. The thing is, he look like how my husband did look, so I guess I am attracted to a type, as Miss McGuire say. And this one have nice talk. My husband did have nice talk, too, and better talk, because he was right there with the politics and community work I was interested in. This one, I don't know. Not so much, I don't think, and that is a pity. This one saying how I beautiful and how I would make any man proud. How I look so… what is the word he use? Elegant. Elegant and upstanding! And he want to take care of me and my children, he say. And I must confess that idea attract me. He tall and black and nice looking like my husband, and he have nice talk. I hope is not just talk. He look like a good man. He is a nice, strong Black man, and from how he talk he could work, too. Ma, I hope I have found someone, *wi*. A man hand could be good for the children. They need another hand – the little ones; the first two drink water already and they could manage themselves. But especially that little one; a man's hand would be good for him. And if truth be told, it would be good for me, too. This body could take a man handling after all those rough days. It would be good to have somebody to listen and somebody to cuddle up to. I not lying, Ma, it would be good. I could talk that talk to you now, because I am full woman and you gone long time! I hope I am being sensible.

I see the children watching him. I see them looking at me, too. I see the little ones watching one another and giggling. I don't want to give a bad example, *non*. Their father dead seven years now, although sometimes is as if I could see him watching me and frowning. Seven years already, yes. And knowing children, perhaps they think their mother too old to have a man. I don't have to admit to it in public, but for myself I know that I am only just forty-one years. Going on forty-two. Not so old, in spite of the fact that I have seven children. Sometimes I think I should find out what is the proper bush to take to stop this nonsense, in spite of what they say the law is, but man does always want their own children. Ma, yes, I know. You didn't talk to me about things like that. But, Ma, even with seven children, I know I'm not old. My body tells me I am not too old. The doctor tell me since before the last two that I have too many children already, that my body suffer from too much birthing, as they say, and that could affect me in all kinds of ways. I will try to be careful, Ma. I will try to be careful. I want support, but I don't want more little children. *Fanm se yon nasyon.* I know you always say that. Woman is a nation. But man is a nation too, *wi*, Ma. Man is a nation, too.

31. A different story.

So now – a different story. That is how it is. My generation – the women in my generation – meaning my family – we don't learn. That is what my grandmother used to say. We never learn. I even fraid to talk to you, Ma, but I thought he was good, and really, I don't know how to be careful. Is either to do or not to do, and – Ma, sometimes I does think, this is dotishness, big woman in her forties still talking to her grandmother about things in her head, but – nobody know me like you. And I come over here early, take man on my account, and is like I never had the time to really find too much friend, and then sometimes friend bring you go, they don't bring you back. I just talking now. But I don't know what to do. It not easy to tell people you business. And now, he not coming around any more. Talk soft. Whisper whisper. The children – they don't even know yet, but I missed my periods. He knows. I told him. And it look like he disappear. This is a disaster. I know this is a disaster. So I create a bigger problem. I didn't solve one. *Papa Bondyé édé mwen.*

My big boy is not mine any more. He disappointed. Just from the relationship he is disappointed. I could see that. You could see it in the way he looks away from me. I hear from Olive that he going away and, he says, or Olive say he is saying that, he's not coming back. Olive says he is going out of town somewhere, to work.

But is not only the relationship or whatever you call it with that man that worrying this whole family and causing confusion. Is all the trouble with not having money for food and everything, because that continue. I still trying to look for work in people houses because I am not getting enough sewing, and I am not getting that because they know whose widow I am. But it's not only that. With the foolishness I do… even Miss McGuire… even Miss Mc Guire. It's only you I could talk to these days, Ma. Miss Mc Guire tell me off. She told me off, *wi.* She used to listen to me and give me advice, but now she asking me how I could not know better! *So you fifteen, then?* That is what she ask me. And now she is telling me more. She says that he saw me driving down the road in – in that old car you insist on keeping. That is what she said to me. She herself said that. He watched me, she said, and her husband told her that is how the story start. I guess he heard it from his friends in the rumshop or whatever it is they call that place here. He wondered who I was, that man who come here and pretend he like me; he wondered if I was white or Negro. That's what he asked them in the shop. And they told him who I was. They told him that I could write minutes after meetings, that me and my husband used to *kick ass* around the place. And he literally followed me home. Literally. That's how he ended up knocking on my front door. He saw the opportunity to make a conquest. Yes. That is what happened. He knocked on my front door and then he invited himself inside. The two big ones were at school or they may have kicked him out, judging from the look on my big boy's face afterward. I guess that child knows more than I do. I guess those children looking out for me and sometimes you have to admit that the young ones know their world better than I know it. I'm ashamed to say it, but that's the way it was. That was the beginning. He came for a conquest and he made his conquest. I don't know what he is saying in the shop now. But it is obvious he gone. Me? Well, I saw a beautiful Black man – another beautiful Black man. And I thought – well, I hoped. I feel so foolish. But that is how it happened.

And it's worse now. They definitely won't offer me work in their houses now. The social worker people are even threatening to take the pension because I – how they say the word? I cohabit, or something like that. They talk to me as if I am the dirt under their shoes. And my big boy is gone or going. And, Ma, I can't even see you, *non*, Ma. The whole place just getting dark. I feel so foolish.

No, Olive. I just talking to myself. Just talking to myself. No, you don't have to go to work, Olive, but… Yes. I went out and tried to get a job again. No. I didn't get anything. I can't find… I will keep looking. I will go out again.

32. 1938/39. *Sé djab pou vwé.* Is real devil.

People are dying in this heat wave, they say. All over Lansing it hot can't done. Heat wave, they say, like a reckoning. And there is nobody. If only there were somebody. And my big boy is going. But anyway, my big girl there, and she taking care of the little ones.

Heat wave is one thing, but there are other things, they say. Times are changing. They are talking about Negroes in the war effort! But it happened once before and not so long ago, at that. It makes me feel old. I have had seven – no, eight – eight children since the last war effort. I can barely feed this last little one. I am here talking to you still, yes, Ma. You listening? I can't see you so well now. You not fed up with me, *non?* Ma, my big girl Olive is such a blessing. Sometimes I think I see tears in her eyes, but I can't watch her cry. I should help her, but truth to tell I can't help myself. I can't watch my children because I can't feed them. That is the main thing. I can't watch them and see what I see.

Things hurt me in a place I can't even reach. Ma, I miss La Digue. I want to walk up Waterfall with Gwen. I want to run back down the hill and shout out to Gwen not to tease the lady who used to be pregnant every Monday morning. I want to see the purple bougainvillea. Ma, I miss La Digue and Holy Innocents School. I miss Sir and Mr Ansel. I miss my life.

Ma, even my big girl Olive, who is a blessing to me, she can't see you and she thinks I'm talking to myself. I want to help her but I can't help myself. I get pregnant just after Christmas, you know. I know that. So this will be an Emancipation baby, born Emancipation month. Ma, everything makes me want to cry these days, and I am not a person like that. You know I wouldn't even cry when Sir beat me and the children watching to see how red my face could get and waiting for break to call me *piti wouj wouj*.

And now I have another baby, they saying I can't take care of my child. But I feed him, Ma, I nurse him, although perhaps I shouldn't do that because my body feels weak. Formula, though, I don't have the money for that. He hurts me and I don't know where he come from, and I can't believe I'm me when I watch him, but I feed him, Ma. Olive washes his bottle for me and everything. And Olive going out to get work sometimes now. She and Wilfred trying to see how they could add to the little pension money, even though Wilfred vex up and gone. A weakness come over me, and I guess my body is older than it used to be, and it will take time to heal and feel better after this one, and I wish I could find the Dr Lang you tell me about a long time ago, but I will be okay. I am just so tired all the time. I want to go out there and work, but they not giving me work nowadays. And I miss the Movement; I miss the organisation, the United Negro Improvement Association – that was really something to work for – and I not hearing nothing much about it now.

The children can't see you, so they say I talking to myself. The big ones ask me if I'm talking to myself again and the little ones crying and telling me to stop it and I can't even watch them, because I know I should feed them. That is the biggest thing for me. Not being able to get work! And they say is the war, but is not only the war, is being Black in a white country, too. And my big son is gone, Ma. My big son is gone. He says he has to find bigger work. But before he up and go away, Ma, he took me to see the doctor and the man said I need a rest. I believe him. I feel it in *me* that I need a rest. But is something deeper that happening to me. He say that if I get a rest I will be all right in a while. I know it. I feel it in me. But right now, there is a tiredness that reach my spirit. I can't tell them and explain to them but I know it and I feel it. The only person carrying the burden now is Olive – is something, eh, how girls does have to carry so much, but I am there. I will be back soon – and those people are in the house all the time – those that say they are social workers. They making matters so much worse. Ma, they just pushing the door open and coming in, as if they have the right, and they don't give us a chance. I tell Olive to try to keep studying – you know, studying something, because the future is all, and I could see she will be a good teacher one day – she good already, and I am so proud of her – but she says she will have to leave the studying for a little while because all is just too much and I can't even watch my children. I know and I don't want her to leave the studying because education is all but it feeling like although I know that, for a little while I can't help myself. And they taking my Malcolm away. But I will pull myself together. I know I just have to stop feeling so bad in my body and my spirit. I will be okay.

"Yes, Olive, child. I just sitting down little bit to see what outside look like. I could see it from here by the gas range. Yes. Give me the baby. I will feed him. Thank you, chile. Yes. I just thinking to myself little bit, you know."

The man down the road, he wanted to give us a whole pig so we would have food to eat, and I say no and the Seventh Day people understand and they help us too, sometimes, when they could, but these others, they don't know that *pork is the meat of the pig or the sow* and that it is forbidden and they think if I don't eat it I am mad. I hear them. They are saying I am mad. If I could work up the energy I would tell them what is what and I will tell them one day but right now my spirit is tired. And is not only because this man leave and go, Ma, because if I could bounce back from man that say he is widower and I find out later he don't have a wife that is dead, I could bounce back from anything. I have seven children and I bounce back every time to work for the Movement and for all of us, but this time it have people who want to make sure I don't bounce back and who want to take the children and it taking all my strength just to figure out how and how to move. Eight children, not seven. Help me, Ma. Don't cry. I know you would help your *own own* child if you could, so I don't doubt you. Don't cry. I glad you come back, Ma, but don't cry.

"No. I'm not crying, Olive. I just trying to keep her from crying. Pass the baby bottle for me."

Ma, the other day a man walk right into the house saying he is one of those that deciding my case. I didn't know I had a case, and, Ma – here the less said the better, even to you. Olive walk in from where she went and shout and ask him what he doing here and say that when everybody out he not suppose to just walk in. Because they just walk through the door, you know, Ma, and if they find a door lock, they talk to me like I have no rights. But these children make me feel good for the next generation. She stand up to him and talk to them like how me and her father talk to them in our day. I know they learn from us, but right now these social worker people know I can't do much without them, and they could take away even the little that they giving, so with me they act like they in charge, but the big ones not afraid of them. If you see how they stand up to them and hold their head up and say their say! I see the future in them, and it looking good. That man, he leave when Olive reach and ask him what he doing here. She tell me to try to feel better; she will cook some chicken soup for me, and she will not go to any kind of study work tomorrow because she want to be sure I'm okay. Ma, I don't know what is happening. I just need to rest a little bit after this baby, and I wish – I wish – I wish you were here. And these people, Ma, they not pretending to be devil. *Sé djab pou vwé.* Is real devil, yes, Ma. *Sé djab pou vwé.*

33. January 1939. They came for her in the morning.

They came to pick her up early in the morning. Who knows what happens with their forms, and their orders, and who has to sign what piece of paper.

She carries with her the spirit of the place she came from. And me, Spirit, I have been here walking with her, watching with her, even finding for her the voice of her grandmother sometimes when dark ocean too rough to let the voice and the seeing cross over easy. I see them enter the house and rough her up and pull her out. I see her struggling to swim in the current that battering her. I see her breathing hard and shallow and fighting to draw breath when the waves tossing her and turning her. I see her trying not to reach sea bottom, struggling not to drown because she want life and she thinking of her children still on the boat. I see her and I remember the children great grandmother and their great grandfather. I watching how the waves battering her and I know she swim strong already and I know she have more swimming to come.

For now, they have her. She didn't even know that some judge say she should be committed, should be taken into asylum for her own safety and the safety of the children that Life had given her. But is spite work. Some who know what talk that talk say that she and her husband, they too uppity from time. They pull her out of a dream in which she was running fast down Waterfall and immediately she wake she think of the dream that she had the day Baron walk out to meet the streetcar that will run over his body and push his spirit out of it. So even though she frightened, she prepared in a way, because she know this is a kind of separation. And she thinking, *I not going to die, though. I won't let them kill me. I have my children.* The question in her head is *What all-you doing? Where all-you bringing me?* And inside her head she invoking the name of the reprobate. *I am famn Norton. Famn Norton na Lamèwik.* She don't know if she say it aloud as they dragging her down the steps but she thinking it.

That doctor said she needed some rest. But you don't drag people out to make them rest? Those social worker people is *djab pou vwé.* Is them. She sure they are the ones with some devil plan. They have been there, pulling open her door without knocking, poking their nose into everything, telling her that she needs to give up what they call *these foolish pretensions* and eat the food she can find. They have been saying she's crazy for not eating the food that is there and can help feed her and her children. They have been telling her that she should be more responsible. What do they know about responsible? Where are they taking her? Her shoes fall off and inside her head she calls to her mother, her grandmother. She'd better not call out loud, because they will say she is mad. But can people do this? Just drag you out of your own house? Is this something they can do because of this thing they call Jim Crow? But is she in the Jim Crow area? Where are they taking her? *Your last child is illegitimate*, they kept saying when they barged into the house, as if she needed to be told. But is that something they can jail her for? *I know, Ma. I know. I have to be careful.* She wants to tell them, *If you would act as if a woman alone can take care of her children and is a person who can have her own ideas and who deserves the pension her husband has worked for, I probably wouldn't be looking for another husband.* She asks herself, what are the rules? How did I get here? Why do I take on these ideas that seem to say you should just let God decide whether he will put a child in you or not? Why don't they make it easier for you to find out what to do not to have children every Monday morning? I suppose they mean don't do nothing unless you is man. Lord, how I lose road from La Digue? Where they taking me? Her shoe. Her shoe fell off and they dragging her. She can't pick it up. They won't stop, won't let her bend down. Oh my gosh! This is not happening. Olive shouting. They are calling me. My children. They won't answer the children. *Yes. Yes. I hear. But where?*

They are dragging her away. This is a depression, that's what they keep saying, so don't they know? Things are bad all around. The car. Would they leave her be if she sells the car? But at least she doesn't have to walk miles when she has to pick up some little something. She doesn't have to walk miles to go look for work. She can park it somewhere a little distance away and then walk the neighbourhood. Would it be different if she didn't have the old jalopy? Or might it be different if she didn't have another baby? Is that it? Black woman with no morals? Is that what they think? Is that why they are dragging her away? Do they still burn women? They come to pick her up early, early morning.

PART V

LEAVINGS AND RETURNINGS

1939 — EARLY 1960s

Why am I here? Sing a Song to me

Something is happening to me.
I need to feed my little baby.
They took me from my children.
They imprison me; a kidnapping.

A savage pulling off my shoes
A getaway vehicle, a driver speeding,
pounding, shouting, stairs, screams.
I keep dreaming this bad dream.

Why am I here?

Sing, bird, sing a song to me;
One there is who cares for thee.
Day by day His strong right arm
Keeps both thee and me from harm.[28]

No-one will answer me

I told you what my name is
and that I was born in Grenada.
I keep asking to be free
but no-one will answer me.

Yes, I have eight children,
I've said they are my life.
Don't ask me the same damn questions
over and over again

I WOULD not in a cage be shut,
Though it of gold should be;
I love best in the woods to sing,
And fly from tree to tree.[29]

My name

Norton, that's my name,
I said my last name was Little.
I need to add something;
it is actually *Norton* Little.

Norton.

I give the white father's name;
I hope it help to set me free.
It must be good for something.
Who knows? The name might be the key.

A boasty name? I don't know.
Is whiteness of the father a boast?
I need whatever might help,
I don't want grief; I'm already lost.

Love not to talk,
Love not to boast;
Grief comes to him
Who brags the most.[30]

1939/1940. In a wood where beasts can talk

They catch me and they have me in a trap
in this bush where beasts can talk.

"You have got a gun, I see:
Perhaps you'll point it soon at me;
And when I am shot, alack!
Pop me in your little sack.
When upon my fate I think
I grow faint – my spirits sink."[31]

354

In a wood where beasts can talk
That is where they bring me to take a walk.

One mad woman sitting in a bush
rush at my big girl when she visit, shouting, "Hush!"

My child bawl out! She fraid! She run,
And that is how this story go on!

In this wood where beasts can talk.
They want me to play stupid and take a walk.

1940s. Love wins love

It is there writ large
in Book One of the Royal Reader:

Love wins love!
It was a girl and a goat
not a girl and a boy.
It say that straight out,
we learned it by heart, so I know:

Love wins love.

Keep this in mind, boys and girls.
Be kind to your pets, and you will find
that they will soon learn to love you.
Love wins love.[32]

There it is in Book One,
big and bold.
A pet is one thing, I suppose.
A woman and a man –
that is another thing altogether.

1939-1943. Tick Tock

Tick, the clock says, tick, tick, tick!
What you have to do, do quick!
Yes, I know I bit her hard yesterday;
if she touch me again I will bite same way.

"TICK," the clock says, "tick, tick, tick!"
What you have to do, do quick:
Time is gliding fast away;
Let us act, and act to-day.

I say, Don't poke around in my hair!
She sat me down, and tried to cut my hair:
I can comb my own damn hair;
I will kick, even if they strap me to the chair.

When your mother says, "Obey,"
Do not loiter, do not stay;
Wait not for another tick;
What you have to do, do quick.

That's the word they use, "delusional",
as if I am not important, so it is personal.
So they are pretending I am mad;
I want to get out of this damn place..

If your lesson you would get,
Do it now, and do not fret:[33]
I don't know what the lesson is
So I will fret over this.

I will fret.

1940s. Kalamazoo. The Place where I am

The place where I am is the Kalamazoo State Hospital!
They think I don't hear the name when they call,
but I know how they pretend and how they scheme,
build cages, create traps to capture my dream.

I remember the bird in the book;
the child calling it, trying all kinda trick
but bird say, *Thanks, little maiden, for all thy care,*
But I dearly love the clear, cool air

Here they say, we have something for you!
How the child promising *fresh ripe cherries, all wet with dew.*
They *jook* up me body with needles, in this Asylum for the Insane
That's what it was before they give it a hospital name.

They want thanks, I suppose, for what they call care
Thanks, little maiden, for all thy care,
But I dearly love the clear, cool air.
Yes. They take me away from the clear, cool air.

Bird smart. They had a clean cage all ready for me.
Like bird say, they take me from my place *by the old oak tree.*
They put so much things in me, I don't know what is what.
Is like they set up to make sure they have me in a trap

But bird say it, when they are not looking, "*Away I'll fly*
To greener fields and a warmer sky:
When Spring comes back with cheerful rain
My joyful song you will hear again."[34]

I lose road

How I lose road
after I leave La Digue?
It's a long way to LaDigue
It's a long way to go
To the sweetest land I know.

> *Goodbye, Picadilly,*
> *Farewell, Leicester Square*

Goodbye Piccadilly, farewell Leicester Square.[35]
Goodbye Lansing, farewell Montreal's Dominion Square,
I want to go back to LaDigue.

Up to mighty US of A
Came this Caribbean woman one day.
All the streets were paved with gold
That is what some say

> *It's a long, long way to Tipperary*
> *But my heart's right there*

It's a long way to LaDigue
It's a long, long way to go
It's a long way to LaDigue land
To the sweetest place I know.

I fraid this mad people place
where every space is full of hate.
Is me that come but how was I to know?
And now, it's a long, long way to go.

If you understand it, tell me about it.
Tell me how I lose road from La Digue,
the sweetest land I know. Tell me,
I am listening. *Mwen ka kouté.*

It's a long way to LaDigue hill
but my heart is right there still.

I lose road, *wi*
Sé sa mwen di.

I lose road, wi
Sé sa mwen di.

Tired, but not insane

Insane is something else
Insane is white sheets and long guns,
breaking windows and lynching people
killing people because they are Black.
The insane people that attack me and my family
have no rhythm, no logic, no reason.

That is insane.

I am tired but
I am not insane.

1940s. Who was he?

My happiness is less today
My heart is broke, that's why I say:
A good man is hard to find
You always get another kind [36]

That new man was like my husband
but really he wasn't the partnering kind,
I thought he would be a body's lover man
so my woman-self reached for a helping hand.

But I admit what the song say: *my happiness is less today.*
Some lessons are hard but they show you the way.

A good man is hard to find;
You always get another kind

I knew it. They tell me my mother knew it.
Don't dwell on it if you can't change it
That's what my grandmother would say.
I will sit here and think of a better day.

But yes. *A good man is hard to find.*
You always get another kind.
But I can stitch, I can repair. I will mend
I will survive.   I'm the sewing kind.

In spite of everything
I am surviving.
Watch me! Watch me!
Just watch me!

1940s. The Honourable Marcus Mosiah

Look for me in the whirlwind,
seek me in the storm.
You mightn't see me
but I will be there
and with God's grace
I shall bring with me
countless millions
of Black men and women
who have died in America
who have died in the West Indies
who have died in Africa,
to aid in the fight for liberty,
for freedom, for life.

The Honourable Marcus Mosiah Garvey
taught himself, they say. Yes.

Look for words in the dictionary,
seek them in the book,
pick up whatever is there,
at first you mightn't understand
whatever is there
but with God's grace
you will learn.

At the 1920 international convention
he brought with him countless millions,
and then persecution,
arrest and imprisonment in 1922.

Look for us in the Caribbean,
look for us in Africa,
look in America,
countless millions of free and enslaved.
In spite of what they think
and say
and do,
not slaves.

Always be a reason for prison or asylum;
they always find a way to put us in jail.
They picked me up one winter morning,
drive me away with my shoe falling off,
trying to make me look mad,
calling me delusional,
say they have to keep me from my children.
My children.
Where are they?

I will bite, I will kick, I will fight.
So yes. I will be mad.

Look for me in the whirlwind.
Seek me in the storm.

We continue the work in Liberty Hall,
we spread the word while he in jail for five years.
We write to President Calvin Coolidge.
He call Marcus Mosiah Garvey
an "undesirable alien",
but he well know him.
We know them.

I will sit here on the chair that is my throne,
here in the corridor where they banish me
because I am disruptive inside of their orderly place,
delusional, royalty in spite of everything.
Be warned that I am only one small part
of the struggle, early in the talking,
and not the last to talk.

Seek me in the storm
long after I am dead and gone.
Don't look back trying to find me,
look for me in the whirlwind,
the whirlwind of our children
and our children's children.
Now we have started to speak
we're not going back to sleep.
Not going back to sleep.

Let me rest a little bit.
With Marcus Mosiah Garvey in my head
I become the storm.
Let me put my head back on my chair,
my throne, and rest little bit.

Look for me in the whirlwind.
Eben, fè sa ou vlé. Ou pèd.
Do what you want.
You lose.

It mightn't look like it
but you still lose.

1940s. The Great Jump

Just look how I jump!
He is just like that,
just like Ben in the *Royal Reader*.[37]

I know I teach them good.
Until
Until

They came to see me.
I don't know where I am
and why I am
when I'm not with them.
They came
Wilfred
Olive
Norton.
I didn't see Malcolm.
They send away Malcolm.
And what is happening to that little baby?
Is mine – mightn't be his
because man don't have to claim.
But he is mine.
What these devils do with him?
They came to see me.
My children.
I want my children.

Royalty

Look to Africa
When a black king shall be crowned.
For the day of deliverance is at hand!

The words of the Honorable Marcus Mosiah Garvey
Every time I say that I am royalty

they saying inside here that I'm delusional.
But he told us!
Value yourself!
Look for us in the whirlwind!

Delusional?
Look for me in the whirlwind!

1940s. *All the people have gone*

All the people have gone.
The moments fly – a minute's gone.
From La Digue – a Langdon.
The minutes fly – an hour is run.

In Montreal, a woman named Norton.
All the people have gone
on the Black Star Line.
A Little in Philadelphia, a man.

The day is fled – the night is here,
what waste, what a woeful affair,
ten years, twenty – all the people gone.
What waste, what woeful want.

Child. Pregnant when they come. Inez?
Malcolm? What day is it today?
My mother. Aunt. Gerda. Grandmother.
Skin. House. All the people have gone.

All the people have gone.
What you have to do, do quick.
So flies a week – a month – a year;[38]
Ella. Ella – a – a? Ella.

I'm in a wood where beasts can talk.[39]
All the people have gone
and there's no-one here to take a walk.
All the people… have gone.[40]

1940s. No birds

The birds have gone.
Not even a bird on the window sill
Pa menm yon jibyé asou webò finèt-la.

Come to think of it
not even a window sill,
no window to look out of,

just these bars.
Perhaps they're trying
to keep those mad ones out there

from coming in here.
No window sill,
so where would the birds land?

Let me take out my sky-lark.
Let me sing my song,
The skylark's song.[41]

Black is Illegal

Land,
land is what the problem is.
They don't want us to have land
and especially not in this area.

When the NAACP has a meeting,
I have to give thanks, because
the UNIA is in trouble now
and the NAACP is standing up with us.
They want to help us keep the land,
they want to help coloured people.
The property is ours, we know,
but in this country, those they call coloured,
and by that they mean all Black people, really,
should not have land.
And although we don't always agree
with each other's approach
the NAACP is trying to help.
Give God thanks!

Land

They don't want Black people to have land,
not in the places that we want.
They think the land belongs to them –
that is Capital Land View, the people in charge.
So the paper – the land paper that we have –
it means nothing.
They tell us to get out!
Even if we have paper showing that we own the place,
it doesn't matter because, they say,
we most likely got it under false pretences.
Colored people cannot legally live in this area.
No access to this property in the Westmont area
because Black is illegal in an area they decide to mark as white.
The children learning that lesson
and that hurting me.
The children telling me the other day –
and they only little – nine, eight, five, four –
they telling me that a man see them working in the garden
and ask them who they working for and where their boss is.

Already they learn that the best thing is to say
that he not there and he will be back soon.
People always snooping around.
And the children learning that
Black is illegal in this area in Lansing, Michigan,
the world, they learning, is supposed to be white.
Think about that in this Michigan here in
One thousand nine hundred and twenty nine.

If I am not mad
with the way the world is
and with the way they try
to rub your face in the mud,
for sure I know they trying every day
to make me mad.

They trying to make you mad!
They trying to make me mad!
What a situation!
Black is illegal!
Black is illegal!

1940s. The tea that they give

I am sleepy again.
What they giving me?
They giving me something!
Did I sleep yesterday?
Something is broken,
something break.
I ka kasé.
Something not right.
Perhaps the tea that they give
make me sleep.
Or that medication they always
shoving down my throat.

I spit it out, I spit it out.
But I can't spit out the injection
that they *tjouké* me body with.
What are they feeding me?
It make me shake,
my face feeling numb,
my arms hurt.
There is something happening,
something happening inside my head.
I don't understand.
I am not sick. I am…

Where is my grandmother?
Ma, where are you, Ma?

I will sleep.
They say I am not sleeping.
Perhaps they are making me sleep.
Perhaps they making me sleep.

Once

Once I thought I might write a poem.
Once I thought I would be
a woman who would lift up my voice
and teach my story.
Well I lift it up
with the UNIA
and I teach my story.

Once I knew I would
have the respect of man
Once I tied my lot
to someone who thought
woman should follow.
But I was finding my way,
not following like a stupidee.

Once I thought I would
write a life, and life
would be a poem I wrote.

Once I thought I would be free
to live a life that I wanted
without bars
without cages
outside of
prison spaces

Once

But something happened,
is happening,
and some people decide
they would stop me
Or try to stop me

Once

1940s. At War

Nwèsè
darkness

Once, long ago
they were just ending war,
now I hear there is another war beginning.

I hear them saying that
men are gone to war,
women nurses gone to war.
Things are bad, I hear tell.

Food, they say, is on holiday,
but I kind of remembering that,
long before the war,
food was causing belly holiday.

There's not much sugar, they say,
few potatoes, they complain.
If they could find some lard,
perhaps I could bake some bread,

but no no no
not here, and not now
for my family, yes, but not here
I'm not doing a thing here –
pa isi – not here.
I could do something at home
on a hill in La Digue.
In… Westmont, Michigan?

My family came to see me.
Auntie Gerda's little boy came to see me.
Malcolm.
And I had a child like him.
Big boy now.
I used to bake for the child
when he was little, that is.
He is a big man
but he say he is that little child.
I fell in love
with a little nephew named Malcolm,
named Malcolm, same way.
Long time ago.
He came to see me.

There is no lard, I hear,
butter, too, is away at war,
and meat is part of the battle.
Even eggs, I am hearing, is part of the fray.

But why? Hens afraid to lay?
And I clean out the fowl run?
They take me away from my house
And what a way things turn ole mas

with the world at war!

But my family from long time
Came to see me.

1940s. *I will not think about it*

I hear whispers
they are bringing a TB unit
to Kalamazoo State Hospital.
I will not think about it.

> No. I don't want no damn knitting
> or sewing
> or nothing.
> Leave me alone.

You lock me up here
Who lock me up here?
Why you have me here?
And then they telling me
I could be disruptive?
Is a helluva thing when people
could just decide to control your life.

And TB is not a thing to play with.
I remember that.
That is not a thing to play with.
My grandmother tell me that
long ago.

1940s. Kalamazoo Musings

I keep myself quiet.
I know there are mad people in here.
They say I am mad,
but I know mad people when I see them,

and that woman sitting near the window
she is mad for sure.
Lord protect me!

I'm hearing whispers:
Someone got hurt
someone was killed,
I hear the whisper whisper.
What a thing!

And there is polio –
whisper whisper in the passageway.
Polio!
Sometimes people say
when you think bad breeze blow
no bad breeze blowing.
But that would be a bad breeze.

They say that TB is everywhere
I hear the whispers
I wonder about that room next to mine
I always hear a *coohoo coohoo*,
a really deep cough.

I hear whispers in the night
and *coohoo coohoo*.
Whispers.
Coohoo coohoo.
Whispers.

1940s. They write me "W"

They whisper and they
write their quick writing
in their little notebooks.
I keep my head down
and I am what they say:
comatose.

They write their quick little notes
and whisper their quick little whispers.
For all the inmates that are white,
they write a "W" in that column.
And I'm what they say:
comatose

Let them write me "W".
You could never trust writing, anyway.
Is not the whole story.
My grandmother tell me.
And I even remember somebody show me.
You can't trust writing.

Is a census, they say.
Let them write me "W" in the census.

1940s. Broken by the war

Something is broken
shaken,
I can feel it
inside here,
broken.

Young men end up here
in the men's section
after wars.

Over there is the men's section,
the army section.
And women, too.
That one in the corner by the window
might be one broken by the war.
Shaking, whole body shaking.

I had a door once. Mine.
My door.
My own front door,
me and my husband.
I wonder if one of those men
was one who stand up in front of my door
with a white cloth covering his face.
It happen, you know:
burning torches, horses.

It happen.
War have a lot of people in here.
I inside here with plenty enemy.
Plenty enemy.

1950s. *They shock me*

They put needles in me,
they put something in my head.
Wilfred?
Olive?
Rex?
I remember somebody.
Where is my Norton?
They shock me.
They put something in me.
I am hurting.
They put some shocking something in me.
Where is my little boy, Malcolm?

Where is Inez?
They put some shocking something inside me.
They put needles inside me.
They are killing me quietly.
Quietly.
They put needles in every part of me.
Deep, deep.
They shock me.

1950s. Be Careful, Wi

I heard something,
something woke me up

crying.
The children?

What are they doing in that room?
They are hurting somebody.

Be careful!
Olive, be careful!

Not Olive. Somebody else.
I must be dreaming?

Olive watching out for me.
Leave her alone!

Be careful, eh, child!
Be careful, oui.

Matjé sa mwen di'w, wi.
Pay attention to what I'm telling you.

Where am I?

1950s. Silence

Dark.
Quiet.
Silent.

All the people have gone.

White coats.
Footsteps.

White coats walking fast.

Swish swish,
roll roll,
rumble rumble,
mumble.

White coats walking,
white hands touching – *steupes* –
bothering people.
They better don't touch me.

And all the people have gone
All the people have gone.

1950s. I feel so ill

I feel so ill.
The walls are falling on me
This is a head-hurting place.
This is a back-breaking station
This is a skin-scratching place
This is a place that hurts my throat
This is a place that makes my body ache.
This is a place that squeezes my spirit.
I feel ill in this place.
I feel nobody in this place.

1902, 1903, and the 1950s. The moments fly

Time to go in, did you say?
It is time. Come this way!

They tell me it is 1952.

The moments fly – a minute's gone.
The minutes fly – an hour is run.
The day is fled – the night is here,
So flies a week, a month, a year[42]

I will not give my grandmother that poem.
It will make her sad.
So flies a year?
And then what, after all that flying?

Where have all the people gone?
Where have all my babies gone?

I didn't do a damn thing
Is worthless people that wouldn't let me live.

Kalamazoo. 1950s. Talking to Myself Again

Yes, Nurse,
you're right:
talking to myself again.

> Yes. Good morning.
> How are you, nurse?
> I am well, very well, thank you.

Some high-up person
must be visiting today,
because they are all smiling
and wanting to know how you are.

I don't take them on usually,
but let me try a thing today,
give them something to write in the book,

asking the same damn question
over and over again.
>   Well, nurse, I'm talking to myself,
>   not because my head is gone
>   but because there is a lot to say to myself!

You know, I remember a doctor yesterday.
Yesterday?
Yes. Yesterday.
That doctor told my big boy
that I needed a rest
and I would be all right again.
The brain needed a space, he said,
to stitch things together.

Yesterday.
Is not tomorrow yet?
What is today?

They still stitching their wickedness together.

1950s. Kalamazoo Musings. The See-Saw

Look at me! I am up in the air!
See, I let go both hands, and yet I do not fall.[43]

I let go both hands
                and I fall!
Right down on my behind!
I feel it hurting.
My bambam hurting me.

Okay.
Now I'm making this doilie.
They bring thread, knitting pins, crochet hook,
everything.

I didn't feel like doing no damn thing
but okay.

I fall, yes,
right down on my backside –
my butt, as they say.
But they push me.
I remember that somebody push me.

Why you watch? *Wi.* Is laugh I laugh.
Sé wi mwen wi. That self.
Sé sa. I laugh. To myself.
I not laughing for you.

Eh bien, wi.
Eh bien.

I tell them I not doing no damn knitting.
Somebody visit and put this in my hand.
Who give me this?
They telling me to try.
They telling me I must do something
and that would help.
Nothing would help
I am not doing no damn knitting.

1904 and 1950s. Lessons

I always tell you
don't look down at the ground.
That's what my grandmother said.
Keep your head up.
My grandmother was no fool
Tjenbé tèt ou.
Tjenbé tèt ou.
Hold your head up.
Hold your head up.

They think I mustn't wear
my earrings and my necklace that people bring for me.
Pretensions, they saying.
That sounding like how they used to say *uppity*.
Tjenbé tèt ou.

I will keep my pretensions.
Pretensions, dressing myself up.
Let me keep my pretensions.

Biting

I will bite them
I will kick them
I hate them to touch me.
They better not touch me.
I see their intentions now.
They make me sick
and they don't want me to get better.
They want a mad woman to keep mad.
Not to send home.
They punishing me.
They punishing me.
They punishing me.

What have I done?
I will bite
I will kick
I know their intentions now.
They better not touch me.

1950s. She took a bottle to church

My teacher made us learn that poem by heart:
Robert Southey, "The Well of St Keyne".

High tower,
trees that watch,
trees that whisper,
tall trees that wait.

And I wait, and I watch
through the bars,
how they reach up, up, up,
everything covered in white.

An oak and an elm-tree stand beside,
And behind doth an ash-tree grow,
And a willow from the bank above
Droops to the water below. [44]

Where is he today, my husband?
Master for life, that's what husbands are.
And me *this* wife did not know enough
to take a bottle of well water to church.

If the husband, of this gifted Well,
Shall drink before his wife,
A happy man thenceforth is he,
For he shall be master for life. [45]

But the husband himself could admit
that his wife outsmarted him – she good, eh?
Some of us don't get the chance. Or perhaps
we don't take the chance? But that husband think he smart.

"I hasten'd as soon as the wedding was done,
And left my wife in the porch;
But i' faith she had been wiser than I
For she took a bottle to church!"

Oh! She took a bottle to church!
I didn't know. In fact, I didn't remember
she took a bottle to church!
What a thing. I didn't remember!

Tongue and teeth don't laugh at good thing!
Laang épi dan!

Kalamazoo. I see the word. And I knew it! I'm in a Zoo.
What kind of zoo is it – a Kalama zoo?
A zoo where they prick you with needles,
where they keep you and watch you in a cage.

Apwé yon sèl fwa, li dé fwa –
After one time, it's two time
Li dé fwa – is two time

She took a bottle to church!
You have to laugh!
She took a bottle to church.

1950s. Kalamazoo

One of the ladies said there are polio vaccines
for children in Michigan if their parents ask.

But who will ask? Parents could ask?
They have rights?
What kinda parents these?

And do I have children?
I saw a man that said he was my son,
but I know that wasn't my big boy.
He too old.

A big man came to see me
and he called himself my son.
But I don't see my children.
Where are my children?

They little.
They only little.
Somebody kidnap them?

My children.

1950s. Kalamazoo: Group Therapy

The man in charge here is called Mr Morter.
There is something called group therapy.

Talk about your problem, they say.

Do I have a problem?
Listen to the problems of others.
Sympathise. Empathise.

If I have a problem – which I doubt –
how do I tell all these white people
what I think my problem is?

That sound like an impossible kind of something.

Perhaps I'll talk to Ma
while they are talking to one another.
I will tell Ma that I had some West Indian friends –
Lyons, McGuire, and some others later, yes!
They helped me but they had to live their own lives, too.
And then one of them wanted to take my boy,
when the devils saying I can't take care of him.
Friend or no friend I don't want nobody taking my children.
Trying to help me. Is not me they helping.
Is who saying I can't manage.
Just tell them I could manage.
There were other people who tried to help me,
and your own people is always your own people.
And even then sometimes you not too sure
What the *feeling* in the help is all about.

I wish Auntie Gerda was around to help me.
I had an Auntie Gerda, yes.
I don't even know where she is today.
I lose track. Life is something.
Even if you could read
you can't read ahead.

Children are not easy.
I tell Ma. And Ma say,
Yes, I know, tell me about it!
I raise you!
I will tell Ma – *wi*?

When something break inside you
you need your own people around.
My children little – that time,
and my own people not around.

I will sit and look at you, yes – and
I will listen, yes.
But tell you my problem?
My *real* problem? I don't think so.

I hearing somebody say something about re-education.
Who the re-education for, I wonder?
Sometimes those who don't think
they need re-education really need it
more than anybody else!

A young man come to see me and he tell me
he is my son. But how could that be?
I have some little children, little children.
I was watching him to see if a little boy inside of him.
Who know? Perhaps there is a little boy inside there?

Re-education? I will smile, I will find something to say.
They tell me I never participate in anything.
I don't want to be here. That much I know,
although I don't remember
everything, everything that happening,
but that much I know!
I don't want to be here
and do the things they want me to do.
That much I am sure of!
I don't know them!

They walking about.
They preparing for the group.

Well, perhaps I will hear what are the problems
people have in this group that they call therapy.

If I listen, that might help me know
what my problem might be.
But I know I should not tell these people
my problem.
That I know for sure.
I know these people are part of my problem.
That I know for sure.

Group therapy, eh!

1950s. *The old man and the dog*[46]

That old man in the book born with his luck.
Which part of the world?
And he give the dog meat.
And the man had a son.
The son dead, they say.
Guard! Or nurse – I not sure which one.
Why I calling them anyway?
I don't trust these people.
Never mind.

Where is my son?
Where are my sons?
And my girls, where are they?
Alouette, gentile Alouette.

Come, old man,
take some bread and meat,
take them out of your bag and eat.

Where is my bag?

Let us go and ask the old man to come in.
Come in, old man, and sit by the fire and rest.

That was the lesson.
That old man born with his luck.
That old man lucky, *wi*.
Come in, young woman,
and sit by the fire and rest.

Old man, you born with your luck, *wi!*
You well born with your luck.

1950s. Visits

My son – I saw him today.
I think it was my son.

He look like my uncle.
I remember my uncle.
We are one people; we can't lose road.
And I saw another one, my son with my same red skin,
not as red as me, but I'm sure he is my son!

I used to tell him
Go out into the sun
and get some colour.
I see my son – but not my son?
Where
is the little stubborn child
that is my son?

A little, little boy
could be a tall strong man like that?
A tall, tall man.
Tall almost like his…
If is him. A man more than 6 foot tall, yes,
this man was.
Moustache and everything.
Tall man.
Couldn't be someone I know.
He call himself my son.
He look like his f…
He look like the man who used to be
my husband.
I don't know what is happening.
I think I see a family face,
and I think I should know
a family face.

Is as if,
is as if,
as if I lose road.
I don't know what is what.

Yes. All the people have gone

I'm in a bush where beasts can talk[47]
The moments fly – a minute's gone
There's no one here to take a walk
All the people have gone.

The day is fled – the night is here
Star. Black. Line. Africa. Sun.
So flies a week, a month, a year
The minutes fly – an hour is run

Montreal. *Chabin*. Chenette. Norton
What day is it today?
All the people have gone
Ten years, twenty. Yesterday.

I'm in a bush where beasts can talk
Do you know Mary?
Valley, grugru, flow, walk
Make a sudden sally[48]

In distant lands, what do you find?
So flies a week – a month – a year;[49]
I'm in a bush where beasts are sick
Let us keep the jewels of the mind...mind...mind[50]

1950s. The Owl

Knit one, purl one.
Knit one, purl one.

I like the owl.

The light of day is too strong and too
bright for his eyes.
So he sits all day long hid in a tree,
Or in a hole in the wall, out of sight.[51]

Knit one, purl one

Now they keep asking me if I still hear voices.
I tell them no.
I don't know I used to hear voices.
Spiritualists hear voices.
I am not a spiritualist.
I tell them that.
You have to be careful with these people.
Now they reducing the medicine
they tell me I need
I hearing them better.
I hear *their* voices
Perhaps now I might start to hear their voices less
But I won't tell them anything.

When I had to travel
I took a dead man's name, is true.
But I am not a spiritualist
I don't hear voices.
We can be many, many people
and not be mad people.
I believe that.
I learn here that you have to be many people to survive,
and don't let them see all the people you are.
So far I don't hear any voices, thank you.

Like the owl
I stay in the wall when the light is too bright
But I don't hear any voices.
I tell them that.

I stay in my hole.
Mwen wété en twou-mwen.
Out there in the field
where they want me to work
I move with no noise.
They'd better not try to snatch me.
I know how to fight.
They can't snatch me.
I ain't going to be quiet.
Not now. Not now.
But I watching.

1950s. The Wind

The wind.
I know the wind.

I hear the wind
outside here, not a raging wind.

The air is crisp,
that's what they say.

I say it damn cold
I know the wind, though –

More than a breeze.

Sir, I lost the rhyme
That's okay. I have the rhythm.

And the rhyme.
I'll get it with time.

The wind is groaning in the trees
It's okay. A little sighing breeze.

Ask of the winds that far around
With fragments strewed the sea[52]

It is good outside.
I know the wayward wind.

1907-1908 and 1950s. That George Washington[53]

That George Washington make me get licks;
I won't forget him for that.
Because of him
my teacher gave me a whipping.
Because of him and the Second Book.
That George Washington and his truth!
Now they tying me up with their truth.

1907, 1908 and 1950s. Evening

This night, when I lie down to sleep,
I give the Lord my soul to keep;
If I should die before I wake,
I pray the Lord my soul to take.[54]

My soul to keep?
Not very sure of that, *non.*
Well, to hold until I wake,
and it is God, so that is good.
And, Lord, though things are bad

I do not plan to die before I wake.
Keep it for a while when I sleep,
but do not take, Lord, not take,
not yet. In spite of everything, I am not ready.
It's up to you, but I have to find my people again.
So not yet, not yet, *non*, Papa God.

In my little bed I lie,
Heavenly Father, hear my cry:
Lord, protect me through the night,
Bring me safe to morning light.

Yes, bring me safe, Lord, to morning light.

1958. The Judge

Judge not that you may not be judged.
That is what the Good Book say.
We have so many judges
Judges who judge the quality of woman
Judges who judge the quality of skin
Judges who decide about the story of race
My son tell me that the judge
Who decided about where we should live
And how I should be as woman
And when sanity should be read as insanity
That is what my son say
How to know who mad and who not mad
My son tells me the judge is dead
I don't rejoice
But think how man forgets
That dust thou art to dust returneth
And man forget that the Good Book say
This was not spoken of the soul.
The judge is dead.
I do not rejoice

Even if I feel like rejoicing
I think about not the one judge
But the whole of man kind
And of woman kind
I think of the powerless
Power of all man
Not only black man
I think of all man
That can seem so powerful
In the midst of powerlessness
My son tell me the judge dead.

1950s. *It is decided*

They hem and they haw
and they haw and they hem
but they tell me – it is decided
I'm going out of this place
for a weekend with my son.
A big one. A big son.
I don't know where the little one gone.
I'm going to stay for a while with a big son.
Those who could decide these things for me
have decided.
And this is good.
What a thing! It is like a miracle.
I remember my grandmother saying,
long, long ago,
if you have enough patience
you will see inside ant's belly,
adan vant fonmi.
I am going to see inside ant's belly with my son.

The Judge

My children get big and they find out.
I remember from long ago that finding out
is a thing you must do.
They find out
that Judge Leland Carr signed to get us
off the property in 1929.
It is because you are a Negress, Mom.
We were a Negro family.
Negro, negress, negro children.
A negress.
And my husband, you see,
he was a Negro.
That was the thing that killed him, they say.
It killed some of his brothers, too,
being a negro.
So we could not legally occupy
property in the white area.
That's why the judge was making sure
to throw us off the land.
We couldn't legally live in the places where they live.
And that same judge, they tell me, get me committed
Tell the… authorities… that I mad,
and he find a doctor that agree.
Judge and doctor, judge and jury.

But my son tell me all of them listening.
Keep quiet, he say, but take it easy in there.
They still have to agree.
So do what they say and take it easy.
Our children are listening
and our children will fight with that word legal one day.

Our children are listening.
That is legal.
Our children are listening.
I have seen them.

I remembering the past
And I seeing the future.
They are listening.
Mightn't be tomorrow,
but look for me in the whirlwind.
They are listening.

1950s. Kalamazoo needs

That lady I talk to sometimes,
now that I'm talking to people
in the corridor out there,
she says she is going out of here.
It will happen for me, too.
One day, I will go out of here.
I feel good to think
of all she will do.

It make me laugh.
Yes, I am excited now because
she is going out of here.
I will go out of here.

She not fraidy fraidy,
and she says when she goes out there
she will tell them to get softer benches.
It make me laugh!
My school benches weren't soft to shout about,
but they were for school, many years ago,
and my young backside was different.
We sit on these things here and is sufferation.

But I feeling excited,
and I thought I forget how to feel that.
So that good.

She says she will tell them to just make it pleasant.
She even say they could spend less on religion
and more on creature comforts.
And she is a catholic, she tells me.
Me, I am everything – and seventh day adventist
because   because   because
they really helped me when – when
water was more than flour,
and they have some of my ideas, too.

I always told my children,
the wall of the church is not the power,
is the people and the feeling.
Catholic or Adventist or whatever she be
I hope she will tell them about caring.

She good. If you spirit strong enough,
the work could continue wherever you are.

You mightn't notice, depending.
But I see how she move in here.
And she white so they will listen to her – perhaps.

1908 and 1950s. Memories at Kalamazoo

Good morning, Nurse. I'm just here talking things through.
Not troubling anybody, and I don't need
any needles in my body, thank you very much.
I won't give any trouble. No. Leave me alone. Just talking.

Chatham didn't hide it. Long time ago, Chatham said straight out
who he was concerned and not concerned about.
And after all this time, no change.
I must remind the children. Be careful.
The profits of this country were never meant to be for them.
They have to fight for it, because is their country.

Good morning, Nurse. I'm just here talking things through.
Not troubling anybody, and I don't need
any needles in my body, thank you very much.
I won't give any trouble. No. Leave me alone. Just talking.

Leave me alone.
It hard.
But I must remember what my children telling me.

1950s. Gardening

Now they have a garden,
they are helping us to grow things,
or we are helping them to grow things?
Therapy, they call it.
I wonder if my grandmother knew?
Gardening as therapy,
to help you get better.
I wonder if that is why Ma
was hardly ever sick?
Oh yes. That *must* be why!
I will grow lilies,
those long red ones,
anthurium lilies.
I must ask them if they could find some plants.
They will like that I'm taking an interest.
Yes, I know.
I wonder if they will grow?
This is a cold place most times.
But they like the cold, those lilies.
Perhaps they will live better here than I can.

I used to let him make his little garden.
Come mom, he used to say.
My children.

I'm seeing them,
I see them.

I wasn't going to do it, *non*.
I would just leave them and their garden
and not bother,
but I will plant,
I will plant a nice little garden.
Even if in this cold place I can't plant
like I want – what I want.

And my husband used to garden too, *wi*.
He used to plant a good garden.
He was from the South!
A good garden.

1950s. All in a row

They want us to make things grow in a row.
I said I wasn't taking on this gardening thing
but okay, today I will do it. Them and their therapy.
Gardening wasn't no therapy for me and my grandmother.
Or was work *and* therapy for me and my family.
They're annoying me.

But the young man who visit me and say is my family,
he say all these things count. Let them see you are
cooperating and they will let you go out, he said.
So I am cooperating.
I am cooperating because they have a say
in my coming and my going.

Mary, Mary, quite contrary
How does your garden grow
With silver bells and cockleshells
And pretty maids all in a row?

They want us to put the plants in a row
You could do it!
That's what they keep telling us,
as if they think they talking to children.

I know what I am doing
Leave me alone, I say.

I will plant all in a row.
I'm such a nice, quiet, orderly person.
That's what they have to know.
I will plant all in a row.

1950s. Whom can you trust?

Today they came to leave gifts;
they left this sewing kit.
Some of us sew,
or we will sew if we feel like it.
Since after my family talk to me
I doing some more.
Did one of them that leaving gifts
have a husband or a brother
who used to burn down houses of Negroes?
You know, there are things my mind
will not let me forget.
Who burned down the house that my husband built?
Today they came to leave gifts for Christmas,
for the birth of the Christ child.
I always used to tell my little ones:
believe in Christ, pray to God.
Pray but don't be fooled by their talk
of Christ and church and pretty things.

I used to tell my little ones,
my little ones.

Who are they?
Where are they?

Guard!
I don't forget that
I must always be on my guard.

Sh-h-h!
Don't call anybody.
Don't trust them.
You don't know anybody.
Shut up, you!

No. I'm alright, thank you.
Yes. Good morning.
Good morning!
See? I'm smiling.
All is well.

Hide.
Don't let them see you.
They not your friend.

1959. She is a seamstress

My knitting pins,
my needles for knitting;
here they are!

Okay. I will use them now.

Knit one, purl one.
I dropped a stitch.
Here it is!

Tongue and teeth don't laugh at good thing.

That's what my grandmother used to say, *wi.*
Lanng épi dan, tongue and teeth,
those two so wayward!
Lanng épi dan.

Knit one, purl one.
I am a seamstress
excellent at knitting.
Do these things
and they help you avoid
other people's kitchen work,
and other people's orders.
Unless it's your man giving the orders.

Knit one, purl one,
knit one, purl one,
reach the end of the row
and begin again.

The *Chaleur,*
that was the boat I travelled on.
Occupation: seamstress.
I signed my name
and then I signed his name
I took *his* name,
the reprobate.

Oops!
I dropped a stitch.
Here it is.
Knit, knit.

In a bush where beasts can talk
I went out to take a walk

Hudson! I reached the Hudson!
How I get there?
I should let my grandmother know

I reached the Hudson!
Other people story
become my story.
But make sure you write it your own way
my grandmother always say.

La Digue
I will go to La Digue.
I'm going home soon, yes.
A long walk.
I will do it.

1903 – 1904 and 1959. She didn't know what to do

There was an old woman who lived in a shoe
She had so many children she didn't know what to do
She gave them some broth and plenty of bread
She whipped them all soundly
And sent them to bed.[55]

Absolutely not funny. Ma said it's only funny
if you are not the old woman!

What has happened to me? What they do to me?
Those big people that are my children,
when they talk to me now
they tell me that a lot happened.
They tell me all the drugs probably make me forget.
All rhythms, all rhymes mix up in my head.
But keep your own counsel, is what Ma would say,
Just take it easy, they tell me, and you will get out soon.

But what did they do to me?
You could do that to people?

I wonder if that old woman in the shoe
ever had time to figure things out:

who she is,
how she is with man,
what to do,
what not to do,
or if they were just always bothering her –
not the children,
those others,
those others,
those others you can't see
when you looking at the shoe.
I sure they were bothering her.

1950s. Waste Not, Want Not

I must not throw upon the floor
The crust I cannot eat;
For many a hungry little one
Would think it quite a treat.

'Tis "wilful waste brings woeful want,"
And I may live to say,
"Oh, I wish I had the bread
Which once I threw away!"[56]

All of these poems are riddles, you know!
How to waste what you don't have,
that is some kind of riddle.
Others waste and we want;
I just realize that is the riddle.

I think I getting better.
If I was sick
I getting better.
I will really get better
when I put this place behind me.
I could feel it in my bones.

1908 and 1959. Write things down

The trick is to be able to get up again when you fall.
That is what I was saying the last time that they visit me –
my children – and that is what they say, too.
That is the trick. Let me write things down.

My son gave me a notebook.
I will have to hide it.
They didn't forget me.
I forget them because I didn't even see them
for a long time,
and they become different people I don't know.
But they didn't forget me.
They carry me inside them.
That is what they tell me.

And year after year they keep asking for me to come out.
That is what I know now.
The devils drugging me and making me mad
and telling them I am insane.
I am not there yet, they tell them now,
I am still delusional, they tell them.
I can't go out.

I was giving up, I thinking now,
because I didn't believe anybody know me anymore.
Truth to tell, I didn't know anybody,
just a set of strange people wanting to do therapy with me.
And now I don't know these big people who tell me
they are my children.
I thought these new people were hiding my children.
But I getting to know them now.
I know them more and more.
Up to two years ago, they tell me, they been asking
and the devils tell them no, my mental health is not good.
I'm not talking, they tell them,
and I kick sometimes still, they tell them.

And I can be disruptive, they tell them.
And I do not participate;
that's what my son tell me they say.
So now I participate.
I am quiet. I don't kick.
I want my family.
My family wants me.
I will even go and work canning things
in the place they have here
My son – Norton, they tell me.
I remember his name but I don't see
the little boy Norton that used to be mine.
The children grow up.
Norton… tell me … go and work,
do what they say.
You will come out, Mom.
He call me Mom.
They call me Mom,
my children.

Rheumatism and Grandchildren

My hand full of rheumatism these days
but perhaps I could write.

My son. A man that say he is my son.
My sons John and Wilfred.
And my daughter, Inez.
And my girl, Olive.
They working they tell me.
I know my big daughter.
Inez tell me she remember me singing to her.

And my grandchildren.
They tell me those grandchildren are mine!
That is like a miracle.

Imagine that!
My grandchildren.
These people that put me here
worse devil than I realise all the time.

Djab pou vwé.
I see Wilfred, I see Olive.
I will have to find out about my family.
I will have to get to know my people.

.

My children?

Stories can be impossible.
Stories are always not possible
until they become possible.
The son that looked like me –
the one the father like.
I remember that.
Well, people could like people
and it doesn't have to be one reason.
Some people could just make you smile
because something in them reach your spirit.
That boy made his father smile
and that is not such a bad thing.
He could make his father smile just by being.
They tell me that one just get married,
that he is struggling hard
and he is powerful like his father
when he preach in the black struggle
Apwé yon sel fwa, sé dé fwa.
After one time is two time.
I can't believe it.
My son is a strong voice in the black struggle.
That is what they telling me.
Perhaps he was walking from a long time ago,
half seeing in front of him what he would become.

I hear he go through a lot
and his teachers told him not to aim too high.
I remember that.
A wife? I don't know the man,
I know the little boy inside him.
He visit me here and I
couldn't see the little boy inside him,
though they tell me he is my same son.
Look for me in the whirlwind!
Apwé yon sèl fwa, sé dé fwa.
Look for me in the whirlwind!

1960-61. *Where did you learn all these things?*

The children – the little ones that were mine –
they used to ask me,
those rhythms, those rhymes,
those stories, those sayings and poems,
where did you learn all these things?
But time is always moving on.
I have the rhythm but sometimes
no long-ago rhyme.
They wondered why their memory of their father
was a different kind.
My husband, their father, didn't like things like that.
It was not his fault that I had more education,
and he knew that! *é ki* more *sa*? How much more?
He did know that!
A Garvey man.
He knew the story of the race
but not the feelings of women of the race.
He couldn't reason with a woman,
talk things over with a woman.
Always had to be telling and ordering.
So that's how it was. We couldn't talk.

407

I hope my grandchildren today
finding a different way:
a different rhythm,
a different rhyme.

1960s. They stole my life

Now my children explain to me
I realize these people stole my life.
That is why I could feel those
empty spaces inside my head,
why all the time I was feeling
so tie up,
so full of vexation
with these people around me.
I could feel I was in a strange place
with people that kidnap me
but I wasn't remembering
exactly how it happen.
They stole my life.

They say I mad and they drug me.
That is a dangerous thing.
They could burn down your house,
take your land,
drag you from your house,
put you in a madhouse prison.
The children tell me to keep quiet
and concentrate on getting out.
Keep your own counsel.
I remember that from long time.
Keep your own counsel.

They explain it to me
I wasn't mad.
Post partum is what my daughter saying.

Just had baby – that is another story.
Other botheration
food and plenty frustration,
war, money, officials that tiefing.
Things bad and I needed support
and time to catch meself.
But I wasn't mad,
that is what my children saying they know!
They stole my life.

The Klan, the judge:
the children keep asking, they tell me,
for them to release me,
but they saying I mad.
Year after year after year
they saying I mad.
The judge that commit me,
my children thinking, was the same judge
that work on the case to take the land.
He and his people
they commit me to madhouse.
They stole my life.

Whether they in Klan costume
Or out of Klan costume
is the same people,
the same same people.
I will stay quiet so I can get out of here
because is still not me in charge.

But they stole my life
Vòlè. Thief.
They thief my life.

1960s. Stronger

The birds are at rest in the trees.
I could feel the quiet in this Kalamazoo.
I give thanks
in spite of every thing.
I give thanks for my boys, grown young men, yes.

Big, big men.
And my girls,
I wonder if they will really know me?
I don't know if I really know them.
But I remember. More and more I remembering.

They take my life, those people in charge,
but if you dwell on it, they will win.
It's not how I woulda want it
but they make my generation stronger.

From the first one to the last one
little boy who lost his mother so early –
who I don't know. Don't know at all.
Not yet. But I will know.
They make my generations stronger.
They make them stronger.

We black women,
women that mad just because they women.
That is what they think.
Just because we are women
and we know the story from every side,
we are mad, they think

But they make all of us stronger.
They make us stronger.

1960. The Pet Bird

I am going out of here,
the singing of the bird become true.

I will not in a cage be shut,
Though it of gold should be;
I love best in the woods to sing,
And fly from tree to tree.[57]

What a thing!

If I laugh they will say I am still crazy.
But what a thing!
A bird so free
that it flies from tree to tree.
So free!

Shh!
They will say you are still crazy.
Don't think the world is safe
because your children now in position
where they could find you
and argue for you.
I hear them talk,
so I know they could argue.

They still Black, though,
still Black,
so danger is not far off
unless some miracle happen.

They think they give you
not what you are due
but what they are pleased to grant.

Shh! Pick sense from nonsense.

I will not in a cage be shut.

1960s. Mental Health

Today, people came to talk to me
about mental health.

My mental health is good, I think.
I tell them that I had my tribulations to bear.

I have borne them, I think.
Now my children are able to talk to me.

They tell me things quietly.
My mental health is improving.

The hospital talked to me about
After Care. After care?

If you are not careful, you will laugh,
a laugh that is not a pleasant laugh.

Not all skin teeth is good grin.
Before care or *after* care?

I will be quiet,
I won't say too much.

A long time ago I learned how not to say a lot,
even before I was married,

and then when I got anxious, nervous,
I was saying too much because they asked.

I told them I was royalty,
and they thought I was mad

I told them I was learned
and I could see their faces saying

Black and learned?
What pretentious nonsense is that?

And my children telling me now
That each time I said something that was me

Those people thought I was more mad
So be careful, they say. I will be careful.

I remember the Black Cross nurses[58]
nurturing and leading,

learning how to follow, how to lead,
how to survive, how to be woman.

I will take the pills I have to take,
now that they have made me mad.

Just take them, my son says.
We will find out more when you are outside.

They will find out more!
Take them – and hide.

You never know what will make
a person in charge decide.

They captured me and they hold me.
And they could do that.

But I am going. I am leaving.
I am remembering the woman of truth.

The man who thought he was the master
didn't free her like he promise,

but she get away and she say
I did not run away. I walked away by daylight.

Woman sojourner. Woman of truth.
I will not run away. I will walk away by daylight.[59]

1960s. Beauty Parlor

Now there's a beauty parlor here
after the gates, bars, cages,
things to sift through, sieve, *wi*.
It's like *I've got the world in a jug;
the stopper's in my hand.*[60]
Plenty things to think through
in this place here now.

There is a parlour for beauty
Tounen! What a thing!
After one time is two time.

Huh! They put a beauty parlor here!

Convalescent

I will go out.
Norton, the one who living
nearest to here,
he told me that.
Olive, I see her, my big girl.
She tells me it is true.
Inside this place, here,
they are saying now
they will be able to give me
convalescent status.
Yes! Is them giving me,
not comatose any more.
Convalescent.

It is coming.
The status is coming.
Convalescent.

1960s. Little Wheel and Big Wheel

SAYS the big wagon wheel
To the little wagon wheel,
"What a difference between us I see!
As our course we pursue,
Can a small thing like you
Keep up with a great thing like me?"

Me? I am royalty!
Even if I have to whisper it to me,
I know I am royalty.

Says the little wagon wheel
To the big wagon wheel,
"You are larger, I own, my good friend;
But my quickness supplies
What I want in my size,
So I keep in the front to the end."[61]

Don't fraid for me.
I keep in the front to the end.

Yes I laughing!
Use the old lines.
Learn the rhythm and the feeling.
Make them your own.
Change and reshape them.

I going out of this place.
As my grandmother would say,
if you live long enough

and just have patience,
you see inside ant's belly
Adan bouden fonmi.
Lanng épi dan!
You live and you learn.

Sometimes the lessons hard but – you learn!
Even when those who don't like you
think the story is theirs, make it yours,
make it yours!
I have my children's hand to hold on to now,
and I keep in the front to the end, *wi.*

I keep in the front to the end.

AFTERWORD

AFTERWORD

When I read *The Autobiography of Malcolm X*, I was immediately drawn to the story of his mother, Louise Langdon Norton Little. Her appearance in that book is brief because the work is aimed at providing the story of her son, the famed political activist. As I looked at the outline of this Grenadian mother's story through her son's eyes, I was interested to know more about the history/herstory that had produced her, and what, from Malcolm's story, I could tell about the mother's influence on her son. I grew even more interested when I heard that Malcolm, at first hesitant to speak to Alex Haley, entered his story most readily when he was asked about his mother.

Among other things, *The Autobiography* informs that his mother tried to warn him that light skin was not something to be particularly proud of, that she used to tell him to go out of the house and *"let the sun shine on you so you can get some color."* Some have doubted that all the things Malcolm "remembered" actually happened in his childhood home, but here I thought I could hear an irate Caribbean voice telling a child just that. The fact that the voice was that of a very light-skinned Caribbean woman added, for me, another intriguing dimension to the narrative. In most narratives influenced by colonialism, and a Grenadian narrative has to be that, light skin indicates some level of privilege, notwithstanding the traumatic circumstances that may have shaped its acquisition. That this light-skinned woman let her children know she valorized blackness indicated to me some complexity in the narrative. It must be acknowledged, here, that a light skin amongst the rural poor is not usually as effective a social currency as a light skin for those who are higher up the social ladder. In *The Autobiography*, I read that the mother told her son, Malcolm, that *her* father, with the last name Norton, was not someone she knew, and that he had raped her mother. Although this story has been challenged, I thought it was entirely in keeping with many other stories of plantation rape and general sexual abuse in the Caribbean and throughout the Americas during the nineteenth century – and both earlier and later. Such stories of both intimacy and abuse, which mothers might tell only to their children, are not uncommon. I felt that the narrative of rape might go some way towards explaining Malcolm's early references to the "white devil". In the autobiography, he mentions that he was known as "Detroit Red" because a "red-headed devil" was his grandfather.[62] I was struck by the contrast with US President Barack Obama's narrative about whiteness in his family history. Obama wrote that when he read *The Autobiography of Malcolm X,* though he found it useful in his early efforts to understand his own racial inheritance, he was troubled by the fact that the early Malcolm referred to the "white devil" and "spoke of a wish to rid himself of whatever white blood ran through him." President Obama wrote, "I knew he was serious. I also knew that his way could not be my way. My road to self-respect would never allow me to cut myself off from my mother and grandparents, my white roots." Obama was able to reflect on his white inheritance with a certain amount of comfort; according to the *Autobiography*, Malcolm's particular experience was that his mother had told him that she came into the world because of her mother's rape by a white man. Since accounts suggest Louise Little had no memory of her mother, the story must have come to her secondhand, suggesting varying levels of unease within the family about the white male character who fathered Louise Langdon. So for Malcolm X and Barack Obama there were different beginnings, different journeys to understanding of self and the other, and toward self-respect.

I was further drawn to the story of Louise Langdon Norton Little when I read what Wilfred Little, Malcolm's older brother, had to say about her influence on their lives. This was recorded in Jan Carew's book, *Ghosts in Our Blood: With Malcolm X in Africa, England and the Caribbean* (1994). I heard in Wilfred's recounting of how his mother quoted long passages from the Royal Readers, elementary Caribbean school texts, echoes of what I had heard

420

my own grandmother and mother recite – lessons remembered from years before. The mother's story, I felt, obviously belonged to the sons (and daughters) but was not theirs alone, referencing as it did the broader history of the 19th and earlier 20th century colonial Caribbean. I thought I recognised, in a personal way, Wilfred Little's mother's voice in some of his stories. Because of the insights provided by his account, I quote freely from the Royal Readers in the novel, recognising its influence on generations of Caribbean people and their children. Some children of that colonial generation don't know that influence is there, but Wilfred Little's comments suggests that he was aware of it.

Some have suggested that Louise Langdon Little was a very educated woman. I agree, but this may not have been the result of extensive formal education. Her socialization within the family in La Digue and political education within Black communities in both Grenada and the United States very evidently contributed to her penetrating and articulate sense of the world. In this, her experience reflected that of political figures she admired, like Grenada's T.A. Marryshow and Jamaica's Marcus Mosiah Garvey. I haven't found evidence that her formal education went beyond what Anglophone Caribbean people would know as Standard Five in the primary school (which then ended somewhere between the ages of eleven to thirteen). For this reason, I spend quite some time in the narrative focusing on the excellence of some of the primary school teachers and the ambivalent influence of the Royal Readers. Here I follow the lead of the fictive "Sir" who enters the story of *Ocean Stirrings* because he has a lot to tell us about attitudes within Grenada at this period – and not because as a character he is a re-creation of any remembered person. However, I do remember, as a child, being amazed at the quantity of poetry, history, and extracts from fiction that my grandmother could recite from memory. By the time I was introduced to the Royal Readers in a still colonial Grenadian primary school, my teachers were less interested in having students learn by rote – though it still happened – but it is clear from my grandmother's performances that *her* teachers made her imbibe huge chunks of material from the Royal Readers.

My fascination with my grandmother's powerful chanting and

the force of her narratives even resulted in my taking a guided tour to visit the Faroe Islands in the 1990s. These islands had so captured her imagination that she chanted about them endlessly when I was growing up and implanted them in my imagination, too. I remember, as well, hearing my mother, her daughter, also chant from memory about these Faroe Islands and other spaces important to the British colonial imagination. My grandmother was chanting remembered lessons from the Royal Readers well into her seventies, and my mother, past one hundred, is still able to chant them. As I pursued references from Wilfred Little's stories about *his* mother, I also found some answers to questions about *my* grandmother's and mother's recited stories. Wilfred Little's stories told me that his mother, growing up in Grenada at approximately the same time as my grandmother, had teachers who were similarly strict and equally focused on student engagement with basic skills. I also learnt that though the colonial administrators of the period were belatedly giving educational skills to children of the labouring population, this was not intended to encourage them to go beyond a basic level, and so ensure their continued availability as a supply of agricultural labour. My novel's historical scaffolding draws on empirical data from a variety of sources, including the Legislative Council records of the period.

Among comments made by Wilfred Little about his mother are the following:

> [She would] *teach us at home when we came home from school. We would give her what we had learned that day, and she would then re-teach it to us and give it to us in a way where it would do away with some of those negative things that they had incorporated in there.*

> ...

> [*She would*] *bring in papers from the West Indies and from other parts of the world, especially where Marcus Garvey had movements throughout Africa. She would have these papers, and we would read them, and we knew what was going on in the other countries where they were being exploited.*

> ...

*[She would] sit us down and have us read aloud passages from
Marryshow's paper* **The West Indian.**

*Marryshow was her countryman and someone she boasted
about all the time.*

. . .

*By reading Garvey's paper and Marryshow's paper, we got an
education in international affairs and learned what Black people
were doing for their own development all over the world.*[63]

*She told me that she'd attended an Anglican school in Grenada
and that the teachers believed that sparing the rod spoiled the child.
So she passed on to us some of the strictness from her own
upbringing, just like my father did from his.*[64]

These and other comments had an impact on my imaginative
creation of the fictive Oseyan of the novel. As I concluded this
work, I discovered that a researcher, Jessica Russell, has had
access to files and stories from Hilda Little, second child and first
girl child of Louise and Earl Little, and this certainly adds to
perspectives put out there by the brothers. Occasionally, too, one
sibling or the other has said something that takes me to the
Grenadian childhood of other Caribbean people. When Yvonne
Woodward-Little, last daughter of Louise Little, two years old
when her father died and ten years old when her mother was
committed to an institution, writes of remembering French songs
sung by her mother during her childhood, I recall (French) Creole
songs that my older maternal relatives and other Grenadian women
of that age, and usually also of rural origins, sang to their young
children. There were also one or two songs in French and these
Louise Little's children may also have heard. Yvonne Little-Wood-
ward's memory takes us on a journey to a rural Grenada shaped by
African people and the influences of both French and British
colonialism. The diaspora memories of Grenadians and their
children help re-create an important period of the Grenada story.

I have always been fascinated by Caribbean history – well, the
fascination started after I left high school – and the intersections
of that history with the literature to which I had been introduced
and to which I later sought to make a contribution. At first, I had

no thought that I was going to produce something motivated by Louise Langdon's story that would be made in a mixture of genres, but the idea began to develop as I read more and saw various images that would be means of presenting the story. Indeed, I began with the digital and only gradually moved to my first love – print and creative writing – as I was thinking of ways to incorporate the Caribbean voice and elements of history; this involved formulating characters based on historical information *and* on perspectives put out there by researchers. But even as I moved towards print, *voice* was constantly at the centre of this interrogation. The fact that I began with the digital, was, at one level, a new approach to the publication of the word, but I have always had an interest in voice and performance. Practically, the digital incarnation of my work on Louise Little, as she is situated within the Caribbean and African American story, was supported by the African American Digital Humanities (AADHum) Initiative of the University of Maryland, its director Marisa Parham, and a developer/designer, Andrew Smith. It will follow the print publication.

As Julia Alvarez notes, some stories "can only finally be understood by fiction" – and poetry, I add, and, increasingly, a mixture of genres. This, incidentally, is what was presented in the Royal Reader series, with its mix of fact, fiction, poetry and visual art. But as a creative writer with an interest in history and politics, I turned also to research done by historians as a way of securing the scaffolding of my work. These included historians such as Caldwell Taylor, Angus Martin and Peter Redhead, whose work focuses on Grenada. When, years ago, I spoke to Caldwell Taylor, public historian and raconteur, with a store of information and an unfailing interest in stories about Grenada and the rest of the Caribbean, he was the one who told me to be sure to follow the writings and ideas of Wilfred Little. He advised me to go to Montreal and made suggestions about people I could speak to there in order to get a sense of the environment and of the Black politics at the time when Louise Little and her uncle Egerton lived there. I also turned to Angus Martin, an unflagging Grenadian archivist whose store of material is always impressive and informative. And then, for this work, there was Peter Redhead, whom I haven't met but whom I encountered in his writing. As I tried to weave together a mass of sometimes apparently contradictory information, Peter Redhead's research suggested complex answers and eventually made me, in effect, read part of the story backwards so that I could more confidently walk forwards. As I read the work of others, I recognised that it was more than likely that they had used the research of Peter Redhead and the archival information so selflessly made available by him and by John Angus Martin. I want to acknowledge that their work of historical research is appreciated.

Remember, though, that as Julia Alvarez suggests, a work of fiction – a creative work – is not a historical document. Beyond historical information, I brought my imagination to work on the invention of scenes and the creation of characters whose depth will hopefully do honour to Louise Langdon Little, whose life I think was of tremendous importance both to the activism of her children, including that of her best-known child, Malcolm X, and to our understanding of ourselves as people in the world.

I also want to recognise the extended family and relatives of Louise Little in contributing to this initiative. I don't mean by that that they gave me their blessing. Researchers can seem intrusive when family members don't really know what you plan to do with their information, and also when they feel that memories of these individuals really belong to them, even though their lives have made them important to the public. I hope I trod carefully. Thanks here also to Catherine Smith-Jones, family member, who graciously gave suggestions about people I might contact. The branch of the family with which I had the most conversation was located in Grenada, and still lives there, in and around La Digue, where Louise Langdon grew up.

There are conflicting narratives in the biography of Louise Langdon Little. People give various dates of birth and various names for the sister who was her mother. These are important elements of the story mainly because they bring attention to the complex interweaving of relationships among various classes of both white and Black Grenadians, and how these interactions, consensual or coerced, had an impact on the shaping of Grenadian communities. As I have said, I based the scaffolding for my fictional narrative on ideas drawn from both Malcolm's autobiography and Wilfred's memories. I also use archival details about Louise Langdon's age and parentage that I researched myself in Grenada and elsewhere, and draw on intriguing conversations with Terence Wilson, a family member in Grenada. As I re-read and reconsidered drafts, I was also influenced by recent work which drew on interviews with Hilda Little and/or discussions with those who survived her. The interpretation of available documentary material is mine alone and, as indicated above, other than this factual scaffolding, what is presented here is a work of the imagination. My object was to make a tribute to the life of Louise Langdon Little *and* to the working people (and particularly the women) of her generation and in particular those from La Digue, St Andrew, Grenada.

After La Digue, I began to look at the setting of the middle part of the story – Montreal, Canada, where Louise Norton first went when she left Grenada. There, she was married to Earl Little. In the documentation of this marriage, Louise's mother's name was entered as Ella. I focused on this detail and some surrounding information and worked back from there to find Ella in the historical records in Grenada. There I found that the name Ella was listed in the 1896 baptismal records of one Helen Louise Langdon. Moving forward again, I noted that when Helen Louise left Grenada in 1917, her age was entered on shipping records as twenty-one, inferring that she was indeed born in or around 1896. Additionally, a passport document, pages of which are included in the book written by Jessica Russell after her interview with Hilda Little's side of the family, gives the date of Louise Norton's birth as 28th November 1895. This is entirely in keeping with the date of baptism found for Helen Louise Langdon in my search through Grenada documents. The archives also refer to a Lillian Langdon born to Mary Jane and Jupiter Langdon (Louise's grandparents) before they were married. This Lillian, supposedly also called Ella, died in Grenada in 1900. She did have a child by Norton, the records suggest. Here, I cannot confirm, of course, that Ella's pregnancy with Helen Louise was the result of a rape, but Malcolm's autobiography suggests that his mother was told, perhaps by her grandmother, Mary Jane, and by other members of the family, that this was the case. However, some members of the family have suggested that it was not this Ella but actually one of the other sisters, registered by another name, who was the mother at twelve and not eighteen at the time of the pregnancy. From researching the archives, but not in my conversations with family members, I came to think about the possibility that the mother was another of the children born before the marriage of Jupiter and Mary Jane. In the light of these different possibilities, in writing the novel, I reflected both on what I discovered through the research, and on what I knew about Grenada that might provide answers to some of the contradictions in the narrative. I know there are stories within families that remain secret, and some that are not told even within the family; that there are stories that younger family members may have pieced together in order to come to their own conclusions; and narratives that differ among various branches of the family. All of these will assuredly be different from my fictive recreation. Ultimately, I based my narrative on my knowledge and perceptions of the complexity of Grenadian culture and attitudes within it.

For instance, it was Helen Louise Langdon who was baptized in Grenada on February 12, 1896, and Louise Langdon who grew up in Grenada, her family says, but the records show that it was Louise Norton who got married to Earl Little in Canada in 1919. Whilst I did not want to dwell on details the family might consider private, I was interested in what this change of naming said about the struggles of working people and perhaps even about the ambivalence of working women in their response to male abuse and to the colonial arrogance of the white plantocracy and those who inherited their socio-economic positions.

The name by which an individual is identified up to the point of travel may not be the name that appears on a birth certificate or other document needed for travel and for introduction to the wider world. This circumstance is not always linked to a connection to whiteness and sexual abuse, but sometimes it is. It is not unusual to find an individual travelling by a name entirely unknown to friends and sometimes even to some members of the family. It is also not unusual to find that a person's name may suggest a relationship with a father figure, who shares that name, that did not exist. Some of this speaks to the ambivalent silences that are a key part of Caribbean – and perhaps many postcolonial – becomings.

What I want my work of fiction to do is tell the story of a working woman, a woman who, like other working women in the Caribbean, had a tough time during her life, and who struggled in spite of her circumstances to change things and had an impact on the future through her own activism and ideas passed on to her children. Hers is a story of one of those everyday women who are not often publicly celebrated – women who quietly nurture, educate and shape those who do make a mark in the world. This work by women is often not appreciated by the wider community because of the lack of official support for it, because of the absence of record in official sources, and because of a social disregard for women's work, and a particular disregard for the lives of Black and working-class women. Like other working women, including the women of her home village, La Digue, both yesterday and today, Louise Little struggled for her own survival and to ensure the survival of the generations to follow, including some who would be celebrated by posterity. Let us give honour to a working woman in struggle.

Beginning with the exploration of events and attitudes set in 19th and early 20th century Grenada, this work of fiction is the story of a woman known to her family and friends as Oseyan, a woman who carries the secrets of the ocean passed down through the generations, a woman who comes on stage not to *be* Helen Louise Langdon, but to perform in celebration of her life of struggle and achievement, and to help focus attention on the many women like her, struggling every day for survival all over the world.

By their comments and generous responses, many people contributed to the realisation of this work. I have already thanked some of them. Here I thank others. I apologise if I miss anyone. I appreciated and found useful each comment by friends and acquaintances, and outreach by all those who heard I was writing and got in touch with some bit of information about La Digue, or Grenada, or something they thought might be of interest. Thanks to Georgene Bess-Montgomery, who drove me out to and around Butler, Georgia, so that I could get a sense of that terrain.

Thanks to University of Maryland graduate MFA student (2020-2022) Lisa Latouche, and Dr Keisha Allan, Comparative Literature graduate and 2021-2022 Postdoctoral Associate in the Latin American and Caribbean Studies Center, who contributed to the historical scaffolding by helping with research on aspects of life in the American Midwest during the 20th century. Lisa Latouche, Dominican (from the island of Dominica), additionally answered my many questions about Creole, much used in Grenada in the 19th century setting of the early parts of the story, and much more current in contemporary Dominica than it is in Grenada. That Francophone Creole – and I name it that here to distinguish it from the Anglophone Creole much more current in Grenada today – was my greatgrandmother's main language and was certainly an influence in the life of Louise Langdon and her grandparents. Lisa was of major assistance as I brought her my own memories of Creole and asked her assistance with orthography and other issues. Thanks to Daunt Curwen who, a few years ago, briefly answered some of my questions about Wilfred Little's visit to Grenada.

The Creole produced in the novel has the essence of Grenadian speech, but as Creole exists in a very limited fashion in Grenada today, it is inevitably also the result of work done by researchers from Dominica, St Lucia and Trinidad & Tobago. In addition to Lisa Latouche from Dominica, I spoke with Morgan Dalphinis from St Lucia, who researches Caribbean and African languages and was of tremendous assistance with my first novel *Angel*, where I tried to render an Anglophone Creole shaped by African languages, French, and English. For this project, too, Dr Dalphinis contributed his knowledge of Creole and African languages and spent many hours discussing aspects of the Creoles of Martinique, St Lucia and Grenada. I'm indebted to him. I took a few months of classes in Creole with Trinidad's Nnamdi Hodge, whose study of the Grenadian Creole is supported both by research visits to Grenada and his interviews with Creole speakers in Trinidad, some of whom can, he says, trace their origins back to Grenada. While I didn't consult Nnamdi Hodge for this project, his research and my classes with him have also helped me think about Creole orthography in this work. As has the interest of Marise LaGrenade, who, with her book *Mwen Ka Alé*, continues to do valuable work researching Grenadian Creole. Her knowledge of French and expertise in translation were of great assistance to me as I wrote and worked through my own memories of my mother's Creole expressions. I must emphasize the importance of the voices of my mother, Helena Collins, and my grandmother Letitia (Lettie) Darbeau. Still in my memory, they remain a constant guide as I struggle to render and interpret Grenadian Creole. Their voices are in my voice when I read or attempt to speak Creole. Thanks also to my St Lucian sister, Veronica (Jean) Glace, who responded to my questions from her own knowledge of spoken St Lucian Creole. Eventually Jean pointed me to a Creole dictionary, and dictionaries from St Lucia and Dominica which, while not always in agreement, were valuable for the writing. This check-in with Creoles from Dominica, St Lucia and Grenada also made me more aware of the differences that exist among these language researchers as all islands try to render in writing a language that has been largely oral. When I couldn't find answers in the Eastern Caribbean Creoles, I also consulted Haitian sources, because all are Creoles born of similar African and colonial experiences, though there are varia-tions. I had in my own thoughts a few phrases inherited/remem-bered from my mother. I found that I had varying levels of satisfaction with orthography as I tried to put them on paper after consulting various speakers. Perhaps the result of all this consulta-tion is a rendering that leans toward a Caribbean orthography not dependent on any one island, not unsurprising since efforts to write the language are largely in this century and the latter part of the twentieth century.

Thanks to Maud Casey, professor in the MFA program at the University of Maryland, who read and commented on early parts of the work and approaches to the whole.

Thanks to my daughter Merissa. While I wrote, Merissa was always thoughtful and supportive. I give thanks. Thanks also to the many friends who gave moral support throughout the process.

Thanks to Terence Wilson for his generous discussions about his family, the family of Louise Langdon in Grenada. I should note that Terence thought, as I did when I started, that the discussions with him would result in a biography. Thanks to Peter Antoine and the Grenada Center for Enlightenment for inviting me to give an Emancipation lecture in 2019 and encouraging my decision to speak about the mother of Malcolm X. Thanks, too, to the many people who were born and who grew up in La Digue, and who answered my questions about location: Irene and William Cenac, Louise Clement, Rawlda George, Lisda and Eugene Sawney. Thanks to Grenadian calypsonian Elwyn McQuilkin (calypso name the Mighty Wizard) for using his skills to compose a song to draw attention to the story of Louise Langdon Norton Little. You will, I expect, hear more about and from the Mighty Wizard when the digital version of my work is released. Thanks, also, to Marisa Parham, Andrew Smith and others in the African American Digital Humanities (AADHum) program at the University of Maryland, whose support for a digital humanities project on Louise Langdon eventually morphed into not only a digital project and an increased focus on the voices of this story but the print product that is this written story.

And thank you, Peepal Tree Press, my publishers, for taking on this work with the keen sensibility the press has for works by Caribbean writers. Jeremy Poynting, Hannah Bannister, Jacob Ross and others of the Peepal Tree Press team, I know that your comments and suggestions made this a better script. I thank you, especially, Jeremy, for your suggestions. Mèsi an pil. Thanks a lot.

Thank you.
Merle Collins
July 2023

Endnotes

1. Royal School Series, *The Royal Readers,* No. I. (London: Thomas Nelson & Sons Ltd), 20.
2. Title and poem in Royal School Series, *The Royal Readers,* No. I, 37.
3. Royal School Series, *The Royal Readers,* No. I (London: Thomas Nelson & Sons Ltd), iv.; *The Royal Readers*, No. VI; The Royal School Series (London, Paternoster Row: T. Nelson and Sons, 1902). The Royal School Series were first published by Thomas Nelson & Sons in 1877.
4. "An Indian's Traps", *The Royal Readers,* No. V., 193.
5. *Royal Readers,* Series No. V, 409.
6. Lord Byron, "The Destruction of Sennacherib's Army", *The Royal Readers*, Book V., 12.
7. "Lord Brougham on Negro Slavery", *The Royal Readers,* Book V, 402.
8. "Chatham on the American War", *The Royal Readers,* Book V, 404.
9. "Rules for Good Reading", *The Royal Readers,* Book V, 369-370.
10. University of the West Indies on Marryshow: https://www.open.uwi.edu/sites/default/files/bnccde/grenada/centre/tam.htm.
11. Marcus Garvey address to the Second UNIA Convention, 1921.
12. "The death of Little Nell" in Charles Dickens, *The Old Curiosity Shop.* 1840-1841.
13. "How to Write Letters", *Royal Reader* No. 5, 141.
14. Book II. "The Timepiece" in William Cowper, *The Task,* pp. 48-49.
15. "How to Write Letters", *Royal Reader* No. 5, 141.
16. Warburton, "The Siege of Quebec", *The Royal Readers*, No. V, 169.
17. James Montgomery, "A Mother's Love", *The Royal Readers*, No. V, 47-51.
18. "The Bear in School", *The Royal Readers*, No. 2, 79.
19. Marcus Garvey, "Declaration of the Rights of the Negro Peoples of the World", 1920. (https://billofrightsinstitute.org/activities/marcus-garvey-declaration-of-the-rights-of-the-negro-peoples-of-the-world-1920).
20. "Around the World – Overland", *The Royal School Series. The Royal Readers No. VI* (Halifax: A & W. McKinlay, 1880), 62.
21. Marcus Garvey Address to the Second UNIA Convention, 1921 (https://www.blackpast.org/african-american-history/1921-marcus-garvey-address-second-unia-convention/
22. "An Indian's traps", *The Royal Readers*, No. V, 193.
23. "Preface", *The Royal Readers*, No. 2, vi.

24. Marcus Garvey, "Declaration of the Rights of the Negro People's of the World", 1920.
25. Marcus Garvey, op. cit., 1920.
26. *Poems by Thomas Hood,* (London: Henry Frowde, OUP). First published in The World's Classics, 1907.
27. Amy Jacques Garvey, *Philosophy and Opinions of Marcus Garvey*, 213.
28. "The Bird's Song", *The Royal Readers*, Book I, 9.
29. "The Bird in the Woods", *The Royal Readers*, Book I, 14.
30. *The Royal Readers*, Book I, 25. Also in George Stillman Hillard and Loomis Joseph Campbell, The Webster-Franklin Second Reader, Hillard and Loomis Joseph Campbell, 1878, 66.
31. "The Rabbit in the Wood", *The Royal Readers*, No. I. First Series, 83.
32. "The Pet Goat", *The Royal Readers*, No.1, 19-20.
33. "What the Clock Says", The *Royal Readers*, No. I, 56.
34. "The Child and the Bird", *The Royal Readers*, Book II, 10.
35. From the early 1900's British Army song, "It's a long way to Tipperary".
36. From a song, "A Good Man is Hard to Find", published in 1917 by the African American song writer, Eddie Green. Recorded by Marion Harris, a white singer, in 1919.
37. "The Great Jump", *The Royal Readers*, No. I, 25.
38. "The Moments", *The Royal Readers*, No. I, 37.
39. "The Rabbit in the Wood", *The Royal Readers*, No. I, 83.
40. *The Autobiography of Malcolm X*, 26. Malcolm X on what his mother said on one occasion when he visited her at Kalamazoo and tried to talk.
41. "The Sky-Lark's Song", *The Royal Readers* No. IV, 119-120.
42. "The Moments", *The Royal Readers*, No. 1, 37.
43. "The See-Saw", *The Royal Readers*, No. I, 7.
44. Robert Southey, "The Well of St. Keyne", *The Royal Readers,* Book V, 187-189.
45. Ibid.
46. "The old man and the dog", *The Royal Readers*, Book I, 10.
47. "The Rabbit in the Wood", *The Royal Readers*, No. I, 83.
48. Lord Tennyson, "The Brook", *The Royal Readers*, No. 5, 20.
49. "The Moments", *The Royal Readers*, No. I, 37.
50. From a song by Dorothy Dainty in Amy Brooks, *Dorothy Dainty in the City* (Boston MA: A Lothrop, Lee & Shepard Co. 1906), 192-193.
51. "The Owl", *The Royal Readers*, Book I, 17.
52. From "Casablanca," a poem by Mrs. Hemans. *The Royal Readers*,

Book 4, 17-18.

53. Referencing thoughts about George Washington related to a story about George Washington entitled "Tell the Truth", *The Royal Readers*, No. 2, 24.

54. "Verses. Evening", *The Royal Readers*, No. 1, 70.

55. "Nursery Rhymes", *The Royal Readers*, No. 1, 32.

56. "Waste Not, Want Not", *The Royal Readers*, No. 1, 47.

57. "The Pet Bird", The Royal Readers, Book I, 13.

58. Uniformed nurses of the UNIA. For discussions on women in the UNIA, see Amy Jacques Garvey, *Negro World*, April 11, 1925. See also Mark Matthews, "Our Women and What they Think", 411 and "Amy Jacques Garvey and The Negro World", *The Black Scholar*, May/June 1979, Vol. 10, No. 8/9; see also THE BLACK SEXISM DEBATE (May/June 1979), pp. 2-13 (Taylor & Francis, Ltd. Stable URL: https://www.jstor.org/stable/41163844.

59. Referencing Sojourner Truth's reported comment to an 1827 slaveowner who refused to uphold the New York Anti- Slavery Law. "I did not run away. I walked away by daylight." (https://www.nps.gov/articles/sojourner-truth.htm).

60. This references Bessie Smith's "Downhearted Blues", 1923: "*I've got the world in a jug, the stopper's in my hand
I'm gonna hold it until you meet some of my demands...*"

61. "Little Wheel and Big Wheel", *The Royal Readers*, No. I, 70.

62. *The Autobiography of Malcolm X*, Kindle version, 252.

63. Wilfred Little, (1995) "Our Family From the Inside: Growing Up with Malcolm X", *Contributions in Black Studies*: Vol. 13, Article 2.

64. Wilfred Little in Jan Carew, *Ghosts in Our Blood* (Chicago: Lawrence Hill Books, 1994), 119-130.

Note: In citing texts from (The) Royal Readers, over the many years of publication both forms, Royal Readers/ The Royal Readers, were used, as were switches between using Roman and Arabic numerals.

Merle Collins was born in 1950 in Aruba to Grenadian parents. She was taken to Grenada shortly after her birth. Her primary education was in the parishes of St Patrick and St George, Grenada. Her secondary education was at the St Joseph's Convent high school, Grenada. She graduated from the University of the West Indies in Mona, Jamaica, where she took a degree in English and in Spanish. After graduating in 1972, she returned to Grenada, where she taught History and Spanish for the next two years. She has also taught in St Lucia. In 1980 she was awarded a Masters in Latin American Studies from Georgetown University, USA. She holds a Ph.D. in Government from the London School of Economics, University of London.

During the period of the Grenadian revolution she served as a coordinator for research on Latin America and the Caribbean for the Government of Grenada. She left Grenada in 1983.

Her first collection of poetry, *Because the Dawn Breaks* was published in 1985. At this time she was a member of African Dawn, a performance group combining poetry, mime and African music. In 1987, she published her first novel *Angel*, which follows the lives of both Angel and the Grenadian people as they struggle for independence. This was followed by a collection of short stories, *Rain Darling* in 1990, and a second collection of poetry, *Rotten Pomerack* in 1992. Her second novel, *The Colour of Forgetting*, was published in 1995 and has been republished as a Caribbean Modern Classic in 2023. A second collection of poetry, *Lady in a Boat* was published in 2003, and second collection of short stories, *The Ladies Are Upstairs* in 2011. She has also published a biography, *Dame Hilda Bynoe: The Authorised Biography of Dame Hilda Bynoe* – the latter three with Peepal Tree.

She is currently Professor Emerita, University of Maryland, College Park.

ALSO AVAILABLE BY MERLE COLLINS

Lady in a Boat
ISBN: 9781900715850; pp. 84; pub. October 2003; Price: £7.99

In poems that express an oblique and resonant disquiet ('people dream of a lady/ in a boat, dressed in red/ petticoat, adrift and weeping') and a sequence that addresses memories of the death of the Grenadian revolution, too painful to confront until now, Merle Collins writes of a Caribbean adrift, amnesiac and in danger of nihilistic despair. But she also achieves a life-enhancing and consoling perspective on those griefs. She does this by revisiting the hopes and humanities of the people involved, recreating them in all their concrete particularity, or by speaking through the voice of an eighty-year-old woman 'making miracle/ with little money because turn hand is life lesson', and in writing poems that celebrate love, the world of children and the splendours of Caribbean nature. Her poems take the 'new dead ancestors back to/ mountain to feed the fountain/ of dreams again'.

The Ladies Are Upstairs
ISBN: 9781845231798; pp. 155; May 2011; £8.99

From the 1930s to the new century, Doux Thibaut, one of Merle Collins' most memorable characters, negotiates a hard life on the Caribbean island of Paz. As a child there is the shame of poverty and illegitimacy, and there are the hazards of sectarianism in an island divided between Catholic and Protestant, the rigidity of a class and racial system where, if you are black, your white employer is always right – and only the ladies live upstairs. Doux confronts all such challenges with style and hidden steel.

We leave Doux as an old lady moving between the homes of her children in Boston and New York, wondering whether they and her grandchildren really appreciate what her engagement with life has taught her.

In these tender and moving stories, Merle Collins demands that we do not forget such lives. If ghosts appear in several of the later stories, they are surely there to warn that amnesia about the past can leave disturbed and restless spirits behind.

In addition to the Doux stories, this collection restores an earlier 'Paz' story to print, 'Rain Darling', and their juxtaposition contrasts two very different responses to the hazards of life.

Angel
ISBN: 9781845231859; pp. 320; pub. 1987, 2011; £12.99

Angel covers the turbulent years during which Grenada both found and lost itself, from 1951, when workers revolted against the power of the white owners of the sugar and cocoa estates, to 1983 when the US invasion put an end to a bold social experiment that turned violently in on itself. At the heart of the story is Doodsie, and her fiery daughter, Angel, product of both her mother's vernacular wisdom, and a university education which exposes her to the ideas of Black Power and radical decolonisation then sweeping the Caribbean.

When the Leader of the 1951 revolt becomes corrupt and authoritarian, both Doodsie and Angel welcome his overthrow by the radical Horizon movement. But mother and daughter take different positions when the popular Chief and the ideological vanguardists of the movement start to fall out. Doodsie knows instinctively where she stands, but Angel is altogether more conflicted about the rights and wrongs of the situation.

Angel richly inhabits the language and life of Grenadian working people, and moves seamlessly between the warmth and tensions of family life and the conflicts that tear a movement apart, provoke fratricide and allow an outrageous breach of sovereignty. As Doodsie says to her fowls, 'If youall would stay togedder, the chicken-hawk won come down an do nutting! Stupes!'

In this new edition of *Angel*, first published to great acclaim in 1987, Merle Collins seizes the opportunity to revise and expand the last part of the novel, not to arrive at different conclusions, but to look again at episodes that at the time of the novel's first writing proved too raw to be handled to her satisfaction.

The Governor's Story: The authorised biography of Dame Hilda Bynoe
ISBN: 9781845232245; pp. 157; pub. 2013; £9.99

This is a richly contextualised and reflective biography of an important Caribbean woman. Dr Hilda Bynoe was appointed in 1968, as one of the very first local governors in the Caribbean in the years just before formal independence, and the first woman, and black woman, to be appointed a governor anywhere in the Commonwealth. All previous governors had been white, male and British.

The circumstances of her governorship in Grenada placed her at the heart of local, regional and international change, and later of conflict. Her appointment was recommended by the Premier Eric Gairy, whose genuine concern to advance women politically was not matched by his commitment to the democratic rights of opposition parties. And though Hilda Bynoe, known in her main career as a caring and socially-engaged doctor, was generally a popular figure, her inevitable but coincidental connection with the Gairy government and its repressive treatment of the radical New Jewel opposition, made her the target of opposition criticism. As a result, she chose to resign.

This is the bare bones of the Governor's story, but Merle Collins probes beyond it for its antecedents and its meaning in a broader Caribbean context. Based on interviews with Dame Hilda, Merle Collins explores the meaning of ancestry, family, the small nation state and regional identities, intra- and extra-Caribbean migration, class and race in the formation of Dr Bynoe's conception of her role. It provides an insightful portrayal of not just an exceptional woman, but the emergence of an aspiring working class into a new Caribbean middle class. It adds to the picture of the education of that class – mostly in the UK – in the 1940s and 50s, but one so far mainly told from a male perspective.

The Colour of Forgetting
ISBN: 9781845235512; pp. 220; pub 2023; £11.99

Set on the Caribbean island of Paz (not a million miles from Grenada), this is a book that creates and occupies a space between epic poetry and the novel in the way its sequence of interludes bring into focus the lives of family and community through time – and in the confinements of small island space. It moves from the days of slavery through to the 1980s, through the difficult inheritance of one family – or rather the disinheritance of those in the family born illegitimate. Throughout, the novel conveys a powerful sense of place, of both attachment and confinement, of the meaning of land in relation to the island's smallness, and the ever-present danger of the communal violence that can spring from the pressures of confinement. Through the novel comes the voice of three generations of the women the islanders know as Carib, warner women, whose prophecies of disaster are dismissed as madness, but who have an unerring sense of what is to come. Signalled in her title, Merle Collins has much to say about the nature of memory and the fatal nature of amnesia when it comes to the lessons of the past. Whilst the book is written in the continuing shadow of Grenada's catastrophe of 1983, it signals hope in small things: in the courage of women like Mamag who will not be silenced; in the reconciliation between father and son that manages to cross the incomprehension between generations; and the capacity of a young man to confront his innermost fears. This novel was first published by Virago Press in 1995 and is here republished as a Caribbean Modern Classic with an introduction by the distinguished Canadian novelist, Douglas Glover.